A SHAMWELL TALES NOVEL

CAUGHT!

JL MERROW

D1303326

RIPTIDE
PUBLISHING

Riptide Publishing
PO Box 1537
Burnsville, NC 28714
www.riptidepublishing.com

Caught!

Cover art: Natasha Snow, natashasnowdesigns.com
Editors: Carole-ann Galloway, Alex Whitehall
Layout: L.C. Chase, lcchase.com/design.htm

ISBN: 978-1-62649-614-9

Second edition
June, 2017

Also available in ebook:
ISBN: 978-1-62649-613-2

A SHAMWELL TALES NOVEL

CAUGHT!

JL MERROW

RIPTIDE
PUBLISHING

To Alan, with grateful thanks for sharing your (mis)adventures in pest control with me—I'm only sorry I couldn't find room for more of your stories! Hanne, thank you for being such a good sport. I hope you enjoy reading about your namesake.

I don't think he expected it, and that's what caught him unawares.
—Trevor Bailey, England Test cricketer and broadcaster

TABLE OF CONTENTS

CHAPTER ONE

"**S**top pushing! Mr. Enemy, she's pushing me!" George H. was crimson-cheeked and close to tears. Destinee had that hard look on her overly knowing face that meant she was guilty as sin, but she was ready to deny it to her dying day.

"Calm down, please, you two." I gave Destinee my sternest glare. "If I see any more of that, you'll be staying in at playtime and sharpening *every single one* of the colouring pencils. Yes, even the boring colours."

"But I didn't do nuffing!" Destinee whined at me, her pathetic tone belied by the evil glint in her hazel eyes. She was probably already planning her revenge, most likely by stabbing me through the heart with a fiendishly sharpened pencil. In sludge brown. We had a short face-off, which ended with her making a tactical withdrawal. I wasn't naive enough to delude myself into thinking it was a retreat.

All was peaceful for a moment as I carried on shepherding form 2E into St. Saviour's Church, tins and jars for Harvest Festival clutched in tiny hands. Thirty pairs of eyes (actually, twenty-nine and a half; Jodie was wearing a patch for her lazy eye) searched eagerly for sight of parents and grannies. I gazed out on the sea of female and/or wrinkly faces in the pews and wondered idly if there was any job in the world, *anywhere*, that was worse for meeting men than the average primary-school teaching post. Father confessor in a nunnery, maybe? Avon cosmetics rep? Or one of those poor sods who went round emptying the sanitary bins they put in ladies' loos?

I gave myself an internal nod of approval. I'd chosen wisely for my first proper job since Crispin—

An outraged squeal pierced my eardrums and reverberated around my skull. My head snapped around, and I winced as my neck cricked. Destinee was kicking off again.

With a wail of "I said *stoppit!*" George H. stumbled into Charlie, a sensitive young man whose mother was no longer in the picture and whose father, I'd realised, didn't quite know what to do with him. I was rather fond of the little chap. I was less fond of his father, who had, with criminal lack of forethought, loaded him up with an enormous, heavy jar of pasta sauce. Inevitably, the jar slipped from Charlie's startled fingers.

I dived for it without conscious thought, launching myself across the stone flags. Time slowed, the jar seeming to fall through treacle, giving me plenty of leisure for a flashback to a long-ago missed catch for the Loriners' first eleven. History repeating itself, oh, bloody hell. I wondered how many weeks it'd take them to scrub the red stuff off the pews—and me, come to that—and whether Charlie would have stopped crying by then.

Then a pair of hefty, leather-clad arms shot out and fielded the jar mere inches before it could hit the stone floor.

I slammed into said floor myself with an *oof* and narrowly missed knocking the blasted thing straight out of his grasp again. Bruised and panting, I stared at the saviour of St. Saviour's—not to mention my Harris tweed jacket—from my supine position six inches away on the flagstones.

He grinned back at me from his. "That was a close one!" Green eyes sparkling in a roguish, ginger-stubbled face, my opposite number leapt back up to his feet and handed the jar back to Charlie. "Here you go, mate."

And then he was gone, startling smile, freckles, and all. Charlie was by my side, clutching the precious burden tight to his chest and whimpering softly. I got to my feet, dusted myself off, and cleared my throat. "Right. Let that be a lesson to you, young Destinee. Now, carry on. We need to take our seats."

Heads had turned. More than that, *the* Head had turned. Thank God disaster had been averted. Losing two jobs in one year would probably begin to look like carelessness. With the uncomfortable suspicion my face must be as red as Charlie's ragù, I carried on herding the children into the pews and was grateful when I could finally slide onto a straight-backed wooden seat myself. And begin courting backache; apparently ergonomics wasn't yet in vogue when the pews were designed. Or maybe they were just the furniture equivalent of the hair shirt.

St. Saviour's was an old church, the present building dating roughly from around the time of the Black Death, when presumably ingratiating oneself with Him on High must have seemed like a jolly good idea. It was constructed on its exterior from the evocatively named Totternhoe clunch, a sort of indigestible porridge of flinty pebbles in mortar, and on the inside from large blocks of pale-grey stone. Thanks to a recent sandblasting, it was rather brighter and cheerier inside than you might expect of a medieval building. The sight lines, though, were dreadful; the chancel was crowded with massive stone pillars at least a couple of bear hugs in circumference and the side chapels were all but invisible to those not actually in them.

Not, of course, that I was in any way straining secretly (and in vain) for a glimpse of black leather, copper-coloured hair, and a ready smile. I wasn't *that* daft. Sworn off men for life, that was me. Or, well, maybe not *life*. Just the next twenty years or so. Maybe thirty, just to be on the safe side. I'd be in my midfifties; surely I'd have acquired a bit more discernment by then.

Was he a biker? I wondered. The man who'd saved us all from the Great Spaghetti Sauce Massacre, I meant. The leather jacket might just be a fashion statement. I frowned. Could he be a parent? I'd had a vague impression of someone around my own age, so yes, it was possible. If he'd embarked on parenthood when I was busy swotting for my A levels. I pursed my lips.

Charlie pulled my sleeve. "Mr. Enemy?"

"Yes, young Charlie?" I whispered back.

"Why are you making funny faces?"

I froze. "My nose itches."

He looked at me solemnly. "You should scratch it. Like this."

A grubby little finger plunged up an only slightly cleaner nose and started to move around vigorously. "Ah. Careful there, Charlie. You'll give yourself a— Oh dear. There we go." I pulled out my handkerchief and did my best to stanch the Niagara Falls of blood from Charlie's abused nostril. Then I glared at the children in the pew in front, who'd turned round to goggle at the poor boy. "Eyes front. Haven't you ever seen a nosebleed before?"

"Is Charlie going to die, Mr. Enemy?" Destinee asked in a tone of relish.

"We're all going to die, Destinee," I said firmly. "Some of us sooner than others. Now hush. We're *supposed* to be listening to the prayers."

The rest of the service went rather as expected—Emily J. forgot her lines, the reception class was adorable but inaudible, somebody's little sister had an unfortunate potty-training accident and Mrs. Nunn, Destinee's mum, got told off by the vicar for chatting loudly on her mobile phone. At least it hadn't been her daughter she'd called.

I pasted on a smile as I strode to the crossing to lead the little darlings in a whole-school rendition of St. Saviour's School's official harvest song, "I Like Baked Beans." I'd spent the last three weeks coaching them in it, and I was quite possibly never going to eat another baked bean ever again. I even dreamed about them, the song running through my head like a radioactive earworm. If it had gone on one more week, I'd have been at serious risk of having a nervous breakdown in the canned-food aisle in Tesco. I could almost hear the Tannoy announcement: *Straitjacket to aisle seven, please.*

Would a redheaded, leather-armoured knight of the road have appeared to save me as I gibbered among the groceries? I wondered, beating time with every semblance (I hoped) of enthusiasm. My gestures became more and more exaggerated as tiny attention spans dwindled and expired in a puff of bad behaviour. Destinee was blatantly not singing, her arms folded and her lips pressed so tightly together they'd turned white. Charlie, bless him, was bellowing out the words loud and clear in his wobbly treble, flat on the low notes and sharp on the high. The terrible twins were playing slapsies with each other, but as I'd had the foresight to place them behind a pillar, nobody would ever know.

As the last notes died away, I lowered my hands, and the parents burst into applause made riotous by their relief it was finally all over. Unless that was just me. I turned to take a quick bow, and couldn't resist scanning the congregation for a glimpse of orange.

All I saw were Edward C.'s pumpkins and Emily G.'s basket of tangerines. Good, I decided. I was safe. And at least Harvest Festival was over for the year.

As was apparently traditional, the parents formed a sort of honour guard along the path for the children as they came out of church, although I noticed one or two sloping off guiltily as soon as they'd been let out. Destinee's mother was back on her mobile already, her highlighted hair tucked behind one multiply pierced ear as she texted with one hand and lit up a cigarette with the other in a rather impressive display of multitasking.

The Catcher in the Aisle, however, was waiting expectantly by the path. Seen for the first time in the light of day—not to mention in a vertical position—he proved to be tall and lean, although nicely broad shouldered. He was wearing a turquoise T-shirt that made his green eyes glow and washed-out denim jeans that looked as soft as velvet and fit him perfectly. His unruly red hair sent a warning—or a promise— of danger that was only enhanced by his battered black biker jacket. He was definitely at least in his midtwenties, I thought, although perhaps a few years older than me. He had a slightly weathered look about him. An outdoorsy type.

I realised he was looking straight at me, a smile curving at the corner of his lips. Oops. He must have caught me staring at him. I stepped up to him before my better judgement could talk me out of it. "Excellent catch, there! Are you a cricketing man?"

He shrugged. "Nah, football's more my game." I could have kicked myself. My better judgement offered to put on a pair of steel-toed boots and join in. Men who wore scuffed motorbike jackets and embarked on fatherhood in their teens generally had other things to do on their Sundays than don flannels and step up to the wicket on the village green.

Suddenly his face broke into a wide grin that just about took my breath away. I found myself smiling back helplessly and then felt like an idiot as I realised he was looking straight past me. "Wills! Harry! Great singing, lads!" Two redheaded terrors—the terrible twins themselves—threw themselves upon him, squealing "You came!"

"Course I did. Wouldn't miss this, would I? Good to hear you're still singing the old song. 'I like baked beans, Brussels sprouts, and tangerines...'"

I slipped away. I had a class of six-year-olds to shepherd back to school. Goodness knows what I'd been thinking, talking to the man like that.

At lunchtime, I sat in the staff room and stared gloomily at my tuna-and-horseradish sandwich. It had seemed like such a good idea at the time. The time in question having, of course, been the moment I looked into my fridge and realised I'd neglected to go shopping. Again.

Rose Wyman came and plonked herself down next to me, which cheered me up a bit. Rose was short and pretty in a well-padded sort of way, with curly fair hair and large blue eyes. She taught year three and was, I thought, a few years older than me. Possibly even six or seven. I didn't like to ask, though. I'd already put my foot in it three weeks into the job when I'd commented on her no longer wearing her engagement ring. Although she'd been fine about it really, once she'd stopped crying. She'd offered to return my handkerchief next day, wonkily ironed and smelling of cheap fabric softener, but, having very little confidence in my ability to avoid future verbal cock-ups, I'd suggested she keep it.

I could see this job really eating into my handkerchief stocks. Maybe I should alert Mother to buy me some more for Christmas.

"Robert?" Rose nudged me, grinning. "I saw you chatting up Sean Grant earlier."

"Sean Grant?" The name didn't ring a bell, although the accusation touched a guilty nerve. Which was ridiculous. Obviously. "Who's he?"

Rose arched an eyebrow. Archly. "The one with the red hair and the cheeky grin? *You* know. Saved us all from smelling like an Italian restaurant for the rest of the day."

"Oh, him." I tried to sound airy. I had a sneaking suspicion I only managed wheezy. "He's the terrible twins' dad, I take it?"

William and Harry Curtis—and really, what *were* their parents thinking of, with those names? I supposed if they'd been girls, they'd have been christened Diana and Camilla. Although, then again, maybe not. They'd been oddly quiet today, considering how much they usually disrupted lessons. I wasn't sure if they were borderline ADHD or just reacting to their mother's illness. I didn't know any details, but her tired, drawn appearance at the classroom door at the end of the school day, not to mention the headscarves she always wore, were something of a giveaway.

"He's their uncle, actually. Surprised you haven't seen him before. Mind you, their mum's been a bit better since the summer, hasn't she? S'pose this means she must be feeling worse again, him being here and not her. He's been great, looking after them when she's poorly." She glared at her own lunch, which, as far as I could see, had done nothing to deserve it and was a perfectly nice pasta salad. "Their dad's been no help at all. Don't think he's even seen the twins since they were in nappies."

"Oh. Um. I didn't get around to introductions. And I wasn't chatting him up either. Chatting, yes. But there was no *up*." I took another bite of my frankly revolting sandwich, gagged, and swallowed as quickly as I could. "Do you, um, know him well?"

Rose shrugged. "Not really. But he seems nice." She forked up some pasta salad, and I winced as my stomach gave a loud, involuntary rumble.

Maybe if I peeled the top layer of bread away from the filling really carefully, it'd be just about edible . . .?

Rose laid a hand on my arm. "Want my banana?"

I nodded gratefully. "Thanks. You're an angel." She even looked a bit like one, with those blonde curls and big eyes. Well, perhaps more in the cherub line. Whatever, she was lovely. I wondered what on earth had possessed that idiot fiancé of hers to call it off.

"You know, you really ought to eat more," Rose said as she handed over the yellow lifeline. "One of the mums called you a manorexic the other day."

Perhaps it had been the nagging. I frowned. "That's not even a word. Or is it, these days, along with *chav* and *well jel*? Anyway, it's ridiculous. My diet is perfectly adequate."

"For a supermodel, maybe. Or a reality-TV star. Not for anyone who's actually human." She narrowed her eyes. "And it's making the rest of us look bad. Tell you what, let's get a takeaway."

"What, now? I've got register in thirty-seven minutes."

"Not now. Tonight, if you like. Or whenever you're free."

"Oh. Er, yes, okay. Tonight would be lovely." It was only half a lie. Her company *would* be lovely. The food, I suspected, not so much. "Your place or mine?"

"Yours, obviously. Seeing as I live six million miles away from the nearest takeaway, and you've got one down the bottom of your garden."

"It's not down the bottom of the garden. It's twenty yards up the road. *And* you only live just up the hill."

"Same difference. It's a big hill. Anyway, I'll come home with you, we can do our marking, and then we'll get an Indian. I want chicken passanda. Oh, and lamb jalfrezi."

I raised an eyebrow. "Do I get to choose anything?"

"Based on your sandwich choices? No. Oh, all right, you can choose the veg. And the rice. As long as it's pilau."

My house, or rather the one I was renting, the Old Hatter's Cottage, was one of the oldest houses in the village, and bang slap in the centre. It was just down the road from the Chinese takeaway, which used to be a bank and before that was a pub, and next door to an estate agent's, which used to be a bakery. And before that, a pub. Next door on the other side was just a house, which had never been anything else as far as I knew. But it could conceivably have been a pub once upon a time.

"Did you know there used to be twenty-one pubs in the village, back in 1901?" I asked as Rose and I ambled up the road after a strenuous round of marking wobbly handwriting. The warm, sunny day had turned into a mild evening, which, at seven o'clock, was still not fully dark, although the nights were closing in fast on us. "That was around one for every twenty-five households."

"How do you even know that? You've only just moved here."

"I have a 'satiable curiosity."

Rose frowned. "If that's a quote, I haven't seen the film."

I *tsk*ed. "It's from a book, actually. Call yourself a teacher, woman? Rudyard Kipling, the *Just So Stories*."

"A book? That's so old, it's practically a stone tablet."

"It's a classic."

"You mean one of those books everyone's heard of and nobody wants to read? Ooh, look—isn't that Sean Grant up ahead? Looks like he's going for a Chinese too."

My stomach went tight. There was a streetlamp right by the takeaway, and the flash of red hair above that black leather jacket was unmistakable as the lean figure disappeared into the old bank building. Then I frowned. "What do you mean, *too*? I thought we were going to have an Indian."

"I changed my mind. Got a sudden craving for crispy duck. And prawn crackers." She grabbed me by the arm and practically dragged me along the street, past the bright-red lights of the Indian and towards the old bank building.

I had a sinking feeling this would not end well.

CHAPTER TWO

"Hello, Sean," Rose chirped as I stumbled up the three shallow steps into the Chinese takeaway. "Fancy meeting you here."

He turned. "Oh—hi. You all right?" he said, looking right at me. His hair was all mussed and flattened in odd places, as if he'd taken off a motorcycle helmet and then run his fingers through his hair. Which, on reflection, was probably precisely what he'd done. He looked dangerous and inviting, like a sleazy club on the bad side of town with a half-price drinks offer you know you'll end up regretting in the morning.

I swallowed. "Fine! Just—you know. Having a takeaway."

He nodded, straight-faced. "Yeah. That's what most people come here for, actually."

I opened my mouth to make a snappy comeback, then shut it again quickly when I realised I didn't have one. Damn it. Rose, treacherously, snorted. She cleared her throat. "Not looking after the twins tonight, then?"

"Nah, I took 'em to the park after school and wore them out with a kick-about, so Debs reckoned she'd be fine with them tonight." He leaned against the wall, all easy relaxation.

Rose cocked her head to one side. "So that means you're on your own, does it?" she asked, her voice innocent.

What on earth was she playing at?

"We can't let him eat on his own, can we, Robert?" She turned to Sean and gave him a honeyed smile. "You'll have to come to Robert's. We can all share. It'll be great."

Oh. *Oh* . . . I just managed to stop myself slapping my forehead in front of everyone. Of course. Just because *I'd* sworn off men didn't mean *Rose* had.

Sean shook his head. "Cheers, but I don't want to be a gooseberry." He gave the two of us a significant look.

Rose snorted again. She really ought to try to break herself of the habit. "Come on! You honestly think him and me are together?"

I hoped I'd just imagined her lip curling as she gestured towards me. "I'm not sure I'm altogether flattered by that remark," I protested.

She smiled at me, looking more toothsome than a crocodile. "Sorry, sweetheart. I don't believe in cradle-robbing."

Icy shock lanced through my chest—then I realised she just meant I was too young for her. *Idiot.*

"You all right, mate?" Sean was staring at me, concern crinkling the corners of those perilously green eyes of his. "Look like you've seen a ghost."

"I— Yes. Of course." I forced a smile. "I'm quite all right, I mean. Not that I've seen a ghost. Hertfordshire's really not that haunted. Not like Gloucestershire. Or the Isle of Wight . . ." I caught myself. "We should order. Will you be joining us?"

I wasn't sure what I hoped his answer would be. I'd been looking forward to a cosy, relaxed meal with Rose, but damn it, the demands of friendship were clear. If she was after him, it was my duty to help her. It'd do me good too to concentrate on someone else for a bit. If nothing else, it'd be a constant reminder to me that I was *not* looking for anyone for myself.

Even if it would be hard to watch them getting closer . . .

"Nah, thanks," Sean was saying, "but it's been a busy day. Think I'll just have a quiet night in with the telly." He grinned suddenly. "'Sides, Wills and Harry'd never forgive me if they found out I'd been fraternizing with the Enemy."

"My name's actually Emeny. Em. En. Ee." I sounded it out with resignation. "But to ninety-nine percent of the school, yes, I'm the Enemy. And that's including the teachers. Still, it could be worse," I added more optimistically.

"Yeah?"

"I was a supply teacher for a week in a London secondary school, where the year elevens delighted in dubbing me *Mr. Enema.* It was the longest week of my life. Also, quite possibly, the most educational. Although not in matters I'd care to elaborate on."

Sean laughed. All right for him, with a gift of a name like *Grant*. "Guess it's not easy being gay and teaching in a place like that."

I blinked at him. He knew I was gay? Who'd told him? No. I must have misheard him. He hadn't said that. Had he? "Pardon?"

Sean took a step back. "Uh, sorry, mate. No offence. It's just you look . . . Sorry."

Oh. "That's quite all right," I muttered to my brogues. My face was hot. I supposed it was only fitting that it should turn a fetching shade of pink, seeing as the rest of me apparently proclaimed my sexual preferences to the world at large. That year-eleven joke on my name took on a whole new meaning.

"We're not really used to someone like you here," he said, which made me feel even worse.

"Shamwell has hitherto been a queer-free zone, has it?" I snapped.

"What? No, you got me wrong. I just meant, you're a bit of a cut above, you know?"

"A cut above what?" I asked, suspicious. If there was a circumcision joke in the offing, I was . . . I was getting paranoid, I decided.

"Well, the way you talk—the way you dress, come to that—I'd have thought you'd be teaching royalty at Eton, not slumming it here with us."

My blood ran cold. "I don't know what you mean. Why shouldn't I be here? There's nothing sinister about it."

Sean had stepped back, his hands raised. Why was he smiling? "Whoa. Hold on, who said it was? Just surprised, that's all. You got family in the area?"

Oh. "Er, no." I essayed a nonchalant shrug, and something in my neck twinged painfully. "Ow. I just saw the post advertised and thought it sounded interesting."

"You all right there?" Sean asked as I rubbed my neck, which had reached the pins-and-needles stage.

"Quite fine. Thank you." I rolled a shoulder gingerly.

His mouth quirked in a *suit-yourself* sort of way. "So do you live in the village?"

"Um, yes. Thank you. And yes. I'm renting the Old Hatter's Cottage. Just down the road. You know it?"

"Yeah? Hey, that's great."

He seemed a tad more pleased than I'd have expected. "Why?"

"He was my great-great-grandad. The Old Hatter, I mean. He lived in that cottage all his life—least, that's what my mum always said. Big industry in this area, hats used to be."

I had visions of the village in days gone by, half the population high on mercury fumes. And the other half, of course, drunk on beer from the proliferation of pubs. It'd certainly explain one or two architectural idiosyncrasies, like the strangely undulating wall just down the road from the church. "Oh—so your family is my landlord?"

"Nah, the house was sold way before my time." He raised one eyebrow a couple of millimetres. "You know, you probably ought to order your food, if you want to eat tonight."

"Done it," Rose interrupted. "Hours ago."

I'd wondered where she'd got to. "Oh? What are we eating?"

"Oh, the usual. Sweet-and-sour pork balls, cashew chicken, and crispy beef. And monk's vegetables, 'cause you look like you could do with getting your five a day."

"What happened to the crispy duck?"

"I decided to let it live to quack another day."

Sean grinned. "Don't want to disappoint you, but I reckon it was dead already. I don't think they just run down to the river and nab one of the ones the kids like to feed."

"Dunno why not," Rose said with a shrug. "There's enough of them."

I frowned. "I've never seen more than twenty-eight, and that was only the once. Usually it's between twelve and seventeen. That wouldn't keep this place going for more than a fortnight." I realised they were both staring at me. "What?"

Rose patted my arm. "Just so's you know, most people *don't* count the ducks every time they walk past the river."

"Oh." I thought about it for a moment but decided not to ask *Why not?* They'd only have given me funny looks again, I was sure of it.

There was a brief silence, thankfully broken by the Chinese lady behind the counter. "Order for Grant."

Sean pushed himself off the wall. "Right, that's me. I'll see you around, all right?"

"If you're sure you wouldn't like to share our, um, pork balls?" I said, making an effort for Rose's sake.

"That's okay. Wouldn't want to get between a man and his pork balls."

Sean grabbed the carrier bag from the lady, smiled at us, and left.

"Bloody hell, have you never heard of playing it cool?" Rose muttered to me as the door closed behind him.

"What do you mean?"

"He already said no once. You don't have to act all desperate for his company."

"So-*rry*." I jammed my hands into the pockets of my jacket and turned to examine the cards and flyers from local businesses on the windowsill, which hoped to persuade me into parting with my cash for, variously: tree surgery, computer services, and bikini waxing in the comfort of my own home. I winced. Not that I'd ever been waxed, but I had a very good imagination, and I wasn't sure where the *comfort* part was supposed to come in.

Rose peered over my shoulder. "Ooh, that's quite a good price for a Brazilian. I'll have one of them."

I handed over the flyer for Ruby's Waxing. "You know, I could have lived without the knowledge of exactly how you cultivate your lady-garden."

Rose snorted a laugh. "*Lady-garden*? Ew. You make it sound like it's got things living in it. So what about you? I've heard gay blokes are all into manscaping."

"Some of us prefer to buck the trend. And why am I even telling you this?" The door opened, and I got *another* crick in my neck turning to check if it was anyone from the school. "Ow," I said, rubbing my neck.

The man who'd just walked in (fifties, unshaven, thankfully a total stranger) gave me a funny look.

"Order for Wyman," the lady at the counter announced. I breathed a sigh of relief. *Finally* I could escape to relative privacy before Rose got it into her head to ask if I had any intimate piercings.

I didn't, by the way. Mother thought piercings were common. Which meant, naturally enough, that when I was fourteen, I got my best friend at school to pierce my ear for me with a sewing needle.

At least, Fordy had said it was a needle. I wasn't altogether sure he knew the difference between needles and pins. Or, for that matter, sharp and blunt, or sterile and more germ-laden than a rat with bubonic plague.

One very nasty infection and two courses of antibiotics later, I'd decided that (a) this particular rebellion wasn't worth the upset it caused to Mother and (b) over my dead body would anyone ever get near my intimate bits with anything sharp and pointy.

I had, as it happened, allowed Fordy near my intimate bits, although not with anything sharp and pointy. That hadn't ended particularly well, either.

"Do you think I'm really that obvious?" I asked when we were safely back inside the Old Hatter's Cottage. Rose took off her anorak, a padded one that looked like a sleeping bag with sleeves, before I could offer to help her, and slung it over the banister. I tried not to be too pointed about removing my greatcoat and hanging it on a coat hanger.

"Obvious about what? Being posh? Being a bit eccentric? Fancying Sean?"

What? "What? No, about being gay. *Obviously*. I mean, from what Sean said . . ."

"Well, it's your gaydar, innit?"

Oh. *Oh*. "He's *gay*?" I blurted out. Had I got this all wrong?

Rose seemed blithely unconcerned. "Well, I couldn't say for *sure*, sure, but I'm pretty certain he swings both ways. I've seen him around the village with men just as much as with women. Are we going to eat or just stand around in the hall yakking?"

"They could be just friends," I said, grabbing the takeaway bag from the hall table. "The men, I mean."

"Yeah, right. The sort of friend you see all the time for a few months and then never hang around with ever again?" Well, she might have a point there. "Front room?" she carried on. "Or are we going to be all posh and sit at the dining table? Again." We'd used the dining table, which was large, sturdy, and scratched, to do our marking on.

"Which would you prefer?"

"Duh. What do you think?"

"Fine. You go on through and sit down, and I'll bring some plates." I detoured into the kitchen and grabbed the requisite crockery and cutlery. "But he's definitely had girlfriends?" I asked, joining her in the lounge. Or *front room*, if one preferred.

Rose had already made herself at home on the sofa and was flicking through the book I'd been reading, which happened to be a copy of *Maurice* by E. M. Forster. "God, is all your stuff a hundred years old?" She tossed the admittedly battered paperback onto my piano stool, then regarded the instrument itself, which had been an unexpected and touching moving-in present from my stepfather. "You know, I'm still waiting for you to serenade me with that thing. How about some entertainment while I eat?"

"What, so you can steal all the pork balls? I'm not that much of an idiot. Now focus, please. Sean. Girlfriends."

Rose made a grab for the takeaway bag as I set out the plates and forks on the coffee table. "Oh, right. Yep. He went out for a while with Destinee's aunt-who's-her-cousin."

I goggled, arrested in the act of sitting down beside her. "Pardon?"

I'd known they did things differently in the countryside. I hadn't realised they did them *that* differently.

Rose looked up from the bag, holding a prawn cracker. "Oh, you know. Her mum, that's Destinee's mum's sister, had her when she was still at school, so she was brought up by the grandparents. So Destinee calls her Auntie Chelsea. Happens all the time." She gave me a sidelong look. "Okay, whatever *you* were thinking, I don't think I want to know."

"I . . . wasn't thinking anything. At all. Do you know the family well?"

"I taught your class last year, remember? Believe me, you've got off easy so far. You're going to see plenty of Destinee's mum in the next few months."

"Oh joy," I muttered, opening up one of the little plastic tubs. "Um. What's this one supposed to be?" The dish inside appeared to be mostly composed of bright-orange grease, with a lot of sticklike things poking out.

"Crispy chilli beef. Go on, have some. It's yummy."

"Is it supposed to be this oily?"

"Come on, it's not that bad. Takeaways are always greasy. That's part of the attraction." She emptied out half the container of rice onto her plate and the rest onto mine.

"It is?"

"Well, yeah. Knowing you're being a bit naughty is always fun. And hang on, are you telling me you've never had a takeaway before?"

My shoulders tensed. "Um, no? Why would I want to tell you something like that?"

"Oh my God. You haven't, have you? What, did Nanny always cook your dinners right up until you left home?"

"Don't be ridiculous," I muttered, my cheeks burning. "I didn't have a nanny." Au pairs were an *entirely* different thing.

"And what about when you were at uni, for God's sake? I mean, *seriously?*"

"I always ate in Hall. Or at a restaurant, but that was only once or twice a term. And before you ask, my last job was at a boarding school, so I ate in, of course."

"And you never went out for a night's drinking and got the munchies?"

"I don't really drink very much. And I always kept a packet of chocolate Hobnobs in my rooms. Sometimes I used to eat toast."

"Did you have a whatchamacallit, a fag to make it for you?"

"Only very occasionally," I said drily. "And then only in the pejorative sense."

"What? And, you know, *what?*"

"Fagging, as in junior boys performing menial tasks for their seniors, is a school thing, not a university thing. And not at my school, in any case. The most the junior boys ever have to do at Loriners' is serve tea and crumpets to the Masters once a term."

Rose made a face. "Public schools scare me. Why are they even called that? Why not just call them private schools? It's more accurate."

"It's a historical thing."

"Snob thing, if you ask me. Pass the chicken cashew thing."

I passed it, and she served herself a generous portion. "Anyway, I didn't go to public school. Loriners' is an independent grammar school. Half the pupils don't even board."

"What, were you not posh enough for Eton? Mm, this is gorgeous. Have some. Go on."

I took a small helping, trying to avoid the limp green bits. "Not really, no."

"Not really what—oh, you mean *posh*? Bloody hell, I was joking. By whose standards are you not posh? The *Queen's*?"

I shrugged. "We're really very middle class. Mother would have liked me to go to somewhere like Winchester, but, well, it just didn't happen." Father's death when I was ten had had quite a few unforeseen consequences. "And, anyway, I don't think I'd have really fitted in."

"No? Aren't they all a load of young fogeys there?"

"Ouch."

"Well, come off it. You wear all that tweed, and honestly, bow ties?"

"Bow ties are cool," I said, confident of this at least. "*Doctor Who* said so."

"Yeah, about three incarnations ago, wasn't it? Not that Matt Smith was cool in the first place. Sweetheart, you need a new style icon."

I had horrible visions of being dragged around Burton's in an upside-down version of *Queer Eye for the Straight Guy*. "I'm fine how I am," I said stiffly.

She shrugged and forked up a pork ball. "Your funeral."

When I was sure she wasn't looking, I glanced down surreptitiously at my checked shirt and corduroys. What was wrong with my clothes? Lots of people I knew dressed like me. My *stepfather* dressed like me.

Hmm. Possibly that was her point? "So what do you think I should be wearing?" I asked. "In the purely hypothetical event I might want to change my image."

"Well, that long coat of yours is okay—quite swish, actually, very *Sherlock*—but what's underneath could definitely do with an update. Have you even owned a pair of jeans? And try wearing shirts without ties. *Especially* bow ties. You know. Just normal stuff."

"Jeans are uncomfortable." And they made me feel alarmingly like I was on display.

"Not once you've worn them in, they're not. Or you could start slow, maybe with a pair of chinos? But ditch the bow ties."

"What, all thirty-one of them?" Quite a lot of them had been presents.

"Oh my God. Only you, Robert, could *literally* have a bow tie for every day of the month. Do they have little numbers on, so you know which one to wear each day? Or do you wear them all in strict rotation, so numbers twenty-nine to thirty-one don't feel left out when it's a short month?"

"They don't have numbers!" I told her indignantly. "I just wear what I happen to be feeling like on the day, that's all." So what if I occasionally wore my least favourite ones on purpose so they didn't feel neglected? "Anyway," I said, rallying, "I bet you've got at least that many pairs of shoes."

"No. Nowhere near." Rose stopped eating for a moment, though, her head on one side. "Actually, I haven't got a clue."

I stared at her. "How can you *not know* how many pairs of shoes you've got?"

"Because I've never counted? Anyway, you know what it's like. There's always a few pairs that get kicked under the bed or shoved to the back of the wardrobe, and when you find them you think, *Oh yeah, I remember you, let's take you out for a stroll.*" She smiled fondly, visions of kitten heels presumably dancing in her head.

I tried to imagine what it must be like to have hitherto forgotten pairs of shoes popping up all over the place. And failed.

Rose served herself an abstemious portion of monk's vegetables. "So how many pairs of shoes have you got?"

"Seven," I replied promptly. "There are my black dress shoes, my best brogues, my other brogues, my walking boots, my gym trainers—"

"Bet they're bright white without a speck of dirt," Rose interrupted.

"Well, obviously I don't wear them outdoors. Then there are my running shoes—"

"I tried running once. Nearly killed me."

"And finally, my cricket shoes. I left my tennis shoes at Mother and Peter's house."

"Do you seriously have a different pair of shoes for every single sporting activity?"

"You mean you don't?"

"Robert, look at me. Does this figure scream *sporty* at you?"

For my sixteenth birthday, Mother arranged for me to go deer stalking. It was horrible—not because of all the blood and gore, because there wasn't any. It was spectacularly unsuccessful, as deer hunts go. No, the worst thing about it was the man leading the hunt. He'd been a gamekeeper on one of the big estates, and I could tell he didn't think much of the plebs who paid for a day's hunting "experience." Oh, he was all politeness when he thought anyone was watching, but I caught him laughing at Mother behind her back just because she said something that wasn't quite right.

But I'm getting off track. What I *meant* to say was, right at the end of the day, when we were all about to give up, I sighted down my gun and a young stag just walked into view—and turned to look right at me, his antlers curving proudly over his fine-boned, regal head. I swear those sensitive brown eyes could see the danger he was in, but he just stood there, staring death in the face.

I didn't shoot him, obviously. I'd rather have shot the hunt leader. From the look on his face when he realised I'd let one get away, I gathered the feeling was mutual.

But anyway, right now, I knew exactly how that stag had felt. I only hoped Rose would show me the same mercy I'd showed the stag when I, inevitably, said the wrong thing. "Well, you do have a touch of embonpoint."

She frowned. "Is that like cellulite?"

"Er . . . It means you're voluptuous."

"Like Nigella Lawson?"

"Yes?" I said, hoping it was the right answer.

"Oh. Cool. But yeah, I'm not really into sport. Doing it or watching it. The one thing I don't miss about Bastard Shitface"—I assumed this was the new pet name for the ex-fiancé—"is the endless hours of TV football. I mean seriously, what's the big deal about watching a load of blokes chase a ball around a field?"

"It's not just the game itself. It's . . ." I struggled to express the concept and stalled for time by serving myself some more cashew chicken, although since Rose's repeated depredations, the second half of the dish's name was largely inaccurate. "It's symbolic."

"What, of men playing with their balls?"

"*No*. It's a battle for supremacy. Men competing to prove themselves better, stronger, more skilled. It's a primeval urge."

"So it's basically comparing dick size?"

"There's a bit more to it than that. Men united in hard, physical struggle—"

"Oh, it's an acceptably straight way for men to express their repressed homosexual urges. Gotcha."

"Well, you might have a point there. But it's about camaraderie, team spirit, honour…" I gave up. "Noted. No sport-viewing marathons while you're in the house."

"There. That wasn't so difficult, was it? So what did you think of Sean, anyway?" she asked me in what was probably supposed to be a casual tone.

I wasn't fooled. "He seems nice."

"I mean," she went on quickly, "I know he's probably not happy-ever-after material, but he'd make a good rebound fling, wouldn't you say?" She crunched on some orange sticks.

I felt she was being a bit callous. Still, maybe she'd change her mind if they ever got, well, involved. "You don't think he's a bit young?"

"What, seriously? He can't be that many years off thirty, for God's sake." She frowned. "Why, do you?"

Uh-oh. I was firmly in Faux Pas City tonight, taking up residence in Foot-in-Mouth Mansions, on the corner of Oops Avenue. "No, no. Absolutely not. More, um, beef?"

"No, ta, I'm stuffed. No, I'm pretty sure he's in his late twenties at least. Him and the twins' mum are twins too. Runs in the family."

"Like the hair." I looked at the container of crunchy, sweet, sticklike things masquerading (not very successfully) as beef. It'd be a shame to waste it. I tipped the rest onto my plate.

"Yeah. Although I heard the twins' dad was a ginge, too. Poor little sods had no chance."

"Are you implying there's something wrong with having red hair?"

"Depends, dunnit? Some blokes make it look good. Sean, fr'instance," she said with a sly look at me. "But others, you just look at them and think ew, ginger nuts."

"I never realised that when a lady looks at a man, she's picturing his, ah . . ."

"Man-garden?"

"Thank you. *Not.* I think I preferred not knowing." I pushed all inappropriate images of Sean firmly out of my head and looked down at my plate.

Unfortunately, the orange tangle of crispy beef was just a little too suggestive for my peace of mind.

CHAPTER THREE

Going out of the house the next morning, I was accosted by Hanne, my small Norwegian neighbour. Milly and Lily, her two giant schnauzers, strained at their leashes, inexplicably failing to pull their mistress along the street after them. "Did you enjoy your takeaway last night?" she asked with a smile, holding back Cerberus's sisters with no apparent signs of strain.

Why I'd thought moving out of boarding school to teach in a village would make a scrap of difference to everyone knowing my business, I couldn't presently imagine. "Yes, thank you," I said politely, trying to get past her without getting tangled up in the dogs' leads. Milly, or possibly Lily, took the opportunity to get a good sniff at an area a well-brought-up dog, I felt, would have had the delicacy to avoid.

"And your friend, she works with you?"

"Rose? Oh yes."

"She looks very nice. Will she come again?"

"Er, probably, sometime." I wasn't quite sure what Hanne was getting at.

"You tell me when she's coming. I'll show you how to make lamb-and-cabbage stew. It's easy, you can't go wrong." I was baffled by Hanne's apparent faith in me. Still, she didn't know me all that well. "And maybe deer antlers. They're very tasty, and fun to share."

Deer antlers? You couldn't *actually* eat those, could you? Wouldn't they be rather, well, chewy? Or maybe crunchy? "That's very kind, but you really don't—"

"A nice young man like you shouldn't be alone all the time." She smiled again and effortlessly pulled the dogs to heel as she walked on by. Maybe she power-lifted in secret.

I strode on up the hill and towards the school. I *wasn't* alone all the time. I saw people every day. At work, and in the village shops, and . . . All right, so I didn't have much of a social life, but I was far from a hermit. I just didn't know many people in the village yet.

And it was entirely my business, I decided firmly, whether or not I made any effort to get to know people. Checking my watch to find that yes, it was eight thirteen, and no, the church clock still wasn't telling the right time, I quickened my pace. If I didn't get a shift on, there would be parents outside the classroom already by the time I got there, eager to offload their little darlings for the day.

They tended to get a bit stroppy if you kept them waiting.

When, having armed myself with a cup of coffee from the staff room, I opened the classroom door to let in the marauding hordes, I soon spotted three matching flashes of orange. Sean was dropping off the terrible twins. He shot me a grin as they got to the front of the higgledy-piggledy line. "All right?"

I'm never sure what the correct reply to that is. Should one say, *Yes, thank you, I'm fine*, or does one just repeat the greeting? After all, nobody who says *How do you do* ever expects to be told how, in fact, one is doing. Perhaps it would be safer to go with a simple *Good morning*. I opened my mouth—then a plaintive chorus of "Mr. Enemy" sounded from behind me, and I was forced to turn away from Sean.

Obviously not recovered from the previous day's ill-advised excavation, Charlie's nose had started to bleed again. By the time I was able to look up from him, Sean was long gone.

I did my best to quell the rising disappointment. There would be plenty of opportunities to talk to him again. For the purposes of getting him together with Rose, I reminded myself sternly. I did a quick head count, closed the classroom door, and got out the register.

At lunchtime, I once again sat next to Rose in the staff room. "What's in the sandwiches today?" she asked, peering at them as if she expected the filling to crawl out from between the slices of bread and start doing a song-and-dance routine. Probably to something like "Thriller."

"Just butter." I'd decided to play it safe, after yesterday's debacle.

"Just butter? Robert, two slices of bread and butter wouldn't keep a baby sparrow alive."

"I'm still full from last night," I protested.

"You can't be. That was yesterday. Your stomach reboots itself when you go to sleep, everyone knows that."

"Sounds nauseating. Anyway, I had three Weetabix this morning."

"Ugh. Don't know how you can eat that stuff. You put a drop of milk on it, and it turns to complete mush."

"It was on special offer," I defended myself weakly. "Tesco had family packs going for half price."

"So leave 'em for the families who've got kids who actually *like* mush. And anyway, since when do you have to keep your hand on your ha'penny?"

I threw her a startled look. "I think you mean 'watch the pennies,'" I said cautiously. At least, I *assumed* she wasn't talking euphemistically about my in any case long-departed (and not in the least mourned) virginity.

"Pennies, ha'pennies, whatever. It's not like either of them are worth tuppence these days. Anyway, it doesn't matter. I brought extra today." She held out a plastic tub and a fork that looked like it had come from a picnic set. "Go on, take it. I've got another one for me."

I took it, not without reservations. "Is there some conspiracy among the women of the village to feed me up?"

"Yeah, we discussed it at the last naked sabbat. We're planning to fatten you up and roast you on a spit at the next solstice. Everyone's looking forward to it."

"People warned me about moving to the country, you know." I opened the tub. It seemed to be rice salad, with vaguely recognisable bits of vegetable and, because this was Rose, large lumps of meat.

"So who else is feeding you for the slaughter?" Rose got out a matching tub and fork and tucked in.

"My neighbour. Hanne. I think she thinks you and I are going out together, by the way. Or at least that we ought to." I forked up a bit of rice salad.

"You haven't told her you're gay?"

"It's never come up."

Rose smirked. "Maybe now you've met Sean, it'll *come up* a bit more often."

I made a face at her and dug back into my rice. My fork halfway to my mouth, I smiled, suddenly realising something. "At least this means I'm not as obvious as all that." Not that I was ashamed of being gay or anything, but I was rather uncomfortable with the idea that everyone I met was speculating over what I got up to in bed.

Especially seeing as what I got up to in bed these days largely consisted of sleeping.

"Hmm. She's not been in this country very long, has she? Maybe it gets lost in translation."

"And here I was, thinking the language of camp was universal."

"Meh. She probably thinks you're just particularly British or something."

I swallowed my mouthful of rice salad. "I feel as if I should make a public apology to the rest of the nation's manhood. This is very nice, by the way. Thank you."

Rose beamed. "Nobody starves on my watch. So, did you speak to Sean this morning? I saw him go past with the twins." The classrooms for the infants at St. Saviour's were arranged in a long line, with a glass wall and doors looking out onto the playing fields. Anyone hoping to pass unnoticed would probably need to dig a tunnel.

"Didn't get a chance. Well, we said hello."

"Men! You're so useless. You need to strike while the iron's hot."

Was the iron hot? I'd have thought lukewarm, at best. "What am I supposed to say?"

Rose heaved an exaggerated sigh. "Do I have to breast-feed you?"

I winced. "You mean spoon-feed, don't you? *Please* say you mean spoon-feed."

"Oh, whatever. Get him talking about himself. Men like doing that."

I had the distinct impression she didn't find this an altogether admirable quality. "And then what?"

"Then you ask him out."

"Me?" Hang on a minute. Friendship was one thing, but was she really expecting me to do all the work for her?

"Yes, you. Tell you what, that wine bar that used to be an antiques shop has just reopened after their refurb. Why don't you ask him to meet you there for a drink Saturday night?"

Ah. I realised where this was going: she'd get me to invite him for a friendly drink, and then oh-so-casually drop in to join us on the night. I could see a potential fly in the ointment, however. "I'm not sure he's really a wine bar sort of person."

"Yeah, but you're definitely not a pub sort of person."

"Does that matter?"

"Yes. *Obviously*. How long have we got to the end of lunch?"

Having the tub in one hand and a laden fork in the other, I couldn't easily look at my watch. "Um, about twenty-six minutes, I think?"

"You do know you're weird? Right, I'm going to love you and leave you. I've got to try and track old Arfur down and get him to do something about the loo in my classroom."

Old Arfur was Mr. Minnit, the only other male member of staff at St. Saviour's School. He acted as caretaker and general dogsbody. Having checked the school records and found out his first name was in fact Winston, I could see why he preferred to be known by his nickname.

"Any day now the UN's going to declare war on class 1W for stockpiling chemical weapons. Now, don't forget: you grab Sean Grant at the end of school and don't let go until he's agreed to a date, got it?"

My mouth now being full, I snapped off a salute—and nearly took an eye out with the fork I'd forgotten I was holding.

At least it had been empty, I consoled myself as I caught the Head giving me a frankly worried glance.

When the bell rang for the end of school, the children weren't the only ones in the class whose heartbeats starting racing. I wiped my palms on my handkerchief and, figuratively speaking, buckled on my breastplate like a knight of old preparing to do battle for a lady's favour. Except, if all went well, it would be Sean winning Rose's favour—or did the fact that he was the one being wooed cast *him* in the lady's role here? A swift vision of Sean in a wimple and Rose in full chivalric armour almost surprised a nervous laugh out of me, but I managed to turn it into a cough.

"Choke up, chicken," Emily G.'s gran, who was first in line for child collection, said with a wrinkly smile.

Charlie, who was standing close by my side, pulled on my sleeve. I bent down to his level. "Why did she say that?" he whispered.

"I have absolutely no idea," I whispered back. "But you should always be polite to older people." I straightened to nod, smiling, at Emily and her gran.

Granny G. narrowed her eyes and hurried Emily away rather more abruptly than I would have considered necessary.

The line continued, parents and other nominally responsible adults picking up their infants, exclaiming over stories of childish achievements and being pestered to go and buy sweeties and/or visit the swings on the way back home. Luck was with me, although possibly not with the twins' mother, as it was Sean who came to pick up Wills and Harry. I stood aside to let the twins barrel past me and launch themselves at their uncle, who bore the onslaught with only a minor look of discomfort as one of them head-butted him in the solar plexus.

I winced in sympathy and stepped forward again. "Sean? Could I, um, have a word? If you don't have to rush off, of course." Maybe he did have to rush off. I wondered what he did for a living that he was able to bring his nephews to and from school. Perhaps he was unemployed? I wondered if Rose knew. Would it be a deal-breaker for her, as the common parlance was?

"Yeah, sure." He frowned down at the twins. "What have you two been up this time, then?"

"No, no—it's nothing to do with them." I was struck with a brainwave. "Actually, why don't you two go and play on the climbing frame while you're waiting?"

"Yeah!" they shouted in unison, and ran off without a second glance at their uncle.

Sean waited while I offloaded the last of my charges, save for the twins and Charlie. Then he turned to me, a question in his eyes. Actually, the question was in his entire body language. It seemed to give the moment a weighty importance I could, frankly, have done without. It was ridiculous. All I had to do was ask him to go for a drink, and it wasn't even for *me*. "Er," I began. My throat caught, so I coughed to clear it.

"Choke a chicken," Charlie piped up politely from beside me, having evidently decided it was just one of those things people said for no apparent reason, like *bless you* to a person who'd sneezed, or *sorry* to someone who'd trodden on your foot.

"Thank you." I turned back to Sean. He seemed a bit distracted and tore his gaze away from Charlie with a start when I spoke. "I, ah, just wondered, if, you know, you'd like to, um, go for a drink? Just, just a friendly drink," I added, to make things perfectly clear. "To see what the place is like now? The wine bar, I mean. Badgers. It's been refurbished. Um. You probably knew that."

Sean arched one copper-coloured eyebrow. "Yeah, okay," he said slowly. Something inside my chest performed gymnastics that were, in the circumstances, *totally* unwarranted. "Tonight?"

"Tonight would be lovely."

"Eight o'clock all right? I'll come to yours first."

"No, no, you needn't do that." I was fairly sure that was more, well, *date* behaviour. Not friendly-drink behaviour. "We can meet there."

He shrugged. "I'm going to need somewhere to park the bike, anyway. Your place is nearer than the village car park."

"Oh. Well, in that case, *mi entrada es su entrada*." Sean looked blank. "Um. My driveway is your driveway? I mean, feel free. Park away." God, why did I turn into a blithering idiot around this man? The sooner I got him fixed up with Rose the better. *Then* maybe my subconscious would stop getting its knickers in a twist every time I saw him.

There was a painful knot in my stomach. Clearly I'd eaten too much of Rose's rice salad.

"Great. I'll see you then." Sean smiled and turned to amble over the field to where the twins were hanging upside down from the climbing frame.

I looked down at Charlie. "Looks like it's just you and me, then. Want to sit down and do some colouring while I see if Mrs. Ormley can find out what's keeping your dad this time? Don't worry, I won't make you sit with her." Mrs. Ormley was known for her excellent manner with the parents and extreme surliness with anyone else. Including the teachers, whom she seemed to see as somewhat larger and therefore more troublesome schoolchildren.

Charlie nodded but didn't say anything.

"I'm sure he's just got held up in traffic. Or lost track of time."

Charlie nodded again, blinking rapidly.

I hid a sigh as I got out the colouring pencils.

By the time Charlie's monolithic dad lumbered up to the classroom door, sweating and apologising in equal profusion, it was too late to catch Rose still in school, so I sent her a text: *Mission accomplished. Badgers @ 8 tonight.*

Her reply was somewhat cryptic: *TFIF. Jst rmmbr: YOLO.*

I sent back: Translation, please?

Her response wasn't much better. *Lrn txtspk, FFS. DDAIWD.*

I gave up.

As I sat at my dining table that evening, tapping idly at my laptop and burning my mouth on my Tesco microwave lasagne, I couldn't help thinking about what Hanne had said. Was it really unhealthy to be alone? Should I start looking for another relationship?

Sean's smiling face popped into my mind. I suppressed it ruthlessly. Then I recalled it and stamped a mental *Property of Rose Wyman* on top of it.

The trouble was, Sean duly disposed of, I found my thoughts turning inevitably to Crispin. He'd had that colour of hair that was commonly termed "dirty blond," but the bare description didn't do him justice. He'd worn it long on top, so it just flopped over his eyes. God, his eyes. They were blue, and clear, and twinkled with devilry when he smiled . . .

Damn it. I was *not* still hung up on Crispin. I was *not*.

At any rate, it was safer for me to steer well clear of men for the foreseeable future. So that was what I would do.

I looked at the computer screen and went cold all over as I realised I'd absentmindedly called up the Gentlemen's Relish dating website— their motto, Huntin', Shootin' and Cottagin'.

I shut the laptop with a snap.

CHAPTER FOUR

I was glad when it was time to get ready for my evening date—no, not date, *friendly drink*—with Sean. But that brought its own problems. I wanted to put him at his ease; to make him feel he was among friends. And after Rose's comments about my bow ties, I was starting to wonder if I should experiment with more popular neckwear. Or even none at all.

I tried wearing a shirt with no tie, but with the collar unbuttoned, my throat seemed absurdly naked, my neck too thin and scrawny, my skin glaringly white and my Adam's apple the size of a grapefruit. But with the buttons all done up, it looked like my mother had dressed me. Also, that she didn't like me very much.

As I was almost certain she was actually quite fond of me, it would hardly be fair to go around giving erroneous impressions. I sighed and rooted around in my wardrobe for a tie of the non-bow variety. I knew I *had* some. At least, I'd had some before the move—four, to be precise—so presumably they were here somewhere. I glanced at my watch and started rooting a bit more speedily.

I breathed a sigh of relief when I eventually located them, strung on a coat hanger with my second-best waistcoat. Now I saw them, I even had a vague recollection of putting them there with the thought that all the things I was unlikely to wear might as well stick together. I pulled them off the hanger and regarded them thoughtfully.

The old school tie was out, obviously; that eye-piercing combination of lime and magenta would probably get me refused admittance to the wine bar. It certainly wasn't going to put anyone at their ease. The college tie was acceptable in appearance, being plain navy with an understated pattern of little crests, but I didn't want to seem like an intellectual snob. Especially as I was fairly sure Sean had never gone to university.

I hesitated over the next tie. I didn't know why I'd kept it, to be honest. It was ivory in colour, with an elegant cursive script that read "My other tie is a bow tie." I'd loved it from the minute Crispin had given it to me . . .

I shoved all three ties back into the wardrobe and shut the door. The fourth and final tie would have to do. Even if it *was* plain black and had only previously been allowed out to funerals.

Now, how to tie it? A full Windsor would clearly be too ostentatious. A four in hand, though safe, might imply a lack of care. A half Windsor? That just screamed *boring*. Ah! I had it. The Prince Albert. Debonair, yet with a touch of individuality. Perfect. I had to make several attempts to get it tied to my satisfaction—I was sadly out of practice—but in the end, I thought, it didn't look too bad: nonchalantly asymmetrical, with the slenderest of extra folds peeking coyly out from the bottom of the knot. That would look nicely informal.

I ran lightly down the stairs and settled in an armchair to await Sean's arrival. It was a minute to eight, so he'd be here directly . . . I caught myself and told myself firmly that to other people, *eight o'clock* meant anything from eight to half past, not *just as the Greenwich pips fade into the ether.* I would *not* allow myself to become anxious over any lack of punctuality.

Then I heard the roar of a motorbike engine. It Dopplered towards me in an ever higher-pitched crescendo, then faded to a purr and stopped, as Sean parked his bike in *mi entrada.* I watched, entranced, as he pulled off his helmet and shook out his hair. Rippling softly in the streetlamp's yellow glow, it shone like liquid copper. There ought to be swelling music, I thought. Possibly birdsong, if anyone could persuade the lazy little blighters to twitter after sunset. The clouds should part, and the light of the full moon should break through and limn his form with silver . . .

No.

No, no, no. I wrenched the curtain shut, wincing as a hook cracked under the pressure. Sean was here for Rose's benefit, not mine.

I flung open the front door a bit more dramatically than I'd intended and yelped as my hand got jammed between the doorknob and the wall. "Ouch. Come in."

"You all right there?" Sean's gaze fell upon my tie. "Oh, sorry, mate—have you just been to a funeral?"

"No, no. Just thought perhaps I should give the bow ties a night off." I made a face. "It's been pointed out to me they're not very trendy."

Sean frowned. "Who said that? I like your bow ties. Bow ties are cool."

A warm, fluttery feeling spread through my chest, as if a dozen animated bow ties flitted like butterflies inside me. "That's exactly what I told her!"

"Who?"

"Er, Rose." Too late, I realised I shouldn't be saying anything that might make her look bad. "But I'm sure she meant well. She doesn't seem to think much of Matt Smith's Doctor Who."

"What? He was one of the best ones. Well, him and David Tennant." Sean pursed his lips and nodded. "You could fancy David Tennant, but Matt Smith was the one you'd take home to your mum."

"You didn't like Christopher Eccleston?" I'd always considered him the sexiest Doctor. Certainly, he could have enticed me into his deceptively large blue box for a ride anytime. "I'd have thought, being a fellow fan of black leather . . ."

"Nah, well, he was okay, but he was like a transitional Doctor, wasn't he? The one just after the Time Wars, when he's all PTSD and stuff. Bit too serious for my liking. Can't imagine him in a bow tie, can you?"

"Good Lord, no." I shuddered at the very thought. "You know, I've been searching forever for a bow tie that actually has Bow Ties Are Cool on it. Somebody in the neckwear business is definitely missing a trick there."

"Too right. Hey, are we going to stand on your doorstep all night, or are we heading out for this drink?"

We were still on the doorstep? Oops, so we were. Had I forgotten to invite him in? Or just forgotten to move so he could actually get in? Probably both, I decided. "Sorry about that. Er, I won't be a tick."

I turned to shove my feet into my second-best brogues. "There. All ready. Shall we?"

He grinned. "I feel like I ought to offer you my arm or something."

"What, in case I totter in my high heels?" I glanced down at a pair of rather delicious-looking black biker boots as we walked down the exceedingly short garden path to the pavement. "Come to think of it, your heels are higher than mine. Perhaps I should offer you *my* arm."

"Nah, I'm taller than you. Wouldn't look right."

"I'm sure we'd be exactly the same height if we were barefoot." My face grew a little warm, for no apparent reason I could fathom. After all, I hadn't meant *completely* bare. Just our feet. Which I in no way had any kind of fetish about. "Five foot eleven?"

"Six foot," he countered smugly.

"Damn it."

"Yeah, it's the extra inch that makes all the difference."

"Surely it's what you do with it that counts?" Bugger it sideways, I was *not* supposed to be trading innuendo with the man. That was Rose's job. "Ahem. Nice evening, isn't it?"

Sean looked up and down the street as we ambled on. A light drizzle was falling, making the pavement glisten in the lamplight as if an obscenely large slug had happened to pass that way. "Well, it's an evening."

I glanced at him and tried unsuccessfully to stifle a grin at the merriment in his eyes.

Badgers wine bar was another forty-five or so yards up the road from the Chinese takeaway, on the corner just across the road from the churchyard. Its large windows glowed with an inviting, warm light. The entrance was set off to the side and looked confusingly like the front door to one of the terraced houses, a row of which directly adjoined the business. The effect was rather as if the owner of the end house had come into money and splurged the lot on building a conservatory with more floor space than the house itself.

"This is definitely the right door, isn't it?" I asked, my hand on the large brass knob. "I don't want to walk into somebody's house."

"Yeah, just imagine if it was one of the kids in your class. Poor little sod would have a heart attack thinking you'd come to check they were doing their homework properly. Nah, we're good here."

I opened the door and found myself stepping into a cosy little vestibule that led, via a somewhat winding route, to the wine bar proper. This was a large rectangular room with floor-to-ceiling windows on two sides and colourful artwork on the other two walls. We sat at a table next to the window—actually, it was more like what I believe Americans call a booth, with red plush diner-style seats perpendicular to the wall or, as in this case, window. Sean slid onto one bench and I onto its opposite number. Our knees jostled for position under the rectangular oak table, and I forced myself to remember Rose.

His leather jacket discarded, Sean was casually dressed in a dark-blue shirt with the top few buttons undone to reveal a T-shirt underneath. Apparently the open collar held no horrors for him. Perhaps I should have dispensed with the tie after all? At any rate, I could take off my jacket, I decided. I shrugged it off and laid it on the seat beside me.

The world's smallest waitress—really, I was certain several of class 2E outweighed her—came with a bounce of blonde curls to take our order. I perused the wine list and ordered a large glass of sauvignon blanc, hoping she wouldn't buckle under the weight when she brought it over. Sean chose a bottle of something called Wormold's Woe, from a local brewery.

"Ah, you're a fan, I take it?" I commented as the waitress tripped off with soundless steps.

"Yeah, they do a good beer, this brewery. Haven't tried this one yet, though."

I mentally kicked myself. Of *course* he wouldn't recognise the literary allusion in the name.

Sean grinned. "Or were you talking about *Our Man in Havana*?"

"Oh, you've read it?" I tried to keep the surprise out of my tone. The merriment in Sean's eyes told me I wasn't entirely successful.

"Yeah. *Brighton Rock*'s my favourite, though. He came from round here, you know, Graham Greene."

"Really?" I hadn't known that. Why hadn't I known that?

"Yeah, born in Berkhamsted. Bit of a git, or so they say, but a good writer. Go on, admit it, you thought I'd never heard of Graham Greene, didn't you?"

"Um . . ." I really, *really* wished the waitress would hurry up with our drinks. Fiddling with the salt and pepper pots just wasn't the same.

"Don't worry, I get that all the time. People just make assumptions—like, they see me, they reckon I never open a book. Then they see someone like you, and—"

"Here you go, one large sauvignon blanc," the waitress interrupted him, balancing a tray precariously on one hand as she put my wine down in front of me. Damn it. I'd wanted to know what Sean had been about to say. What *did* people assume when they saw me? "And one Wormold's Woe."

"Cheers, love." Sean raised his glass. I took a fortifying sip of wine. "Is it good?" I asked, as he set his glass down again.

"Not bad. Yours okay?"

"Very passable. Um. You were saying?"

"What was I saying? Oh, yeah, books. I did A-Level English, but I'd had enough of it by then, so I didn't bother with uni. Wanted to get out in the real world." He shrugged. "Fancied earning a bit of money, not getting into debt."

"So what do you do? For a living, I mean," I added quickly, just in case he thought I was asking something prying and inappropriate.

"Me? I'm a pest-control technician."

I almost dropped my glass. He didn't mean . . . Did he? "That's, a, er . . . ?"

Sean grinned. "Ratcatcher. But I deal with loads of other pests too."

"That must be, um, interesting." It could be worse, I told myself firmly, resisting the urge to draw back in my seat. He could have been a sewage worker. A hospital cleaner. An undertaker. And he'd almost certainly washed his hands before coming out tonight.

"You'd be surprised. There's plenty of variety in my line of work."

I tried not to grimace at the images of humming rubbish dumps that were dancing noisomely in my head. "So how did you get into it? Did you always know you wanted to be a, er, pest-control engineer?"

"Technician. Nah, I don't think anybody ever just wakes up one morning and decides, *Right, I fancy catching rats and clearing wasps' nests for a living.* I had a mate who was doing it, and he said there was an opening, so I went for it. Haven't regretted it."

"Really? I mean, that's wonderful." God knew I had enough regrets over my own career.

Sean leaned forward, and my stomach performed a strange somersault as his gaze met mine. "How many jobs do you get to work somewhere different every day? I've seen places the public never gets to see."

"Not wishing to be rude, but would they want to?"

"Hey, I'm not just talking about the sewers. What about the roped-off areas in Westminster Abbey and the British Library? Plus some other places I'm not allowed to mention 'cause of the nondisclosure agreements, but trust me, if you've ever read *OK!* magazine, you'll know the owners. Know *of* 'em, anyway."

"I stand corrected. Well, sit corrected. So all these places have had, um, problems?"

Sean shrugged. "Not all of 'em. You see, a lot of these places— 'specially where they've got historical relics—they can't afford to have an infestation. So we do the preventative stuff, lay out the insect monitors or the traps, depending on the type of place it is, and check 'em up several times a year. It's the bread-and-butter work. Contract stuff. Then there's the call-outs on top of that."

"Isn't it a bit, well, cruel? I mean, exterminating poor defenceless things for a living?"

"So you'd rather we let the cockroaches roam free?" Sean cast a glance around the bar. I followed his gaze nervously, half expecting to see a seething mass of black carapaces carpeting the parquet floor.

"Well, no."

"Let the wasps take over your loft?"

"If they weren't doing any harm, maybe . . ."

"Wasps are vicious bastards. And they damage your ceiling."

"Oh?"

"Yeah, the plaster underneath the nest gets damp. Weakens it." He half smiled. "Had a technician on my team fall foul of that, not so long ago. It was his own fault, really. Daft bastard tried to take out the nest from inside the bedroom. It was in the loft, see, but they were coming in the house through a sunken light fitting. Kevin, that was his name, he's a bit of a lazy sod. Can't be arsed to go up in the loft and do it properly. So he tells the customer, 'Trust me, love, I'm a professional,' and shoos her out of the bedroom. Shuts the door, gets out his duster, shoves the lance through the hole in the ceiling and puffs out the dust."

I winced. "I think I can see where this is going."

"Yep. Down comes a chunk of ceiling, right on top of his head. With it comes the light fitting, half the wasps' nest, and oh, about two hundred pissed-off wasps. They get all over his head, inside his suit . . . You get the picture. Stung all over, poor sod. And I mean *all* over. You think a wasp sting on your arm is bad? Try one on your bollocks."

I shuddered. "Ouch."

"Just a bit. Now Kevin, not being the sort to suffer in silence, makes a bit of a fuss. Which you can take to mean screams his bloody head off. So the customer opens the door, takes one look at Kevin, trapped in there with the wasps, and what do you reckon she does? She shuts the door on him and leaves him to it. Well, like she said, he'd told her he was a professional."

"Oh God." I tried not to laugh and failed. "Um. I'm sorry. He was all right? Eventually, I mean?"

Sean nodded, grinning. "He got out of the pest-control business after that. We all thought it'd be best. Works in insurance now. But going back to what you said, it's usually pretty humane. There's the Countryside and Wildlife Act 1981 that lays down all sorts of rules for how you can get rid of pests. And there's people keeping an eye on us too. You know how we get a lot of roadkill round here? How many times have you seen an owl or a red kite by the side of the road?"

I'd never really thought about it before, but now he came to mention it, they *did* seem rather conspicuous by their absence. After all, I'd seen more badgers, bunnies, and foxes lying in sad furry heaps by the roadside than you could shake a bloodstained stick at. "Um, none?"

"That's because Natural England scoop 'em all up so they can test them for secondary poisoning. Make sure we've been clearing up all the dead rats and not letting 'em get into the food chain." He smiled and took a gulp of beer.

I found myself smiling back, a warm glow suffusing my insides that I suspected had very little to do with my sauvignon blanc. This was all rather unexpected. I mean, obviously I'd admired his looks, his smile, and his capability in a crisis, but I'd never thought I'd be drawn to him quite so personally.

A lump of ice seemed to settle in my stomach. I wasn't here to be drawn to him, was I? I was here to help him get drawn to Rose. Which was for the best, wasn't it? I didn't *want* another relationship. Not now. Maybe not ever.

The thought was confusingly depressing. I picked up the cocktail menu, hoping to distract myself by speculating what might be in a Broken Brock. From the look of the ingredients list, everything.

Sean put his glass down. "So what was it like for you? Did you always know you wanted to work with kids?"

"Oh yes. Education gets a bad press, but it's so important." I roused myself to give him a twisted smile. "And I'm going to apologise in advance in case I start ranting on at you about tuition fees and student loans."

"Not a fan?"

"God, no. So many bright young people from poorer backgrounds are being put off going to university, while the places are taken by better-off students who don't really want to study; they just want to have fun for three years. It's criminal, the way it's stifling social mobility to the detriment of those worst off." I realised I'd crumpled up the cocktail menu in my hand and, horrified, tried to straighten it out. "Oops. Um. Sorry about the rant." I shoved the menu in my pocket, hoping no one would notice.

Sean was smiling at me. "Hey, no worries. You already apologised, remember? And it's great that you care. Especially seeing as it's something you've obviously never had to worry about personally."

"That's what everyone assumes." I looked down at the table. "Actually, I was a scholarship boy at Loriners'. You see, when Father died, he left Mother and me in a bit of a state. He'd been— Well, nobody actually said the word *fraud*, but he'd made a few unwise decisions on behalf of his firm. Very unwise. And he hadn't wanted people to know, so he tried to make up for it by mortgaging the house, among other things..." I drew an abstract pattern in the condensation on the side of my wineglass, then smudged it out. "Anyway, for five years, we were, well, not well off. At all. The scholarship covered my tuition at Loriners', but Mother still had to pay for my uniform and all the other things. If she hadn't had her job at the school, which meant they let me off the boarding fees, well . . ." I trailed off. I honestly didn't know why I'd told him so much.

"What about now?"

"Oh, Mother's fine now." I smiled, relieved to be off the subject of our stint as paupers. "She met Peter, who is now my stepfather, and he's taken tremendously good care of her ever since."

"That's great. You get on with him okay?"

"Oh yes." I shrugged, a little self-conscious. "He's been very kind. You've probably gathered I shouldn't be able to manage the rent on the Old Hatter's Cottage out of my teacher's salary. Most of the other staff can't afford anywhere in the village." I was reminded once more what I was actually here for. "Rose has a flat here, though. It's just up the road."

"Right." Sean nodded. "So are you planning on getting involved in village stuff? There's a cricket team, if you're interested. Wrong time of year for that, though, I s'pose."

"At least it'll give me time to get in training for the start of the season. After fumbling that catch in the church, I'm not sure they'll want me if I don't pull my socks up."

"Hey, I just got there first, that was all. You'd have made it if I hadn't been there."

"No, I'd have been lying on the church floor covered in tomato sauce and reeking of garlic."

He grinned. "Okay, so now I wish I *had* just let the jar fall."

Was he flirting with me? It *sounded* like he was flirting. And the way his eyes crinkled up at the corners was awfully suspicious . . . "David Tennant," I said quickly. "Why wouldn't you take him home to your mum? Because you'd be worried she'd be all over him?"

"Well, that too. Nah, I don't know. He still had a bit of that darkness, I reckon. No second chances, remember?"

I swallowed. Yes, I remembered. "Some people would say an uncompromising nature is a good thing," I said cautiously.

"Nah, everyone deserves a second chance."

I smiled and picked up my glass, only to realise it was empty.

"Oh, sorry—fancy another, Rob?"

I looked up, startled. Apparently I was an open book to Sean.

"Don't mind me calling you that, do you?"

"No, no. It's just, I've never been a Rob before. I've always been Robert to my family."

"Yeah? What did your mates at school call you?"

"Emeny, mostly."

"Bloody hell. They still do that?" Sean leaned back in his seat and signalled to the waitress, who was busy with a table of fortysomethings—thankfully, none that I recognised as parents—but acknowledged him with a nod.

I waited until he turned back to me. "At Loriners', yes. It's a bit old-fashioned like that. I think that was why Mother chose it." Well, that was one of the reasons.

"Didn't you have a nickname or something?"

"Well, there was Fordy, who was *completely* obsessed with *Blackadder* for a while. He used to call me Bob." I emphasized the *B*s as Fordy had used to. I decided not to mention the rather large number who'd called me Emsy. Some people seemed to think it was a bit girly, which was not at *all* the impression I wanted to make. "And some of the others called me Eminem."

Sean laughed. "Sorry, mate, can't see the resemblance."

"Good. I watched one of his videos once. Revolting. Does the man *have* to be so coarse?"

The waitress returned to us at this point, with a chirpy smile and a "What can I get you?"

"I'll have another Wormold's Woe, please," Sean told her, leaning back in his seat. It struck me that for a not-really-a-wine-bar person, he seemed remarkably at ease here. "How about you, Rob? Same again?"

"Oh—yes, please." I waited until she'd gone. "Are you sure you're going to be all right on your bike?"

"I'll be fine—this stuff's not that strong. Two's my limit, though. Course, if you're worried, I could always leave the bike at yours and . . . walk back home."

There was the barest suspicion of a wink, and for a moment I had a strong feeling he was suggesting something else entirely. I looked down, my unsettled gaze falling on my watch. Where on earth was Rose? She hadn't forgotten, had she? I shot a glance at the door. Rose resolutely failed to materialise.

"You expecting someone?" Sean asked.

"No! I mean, of course not. I was just looking for the, um, little boys' room?"

"The gents'? I think it's out the back. Past that sign that says *Toilets*, with the big arrow." He gestured, not without a teasing smile, to a sign that couldn't have been more obvious if it had been flashing neon.

"Oh yes. Of course," I said, as if I could have possibly missed it. Bother. Having asked, I'd now have to actually *go*. Then again, this could be the perfect opportunity to call Rose and find out just what the hell was going on. "Be right back," I said breezily, stood up, and walked over in the direction Sean and the arrow had indicated.

Halfway there I remembered my phone was in my jacket and my jacket, uncharacteristically, was on my seat. Damn it. I strode back again. "Might be cold in the gents'," I said, avoiding Sean's eye as I grabbed the jacket and got out of there as swiftly as I could.

My luck was in, and there was no one else using the facilities. I dialled Rose's number and paced the tiles until she picked up.

"Hello?"

"Where are you?" I demanded, as quietly as I could.

"What?"

"Where *are* you?"

"Robert, is that you? I can't hear you. You've got to speak up."

Could I risk speaking more loudly? How far would it carry? The question became academic as a middle-aged man walked into the gents' and cast me a deeply suspicious look. Damn it, damn it, damn it. "I'll call you back."

I heard the faint strains of another "What?" as I took the phone from my ear and thumbed the call off. What to do now?

The way back to the vestibule involved skirting one edge of the main bar, but apparently I was, as they say, on a roll as Sean's head was bent over his mobile. I made it to the vestibule unseen, only to find it occupied by a raucous gaggle of short-skirted, precipitously heeled young women who gave me a frankly assessing glance, then looked away dismissively.

I was never wearing this tie again, I decided as I made a break for freedom straight through the door and down the steps.

The drizzle had stopped, leaving the air cool, fresh and a blessed relief on my somewhat heated face. I dialled Rose's number again. "*Where are you?*" I'd said it so often the words were rapidly losing all meaning for me.

"At home." Her tone was petulant. "I've finished mowing my lady-lawn and now I'm *trying* to watch a DVD. We don't all have hot dates tonight."

"Yes, you do!" The pavement was narrow in front of the door, so I strolled to the corner to allow a man in a mobility scooter to pass by. He raised a hand in acknowledgement and trundled on.

"Sweetheart, the only hot date I've got tonight is with my good friend Mr. Shiraz. Although I've been thinking of maybe inviting his mate Merlot over for a threesome." Rose was already slurring her words. This was a disaster—no way could she drop in on us casually now.

"You're supposed to be turning up unexpectedly at the wine bar to join me and Sean!"

"What, for a threesome?" There was a suspicion of a giggle.

"There will be no threesomes!" I raged. A burst of laughter rang out from a gang of teenagers hanging around on the corner by the churchyard. Mortified, I strode a few yards up the street and lowered my voice. "I thought we had a plan. To get you and Sean together."

"No, we had a plan to get *you* and Sean together. Ooh, did it work?"

"No! Rose, for God's sake, I thought I told you I didn't want to get into a relationship." My words sounded hollow in my own ears. It must be the phone, I decided.

"Yeah, but that was before you met Sean."

I bolstered my resolve. "When did I *ever* give you the impression I wanted to go out with Sean?"

"You ever watch cartoons? You know when Bugs Bunny sees Jessica Rabbit, and the eyes light up and the tongue rolls out? That's you whenever you see Sean."

"That's not true!" Oh God. It wasn't true, was it? I frowned. Bugs and Jessica? That wasn't right. "Hang on, he's from an entirely different world. Rose, listen very carefully—"

"I shall say zees only once?" she interrupted and cackled.

"I do *not* want to go out with Sean!" Realising I'd raised my voice again, and had probably been gesticulating like a madman too, I looked up to make sure there wasn't anyone I knew within earshot.

Straight into the eyes of Sean, staring at me through the wine bar's window—the *open* window—with an unreadable look on his face.

CHAPTER FIVE

For one horrible, shameful moment, I seriously contemplated doing what Rose would probably term "a runner." But to leave Sean like this—with the unpaid bill, to add insult to injury, or was it the other way round?—would be unconscionably rude.

Also, his motorbike was parked in my *entrada*. There really was no escape.

I walked back into the wine bar, the speed of my steps inversely proportional to the closeness of our table. "Sorry," I said as I slid back onto the bench seat, the uncaring ground having utterly failed to open up and swallow me en route. "Phone call."

Sean stared at me, stony-faced. The waitress had replenished our drinks while I'd been away from the table, but he didn't appear to have touched his. "Yeah. I saw. And heard. Come to that, so did the rest of the village. Although you might want to Facebook it when you get home. There's probably one or two people in the next town who didn't quite get just how much you don't want to go out with me."

I cringed. "It's nothing personal . . ."

"Yeah, I get it. It's just that I'm *from a different world*, isn't that what you said?"

"That wasn't— I wasn't talking about you!"

"So who were you talking about, then?" Sean picked up his beer glass, frowned at it, and put it down again.

"Um. Bugs Bunny?" I cringed. It sounded so totally implausible, now I came to say it out loud.

"Yeah, right." He got out his wallet, pulled out a couple of notes and slipped them neatly under his beer mat. "You enjoy the rest of your wine. I think I can remember the way back to my bike." Then he stood.

"It's not . . ." I started. But it was, wasn't it? At least, even if he'd mistaken my motives, the end result was the same. I *didn't* want to go out with him, did I?

So I should let him go.

"I'm sorry," I said, meaning it.

It only seemed to make him feel worse, if the hurt that flashed across his expression was any indication. "Yeah. Me too. I'll see you around."

And then he was gone.

"Robert, you do realise you're a total, utter lady-garden?"

I cringed. "I wish you'd stop using that phrase." I was beginning to question the wisdom of having hared up the hill to Rose's little flat following my ignominious departure from Badger's. Mr. Shiraz was no longer in residence, and Mr. Merlot was only half the man he used to be. Granted, I'd had some hand in reducing his circumstances. I hadn't been able to stomach my sauvignon blanc after Sean's departure.

Much as he hadn't been able to stomach his beer in my presence.

"When—'scuse me," Rose said, having interrupted herself with a burp. "When did I *ever* tell you I wanted you to set me up with Sean?"

"You told me to ask him out," I protested. "And you were the one flirting with him in the Chinese takeaway."

"Yeah, because if I'd waited for you to get your act together, we'd both have ended up dying alone."

"You might have asked me if I *wanted* to get my act together!" I took a fortifying swallow of Tesco's cut-price merlot. Hopefully the high alcohol content would numb my taste buds sometime soon.

"Well, why don't you, then? You're not telling me you don't fancy the pants off him."

"I . . . Well . . ." A further mouthful of merlot aided the brain power. "If you don't want him yourself, why are you so keen for *me* to get together with him?"

"Because you *want* to. Don't you? And he'd be good for you. Chip a few corners off that ivory tower you grew up in." She lolled back on the sofa, her fuzzy pink dressing gown parting to show a sticking plaster high on one leg where I presumed she'd cut herself shaving. I reached over and adjusted the fluffy material to a more respectable position.

Rose rolled her eyes in exaggerated fashion. "Worried you're going to get a glimpse of my la—"

"*Don't* say it."

"Prude. I am wearing knickers, you know. My mum taught me always to wear undies when entertaining gentlemen callers. You know, cos they like taking 'em off themselves." She sniggered. I ignored her.

"So you knew about his profession, then?"

"The pest control?" She smirked. "Might have. Did you do a spit-take when he told you?"

"I did *not.*"

"Bet you did really. Did they have to get out the smelling salts?"

"Rat-catching is an ancient and honourable profession," I said stiffly. "I don't think you should be making jokes about it."

"See? I told you, you fancy him. So what's all this about not wanting to go out with him?"

I sighed. "I just don't want to get into a relationship right now. Not with anyone."

"Hang on, I thought I was the brokenhearted man-hater, here. All my hopes and dreams shat on by that bastard. What's your excuse?"

I stared into my glass. The wine being somewhat murky, I didn't find much in the way of inspiration there. "Apparently there's something of an epidemic."

"What, are you serious? Why didn't you say anything before?"

"About Crispin? Not really my favourite topic of conversation."

"So go on, tell me about him." She leaned forward, and her dressing gown gaped at the top this time.

I shielded my gaze politely from the expanse of pale cleavage and purple lingerie that was revealed, and got another eye roll for my trouble. Huffing, Rose made a show of adjusting her dressing gown.

"There's nothing much to tell." Lies, all lies, but I couldn't face her knowing the truth and despising me. "He was a fellow teacher at my last school, and we were together. I, well, I loved him." It still hurt to say the words, as if I were ripping off a plaster from the half-healed wound in my chest. "And I thought he genuinely cared for me too. But I was wrong." That, at least, was the truth.

"Is that why you left your last job?"

She didn't know anything, I reminded myself. It was a perfectly reasonable supposition to make. "It's . . . related to it," I said and drank some more merlot. Worryingly, it was starting to taste almost nice.

"Poor you. Don't s'pose I'd have wanted to stick around somewhere I'd keep bumping into Shitface. Hah. No chance of that, with him buggering off to Dubai."

I leaned forward, gazing at her with focus. "Is that why you split up? Because you didn't want to go out there?"

"Not exactly. More to do with him just deciding he was going because that was what *he* wanted to do, and sod what I thought about it and whether or not I fancied tagging along as the dutiful little wifey, smothering myself in a burqa and giving up alcohol."

I frowned. "Would you really have had to wear a burqa?"

"That's not the point, is it? The point is, him just deciding he was taking this job and me having no say whatso-bloody-ever." She hiccupped. "So I told him he had to choose. Dubai, or me. Bastard. Pass the bottle."

"Are you sure you haven't had enough?"

"I'm positive I haven't had enough. And I'm double positive you haven't had enough." She cocked her head on one side. "Does a double positive make a negative? One of the kids is bound to ask me one day."

"You're a credit to the state education system," I told her gravely as I refilled her glass.

"That's a *no*, isn't it? Gawd, it's true, isn't it? Those who can, do, and those who can't, teach." She stared morosely into her glass.

"I'm taking that away if you're going to get all maudlin."

She handed it to me anyway and lurched to her feet. "I think I've had enough. Gotta pee. Sorry, tinkle. Heh. Gotta tinkle, twinkle." I watched in concern as she swayed across the room, nearly tripping over her handbag at one point, but with two full glasses of wine in my hands, the logistics of leaping to her aid were eluding me.

It might also, it has to be said, have had something to do with the amount of alcohol currently coursing merrily through my veins. I put the glasses down carefully on the table and leaned back on the sofa to await Rose's return.

Five hours later, I woke up frozen and alone. Worried she might have passed out in the bathroom, I took my aching head and queasy stomach to investigate.

Rose was curled up in bed, sleeping like a baby and snoring like a foghorn. Miffed, I stole the throw from the bottom of the bed and went back to sleep on the sofa.

CHAPTER SIX

I didn't see Sean for the next couple of weeks. His sister, clearly feeling better, was back on the school run with the twins, sporting a succession of ever-funkier headscarves.

I'd thought the one with the skulls on was a laudably defiant reference to her own illness, but Rose informed me it was just the fashion.

I wasn't sure how much, if anything, Sean had told his sister about our disastrous night out. I *thought* she seemed neither more nor less friendly to me than usual, but as her moods had always seemed somewhat changeable, it wasn't easy to tell. I told myself it was ridiculous to miss him. We'd spent, in total, including all school pickups, less than three hours together. We'd had one drink together.

But he'd liked *Doctor Who*. And bow ties. And Graham Greene. And when he'd smiled, his eyes had crinkled up at the corners . . .

No. It wasn't meant to be. Although I hadn't intended it at the time, there had been a grain of truth in what Sean had thought I'd said. We *were* from different worlds. His was filled with small, scurrying creatures that had to be firmly controlled lest they cause a nuisance. Mine was filled with . . . All right, maybe our jobs weren't so very different. But anyway, Sean was bisexual, wasn't he? People always warned you about bisexuals—said they'd end up leaving you for a woman when they wanted to settle down. That was what Fordy had always said, anyway. And he was married now, to a girl called Linette, who'd recently given birth to their first child, an alarmingly blob-like infant whom they'd shortsightedly christened Georgie, so he should know. Although Fordy was only bi-curious, really. He'd made that quite clear.

I missed Fordy.

And Sean.

No, no, I didn't miss Sean. I *didn't*.

Things always went wrong when I started getting attached to someone.

Sean didn't appear at the classroom door again until the very last day before half-term. Although school closed early, at two o'clock, the children were all overtired and hyped up in anticipation of Halloween. The twins had been particularly trying. It didn't make it any easier to face their uncle.

"All right?" he said warily when he reached the front of the line. Possibly my face had betrayed my misgivings over speaking to him again. "These two been behaving themselves?"

I made a bit more of a business about letting them out than it really warranted: straightening coats, making sure they had their PE kit and generally doing anything I could think of to avoid looking Sean in the eye until I felt a little more equal to the task. "Um. There's been a bit of high spirits," I confessed to the doormat.

"Oh yeah?"

"They pretty much spent the whole day hiding around corners and jumping out at people shouting 'BOO!'" I said, looking up in resignation.

Sean met my gaze with a wry smile that lifted my spirits far more than it should have. "Sorry. Bit disruptive, was it?"

I fought the impulse to grin back at him moronically. "Not only that, apparently several of the reception class wet themselves in fright." Lucy Kemp, their not-very-gruntled teacher, had glared daggers at me as she'd complained. Of course, *she'd* only been at the school a year, so she hadn't had to deal with having the twins as her responsibility.

Sean gave his charges a stern look. "Oi, you two. You shouldn't go scaring the littl'uns."

"We was just having fun," they chorused in stereo.

"Were. You *were* just having fun," I corrected automatically.

"See?" Wills grinned, triumphant.

"Even Mr. Enemy says so," Harry finished for him.

"It's Emeny," Sean said firmly, surprising me. "Em. En. Ee. And no, he doesn't. You're not getting away with it that easy. Come on, I want you to say you're sorry." He stared unmoved at their mutinous little faces, Wills's still with a smear of tomato sauce on his cheek from lunch. "*Or* I won't be taking you trick-or-treating on Halloween."

"Sorry, Mr. Enemy," they muttered in sullen unison, staring at identically scuffed shoes.

"Mr. *Emeny*," Sean insisted.

The muttering this time was barely audible, but it could conceivably have been "Sorry, Mr. Emeny." Actually, it could equally well have been *Sod off, Mr. Enemy*, but one soon learns, as a teacher, that there are some things it's better not to hear.

"That's better," Sean said, clearly having learned that lesson too. "Right, let's get you home." He paused and looked up at me. "They, uh, got all their kit?"

I nodded. "Have a good half-term."

"Yeah, you too." There was another pause, and then they were gone.

I felt unaccountably flat. Half-term blues, I told myself, and after I'd dispatched the last of my charges, I wandered next door to see if Rose fancied getting another takeaway tonight. Or any of the next nine nights, come to that.

Rose was alone in her classroom. She clearly had her parents well trained out of tardiness. She was singing to herself and putting potted plants in a box to take home for the week's holiday. At least, I assumed that was her intention. Possibly she was planning to chuck them over a hedge somewhere and trust her little darlings would have forgotten them by Monday week. The last verse of "I Want to Break Free" faltered on her lips as she glanced up at me and frowned. "Cheer up, for God's sake. We've got a week off."

I shrugged. "I know, I know. I just—"

"Shush!" Rose interrupted me.

I frowned at her, a bit hurt, as she cocked her head on one side. Then I heard it too.

Coming in through the open classroom door, there was a chant I remembered only too well from my own school days.

"Fight! Fight! Fight!"

Rose and I exchanged looks of alarm. "I'd better go," I said, asserting my manhood.

"I'll come with you," she replied, which I chose to interpret as a gesture of solidarity rather than a comment on said manhood.

We sprinted past the classrooms and across the playground, dodging buggies, skipping ropes and little clusters of mums who'd lingered to chat. A crowd of parents and children had gathered at the school gates, and in the centre I could see two furiously struggling figures. One had hold of the other's long, bleached-blonde hair, while the second appeared to be trying to tear the sleeve from her opponent's shirt and mostly succeeding.

"Isn't that Mrs. Nunn? You know, Destinee's mum?" Rose said, breathing hard beside me. "Who's the other woman?"

"Not sure." I took a deep breath and stepped in. "Ladies! Please! There are children present. Calm yourselves." I ducked as the one that wasn't Destinee's mum took a swing at me, her bright-red acrylic talons outstretched.

Destinee's mum shouted, "Oi! You leave 'im out of it!" followed by a few words I really hoped the children couldn't understand—at least, not the reception class—and made another grab for the other woman's hair.

I winced as a thick, blonde handful came free. "Mrs. Nunn! We'll have . . ." I trailed off, realising that "none of that" would sound like I was making fun of her. "That's enough." My hand hovered by her shoulder, fearful of landing on the bare flesh exposed by the ripped seams.

"Tell *her* that, why don't you? Bloody home-wrecking bitch!"

Oh. Evidently the other woman was, in fact, *the other woman*. I vaguely remembered Rose telling me that Destinee's father was a little freer with his favours than was usually appreciated by a man's wife, but surely that was all in the past now? Mrs. Nunn had had, ever since I'd known her, a new partner in the form of the deeply tanned and worryingly fit village tennis coach.

Apparently not. The other woman bared frighteningly white teeth, one of them smeared with lipstick the same blood red as her nails. At least, I hoped it was lipstick and not actual blood. "You're a fine one to talk. Shacked up with that bloke before Kev was even halfway out the door. He told me *all* about you, with your drinking and your bloody eating disorders—"

Mrs. Nunn went crimson. A safe distance behind her, I could see Destinee's normally pert little face, absolutely white and looking much younger.

"Enough," I said sharply, stepping between them and hoping I wasn't about to lose the eye I'd fixed on Mrs. Nunn's tormentor. "The school gates, with so many young children present, are not an appropriate place for this sort of discussion. Please leave, or I shall be forced to call the police."

For a tense moment, she stared me down, her clawed hands still upraised to strike. I reminded myself to stand firm. So what would it matter if I gained a few battle scars? Some people found that sort of thing quite attractive. I hoped. Then she deflated. "Oh, I'm going. Don't want to stick around here with the likes of *her*."

"And you can take your cheap hair extensions with you," Mrs. Nunn yelled, throwing the handful of blonde tresses after the other woman.

Hair extensions? Thank God.

The *other woman* stalked off with barely a backwards *V* sign. Mrs. Nunn clung to my arm. "You all right there, Mr. Enemy? That cow didn't hurt you, did she? You could have the law on her for that," she added, looking hopeful.

"I'm fine," I assured her. "But what about you?" Mrs. Nunn tended towards the petite, and the other woman had been easily twice her weight.

"Oh, don't you worry about me. I know how to look after myself. But you ought to watch it, she's a vicious cow."

Her implications weren't entirely flattering, but I let it pass. She meant well, at any rate. Apart, obviously, from the violence and profanity.

I suddenly became aware of the sounds behind us. Was that . . . applause? I turned and was horrified to find a ring of parents smiling and clapping—Sean among them. Back at the school building, I could clearly see the Head looking out of the window. I must have blushed as red as the other woman's nails.

Emily's grandmother was beaming at me. A couple of the other mums—and not a few of the older children—appeared to have been filming the event on their phones. I made a firm resolution not to go anywhere near Facebook for the next couple of days. I heard someone saying, "See? I told you it'd be good to have a man on staff. Even if he is a bit . . ." Thankfully, the general hubbub swallowed the rest of her sentence.

"Hey, nice work, there," Sean's low voice said in my ear.

Startled, I spun round. "Um. Thanks? I, ah . . ."

He gave a crooked smile. "Sorry. Gotta go. The twins have got an appointment."

It was probably just well, I told myself as his leather-clad shoulders hove out of sight. I hadn't had the faintest idea what I'd been about to say to him anyway.

CHAPTER SEVEN

I put the first Saturday of half-term to good use by having a lie-in.

I was just enjoying a leisurely cup of coffee when there was a knock on my door. I opened it to find Hanne standing there with a sunny smile and a large bowl covered with a tea towel.

"Have you had lunch?" she asked.

"No," I said cautiously.

"Good! We're going to do some cooking. Pølsefocaccia. It's very easy. I made the dough already, and it's risen." She handed me the mixing bowl and pulled a can of hot dog sausages from one voluminous parka pocket. Unlike the dough, my alarm was very definitely still rising. "Now, you have cherry tomatoes?"

I winced at her assured tone. "No. Sorry."

Hanne frowned. "Olive oil? You must have olive oil."

"I, um, ran out," I lied quickly.

"Hmm," she said. It spoke volumes. "But you have salt, at least?"

Apparently my face was also fairly eloquent. Hanne sighed and handed me the sausages, clearly far more confident than I was in my ability to handle them and the mixing bowl without dropping something. "Put these in the kitchen and get your coat. We're going shopping."

Once the supplies were safely deposited in the kitchen, Hanne dragged me round the village Tesco at lightning speed. She frowned at the fresh produce and tutted at the meagre array of olive oil, although why anyone would need more than two varieties to choose from was beyond me. I walked out burdened equally with carrier bags and misgivings.

Back at my house, Hanne searched my kitchen cupboards until she came up with a roasting tin, which she oiled liberally. Then she divided her dough roughly in half (actually, it was more like 55:45, but she assured me that (a) it was supposed to be in halves, and (b) it didn't really matter if it wasn't exact). The first portion she told me to spread out on the bottom of the tin and press down firmly.

It was harder than I'd thought; the stuff was elastic and springy and kept retreating from the corners. I subdued it ruthlessly.

"Okay, now you put the sausages on top." Hanne handed me the can, which I opened and remembered to drain before tipping the sausages onto the dough. They slithered for a moment in alarmingly wormlike fashion, then were still. I started to rearrange them into an orderly array.

Hanne watched me for a moment. "You know, it doesn't matter if they're not quite even."

"Are you sure?" I frowned at the last two sausages, which were still a little higgledy-piggledy for my liking.

She smiled. "But it's your bread. You do it how you like it."

Relieved, I straightened the last two sausages. "Now what?"

"You put the rest of the dough on top. Like a sandwich."

Like a sandwich? I could do this. I'd made lots of sandwiches. Some of them even successfully. It was a bit tricky to do without messing the sausages up again, but I didn't do too badly, I thought.

Hanne seemed to be tapping her fingers on the worktop by the time I'd finished, but some people are just restless like that.

"And now?"

"Now we add the tomatoes. Like this, you see?" She demonstrated, halving one of the tomatoes with a serrated knife, then using her thumb to poke holes in the top of the dough, into which she inserted the tomato halves. "Now, you do the rest." She glanced at her watch. "And it doesn't matter if they're a bit all over the place, okay?"

"Okay," I said and set to work. It was actually quite fun, poking little holes in the dough and pushing the tomatoes in. Charlie would enjoy this, I was sure. Perhaps I should ask Hanne to write the recipe out for his father—like she'd said, this was *easy*. I couldn't imagine why I'd always thought cooking was so difficult.

"Now, we pour on the olive oil—that's right—sprinkle on the salt . . . Perfect. And now we leave it to rise."

"Oh. How long for?" I was a little disappointed to find we weren't going to cook it immediately.

"Oh, about three quarters of an hour or so. Then you put it in a medium-hot oven for half an hour. You let it cool for ten minutes, and then it's ready to eat."

I frowned. "How many minutes is *or so*? And what temperature is *medium hot*?"

She smiled and shrugged. "It doesn't have to be exact."

I stared at my cooker dubiously. If appliances had expressions, I was fairly sure the cooker's would be mirroring mine. "So . . . it goes from one to nine. So medium hot would be four and a half?"

"You know, the numbers are only a guide. Every oven is different." She gave me a searching look. "You have used the oven before?"

My gaze darted guiltily to the microwave in the corner.

Hanne sighed. "Try it on gas mark five or six. If it looks like it's burning on top, turn it down a little." She wiped her hands on a tea towel and picked up her bowl.

"Aren't you staying?"

"No, I must get back to the dogs. And I have the other half of the dough at home for my own lunch."

"But . . ."

"You'll be fine. Just half an hour in the oven, remember? You could check it after twenty-five minutes. You have an oven timer? Maybe an alarm on your watch?"

"Oh, I won't need that." At least one thing I could be confident about.

"Then it's no problem. Enjoy your lunch. Maybe next time we'll make deer antlers?"

"Yes, all right." Hah. I'd be safe next time. I was pretty sure they didn't stock *those* in the village Tesco.

"Good. Now, you tell me when your pretty friend is coming round next time, and we'll make something special, okay?" She swept out with her mixing bowl, leaving the kitchen feeling empty without her cheerful presence.

I found myself missing her—and envying her too. Hanne seemed so sure of her place in the world—and she seemed to manage living alone much better than I did. Of course, she had the dogs. Maybe I should get a dog? I pictured myself, Barboured and wellied up to the gills, striding confidently over mizzled fields, my faithful companion at my heels. Just like any other country dweller. Yes, definitely something to think about. We could play Frisbee, and I could throw tennis balls for him—or her—to catch. It would get me out of the house more.

I might even bump into Sean once in a while, a sly little voice whispered in my id. He seemed the sort to get on well with animals; after all, he seemed to have no problem wrangling the twins.

I gave myself a mental slap on the wrist even as I grinned at the thought.

Right. The bread thingy was going to need another thirty-six minutes to rise. Time to get on with the laundry. And this time, I was going to do it perfectly. My record of thirteen days without a mixed-wash accident couldn't stand unbroken *forever*.

I put the bread in the oven at 12:42 on the dot, turned it on to gas mark five and sat down with the paper. Then at 12:48, a thought struck me. Weren't ovens supposed to be preheated? I had a vague memory of that from long-ago home-economics classes. Damn it.

I took the bread out of the oven. How long would an oven take to heat up? Five minutes? Ten? Twenty? If I left it that long, wouldn't the bread be too risen?

And now I came to think about it, had I just made a catastrophic mistake, removing the bread from the oven after it had already been in for six minutes? Would it collapse in on itself like soggy papier-mâché?

Maybe I should put it back in. I nipped back into the kitchen and did just that, careful not to burn myself on the oven door. But, damn it, how long would it need *now*? Should I count the previous six minutes it had had? Or did the cooling-off time, plus the not-actually-heated-up time cancel that out . . .?

Get a grip, Emsy. I was overthinking this. It was a loaf of bread with sausages and tomatoes in, not a medley of raw uranium, plutonium, and whatever else they put into nuclear reactors shortly before national disasters were declared. I took a deep breath and walked out of the kitchen, shutting the door behind me. Then I sat back down with the *Times*, turned it to the crossword page and told my brain sternly not to think about anything even vaguely bread related for the next half an hour.

The crossword was actually rather good today. The compiler was new to me, and his clues were consequently that much harder to unravel. He slipped up badly with one of them, though—"Animal liberators captured (3)" was so obvious I was sure not a single child in my class could have failed to get it. Well, the ones that could read well enough, at any rate. I wrote *R-A-T* in the grid with a sardonic pen.

I wondered what Sean was doing today. Did he work Saturdays? After all, presumably infestations didn't keep to office hours. Then again, one quite frequently saw mice in the London Underground. And city life was sometimes referred to as *the rat race*. I smiled to myself at the thought of little dark-suited rodents with miniature briefcases scurrying back to their commuter-belt homes at six o'clock.

Then I remembered I was living in the commuter belt, and the thought didn't seem quite so amusing. I swept a glance around the corners of my front room, but no furry creatures waved cheekily before going back to nibbling at the wiring and peeing on the carpet, thank God. Unless—was that something moving behind the curtain? I froze—then realised, embarrassed, that it was just the curtain itself, shifting in the draught from the imperfectly sealed window. I could feel myself blushing even though there was no one here to see. *Get a grip, Emsy*, I told myself again—and, oh dear Lord, I'd forgotten the bread. Half an hour had been over a scarily long time ago.

I sprang up from my chair and threw open the door to the kitchen. Then I squinted. The kitchen, and everything in it, looked a bit . . . fuzzy. This, my nose informed me, was because it was steadily filling up with greyish smoke that billowed from the cooker in ominous waves.

I might not have a great deal of experience with baking, but I was fairly certain this wasn't supposed to happen.

I flew to open the back door, then darted back to the oven to turn it off. Damn it, why did the bloody thing have to have so many knobs? Flapping at the smoke with my left hand, I squinted at the tiny little icons and numbers. Yes—that one. I turned the knob as far as I could to the right.

Then, cursing, turned it as far as I could to the *left*. A reassuring zero appeared. Should I open the oven door? It'd probably be safer to leave it for a while. A *long* while.

I escaped from the kitchen and leaned back on the door to heave a sigh of relief, only to have it turn into a hacking cough that left my chest aching and my eyes streaming.

Oh God. I mopped my face with a mortified handkerchief. Hanne would never speak to me again if she found out I'd burned her unpronounceable bread to cinders. I'd have to lie if she asked me how the baking had gone, I decided. And just hope she hadn't happened to look out of her window while smoke was billowing into my back garden. Perhaps I should light a small bonfire by way of camouflage? Then again, on current form, I'd most likely end up burning down the whole village.

What the hell had I been thinking of earlier? I couldn't get a dog. I could barely look after myself. I'd probably kill a pet within a week by feeding it the wrong thing, or letting it out to play with the traffic.

I felt so depressed about the whole thing, I had half a mind to go out and play with the traffic myself. Then again, this was Shamwell. The traffic on the high street generally trundled along over the speed bumps at around fifteen miles an hour. Anyone serious about suicide would be better off popping down the road and jumping in the river.

Granted, you'd be hard-pressed to drown yourself in its usual four to six inches of water (rising, I'd been told, to four to six feet at times of heavy rain, though I found this hard to envisage) but no doubt you could take your pick of unpleasant waterborne diseases to expire from. Eventually.

Bizarrely cheered by these morbid thoughts, I decided to go out for a run. Having slept late today, I hadn't been out yet. I'd changed into tracksuit bottoms and a long-sleeved T-shirt and was lacing up my running shoes before it occurred to me it would perhaps be a bit risky leaving the kitchen door wide open while I was out. A quick peek into the kitchen confirmed the smoke—and the smell—hadn't yet dissipated. Still, the back gate was bolted, it was broad daylight, and I lived in the middle of the village, for heaven's sake. How likely was it that anyone would break in? Or rather, walk in, seeing as no breaking would be required in this instance.

In any case, they'd probably take one look at my meagre possessions, decide, as Rose had, that they were all around a hundred years old, and walk straight out again. Not having been used to having a whole house to myself, I hadn't really accumulated much in the way of portable goods, and the television that had come with the rest of the rented furnishings didn't look as though it would make enough on resale to be worth the bother of carting it away.

I carefully hid my laptop under the sofa cushions and set out, crossing the road and taking the back lane up the hill to the park.

It was a glorious autumn day, the leaves still largely on the trees but turned to gorgeous hues of red and gold. Every time the gentle breeze gusted, a few leaves drifted down lazily to dapple the grass. The air smelled fresh, moist, and earthy. In the enclosed playground in the centre of the park, bundled-up toddlers and older children in anoraks shrieked as they ran between the swings and the roundabout or bounced around on strange springy things that were supposed to look like horses or motorbikes.

My steps faltered as I passed the playground and spotted a trio of redheads: one tall, two small. Sean was playing football with the twins. As I watched, he booted the ball past his two opponents and between a woolly hat and a piled-up scarf lying on the ground. He drowned out their disappointed cries with a loud cheer, pulled his shirt up over his head and ran around the makeshift pitch doing an aeroplane impression.

I couldn't help laughing at the sight. Part of me also noticed his actions had exposed a taut abdomen with a light sprinkling of ginger hair. It started around his belly button and trailed enticingly downward, leading inevitably to recollections of Rose's *ginger nuts* comment . . .

"En-em-ee, En-em-ee," the twins chanted. Sean skidded to a halt and pulled his shirt back down as I realised I'd been standing there, staring. Probably with a silly smile on my face. Or a creepy leer. I wasn't sure which was worse. Mortified at the questioning look in Sean's eyes, I gave him an awkward wave and ran on.

My route led down a gentle slope to the river. I imagined this must be a popular spot for families in warmer months, but now there were only a couple of dog walkers. I stopped to do some stretches by a willow tree, its melancholy branches dipping golden leaves to caress the sluggish water. I did a few more than usual—for some reason my heartbeat was a little slow to return to its resting rate of fifty-four. I must be getting unfit, I thought. Rose, though lovely, was in some respects not the best influence healthwise. Still, it was running that would sort that out, not stretching. One last go at the hamstrings, and I unfolded myself, ready to be on my way.

Except now Sean was right in front of me, Startled, I stared at him for a moment. The twins trailed a long way behind him, kicking the ball between them as they zigzagged across the grass.

Sean stared back. Then he shook himself almost imperceptibly. "Hi."

"Hi," I said back. Oh God, what should I say? "I'm, um, out for a run."

He smiled, his gaze travelling pointedly down my running-gear-clad frame. "I'd never have guessed."

God, he must think I was a complete moron. He'd probably be up at the school after half-term, demanding to know why his nephews were being taught by someone so clearly intellectually challenged. "So I'd better, um, run." I gave him another hideously awkward wave.

Then I ran.

Over the bridge, along the riverbank—looking resolutely in front of me, and *not* to the right, where I might possibly have spotted a flash of red hair out of the corner of my eye. Up the slope and onto the old railway line.

I was halfway to the next village before I felt safe to stop for a breather. What the hell had that been all about? I leaned on an old brick gatepost (now sans gate) and did a quick quad stretch. Had Sean followed me to demand to know why I'd been ogling his midriff? A thought crossed my mind—but it was ridiculous, so I banished it immediately, and switched legs.

But Sean had seemed a bit . . . distracted, down by the river.

No, I decided, and jogged up the steps to the wheat field above the track, its harvest long gathered in for the winter. A footpath led along the side of the field, eventually crossing a bridleway that would lead me back to Shamwell. It was bordered by rough blackthorn hedges now covered in plump, blue-black sloes. Their vicious spines stood sentry, ready to impale any would-be gin makers who might venture this way.

There was *no way* Sean had been ogling me in his turn as I did my stretches.

For a start, I told myself as I scrambled over a stile, dressed in my scruffy running clothes, I was hardly ogle-worthy. For much of the village, I'd found on previous excursions, I wasn't even recognisable as Mr. Enemy from St. Saviour's School. The children in my class could usually work it out, particularly after I'd spoken, but their parents, if I greeted them mid-run, generally just gave me puzzled frowns.

Ah. That must be it. I turned into the single-track lane which led down to the ford. Sean had just followed me to get a closer look at the weird stranger who'd been staring and waving at him.

Over the ford, the road at present bone-dry as much of the river water was channelled underneath. Then a right turn down a narrow path bordered by the dual hazards of prickly, red-berried hawthorn to the right and stinging nettles to the left, and I was back in the park, this time higher up by the tennis club. Cautious glances yielded neither Sean nor the twins.

Of course, *they'd* recognised me. They'd been chanting my name— more or less. So Sean must have known who I was before he followed me down to the river.

Oh, bugger it. He'd probably just taken them down to the river to play Pooh-sticks on the bridge. *Everything*, I told myself firmly as I padded down Mill Lane and back to the high street, *is* not *about you*.

The Old Hatter's Cottage, I was pleased to see as I kicked off my running shoes, appeared unburgled. As it was starting to get chilly now, I shut the back door. The kitchen still smelled a bit charcoal-y, but that was probably because I hadn't had the nerve to open up the oven yet and deal with whatever was left inside. I supposed I ought to bite the bullet and get it over with, but . . . No. Shower first. After all, I could hardly clean the oven when I wasn't clean myself, could I?

Procrastination successfully justified, I jogged upstairs for a shower.

Thirteen minutes later, scrubbed, shaven and smelling faintly of sandalwood, I wandered back into the living room. My stomach reminded me with a rumble that I'd never actually managed to have lunch. There probably wasn't a lot of point, now. I might as well wait until teatime. After all, I'd eaten my Weetabix—which, I had to admit, had tasted an awful lot like mush—several hours later than usual this morning.

I threw myself at the sofa—and remembered at the very last minute I'd hidden my laptop under the cushions. Twisting midair to avoid crushing it, I bounced off the edge of the sofa and landed on my arse on the carpet.

Ow. I rolled my eyes at myself, darted a quick glance at the window to make sure no passersby were gazing in at me in concern or, as it might be, mockery, and heaved myself to my feet. As I did so, I caught a flash of movement out of the corner of my eye. It had been by the fireplace. I jerked my head round to look more closely— and a small, furry, brownish-grey blur streaked across the carpet and through the open door into the kitchen.

Oh God.

I'd got a rat.

CHAPTER EIGHT

I'd got a rat. In my *kitchen*. No doubt even now nibbling at my chocolate Hobnobs and doing unspeakable things on the work surfaces. I was never going to eat again. I slammed the kitchen door shut to at least keep the wretched creature out of the rest of the house, and went to collapse on the sofa.

And nearly sat on my laptop *again*. Damn it. I pulled the thing out from under the cushion and quickly looked up *rat infestation* on the internet.

Six queasy minutes later, I shut the laptop with a snap, my skin crawling. Possibly it had been a mistake to search *images*. At any rate, it was clear I needed to do something about my uninvited guest before I was knee-deep in droppings and/or got nibbled to death in my sleep. But whom should I call?

There was an obvious answer. Obviously. But calling Sean would be . . . awkward. After all, only a couple of hours ago, I'd found it necessary to run several miles to get away from having to speak to him. And if I called him, he might read things into it. Things like I wanted to see him.

Which I didn't, of course, I told the tight feeling in my chest.

Did I?

Why did relationships have to be so complicated?

No, I told myself. I'd merely be calling upon Sean in a professional capacity. I could just picture his look of bemusement if I accused him of reading into my plea for help things which were not, in fact, there. He'd frown, a crease appearing between those copper brows. *Why on earth would you imagine I'd infer something like that?* he'd ask.

Well. He probably wouldn't say *why on earth*. Or, for that matter, *infer*. But the principle still stood. Decision made, I grabbed my phone—and realised I didn't, in fact, have Sean's number. Or the name of the company he worked for. Both those pieces of information would undoubtedly be available in a file somewhere, listing Sean as emergency contact for the twins, but said file was now firmly locked up in school for half-term.

Sighing, I called Rose.

"Well, what are you calling me for?" she demanded after I'd explained my situation. "Why aren't you calling Sean?"

"I haven't got his number. And anyway, I don't want to call Sean," I added, my resolve having faltered in the time it had taken to make the call. "That's why I'm calling *you*. There must be other ratcatchers in the area."

"Yeah, but he's right in the village. You want prompt service, don't you? Are you telling me you'll sleep tonight if you don't get it sorted?"

Oh God. She had a point. "I could stay with you?" I suggested hopefully.

"No way. Last time you stole the blankets, and we weren't even sharing a bed. 'Sides, I'm not enabling your avoidance tactics."

"Have you been reading self-help books again?"

"Might have been. Stop changing the subject. Just call Sean. You want someone you know and trust, don't you? And it's not like he's still going to be peed off about that date you went on. He's not the sort."

"I suppose . . ."

"Look, have you got a pen and paper? I'll give you his number."

"I'll remember it."

"Weirdo."

"Having a good memory for numbers isn't actually a failing, you know."

"It is when it's weird. Are you sure you're gay? I'm beginning to think you're mathmosexual."

"You mean I'm an arithmophile. Which, for the avoidance of all possible doubt, I'm *not*. It would make teaching maths extremely embarrassing. Are you ever going to give me this number?"

"Hang on, don't get your bow tie in a bunch. Let me find it . . . Here you go. Ready?"

"Go on, baby," I growled. "Talk dirty to me."

I should have known. Rose proceeded to recite the phone number in the sort of voice Fordy would have called "porntastic," punctuating each digit with a breathy moan and ending on a long-drawn-out *two-ooo-ooooh*.

"Enjoy that, did you?" I asked drily.

"Oh, yeah. Think I'm going to have to go and do some sums now. Some really long, *hard* sums. How about you?"

"I think I'm going to call Sean."

"See? I knew that'd get you in the mood. Good luck finding your lowest common denominator. Just remember, no multiplying until the third date."

"I think we're going to have other things on our minds. Rat, remember?"

After I'd hung up, I stored Sean's number in my phone and was about to hit Call, but my finger veered off to one side. Was it fair to call him in after the way I'd hurt his feelings? After all, he'd stayed off the school run for so long. Perhaps he'd been avoiding me?

Then I realised what an idiot I was being. "Yes, Emsy," I said to the phone in my hand, "he's been pining for you so pitiably he dragged his sister out of her sickbed to take the twins to school, all to save his delicate little feelings. Which, by the way, he was merely repressing manfully when he spoke to you earlier with absolutely zero appearance of romantic woe." I rolled my eyes and hit Call.

"Yeah?" Sean's voice sounded cautious.

"It's me. Robert. Emeny," I explained, cringing. But at least I'd managed to avoid putting the automatic "Mr." in front of my surname. "Rose gave me your number."

"Oh, yeah?" Now he sounded intrigued. And slightly mocking, although maybe that was just my paranoia.

"I've got a rat."

There was a beat of silence so loud it nearly deafened me. "Okay," Sean said briskly, and this time his tone was all business. "So you want me to come round?"

"If you're not too busy . . ."

"Nah, I'm not working today, and the twins are back home with Debs. I can come straight over."

"Thank you so much—"

"Not a problem," he cut me off. "See you in five minutes."

It was, in fact, nearer eleven minutes before he turned up, but I've noticed people always underestimate these things, so it was actually sooner than I'd expected him. I heard him before I saw him, but while I'd been listening for the roar of a motorbike, it was a quietly purring van that pulled up in front of my house.

I had the front door open before he could knock. "Thank you so much for coming," I greeted him. "Especially on your day off."

"No problem," he said, still with that off-puttingly businesslike tone he'd had during our phone conversation. I'd wanted to open with an apology, but his manner wasn't encouraging. "Right. Did you see the rat? Or have you just seen where it's been?"

"You mean, its droppings?"

"Yeah. Rule of thumb—if they're the size of a grain of rice, it's mice. If they look more like raisins, it's rats. So if you show me where you found them, I'll—"

"I didn't," I said quickly. "I mean, I didn't see droppings. I saw the rat. By the fireplace." I led him into the living room and pointed. "There," I said, in case he was having difficulty identifying the hearth.

Sean looked. "Well, it's not there now," he said after a few exceedingly long seconds. He gave me a teasing look. "You know, I was planning on giving you a call anyway, seeing as you were too busy to stop running earlier. You don't have to make up excuses to call me."

Fabulous. So now he suspected me of compounding my errors from the other night by dragging him out here on a wild-goose chase.

"I didn't make it up! The rat was *there*." I jabbed a finger at the fireplace, as if by pointing hard enough I could somehow summon the recalcitrant rodent. "Obviously it didn't *stay* there. I startled it."

Wait a minute. He'd been planning to call me? Why?

"So where did it go?" Sean asked. Damn it, I'd missed the chance to question him.

"Into the kitchen." I was sure on that point, at least. "I shut the door behind it," I added, to show I hadn't been *completely* useless.

"How fast?"

I frowned. "As fast as I could, of course."

"How fast was the rat going?" Sean asked with infinite patience.

I stared at him. "At the speed of rat? *I* don't know. I don't actually keep a radar gun handy for measuring rodent velocity."

"Did it look like it knew where it was going?" He held a hand up to forestall whatever I was going to say next. "You see, rats like to stick to their usual routes. And they don't see too well. So if it was moving quick, it was probably taking its route in and out of the house. Which means it's long gone now."

"Oh. Um." I suddenly felt very small and rather hot. "I, well, I only saw it out of the corner of my eye. I *think* it was moving fast, but, well . . ."

Sean was nodding. "Not to worry. I'll give the kitchen a thorough check before I go, anyway. Even if I don't find the rat itself, hopefully we'll be able to see where it's been coming in."

"You mean, you think it's been in more than once?"

"Oh yeah. Most like."

I shuddered. Then I frowned. "Wait a minute, wouldn't I have noticed something? Raisins, so to speak?"

"Not always, if it's rats. In some ways, you're better off with rats than mice. Mice are incontinent little sods. They'll pee and crap all over the place. Rats, now, they often have their own toilet area. And a separate eating area."

"Oh? I'm surprised they're held in such low regard, then. They seem the perfect houseguests." I thought about it. "Bubonic plague notwithstanding."

"Yeah, not to mention Weil's disease, TB, foot-and-mouth and a whole load of other nasties. Plus there's the damage they cause. Had a case once where they'd got into the loft and gnawed a hole in the water tank."

"Shall we get on and look for it, then?" I said quickly, making a mental note to boil all water before washing in future.

"Well, if you're sure you don't want to keep it as a pet . . ." Sean grinned.

"Positive," I said firmly and led the way into the kitchen. The subtle aroma of eau de charcoal wafted into my nose, and I realised guiltily I still hadn't dealt with the failed focaccia. I casually tiptoed to the back door and opened it wide, hoping Sean wouldn't notice.

We looked *everywhere* for that bloody rodent. Sean even removed all the kickboards from the bottom of the kitchen cabinets, got down on hands and knees and risked life and limb by shining his torch underneath. All to no avail.

"No sign of it," he reported, getting back to his feet. I shuffled hastily back and tried to look like I *hadn't* just been ogling certain parts of his anatomy. Specifically, those parts that filled out a pair of denim jeans rather nicely. "I'll shift the cooker out—sometimes they like to hang around behind those. It's nice and warm for them, and you get food spillages."

I didn't like to admit that my cooker didn't, as a rule, see a lot of either warmth or food. And, after all, it *had* been in use today. "Need a hand?"

"Nah, I'm good." Sean crouched down and took hold of the bottom of the cooker.

More from a feeling that I ought to be doing something, rather than just standing around being useless while "man stuff" was being done than out of real expectation I'd find something, I started shifting stuff around on the worktops. There wasn't, to be honest, a great deal of stuff to shift; most of my groceries, such as they were, were in cupboards. I was *not* looking forward to helping Sean search their dark corners.

The family-size box of Weetabix, which would probably last me until retirement, however, had been too big to fit, so it squatted on top of the fridge-freezer. I reached out a hand to pick it up. Wasn't it a little heav—

In a greyish blur, something erupted from the top of the box, ran up my arm, *over my head*, down the other arm and, with a leap, scurried to the floor and out through the open kitchen door.

There was a long moment of absolute stillness. I was rooted to the spot, physically unable to move. Unless you counted the shaking. I could still feel its little claws skittering across my skull.

"Well, he's gone, anyway," Sean said into the silence.

"R-r-r . . ." I forced out through chattering teeth. "R-r-r-r—"

"Actually, it was a squirrel," Sean said. "Sorry."

"Sq—" I caught myself before I could get stuck in another Möbius loop of stuttering, and took a deep breath. "Squirrel?" It came out a little squeaky, as if I'd decided it would be amusing to mimic my rodent visitor.

"Yeah." Sean shrugged and moved forward to give my rigid shoulder a cautious pat. "It had a pretty thin tail, mind, for a squirrel. And some people reckon they're just rats with better PR."

I shuddered. "Are you trying to make me feel better or worse?"

He smiled. "Better. Seriously. You want to sit down?"

"Not sure. I, er, I'm not entirely certain I can move."

Sean squeezed my shoulder, and warmth pulsed through me from the point of contact, freeing me from my paralysis. I had the ridiculous urge to pull him closer, so I covered it with a cough. "Um. Tea?"

"Yeah, that'd be great." His hand dropped away.

Feeling bereft, I went to fill the kettle—then did an about-turn to shut, bolt, and lock the back door en route. For some reason, my hands weren't really cooperating, seeming to favour a sort of localised Saint Vitus's dance over actually doing what I asked them to, so by the time I'd finished rattling the key against the lock and was able to return to the kettle, I found it already steaming. Sean had also had time to get out a couple of mugs and locate the teabags. He gave me a kind smile and poured in the water. "Milk?"

"Yes. Please. Sorry, I'm being a terrible host."

"Scare up a couple of biscuits and I'll let you off. Come on, I'll take these through."

It was just as well Sean was carrying the drinks. I fumbled the packet of chocolate digestives and almost dropped it twice en route. The first time was because my hands were still shaking; the second because I saw something move on the floor out of the corner of my eye.

I was mortified when I realised it had been my foot.

"You must think I'm an absolute wimp," I muttered sadly as I dropped onto the sofa. "A squirrel. Any of the little girls in my class would think all their Christmases had come at once if they found a real live squirrel as the hidden surprise in their Weetabix. And here I was, practically wetting myself in terror."

Sean sat down beside me. "Nah, don't be so hard on yourself. You were just startled, that's all. And you were expecting a rat. 'Spect I'd have screamed like a girl too if one ran over my head like that."

Oh God. "I screamed like a girl?" I'd have been quite happy to continue in ignorance of that.

"It's just a figure of speech. You sort of yelped. A very manly sort of yelp. Almost a grunt, really. Or a growl." Sean's smile was teasing.

I glared at him and pointedly took a chocolate biscuit without offering him one. "Now you're patronising me."

"If it helps, I once saw a bloke go into a dead faint when he saw a rat running straight at him."

"They do that? Rats, I mean?"

"Not really. Like I said, rats keep to their usual routes, even when there's danger around. So it was actually going for the doorway, trying to escape. It wasn't the rat's fault he was standing in the way, though the bloke swore blind when he woke up the rat had been going for his throat." He cocked his head to one side. "Feeling better?"

"A bit." I took a deep breath and let it out again slowly. "What I don't understand is how the wretched thing could have got in here in the first place. Wouldn't I have noticed if there were holes in the walls?"

"Sometimes they just see a chance and take it. Did you maybe have the back door open today, let a bit of fresh air in the place?"

"No, of course— Oh." I remembered the baking incident. "Um. Maybe?"

"There you go, then. Opportunistic little sods, squirrels. Speaking of which, can I get a biscuit, here?"

"Just one," I said, passing him the packet. "And no dropping any crumbs. I don't want to encourage the rodent invasion. You know, I always used to like those internet videos of resourceful squirrels getting into bird feeders. Now I have visions of them teaming up to find a way of picking my locks." I shuddered.

Sean grinned and helped himself to two. "It'd give you an excuse to call me again, though, wouldn't it? If you think you need one."

All at once I felt a good bit hotter than the mug of tea in my hands could reasonably account for. "Um," I said, my resolve wavering.

Would it really be such a *very* bad idea to see Sean again? He wasn't Crispin, after all.

"Look," he said, gesturing with a biscuit. "That night at Badgers—"

"I'm so sorry about that," I interrupted desperately. "Really I am. I just, well, it was all a misunderstanding, really. I mean, I know what I *said*, but..." I trailed off, my throat tight. In any case, I wasn't entirely certain how I'd have finished the sentence without digging myself an even bigger hole.

Sean's eyes were kind. "Well, maybe I overreacted, okay? I mean, I talked to Rose about it, and she reckoned we both got the wrong end of the stick, and, well, I thought we got on okay, didn't we? So maybe we should give it another go? I know you just came out of a bad relationship, but you gotta get back on the horse sometime, right?"

I stared at him. Had Rose told him *everything*? I was intensely relieved I hadn't shared any of the more painful—not to mention shameful—details of my breakup with Crispin. God, if Sean ever found out about Oliver... I swallowed.

Sean leaned towards me. He put a hand on my knee, sending a curious kind of tingling heat through the fabric of my trousers. "Look, I'm not a bad bloke. Honest. Whatever that git did, I promise you I won't do that. I like you, okay? You're funny." He smiled. "And different. I like that. And I think you like me, even though you're trying not to. So how about it?"

"I . . ." I took a delaying mouthful of tea. "What, precisely, are you proposing?"

"Bit soon for a proposal, innit? Hey, only joking," he added as I spluttered on my tea. "How about this? The local am-drams are doing a production of *Pygmalion* this week in the village hall. Fancy going along? They mostly remember their lines, ones I've seen before, and some of 'em can even act."

"Well..."

"Gotta support the local community, haven't you?"

He had a point there. And, really, what could be the harm in spending a couple of hours in the company of Sean, a hall full of villagers, and a dubious interpretation of George Bernard Shaw's comedy of class? "What day is it on?" I asked.

Not that my social calendar was exactly booked up. Or even existed, for that matter, outside of my own mind, but if it *had* had physical form, it would have been a pristine set of blank white pages.

"Thursday, Friday, and Saturday. Saturday is their gala night, and you get a free cup of tea and a biccie in the interval. Tends to bring the grannies out in force, that does, so I was thinking maybe Friday if you're free?"

"I . . . think I might be," I said. After all, one should support local theatre. And accepting his invitation was hardly tantamount to throwing caution to the winds. It was barely even allowing it to be ruffled by a gentle spring zephyr. Moreover, Sean *had* been very understanding about the whole Badgers debacle, the memory of which was still tying my stomach in guilty knots. Not to mention the squirrel. One might almost think he was rather taken with me, a prospect that left me less alarmed and more gratified than I would have imagined.

At any rate, such generosity of spirit should, I thought, be encouraged. I smiled, pleased with my logical analysis of the question.

Sean smiled back. "Great. I'll get the tickets, and I'll see you about half past seven. We can walk up from here."

CHAPTER NINE

"**S**o how'd it go, then? Your rat date yesterday." Rose mopped up some passanda sauce with her keema naan. She was round at my house for Sunday dinner, apparently determined to keep on widening my horizons with regard to takeaway food.

We'd passed Hanne on the way in. She'd sent me a smile of approval when she saw Rose, which had swiftly turned to a frown of displeasure when she saw our carrier bags full of unmistakeable rectangular plastic tubs. I had a sinking feeling I was going to be getting another cookery lesson in the near future.

"It wasn't a date." I blushed. "It wasn't even a rat. It was a squirrel." There was a Brussels sprout in my chicken biryani, which was not what I'd have considered a typical ingredient in Indian food. I poked it with my fork, then decided to hell with it, and bit, so to speak, the bullet. It actually tasted rather nice.

"See, you go on about my education," Rose was saying, waving her naan at me, "but at least I can tell a rat from a bloody squirrel. Are you serious? I mean, every kid in reception can tell a rat from a squirrel. There are probably unborn *babies* who can tell a rat from a squirrel."

"I only saw it out of the corner of my eye, the first time," I protested. "And it was a little hard to see the second time, when it was *running over the top of my head.*"

"Ew. I hope you've washed your hair since."

"God, yes. And scrubbed the kitchen so clean—"

"You could cook your dinner in there?"

"I was going to say, there's absolutely nothing to tempt any more rodent raiders into the place. Not a crumb to be found. And no more boxes of cereal left where the little blighters can see them either."

I took a swallow of Tesco chardonnay. Again, not something I'd have associated with spicy food (or any food, to be honest) but Rose had insisted that cheap alcohol was an essential part of the Indian takeaway experience. Actually, she'd tried to persuade me to drink lager, but I'd explained firmly that although I loved her dearly, there were limits.

"Heh, now I'm imagining a gang of squirrels lined up on your windowsill, pressing their twitchy little noses to the glass while they stalk your breakfast."

"Do squirrels even have twitchy noses? I thought that was bunnies."

"There'd probably be some of them as well. Just make sure you don't leave your carrot out where they can see it." She sniggered. "Or your Brussels sprouts."

"You know, it's rather disturbing to have you use those vegetables as euphemisms while we're actually *eating* them."

"First time a woman's ever had her lips round your meat and two veg, is it?" She took a large swig of chardonnay and grabbed the bottle to refill her glass, making a disappointed face when the wine ran out two-thirds through.

"You know, I'm going to have to start rationing your alcohol intake. Half a bottle of wine and—"

"I'm anybody's?"

"I was going to say, a little inclined to vulgarity."

Rose held up an admonitory finger. I could tell it was intended as an admonishment, as it was her middle finger. "That, darling, is sexist. Ah-ah-ah," she added, cutting me off as I opened my mouth to defend myself. "See, you may not *think* you're being sexist, but you are. If a bloke makes a dirty joke, everyone laughs. If a woman does, it's vulgar." She paused and then belched loudly. "God, your face. But if *Sean* had done that, you wouldn't think anything of it, would you? It's just double standards, innit?"

"Maybe," I said cautiously. "Although I'm fairly certain I'd think *I* was being vulgar if I burped in public." It was an interesting point, though. *Was* Sean the sort to do that sort of thing? And would I mind if he did?

Somehow, I couldn't imagine myself having a problem with anything he might do. Which was a disturbing thought in itself.

Rose was speaking again. "Yeah, well, you're you, aren't you? Anyway, stop changing the subject."

"I hadn't realised I was. Changing the subject, I mean. I'm well aware I'm *me*." I was beginning to wonder if the wine was stronger than I'd thought it was.

"So go on," Rose continued, fixing me with a piercing gaze. "*Have* you ever done it with a girl?"

"No," I muttered to my biryani. I lifted my head to give her a challenging look of my own. "Have you?"

"Ew. *No*." She frowned. "It must be weird, liking both. I mean, do you think bisexuals ever wake up feeling frisky and go to grab a handful of boob, then think, 'Oh, bum, this one hasn't got any'?"

"I wouldn't know, would I? Not exactly my area of expertise, breasts." I stood, feeling suddenly depressed. "I'll go get the other bottle of wine out of the fridge."

"So what are you all mopey about?" Rose asked when I slumped back onto the sofa.

"Nothing." Silently lamenting the lack of a proper cork—Peter would be quietly horrified—I opened the bottle of wine with a sharp twist to the screw top.

"And I'm a supermodel. Come on, what is it?"

I *humph*ed. "Oh, I don't know. Maybe the way you so thoroughly dismissed the idea that anyone could have a successful long-term relationship with a bisexual?"

"So? It's not like you're actually going out with one." Her eyes became piercing little slits. "Are you?"

"I. Um. I may just possibly be going out with Sean on Friday, yes. But we're not necessarily *going out*," I added quickly. "I mean, we're just going to see a play together. It's not really a date. Probably."

"And you didn't *tell* me? You cagey sod. I can't believe you didn't tell me you were going out with Sean."

"Yes, how dare I keep you in ignorance of any aspect of my life for as long as, oh, twenty-four hours?" I rolled my eyes and topped up my glass.

"So what changed your mind, then? I mean, up till yesterday you were all, *Oh no, I don't want a boyfriend.*"

I winced at her impersonation of me and sincerely hoped it wasn't accurate. "I . . . Oh, hang it. I shouldn't go, should I? I should ring him and cancel."

"What? Screw that. Why the bloody hell would you want to cancel?" She grabbed the chardonnay from where I'd left it on the table and refilled her glass once more.

"Because you were right. Nothing's changed. I just . . . I don't know what I was thinking." Mostly, I suspected, I *hadn't* been thinking. Or at least, not with the appropriate organ.

"I still don't get it. This Rice Crispy bloke was over half a year ago—did you take a vow of celibacy after him or something?" Rose ripped off another chunk of naan with casual savagery.

"It's . . . complicated." I took a swallow of wine. I'd rather lost my appetite for the food. Then I took a deep breath. "Rose, do you think people in a relationship should be totally honest with one another?"

"What about?"

"Well, you know. Everything. Say, one of the parties had done something—no, not *done* something, been *suspected* of something—that might lead the other party to despise the first party. If the second party found out about the suspicions surrounding the first party, and, obviously, believed the first party to be culpable."

"What is this, a legal document?" Her eyes narrowed, and a drop of curry sauce teetered perilously on the bottom of the piece of naan that had stalled halfway to her mouth. "Why? What've you done?"

"Nothing!"

In an unprecedented move, Rose put the naan back on her plate, uneaten. "Oh my God, are you cheating on Sean? I can't *believe* you're cheating on Sean."

"I'm not cheating on Sean! How could I possibly be cheating on someone I'm not even going out with?"

"You lied on your CV? Everyone does that, you don't need to worry about it. Nobody ever checks up on GCSE grades."

"I didn't lie on my CV, either."

"You didn't? Why the hell not?" Her eyes went wide. "Oh my God—you're really a woman?"

"That doesn't even make sense with what I told you! And no, I'm not trans, all right? *Please* stop trying to guess."

"So what is it, then?"

"I don't want to say."

She glared at me.

"I mean it, Rose. Stop pushing."

"You realise whatever I'm imagining is probably worse, don't you?"

It couldn't be. "I'll just have to live with that," I said firmly.

"You're no fun," she muttered. "One last guess, and then I'll leave you alone, all right?"

"I'd really prefer—"

"You had an affair with a pupil."

Oh God. There was a rushing in my ears. You'd think I'd be used to the sound of my life collapsing.

I couldn't do this. I couldn't face it all happening again. Rose would despise me. Sean wouldn't want anything to do with me. The Head would sack me, and the parents from the school would probably lynch me . . .

"Robert? *Robert*," Rose was saying. "Come on, sweetie, just breathe."

I slowly became aware that I was huddled on the sofa, Rose's arms around me, crushing my face to her ample bosom in a way that made it almost impossible to obey her verbal instructions. She was patting my back as if I were a small child, which, given my near-foetal position, was perhaps understandable. A few moments' futile struggle on my part eventually ended with her relaxing her grip, and I gulped in air.

"Is that what they thought you'd done? It is, isn't it? That's why you stopped teaching secondary, isn't it? Come on, you know I'd never believe you'd do anything like that." She paused. "You *didn't* actually have an affair with a pupil, did you?"

"No! No, I swear I didn't." I looked up at her then. "On my mother's life."

"Hmm." She pursed her lips. "Swear it on your favourite bow tie, that black one with the pinstripes?"

I managed a weak smile. "That's not my favourite. I just wear it a lot. It makes me look professional."

Rose coughed. It sounded a lot like, "You *think*?"

I ignored her. "And I swear to you on *all* my bow ties. Which, I'd like to point out, are not actually dearer to me than my mother's life."

"All right, all right, I believe you." She stared thoughtfully at her plate. "So that's why you split up with Crispy Crackling, then? He didn't believe you hadn't done it? And you're worried Sean might find out and do the same?"

I nodded. It had been a bit more complicated than that, but, well, that was more or less the gist of it.

"Well, for one thing, I can't believe Sean's got one single thing in common with anyone called Crispin. Don't interrupt," she added as I opened my mouth to tell her they were actually of a rather similar height and build. "And for another, no one knows except me, do they? And *I* know the whole thing's bollocks, so I'm not going to go spreading it around. So you're sorted, aren't you? Just forget about it."

"Ea-easier said than done." My traitorous voice cracked, calling me a liar.

"Look, you came here to make a fresh start, didn't you? So sodding well make one."

CHAPTER TEN

I t was all right for Rose to talk about making a fresh start, I thought
grumpily to myself as I sat down to a mountain of lesson planning
on Monday morning. It wasn't like *she'd* just broken up with the man
she'd thought to be the love of her life . . . Oh. Well, maybe she had,
but at least I wasn't bullying her into dating again already.

Although, come to think of it, her breakup was barely six weeks
old, whereas mine was that many months. I sighed. Fine. I'd concede
she had a right to bully me. It didn't mean I had to actually do
what she said.

Still . . . I'd looked out for Sean in the park while on my run this
morning, but the only redhead I'd seen had been the alarmingly
henna'd wife of the vicar, walking her Yorkshire terriers. When
I'd thought about it afterwards, I'd realised that eight o'clock on a
Monday morning in the school holidays was probably way earlier than
any sane person would want to get the kids out and about. And, of
course, there was the little matter of him having a job to go to.

He hadn't mentioned taking any days off to look after the twins.
It just seemed the sort of thing he might do, that was all. He was that
sort of person. Caring. Affectionate. Hot as hell in that leather jacket
of his . . .

And this was *not* getting my lesson plans done. I made myself a
cup of coffee so strong the spoon practically melted, and settled back
to work.

Feeling I deserved a break (and to be honest, at a bit of a loose
end) I called Rose in the evening. "Are you busy tomorrow?"

"Why? Need me to go shopping with you for an outfit for your hot date with Sean?"

"Thanks, but I've been buying my own clothes for some years now."

"Yeah, and look at the result. Can't, anyway. I'm having a day out with the girls. I'd ask you along, but it's been booked up for months."

Oh. A spa day, I presumed. They seemed inexplicably popular among women. Even Mother had been on one of those recently, although I was sure she'd always used to say they were common. "I'll try and contain my disappointment at not getting to spend a day having my toes nibbled by fish and getting my eyebrows threaded."

"You know, you should think about it. The eyebrow thing. You don't want to end up with a unibrow."

"I'm in absolutely no danger of getting a unibrow." I peered into the hall mirror, relieved to find no unruliness in evidence. "My eyebrows are perfectly discrete."

"What, small, inconspicuous and won't give away your secrets?"

"That's *e-t-e*, not double-*e-t*. Meaning discontinuous and individual."

"God, I bet when you were little, you used to ask Santa for a dictionary for Christmas."

It had been the *Encyclopædia Britannica*, actually. I decided not to mention this. "Well, you enjoy yourself getting plucked like a chicken."

"Yeah," Rose said, sounding strangely amused. "I'll do that. Me and the girls. Doing girly stuff."

Tuesday evening, I went onto Facebook and found she'd uploaded a new photograph with the title *Girly Day Out*. It showed her in helmet and lifejacket, hurtling down the Olympic white-water course on a raft with seven other women, some of whom I recognised from St. Saviour's School. Their expressions ranged from abject terror through grim determination to demonic glee (Rose).

Feeling properly chastised for my presumption, I *liked* the picture and added a comment: *Mea culpa. Skydiving next?*

*Her reply bloop*ed *in a few seconds later: I'm game if u r. Will see if can arrange.*

Ye gods.

I hoped she was joking.

CHAPTER ELEVEN

Halloween this year fell smack in the middle of the half-term holiday. The Old Hatter's Cottage being smack in the middle of the village, I thought I'd better get in a goodly supply of sweets or risk the consequences. After further deliberation, I also purchased a small and somewhat oddly shaped pumpkin, which was all that was left in the village Tesco.

Scooping it out was a lot messier than I'd imagined, and I was covered in slimy, stringy, orange stuff when I'd finished, but I also had a perfectly functional jack-o'-lantern to place outside my door. The internet had been a mine of intimidatingly complex ideas for carving the thing, but I went for the classic triangular eyes and nose, with a very approximately crescent-shaped mouth, and it didn't look too bad.

At least, I was confident very few of class 2E could have done much better. Not without help, at any rate.

After a seasonal meal of canned spaghetti on toast—when plated, it looked uncannily similar to pumpkin innards, which didn't help my appetite overmuch—I settled down with a copy of M.R. James to await my visitors. I was barely four pages into *Oh, Whistle, and I'll Come to You, My Lad* before the first knock came. I flew to the door and found two miniature demons standing on my doorstep, accompanied by a very large and rotund ghost.

"Trick or treat!" they chorused. The demonic voices were infantile and lisping; the ghostly one gruff and manly, which at least solved the question of whether I was looking at a pregnant spirit or one with a fondness for ectoplasmic beer.

I cowered in mock fear and held out the bowl of sweets at arm's length. The demons giggled and very politely took one sweet each.

"Oh, go on, take a handful," I encouraged them. "You deserve it for being so scary."

"Thank you," they chorused.

"Cheers, mate," their ghostly guardian added. "Oh, and good costume. Matt Smith's Doctor Who, right?"

"Right," I said, with a somewhat fixed smile.

It would only have embarrassed us both if I'd admitted I was in my usual clothes.

"You ought to get a fez," was the spectre's parting shot. "Be even better then."

"I'll bear that in mind. Thanks." I shut the door and sat back down with old Monty's ghost stories and a miniature Mars bar to await the next callers.

An hour or so later, by which time two separate fathers of preschool children had informed me they'd liked Tom Baker better, I opened the door to a loud, confident knock and found two redheaded spiders and a six-foot-tall black rat standing on my doorstep.

"Trick or treat!" the twins yelled at high volume.

Sean lifted the snout of his costume to grin at me through the mouth. "How's it going? Had any more visitors? Little furry ones, I mean."

"Up until now, my house has been refreshingly rodent-free," I said, smiling back at him. "Although there seems to be a bit of an arachnid infestation right now. I don't suppose you've got any tips to deal with that?"

"Chocolate. Give 'em chocolate, and they'll go away. Won't you, lads?"

"Yeah!" they shouted as one. I duly held the bowl out, and they dived in. Fortunately with only one hand each, not the twelve they now seemed to possess between them.

"Are you having a good half-term holiday, boys?" I asked them.

There followed an excited competition between them as Wills and Harry each tried to tell me in his loudest possible voice all about his own particular favourite half-term activity. The net result was that I was no wiser when they finished speaking than when they'd started as to what they'd actually been doing. But I got the general impression they'd been enjoying themselves.

"How about you?" Sean asked, his voice warming me despite the chill in the night air.

"Good," I said. "Cunning marketing ploy, by the way."

He laughed. "Yep. Any excuse to drum up trade. Debs made the boys' costumes. They wanted to be zombies at first, but we persuaded them spiders are scarier." He didn't add *and less morbid*, but I strongly suspected that might also have been a factor.

"Absolutely," I said firmly. "After all, how many people do you know who've ever been terrorised by a zombie in the bath?"

The giant rat head nodded. "Although fair dues, they'd be a lot harder to wash down the plughole."

There were predictable yells of "You're not washing me down a plughole!" Then the left-hand spider (Wills, I thought, but it was hard to be certain with them in costume) asked, "Why didn't you dress up, Mr. Enemy?"

"*Emeny*," Sean said. "And not all grown-ups like dressing up."

"On the contrary," I said drily and recounted the compliments I'd received on my "costume."

"But Doctor Who's not scary," Harry (or possibly Wills) complained.

"Oh? You tell that to a Dalek. Daleks are *terrified* of the Doctor." I folded my arms.

"Are they scared of spiders too?" Wills/Harry asked.

"Probably. Actually, yes, definitely. Spiders creep inside their metal cases where they can't exterminate them and crawl *all over* their squidgy alien bits. And there's nothing the Daleks can do about it." I smiled.

Four arachnid eyes opened wide. "Yeah! We're going to scare the Daleks!"

I looked up from the twins to see Sean gazing at me from beneath the rat's snout. The costume cast a shadow over his expression, leaving me unable to interpret it, but it seemed like something important had been said, nonetheless. We didn't speak for a moment. Then Sean let the snout fall to cover his face almost completely. "Come on, lads. We'd better get on to some other houses before they run out of sweets, yeah? Say thanks, now."

"Thanks, Mr. Enemy!" they yelled, and then they were gone, Sean with them.

It was only as I closed the door that it registered they'd come a very long way from their house. Sean must have driven them down in the van. Were pickings really that much better in the village centre?

Or had he wanted to visit me in particular?

It was probably just wishful thinking. But the thought warmed me, nonetheless.

After that, the trick-or-treaters died down to a mere trickle of treaters. There were a few more witches and vampires, an absolutely adorable pumpkin-in-arms, and then that seemed to be it for the night.

I settled back down with my bowl of sweets and thought about Sean. He should have looked utterly ridiculous in that rat costume, but somehow he'd managed to carry it off.

Although possibly I was biased.

CHAPTER TWELVE

I t seemed amazing, in hindsight, to think I'd been concerned the week-long half-term holiday would drag. In fact, what with all the preparations for the next six weeks of school, coupled with sorting out a few things in the house I'd let slide while I was still finding my feet, it seemed no time at all before Friday evening rolled around. Of course, I'd also finally had the chance to give Peter's piano a proper workout and dust off my collection of Scott Joplin rags. The Head had been kind enough to allow me to play the children out of assembly with the occasional burst of "The Entertainer," but it wasn't quite the same as playing on my own instrument.

I gave the top of the piano an affectionate stroke as I wondered if Sean liked ragtime, or could be persuaded to.

It would probably be best not to spring it on him too soon, I decided.

Dressing for my second date with Sean was significantly easier than for the first. (Not, of course, that the first date had actually *been* a date. Or, indeed, anything that I really wanted to dwell on, in retrospect.) For one thing, I already had the assurance that Sean liked my bow ties. For another, I could be confident in advance he'd get a kick out of this particular tie: it was a subtle grey, with a tasteful print of little blue TARDISes spinning jauntily along the space-time continuum.

Of course, we hadn't actually *said* this date was, in fact, a date. Had we? Perhaps Sean just wanted to be friends. Which would be fine, obviously. Friends were good to have. And usually significantly less complicated to deal with than people you actually got to share your bed and your life with.

I imagined waking up with Sean on a weekend morning. Would he be a cuddler? Yes, I was sure he would be. We'd wake up entwined, all warm and drowsy, and he'd be hard and so would I, and we'd have all morning to—

I cut off that line of thought ruthlessly. Any more of that and I'd need to take another shower. A cold one.

At 7:28, I heard the roar of Sean's motorbike as he pulled up in what I was now doomed to think of for all eternity as *mi entrada*. I took a deep breath, checked my reflection in the hall mirror, and threw open the door.

Lit from above by the streetlamp, Sean pulled off his helmet, ran a hand through his copper hair, and smiled. The shadows gave his roguish features an almost demonic air that had me in serious danger of needing that cold shower after all. "Honey, I'm home."

I couldn't have stopped myself from smiling back if I'd wanted to. "And what sort of a time do you call this?" I paused, mentally replaying how that might have sounded. "Um. We were quoting *Doctor Who*, weren't we? Because actually you're right on time."

His smile broadened. "We were. Although I probably should have been River and let you have the Doctor's line, seeing as you're the one in the bow tie. Are you ready to go? If we're quick, we can get a drink in before it starts."

"Yes, absolutely." Manfully resisting the urge to pull him into the house and say to hell with the amateur dramatics, I patted my pocket to make sure I had my keys, slipped my feet into my brogues, and joined him outside. The stiff autumn breeze made me shiver, but on the plus side, it had a distinctly cooling effect on my ardour, which was probably just as well, seeing as we were going to be out in public.

"Sure you don't want to grab a coat?" Sean asked.

"No, no, I'll be fine. It's only a six-minute walk. Nearer five, if we're walking briskly. What?" I asked. Sean's smile had taken on the sort of look I often saw directed by mothers at the least intelligent of their offspring.

"Nothing. Just, you know, most people aren't that exact about timings. Come on, we'd better get moving. We'll only have—" he looked at his watch "—twenty-three minutes to get those drinks in."

"Are you making fun of me?" I asked suspiciously as we crossed the road.

"Would I?" His eyes were wide and guileless.

"Yes," I decided firmly. "Yes, you would."

"Well, only a little bit. Just to keep you on your toes." He grinned. "If nothing else, that'll even out the height difference."

I mock-glared at him. "I'm sure you were exaggerating anyway. I strongly suspect if we measured you now, you'd only come up at five foot eleven and three quarters. Possibly only five foot eleven and a half."

"Ah, but we're all the same height lying down. Least, that's what Debs always says."

"How is she?" I asked, aghast at myself for having failed to do so earlier. We'd just passed the pub, a burst of chatter and laughter reaching our ears as someone opened the door, and were heading up the sparsely lit back lane towards the park.

"She's doing really well." He shrugged. "Well, you know. Considering. She's been enjoying half-term with the twins."

Really? I thought, but didn't say aloud. Personally I'd have thought the company of two young tearaways was the last thing an ill woman needed, but presumably it was different for their mother. "I'm glad to hear that."

"Yeah, it's been a while since she's been feeling up to taking them out places. And they've had a couple of cinema trips—you know how they do these Kids' Clubs in the school holidays, with cheap seats—so she's been able to take it easy some of the time as well. But she's been a lot better since she finished the chemo."

"I'm glad." We rounded the corner and walked up the narrow lane alongside the park, its other side lined with houses whose owners had no doubt paid a pretty premium for their uninterrupted view across the fields. All that could be made out at this time of night, of course, was the string of moving fairy lights made up from the headlights of cars driving along the distant village bypass.

The village hall loomed at the very top of the park, standing guard over the tennis courts and the kiddies' playground. Inside, it was quite large, with a wide permanent stage at one end, raised high enough from the floor that the lack of banked seating wasn't a problem. Ranks of orange plastic chairs had been set out with a central aisle, giving an effect somewhat similar to a registry office, although without the tense atmosphere usually imparted by feuding relatives.

The bar was in a little side room, separated from the main hall by a folding partition. We ordered drinks for now—wine for both of us this time, as apparently the extremely limited bar didn't stock the right kind of beer—and more for the interval. I was a little concerned about Sean riding his bike after a couple of glasses of wine, but I needn't have troubled myself. The plastic "glasses," when they arrived, were exceedingly small.

"Are they worried people will get drunk and heckle the performers?" I whispered to Sean as we took our drinks to a quiet corner.

"Nah," he whispered back. "I reckon it's just that a lot of the old folk who come to these things aren't all that steady on their feet to start with."

And, indeed, the crowd milling about seemed to consist mainly of a rather older demographic than I had expected, given that this was Friday, and Saturday was supposed to be grannies' night. I wondered if they'd be shocked to see two men on a date together. Or if they just wouldn't realise we were, in fact, on a date together. Which, upon reflection, was far more likely. I'd had it drummed into me from a very early age that public displays of affection were vulgar, and although I'd gone past the stage of holding rigidly to Mother's teachings, I really didn't think this was either the time or the place to start snogging in public.

Assuming, of course, Sean was even interested in snogging. In public or otherwise. Maybe this wasn't a date. Maybe he'd just invited me here as, well, a friend. Hadn't I stressed just that when I'd asked him to Badgers?

Feeling a little depressed, I put my thimbleful of wine down on a table and flicked through the programme, which had cost me a pound on the way in. As the content was almost entirely made up of adverts for village businesses, I wasn't totally certain I'd got my money's worth.

"In the interests of full disclosure," Sean said quietly in my ear, "I probably ought to mention Eliza Doolittle's my ex."

Eliza Doolittle, my programme informed me, was played by Heather Matthews. She was, presumably, the dark-skinned, pretty young woman adorning the posters which had been placed all over the village to advertise the event.

I knew there had been something about her I disliked.

"We're still friends, but that's all it is," Sean went on. "And if you could, you know, say something, I might feel a bit less like I've just ballsed things up completely."

"I . . ." I stared at the programme. "Is this a date? I mean, well . . ."

"Yeah," he said and took hold of my hand. "It's a date."

I darted guilty glances around the hall. Most people, either huddled in their little conversational groups or already seated, had their backs to us, but Emily G.'s granny caught my eye and waved. I waved my programme at her awkwardly, left-handed, as Sean still had my right hand in his disconcerting grasp. I was certain my face must be worryingly red.

"Are you sure this is, well, appropriate?" I hissed in Sean's ear. Oh God, would it look like I was kissing him?

"We're holding hands, not shagging," he whispered back. "Didn't mean to make you feel uncomfortable. Anyway, we probably ought to go and sit down. You can take your glass in, don't worry."

He let go of my hand. Freed of his grasp, it felt smaller, and bereft, as he led me to a pair of seats quite near the back. "That's all right," I said inadequately, but couldn't quite muster the courage to take his hand back once we'd sat down.

The lights dimmed, and some poorly reproduced music began to play, swiftly followed by the opening of the curtains to disclose a mocked-up Victorian street scene, where a young lady in tattered period garb was attempting to sell some rather modern-looking artificial flowers.

I soon realised Sean had been right when he'd said that *some* of them could act. Eliza (curse her) was rather good, as were Professor Higgins and Mr. Doolittle, but Freddy was more wooden than the scenery and far too old for the role. He and Colonel Pickering were much of an age, instead of at least a generation apart. Still, it was entertaining enough to a crowd who had come willing to be pleased. Eliza's timing and delivery on the iconic *Not bloody likely* line was impeccable, and I roared with laughter with the rest of the audience. Crispin, I thought, wouldn't have been seen dead here. I felt an unwonted—and to be honest, unwanted—pang of sympathy for him.

"Do you come to a lot of the local productions?" I asked Sean in the interval, after we'd picked up our drinks. We wandered over to one side of the hall, where there was a wall covered with black-and-white photographs of Shamwell in days gone by.

"Most of them, yeah. I just think if people are going to go to all that trouble to put something on locally, you should support that, right?" He shrugged. "Theatres in London, yeah, they've got the big-name actors and all the money behind them, but that's not what it's all about, is it? It's like, stuff in a place like this is just as important as what happens in the city."

"An admirable sentiment, although I'm not sure everyone would agree with you there," I said, rather hoping he might convince me of it. Having banished Crispin more or less successfully from my mind, I couldn't help thinking of Fordy. He'd been appalled to hear I was taking a job in a village primary school. He'd told me flat out I was flushing my career down the toilet.

Of course, he hadn't known why I'd— No. I wasn't going to think about that now. I studied a view of the village high street from 1904. It was remarkably similar to how it looked today, save that the photograph showed rather fewer cars (i.e., none) and rather more young lads loitering in flat caps (i.e., some). Perhaps Fordy had been right when he'd called the place "so sleepy it was practically bloody comatose."

"Yeah, well. They can have their opinion. I'll keep mine." Sean sipped his wine. "So what brought you to Shamwell, anyhow? I mean, no offence, but I'd have thought you'd have gone for a job in a private school. Like the one you went to."

"I . . . Well, I did. But I decided it wasn't for me. Teaching older pupils, I mean." My hands became uncomfortably clammy, and I took a restoring sip of wine.

Sean didn't appear to notice my discomfort, for which I was grateful. "Yeah? I guess it's got to be a lot different. You don't miss it, then? Teaching your subject at high school level, I mean?"

I thought about it. "Not really. Nothing like as much as I thought I might." I hadn't actually realised how true that was, until now.

"Did you have to do a lot of retraining? I mean, it must be a bit like a hospital consultant deciding to go back into general practice."

"Teaching A-Level maths is hardly brain surgery. But yes, in primary education you don't just stick to your subject, as a rule. Which for me is good, because it means I can teach maths *and* music, which I couldn't before. And there's a lot more pastoral care involved. Of course, the hardest part was persuading the interview panel I was serious about it." I smiled at him, although that wasn't, in fact, strictly true. There had been a *lot* of reading involved, not to mention learning the National Curriculum upside down and backwards. "I signed up for a fortnight's Return to Teaching course, which helped a lot. Although I got a few funny looks from the rest of the class. I think they thought I was a bit young to *start* teaching, let alone return to it."

Sean laughed. "Yeah, I should think you'd stand out a bit among all the mums coming back after career breaks."

"Not to mention the men in their fifties coming back after being made redundant from the better jobs they left teaching for in the first place."

"You didn't have to get any different qualifications, or anything, then?"

"No, fortunately. There's been talk of introducing certification in teaching different age groups, but nothing's come of it as yet." A thought struck me. "How about you? Are there qualifications in pest control?" My mind frankly boggled at the thought of the practical exams. Did they arrange controlled invasions of the exam hall by cockroaches, or send the candidates into single combat with wasps' nests?

"Oh yeah. There's a shedload of Health and Safety stuff you have to know, of course, and everyone where I work has to get their BPCA—British Pest Control Association—level two." He laughed suddenly. "There isn't a level one. Never found anyone who knows why that is. And there's always more stuff you can learn. Safe use of air weapons, that kind of thing. It's all right sending someone out to take potshots at pigeons, but no one's going to be impressed if they shoot the customer instead."

I shuddered and finished my wine.

"Want another?" Sean asked.

"Thanks, but they must be about to start again. We've had over fifteen minutes already."

"Yeah?" Sean raised his eyebrows and looked at his watch just as the bell rang and a loud voice asked us in jovial, reproduced tones to take our seats for the second half.

We trooped obediently back into the main hall. Just before we reached our row, someone jabbed me in the ribs. "Are you enjoying it, then?"

I turned to find Emily G.'s granny's wrinkly face looking up at me. "Oh yes, very much, thank you. And you?"

"It gets me out of the house." Her sharp eyes narrowed as she turned to Sean. "Came to see your girlfriend, did you?"

"Ex-girlfriend," he said easily.

"He told me," I blurted out, awash with gratitude that Sean hadn't left me in ignorance to be blindsided by Granny G.'s no doubt well-meaning interference. Then I swallowed as both of them turned to look at me.

"Did he now?" Her expression didn't soften. If anything, her eyes turned flintier. "I don't hold with these menageries. In my day, you made your choice, and you stuck with it."

Menageries? Did she think Sean and I and Eliza Doolittle were . . . Oh God, had she been around somewhere when I'd been ranting about threesomes?

I refused to even *consider* the possibility Granny G. hadn't, in fact, got the word wrong and was talking about bestiality.

"Good for you," Sean said, seeming untroubled. "How's Mr. G. doing these days?"

"Doing?" She snorted. Perhaps it was a village thing. "Catch him *doing*."

Somebody *shushed* us loudly, and chastened, we scurried to our seats.

The curtain opened, and the broad comedy of the first half gave way to the more painful jibes of the second. Professor Higgins likened Eliza to a squashed cabbage; she threw his slippers at him. For a moment, I thought I was back at school with class 2E.

After the curtain had come down for the final time, and the last of the applause died away, Sean turned to me. "Mind if we hang around and say hi to Heather?"

"Not at all," I lied politely.

We lingered in the hall as the rest of the audience filed out, elderly voices chattering cheerfully. At length the actors started to emerge from a corridor by the side of the stage. Heather was still in costume, and she smiled when she saw Sean. "You all right? I thought I saw you at the back, there." She hitched her bag up on her shoulder and came to kiss him on the cheek. "What did you think, then?"

"You were great. Really rocked it. Hey, this is Robert." He stepped back from her embrace and turned to where I was shifting uneasily in my brogues. "He's the twins' new teacher."

"Yeah? You poor sod." Her natural accent was a lot closer to Eliza's original cockney than to the way she spoke at the end of the play, after she'd been thoroughly Higgins'd. Having acknowledged me, she turned back to Sean. "How's Debs doing? She still having the chemo?"

"Nah, she's finished now. She's gotta go back in for tests next week, see if it worked."

"Yeah? Fingers crossed for her, then. Work going okay?"

They chatted for another minute or two about people I didn't know, while I became intimately familiar with the information on the village notice board. I discovered that, should I need to consult a policeman, there would be one available from two until four on Tuesday afternoons. Hopefully the village criminals would take note and time their activities accordingly. Library services, by contrast, were available four days a week and until 8 p.m. on Thursdays.

I was just perusing the list of Zumba classes at the hall, for which there seemed to be such an extraordinary demand I was starting to contemplate going along to one to see what all the fuss was about, when Sean took my arm. "Sorry about that," he murmured in my ear. "I forgot how much she goes on sometimes. Are we going to go back to yours for a drink? Think we're a bit late for the pub, now."

"Oh—well, I wouldn't want to keep you out . . ." Damn it. *Why* did I say that? Did I *want* him to think I wasn't interested?

"Nah, that's okay. I'm not working tomorrow."

"Oh. Good." Bother. Was I now sounding as if I intended to monopolise his company for the entirety of the next twenty-four hours, whether he wanted me to or not?

We stepped out into the darkness, the air a frigid shock after the hall, which had been heated to almost uncomfortable levels by the number of warm bodies inside. I shivered. Perhaps I should have worn a coat after all.

Then again, perhaps not, I decided, as a leather-clad arm slung itself around my shoulders and pulled me close. "Getting a bit nippy, innit?" Sean murmured in my ear.

"Innit just," I replied. "Um. Did that sound like I was making fun of you?"

"Little bit. Don't worry, I can take it." The eerie shadows cast by the streetlamps lent his smile a devilish cast that sent black-winged butterflies flitting around my insides.

"I wasn't mocking you," I said. "Honestly."

"Don't worry about it." He squeezed my shoulders. "I like a bloke with a sense of humour."

"Hmm. The last man who said that to me then went on to say, 'Which clearly you've got, going by the way you dress.'"

"Heh. Take it that relationship didn't go too well."

"Not particularly." It had been Crispin.

There was almost no one else around, the majority of the audience having dispersed while we were with Miss Doolittle, and the cast having, to a man, jumped into cars to drive home. In the darkness that surrounded us, I even dared to slip my arm under Sean's jacket and around his waist. Hard muscle flexed under my hand as he walked, and stubble rasped my cheek as Sean pressed close to me but didn't kiss me.

Which was good, obviously. After all, we *were* still in public. Technically speaking.

"It's rather startling to think how much things have changed, isn't it?" I said to break the suddenly charged silence. "All the things people could or couldn't do, back in Victorian times, depending on their social class."

"Yeah, not to mention the *people* they couldn't do." Sean laughed quietly, more a breath than anything. "You wouldn't have been here with me, that's for sure."

"Not unless we wanted to join Oscar Wilde in Reading Gaol," I said drily.

"Not what I meant, and you know it."

"Weren't your family landowners in Victorian times?" I countered. "Perhaps *you* wouldn't have been here with *me*."

Sean kicked a stray conker, unaccountably missed by village children, along the pavement. It bounced and rolled merrily into the gutter. "Social mobility, you gotta love it."

"I don't know. Sometimes I just think it makes things even more of a minefield."

As we reached the more brightly lit, central portion of the village, I regretfully let my arm fall from Sean's waist. He took the hint, and we walked on no longer touching. Here, there were still one or two people about, although the corner by the church was bare of teenage gangs. I shivered once more, bereft of Sean's warmth.

Sean spoke again. "So do you reckon they'd have ended up together? Higgins and Eliza?"

"Well, Shaw was adamant that they wouldn't."

"Yeah, but what did he know? He was only the bloke who wrote it. Forget about him—what do you reckon?"

I shrugged. "Well . . . to be honest, I can't see her ending up with either the professor *or* Freddy. Higgins would have been impossible to live with, but after him, settling for Freddy would seem like, well, settling. I'd have thought she could do a lot better."

"What, a girl from the streets with no money and no family? Even if her dad *had* gone up in the world, there'd be plenty who'd still look down on her once they found out where she came from." Sean paused. "Anyway, I thought Freddy was all right. Bit naive, but his heart was in the right place. It wasn't his fault he'd been brought up to think the world owed him a living."

We'd reached the Old Hatter's Cottage. "Will you come in?" I asked, my stomach filling with butterflies once more. Or moths, perhaps, seeing as all good butterflies would be tucked up in bed by now. Possibly with other butterflies, and would that be the way this evening was going . . .? I held my breath as the internal insect swarms threatened to get out of hand.

"All right," Sean said. "Wouldn't mind a coffee before I get back on my bike."

Oh. That meant he definitely wouldn't be staying. Or did he just not want to presume?

"Have you got much on tomorrow?" I asked, opening the front door and ushering him in.

"Promised the twins I'd take them down to the London Dungeon, so yeah, it'll have to be an early start."

"Ah. I have a feeling that'll be right up their street. Lots of blood and gore, from what I've heard." I frowned as we walked through into the kitchen. "It's an odd phrase, that, when you think about it, isn't it? *Gore* being a synonym for blood. It rather fails to add anything to the meaning."

"Yeah, I s'pose not, now you mention it. Like hale and hearty."

"Fine and dandy." I filled the kettle and switched it on.

"Be all and end all," Sean suggested.

I got out two mugs. "Belt and braces . . . No, wait, that one doesn't fit, does it?"

He smiled. "You know, I was surprised to see you're a belt man. I'd have put money on you wearing braces."

"Not recommended when you're a teacher, I'm afraid. Children do so love to snap them." Coffee, coffee, where did I keep the coffee? Oh yes—in the cupboard above the kettle.

"They're not the only ones." Sean leaned in close, one eyebrow slightly raised. "So if you've got some hiding in your wardrobe . . . Braces, that is, not kids."

I swallowed. "S-several pairs. Um. You remember how we decided this was a date?"

"Yeah?" Sean murmured, his face very close to mine.

"Well, I, er . . ." Thinking, *To hell with it*, I closed the remaining gap and kissed him.

It was *delicious*. His lips were firm and yielding in just the right combination, and he tasted of red wine and devilry. His arms slid around my hips, pulling me close to him, and I realised too late I was still holding the mugs in one hand and a jar of coffee in the other. Cursing inwardly, I wrapped my arms around him as best I could, hoping the loud clinking noise that ensued didn't mean I'd just broken something.

Sean pulled back from the kiss, laughing. "You want to maybe put some stuff down?"

"Possibly," I conceded, and gave the mugs a quick once-over as I put them on the counter. "I'll have the chipped one," I said ruefully.

"Whatever. I'm not bothered," he said, pulling me close again. This time I was able to reciprocate in kind. I let my hands roam over Sean's shoulders, their form frustratingly masked by the leather jacket he still wore. His mouth found mine, and this time, his tongue entered my mouth, questing and challenging. I hardened embarrassingly quickly, but was reassured when, on shifting my hips, I felt an answering hard ridge in Sean's jeans. Our kisses grew hungrier, fiercer. I wanted to touch him all over and was rapidly coming to loathe the leather jacket I'd so admired earlier. His hands clenched on my hips with a force that was almost bruising, the heat of them palpable even through my trousers.

The kettle boiled noisily and we broke apart, both of us breathing rather quickly. "Um. Coffee?" I said, my voice shaky.

"Uh, yeah. Wow."

"Wow?"

"Definitely wow. Talk about your hidden depths."

I gave him a sidelong look. "Not *that* hidden, surely?"

"Depends. I mean, don't get me wrong, I like the way you dress—it's different and fun and all that—but yeah, it's not exactly in-your-face sexy, is it?" He gave my rear a gentle squeeze. "Course, when I saw you in your running gear, with your hair all messed up and that . . . I mean, most of the time you're so put together, you know? It was like . . . Shit, this is a bad analogy, cos I liked you before, anyway, but it was like that really corny moment in films when the girl in the lab coat takes off her glasses and shakes out her hair, and suddenly she's gorgeous."

I frowned. "I don't wear glasses. And my hair's too short to shake out. Plus, and I really feel I should emphasise this point to avoid any *possible* misunderstandings, I'm not a girl."

Sean laughed. "I told you it was a shit analogy." He brought one hand up to stroke my face, and I fought the urge to nuzzle into it as his other hand slid farther around my waist. "But you are gorgeous."

Delight and embarrassment warred. Embarrassment, as usual, won. "I think I'd better make you that coffee now. The wine tonight obviously had quite an effect on you."

"Yeah, two thimblefuls and I'm anybody's."

"Anybody's?"

"Nah, not really. I've got pretty high standards." His fingers brushed my throat, and I swallowed.

"Um. You'd probably better let go of me. So I can make the coffee," I reminded him.

"Probably." Sean's hands didn't move.

"Soon?" I hinted. "Before we have to boil the kettle again?"

"Definitely." He leaned in to kiss me, his lips soft, then slowly let go.

I blinked at him for a moment before remembering I was supposed to be doing something now.

"Coffee," Sean said helpfully.

"I knew that." I spooned coffee into the mugs, managing not to spill more than half of it over the counter, which I counted as something of a victory.

"Course you did." Sean leaned in beside me and swept the spilt coffee grounds up with his hands, then brushed them off over the sink. "Milk?"

"Fridge." I inclined my head in the fridge's general direction and poured hot water into the mugs.

"Sugar?"

"Cupboard. I'll get it."

"Top?"

"Bot—" I caught myself halfway through the automatic answer. "I beg your pardon?"

Sean leaned on the counter, an evil grin plastered over his face that gave him a disconcerting resemblance to his nephews. "Sorry—thought we were playing word-association games. I always used to like those when I was a littl'un."

"I bet you were a horrible child." I'd also lay money on my face being a violent shade of crimson right now. I hid it in the cupboard, under the guise of searching for the sugar.

He was unrepentant. "You'll have to ask Debs about that. Course, she reckons I still haven't grown up."

"She's undoubtedly right. Sugar." I turned and presented him with the packet.

"Honey," he acknowledged, unrolling the top. "Spoon?"

"Dish," I muttered, handing him the appropriate item of cutlery.

He frowned at it. "No, that's definitely a spoon."

"I'm beginning to have a lot of sympathy for your sister," I said drily. "Not to mention your parents."

"Yeah, well, don't waste any sympathy on my dad."

I looked up sharply from my coffee.

Sean shrugged and spooned sugar into his mug. He stirred it and stared into the whirling contents. "He buggered off when we were eight. Haven't seen him since. Debs always says she wishes he'd hung around a bit longer so she'd have known the sort of bloke to avoid."

"Oh God. It must have seemed like a sick joke when the twins' father left too." I put down my mug and, hesitantly, put my arms around him.

"Sick's the word all right," he said so quietly I had to strain to hear him. "Makes me want to puke to think if the worst happens, that bastard will have more claim to the boys than I will."

"You've been like a father to them." It wasn't a guess. I'd seen how they were with him—and how he was with them. "I don't know what the legal position is, but surely if she names you their guardian in her will . . . And anyway, it may never come to that. People get better from cancer all the time."

He nodded. "Yeah. Shit. Sorry—turning into a right miserable date, aren't I?"

"Don't be silly." I held him, hesitating, then said it anyway. "I never really knew my father either. He died when I was ten, and before that he was always working, you see—even at weekends, he'd be busy— and I was away at school half the year in any case."

"Yeah? How old were you, when you first went to boarding school?"

"Seven. But I had to leave when Father died, so I was only there three years. I boarded at Loriners', of course, but Mother was there too."

"Must have been rough. Leaving all your mates, right when you'd just lost your dad for good." Sean's hands stroked up and down my arms, their rhythm slow and soothing.

"I . . . I found new ones. Eventually." I managed a wonky smile. "Don't know what I'd have done without Fordy." Entirely failed to weather the bullying, probably.

"Yeah. At least Debs and me always had each other. So you still see him, do you? This Fordy bloke?"

"Not as much as I'd like. He's married now, with a new baby."

Sean laughed. "I remember when the twins were first born. You'll be lucky if you see him at all the first six months. He'll be too busy trying to figure out how the bloody hell the steriliser's supposed to work and wondering if he's ever going to get a full night's sleep again. He works, does he?"

I nodded. "In the city. Stockbrokers. They live in Kent, though, Fordy and Linette. And Georgie too, now, of course."

"So he's got the commute on top of everything. Poor sod." He paused. "You and him ever . . .?"

"Um. Possibly. But I'm fairly certain Linette doesn't know—I mean, not that anything happened after they got together, of course not. But I don't think he'd want her to find out." My insides, like my tongue, felt all tangled up in knots by the end of that.

"Huh."

"What?"

"Oh, just wouldn't have pegged you as the sort to be someone's dirty little secret. Shit, I didn't mean it like that. Come back."

I'd stepped away from him, my hands falling to my sides. "How did you mean it?"

"Just—I don't get that, you know? Keeping secrets from people you care about. Well, I get it, but I don't like it."

"Maybe he thinks she's happier not knowing?"

"Yeah. Maybe. Look, I wasn't having a go at you or anything. I was just surprised, that's all. Come back?"

Sean gazed at me tenderly, and I couldn't resist his entreaty a second time. I stepped forward, and his arms encircled me once more, our bodies pressing together, learning how to fit to one another. He chuckled into my hair.

"What?" I asked, nuzzling his neck. He smelled of soap and shaving foam, with a warmer scent I could only identify as *Sean*.

"Just . . . I'm not usually this heavy and serious and all that. Honest. Not at the start of a relationship, anyway. Course, I've never been in one with anyone like you."

I felt light-headed and strangely tingly inside. He'd said what Fordy used to refer to as *the 'R' word*. "I don't mind," I murmured. I wished he'd move away from the kitchen counter. The way he was leaning against it made it impossible for my hands to stray below his waist. I made the best of a bad job and pushed his shirt up under his jacket, my hands delighting in their contact with the warm skin of his back.

Sean made a loud *mmm* sound, and there were definite stirrings in those jeans of his. I was hard again too, and when we kissed, I got harder still. His kisses seemed gentler this time, but somehow deeper. As if we were inviting each other in, rather than demanding admittance.

When we broke apart once more, both of us were breathing heavily.

"Shit," Sean said. "I'd better go. But I'll see you again, yeah? Sunday? Think I'll be too knackered tomorrow night."

"Sunday," I agreed, not certain I trusted myself to say any more. Part of me—a very definite part of me—wanted to ask him to stay the night. But another part of me felt nothing but relief that we weren't moving so quickly. I'd never been one for casual sex. I never seemed to have the knack of separating the emotions from the act.

And I was utterly terrified of the speed with which I was falling for Sean.

CHAPTER THIRTEEN

'd invited Rose round for dinner on Saturday. In a halfhearted attempt to stem off incipient heart disease from all the takeaways, I nipped out to Tesco and bought a couple of pizzas and a prepacked salad.

Hanne met me on my doorstep and cast a doleful eye at my purchases, clearly visible through the plastic of the gossamer-thin carrier bags the supermarkets were handing out these days. "Your pretty friend is coming over? You should have told me. I could have helped you make something special. Better than the pølsefocaccia."

"Ah . . . Rose isn't actually my girlfriend," I said, visions of burned-down houses dancing in my head. "And she's really not fussy."

"Oh, you young men." She smiled at me kindly. "Women like to be spoiled. Even if they say they don't. Next time, okay?"

"Next time," I agreed. It seemed easier than the alternative.

As I walked into the kitchen with my bags, my eyes making the quick scan for furry invaders that had become second nature, I berated myself, not for the first time, for not just telling Hanne I was gay. After all, even in the unlikely event she reacted in horror and shunned me for the foreseeable future, when all was said and done, she was only my next-door neighbour. Her disapproval would hardly blight my life and might even save me from further kitchen-related embarrassment.

I'd survived Mother's initial disappointment over my coming out perfectly well. And she'd quite come around to the matter now. She'd even been rather fond of Crispin. In fact, she'd been disappointed when we'd broken up, although of course, she hadn't known the full details.

It was probably best not to speculate what she might think of Sean.

I filled the day with all the tedious but necessary chores I'd been putting off all week, such as picking up the dry cleaning and investigating local cleaners. For a room in which one did nothing but wash, it seemed a bathroom could get remarkably filthy if not attended to once a week.

Rose arrived a few hours after sundown, like a fashionably tardy vampire, and we took our pizzas into the lounge to eat perched upon the sofa, despite the presence of a perfectly good dining table. I had to pop back into the kitchen for the salad. Rose had left it languishing on the kitchen counter in a rather pointed manner, I thought.

Rose freed a slice of pizza from the clinging, cheesy embrace of its fellows, and daintily placed a forkful of coleslaw on top. "So go on, tell me all the gory details. Did Sean stay the night?" She took a bite.

"No," I said with a barely suppressed sigh.

"You went to his?" she asked, her hopeful tone somewhat muffled by her mouthful of food.

"No." I cut myself a bite-size morsel of pizza and virtuously added a baby lettuce leaf.

Rose swallowed. "Quickie in the bushes after the show?"

"*No.* I can't think of anything less conducive to a successful career in primary education than being caught in flagrante a stone's throw away from the swings. Also, it was extremely cold." Lettuce and pepperoni grease was not, I decided, a match made in heaven. Perhaps I should follow Rose's lead and stick to the coleslaw.

She gave me an evil smile. "Worried you wouldn't show to advantage?"

"Eat your pizza, woman, and stop speculating about my sex life."

"You're no fun. Fine, just give me the PG version. Did it go okay? You and Sean get on all right?"

"Yes, actually. It went really well." I put down my fork, distracted from pepperoni and cheese by the memory of Sean's kisses.

"You've got the world's soppiest smile right now. Is it *twu wuv?*" she simpered.

I struggled to think of how to reply. "It's very early days. And it didn't *all* go well. He introduced me to his ex, which I could have done without."

"Ew. Awk-ward," she singsonged.

"His *female* ex, which made it even worse." I mercilessly stabbed a cherry tomato in the heart and popped it in my mouth, whole.

"Stop being sexist. Why's a female ex worse than a male one?"

I swallowed. "She just *is*, okay?" My insides were all tangled up with half-formed doubts and anxieties. Not to mention pepperoni. "And she wasn't what I was expecting."

Rose shrugged. "Never met her, but if she's the one I remember seeing around the village, she seemed all right. If you like them skinny." She looked at me. "Which obviously he does. Mixed-race girl, wears really tight jeans?"

"Well, when I saw her, she was wearing a floor-length skirt and frilly blouse, but I suspect she'd dress differently when she wasn't actually in costume. She seemed to get on with him really well. Asked about his family, joked about people he worked with."

"So? They were together for a while, weren't they? Course she'd have met that lot. Just cos you haven't yet doesn't mean anything."

"That's not what I mean . . . I mean, she seemed very much his sort of person." I stared at my plate for a long moment, but there was no wisdom to be found in the arrangement of the pepperoni atop my pizza. Although the pineapple chunks Rose had insisted we add made a pretty pattern. "Not at all like me."

"Why should she be like you?"

"I just thought . . . People have *types*, don't they? Perhaps I'm not really his type."

"Maybe he looks for something different in a girl than he does in a bloke." She cackled. "If he doesn't, he's going to be in for a bit of a shock when the lights go off."

"Well, *obviously* there will be that sort of difference. But I just thought . . . Aren't people bisexual because they don't care what gender people are? So wouldn't they look for the same thing in either gender?"

Rose frowned. "Don't see why. Maybe he likes girly things in girls, and blokey things in blokes?"

"But doesn't that mean, then, that no one person will ever have all the attributes he's looking for?"

"It's not a bloody checklist. Least it isn't for the rest of us. You, maybe. I can just see you with a list of required *attributes* you have to tick off before you go out with someone: taller than you: check; bit of rough: check; enormous—"

"I don't have a checklist!" I cut her off hastily.

"So there you go, then. Neither does he." Rose piled more coleslaw on her half-eaten pizza slice. "So what was he like, then? This last bloke you went out with. Cos if the name's anything to go by, he wasn't a lot like Sean." She snorted. "*Crispin*. I mean, seriously, who names their kid that? I bet he's some long-haired, limp-wristed fairy who flounces around spouting poetry all over the place. And I'm not being homophobic, all right? I'm just stupid-name phobic."

"Crispin was the games master," I said as drily as I could. "He's never flounced in his life, and he's always hated poetry." And he had remarkably sturdy wrists, I remembered with somewhat less of a pang than I'd expected.

"You two don't sound like you were very well suited, then. At least Sean likes stuff you like."

I found myself smiling. "He's something of a revelation, isn't he? I mean, you look at him—boy from the council estate, comes from a broken home, works in a, well, not particularly revered profession. But he doesn't let his background define him or hem him in. And he's not ashamed of his interests."

"God, I can feel my teeth rotting away just listening to you. You'd better not wear that soppy smile in front of the kids. They're vicious little bastards for spotting a weakness. So when's the wedding, then? I need to start saving up for a hat. Unless the Old Hatter left a few tucked away in the attic here? Nah, they'd all be three hundred years out of fashion and made of crinolines and stuff."

"I'm fairly certain a crinoline was a type of petticoat, not a hat. And there's not—" Mortifyingly reminded of that night at Badgers, I lowered my voice substantially. Not that I thought Sean was listening outside my window, or indeed within miles of being able to overhear my incautious outbursts, but once bitten, et cetera, et cetera. "There's not going to be a wedding. We've had one date."

"Two, if you count that night in Badgers."

"Which I'd been trying to forget."

"Three, even, if you count the squrat."

I frowned. "Skwuh-rat?"

"It's short for squirrel-you-thought-was-a-rat. So yeah, you've had three dates already. Actually, when you put it like that, I can't believe you haven't been to bed with him yet."

"It's only a date if both parties *know* it's a date," I said firmly. "And squrats don't count. So we've had one date, that's all. And I'm hardly going to rush into things with someone I've only just met."

"I don't know. I thought you gay blokes were all about casual sex." She took a last mouthful of her pizza, which seemed to have disappeared much more quickly than my own.

"Sorry to disappoint, but some of us prefer it to mean something."

"S'pose I should have expected that from you. I'm a bit surprised at Sean, though. Or did he try it on, and you slapped him down?"

"There was no slapping. We just mutually agreed not to rush into things."

"Huh. First time I went out with Shitface, I had to beat him off with a stick."

"Which only goes to prove he was never good enough for you."

"Well, I didn't beat him that hard." She clicked her tongue. "Shame, really, with hindsight." She looked sad, and I didn't think it was the missed opportunity for violent assault that was bothering her. I cut a generous slice from my remaining pizza and slid it onto Rose's plate.

If I'd been expecting thanks, I was disappointed. She merely set to with gusto and a muttered, "Lightweight."

"If he came back," I said cautiously as she tucked in, "and said he was sorry and it'd all been a terrible mistake, would you take him back?"

There was a heavy moment of silence. Possibly because Rose had her mouth full. Then again, perhaps not. "Doesn't matter, does it? He's not coming back."

"But—"

"Would you take Crispy Beef back?"

Ouch. "Point taken. And don't call him that. He'd probably like it. More coleslaw?"

"Nope, I'm stuffed." She promptly gave herself the lie by forking up the last of my donated pizza. "So when are you seeing Sean again?"

"Tomorrow." I gazed at the last ragged remains of my pizza and put my knife and fork together with a sigh.

Rose swallowed. "Ooh, that sounds keen. What are you doing?"

"Not sure yet." Actually, come to think of it, we hadn't made any arrangements at all, so I didn't even know if I'd be seeing him daytime or evening. "I might introduce him to Portia."

"I'm sure it's cruelty to cars, calling a Nissan that. Poor thing probably has an identity crisis. You know, actually, you ought to get a second car. Preferably one that looks like it was built this century. Then you can get one of those stickers that say, *My Other Car Is a Portia.*"

"Be leaving the teaching profession for a career in stand-up any day now, will you?"

"You can mock. Ten years from now, you'll be telling everyone you knew me before I was famous."

"Somehow I feel certain there was a silent *in* before that last word."

"Yeah, whatever. Are you seriously not going to finish that?"

Wordlessly, I passed her my plate.

CHAPTER FOURTEEN

S unday morning, I got back from my run to hear my phone ringing plaintively from where I'd left it in the lounge. With a final burst of speed, I managed to dive onto the sofa and catch it just before it went to voice mail. It was Sean, and my heartbeat, already racing after my exercise, struck up an odd pizzicato beat, *allegro ma non troppo.* "Hello?" I panted.

"Had to dash for the phone, did you?" His voice was warm and amused.

"Well, yes," I said, trying to calm my breathing. "But I've just been out for a run too. Literally just got in."

"Bloody hell, that's keen. I've only just got up." My brain helpfully conjured up an image of Sean with sleep-tousled hair, of which other parts of me approved wholeheartedly, especially as I'd neglected to supply him with pyjamas. "Do you run every day?"

"God, no. I'm not *that* keen. Three or four times a week, that's all." I kicked off my trainers and put my feet up on the sofa.

"That's a bit vague, for you."

"Well . . . I run Monday, Wednesday, and Friday mornings, and again sometime over the weekend if I'm not busy."

"That sounds more like it. What sort of distance do you do?"

"Really not that far. Five miles at most, usually. It depends if there's a good circular route. I was up around the golf course today."

"Yeah? Managed to avoid the balls flying all over the place, then."

"Don't worry, I always wear very supportive underwear." Oops. Was that a bit too risqué for this stage of . . . whatever this was?

Apparently not, from the sound of Sean's laughter. "Anyway," he said after a moment, "are you still up for doing something today? Thought I could maybe pop round your place about half past two."

"Absolutely. I'll look forward to it. Um, you'll have had lunch by then?"

"Yeah, no worries. Right, I'd better go. I'll see you this afternoon, okay?"

We hung up. I was smiling helplessly. Then I frowned. What, exactly, were we going to do this afternoon? Drink tea? Go out to a pub? Stay in and watch whatever minor-league football was still available to view on terrestrial television? Oh God, would he be disappointed I didn't have satellite? No, that was ridiculous. Maybe he'd want to go to a pub to watch TV there? Still, whatever we were doing, I was fairly certain Sean would have warned me if my normal clothing would be in any way inappropriate.

Comforted by this thought, I went to shower and change. Once clean and dressed in proper attire, I decided to match my bow tie to my mood and swiftly knotted the orange one with the hot-air balloons on around my neck. Yes, that looked nicely jaunty. Sean, I thought, would approve.

I filled the time before half past two with a little light reading. I'd been meaning to delve into *The Road to Wigan Pier* for some time now, and it was, it transpired, quite rewarding, if a little repetitive. Orwell seemed inordinately fascinated by coal miners at their ablutions, dwelling in loving detail (and more than once) upon the spectacle of them washing off the coal dust to display, in his words, *the splendour of their bodies*. Or possibly that was just the part I myself found most arresting. At any rate, the book passed the time agreeably enough.

I splashed out on a roll from the baker's for lunch, and before I knew it, I was listening for the gentle roar of Sean's motorbike as if I were a child at Christmas straining for the sound of Santa's sleigh bells. At least, if one believed Bing Crosby. Personally I thought today's children were more attuned to the sound of parcels arriving from whatever online retailer their parents currently favoured.

Pretty much on the dot of half past two, my patience was rewarded with a knock on the door. When I flung it open, I was struck once again by Sean's sheer physicality. He stood on the doorstep seeming to exude warmth, his tousled hair exerting a powerful magnetic pull on my fingers.

I smiled at him helplessly.

Sean smiled back. "You all right? Nice tie, by the way. I brought the spare helmet—thought maybe we could go for a ride?"

Some of the warmth his presence had engendered seemed to seep away as I fixed the bright-blue monstrosity in his hand with a dubious eye. Like the helmet Sean wore, it was a full-face one with a darkened visor, the sort favoured by armed robbers of village post offices.

It was going to clash horribly with my bow tie. "Are you sure this is a good idea? I've never actually ridden a motorbike before. What if I do something idiotic and cause you to crash?"

Sean's eyes widened. "Seriously, you've never been on the back of someone's bike?"

"Well, no. Everyone I knew had cars." I didn't know why I felt defensive of this fact.

"Right, that settles it. Come on, get your shoes on—and you'll need a warm jacket and gloves too." He tapped one booted foot with mock impatience on the doorstep, leaving me with no option but to comply.

Well, I could have shut the door in his face, I supposed. But that would have been rude. And besides, I didn't want to. My hand hovered by my greatcoat—then moved on, as I was assailed by gruesome images of its tails getting caught in some vital component or even the wheels, bringing our little jaunt to an abrupt and messy end smeared across the tarmac. I selected my Barbour and shrugged it on, then turned to see Sean shaking his head in apparent amusement.

"Only you, mate. Only you."

I frowned. "Mother gave me this last Christmas."

"Yeah, but I bet she didn't reckon you'd be wearing it on a motorbike. Nah, don't worry, it's great. Very you."

"I'll take that as a compliment," I said loftily, patting my pockets to ensure my gloves were inside.

He grinned and stepped through the door. "You should. Come here."

I stepped forward, expecting him to straighten my tie or adjust my collar, and was caught by surprise when he kissed me. His lips and teeth were cold from the outside air, and I barely had time to taste a hint of coffee before he stepped back again, leaving me dizzily off-balance and pleasantly out of breath.

"Right, I thought we'd have a bit of a ride and pop in on Debs for a cup of tea on the way back, if that's okay? Don't worry, the twins won't be there—they're off at a party this afternoon."

I collected my scrambled thoughts as we went outside. "I wouldn't have worried if they'd been there, you know."

"Yeah? Thought you'd want to enjoy your last kid-free day in peace."

"You know, I actually think I'm going to be glad to get back to work tomorrow," I said, shutting the door behind me. "I've been missing class 2E, believe it or not. Of course, ask me again at lunchtime tomorrow and I may have a very different answer for you. But is your sister expecting us? I don't want to put her out if not."

"She won't mind." He hesitated. "You know I live there too, right?"

"Oh—no, I mean, I suppose that must be in the twins' files, but I hadn't . . . No. I didn't realise." Did I have my keys? I patted my pockets. Yes, yes, I did. *Calm down, Emsy, it's only a bike ride.*

"Yeah, I moved in after Wes left. It didn't make sense, keeping two places, seeing as I was round there all the time anyhow. I mean, she'd have been better off with benefits and stuff without me living there, but I wasn't going to keep my place on just so we could screw the system." He smiled and shook his head. "First six months nearly killed me. I was walking around like a bloody zombie at work all day. It was all right once we got 'em sleeping through the night, though."

"Your sister must have been so glad to have you around." How many young men would have done the same? I wasn't sure *I* would have. Then again, my stepsisters were all significantly older than I was and scarily self-sufficient to boot. The idea of me helping any of them out had always seemed rather laughable, but it was probably very different for twins.

Sean shrugged lopsidedly and stared at his handlebars. "Yeah, well. We've always been close, me and her." He looked up. "Now are we going to get on this bike or what?"

Resisting the urge to say a plaintive *what*, I struggled into the helmet by way of reply.

Sean reached up to adjust it. "Okay. Can you still hear me?"

"Yes," I said, my voice sounding muffled.

"Right." Sean threw his leg over his bike and sat. "Just remember to hold on tight with your arms around my waist, and when we go round a corner, you lean with me, okay?"

"Okay." I gave him a thumbs-up in case it hadn't been clear.

"Just relax and enjoy it, all right? I've been riding bikes since I was sixteen. Had Wills and Harry on the back loads of times—not at the same time, though, in case you were worried."

"I'm not worried," I said, in an admittedly rather worried tone of voice. I tried to mimic Sean's easy swing of the leg and managed to mount the bike behind him with only minor protestations from the groin area. "You know, I do have a car, if you wanted to go for a drive instead."

Sean laughed. He probably thought I'd been joking. He started the engine, I wrapped my arms around his waist in sudden alarm, and then we were off.

It was absolutely *exhilarating*. Sean started off slow—the speed bumps in the centre of the village rather necessitated this—but when we crested the hill and open countryside was before us, he opened up the throttle. We zoomed down the road, the wind buffeting us. It was totally unlike driving Portia, even with her top down. I felt viscerally close to the throbbing engine underneath me, and to Sean, his body lean and hard against my arms and my chest. It was as if we were one; not so much as if Sean and I were upon the back of some great beast— I'd been horse-riding and it had, frankly, been nothing like this—but more as if we *were* the beast, all three of us. Men and machine in some bone-deep symbiosis.

Sean turned down a narrow lane. Leaning with him into the corner, I felt like I was putting my life in his hands—trusting him to know the limits of the engine and just how close to the ground we could come without disaster. It was thrillingly intimate. We passed farms, stables, and the ubiquitous pubs, before coming out onto what passed for a main road around here, bordered on one side by the golf course and on the other by large houses with steep gables and ancient trees standing sentry over their well-kept gardens. We turned again, into the eerie, womb-like embrace of a holloway lane. Trees loomed over us, their branches meeting overhead in incestuous, half-naked tangles, and their shockingly bared roots at eye level. My stomach went into free fall as we crested a bridge over the river.

Down a parallel main road, then another turn into a road that was more track than lane. This time, we climbed steadily through farmers' fields until we'd reached the horizon. The view was astonishing—down into the valley and beyond, where cotton-wool sheep grazed in fuzzy felt fields. In the village, St. Saviour's Church, so magnificent from close up, might have been liberated from the reception-class train set. Dotted around the fields were spinneys of gnarled trees whose autumn clothing brought to mind the burning bush of biblical legend. The air here was fresh and earthy, and the only cars I could see were matchbox-size ones trundling along the main road far below.

We pulled into the car park of a pub that stood in a tiny hamlet, only half a dozen houses in all. Sean killed the engine and turned back to me. "You okay?" His voice was muffled by his helmet—or possibly by mine—but audible.

My heart still pounded, and my blood was fizzing in my veins. "Absolutely. That was fantastic. Are we stopping for a drink?"

"Nah, not unless you're gasping. Just wanted to make sure you were okay." His eyes crinkled up behind his visor. "You were holding on a bit tight for some of that."

I flattened a little. "Oh God, sorry. Did I hurt you?"

"Nah, I'm fine. I liked it. Okay, you ready for off? We'll head over to see Debs now."

I attempted a nod and narrowly missed banging our helmets together. "I'm ready."

We set off again, hurtling down into the valley once more until we reached the main road. This time, Sean took the direct route, through the village, past church and school, crawling over the speed bumps and accelerating once we were past them. It felt like coming back to earth after a trip in a balloon.

The house Sean shared with his sister and nephews was small, modern, and semidetached, situated squarely in the middle of a Toytown of identical houses that made up the Hillside council estate. It was, as the name suggested, perched atop the hill that bounded the village, the main road up which was known, imaginatively, as The Hill. As council estates went, I supposed it was rather nice; there was minimal graffiti on the bus stops and walls, and I couldn't see a single boarded-up window. The children's play area we'd passed en route was colourful and in good repair, the benches occupied not by alcoholics but by young mums watching their toddlers at noisy play.

Of course, for all I knew, the mothers could be alcoholics, but the only bottles in evidence contained formula milk, not gin.

"It's not much," Sean said apologetically after parking in the cracked concrete driveway and taking off his helmet. He ran a hand through his hair, reinforcing its usual irresistibly tousled aspect.

"Have you and your sister always lived in the village?" I asked, having dismounted from the bike and freed myself from my own headgear. I ran a hand through my hair, then patted it back down again as best I could. I had a strong feeling *tousled* wouldn't be nearly as good a look on me as it was on Sean. "I mean, I know your family is from around here, but did you ever live anywhere else for a bit?"

"Nah, I'm a Shamwell lad born and bred." He shrugged. "Thought about moving when Debs got married, but I couldn't see the point. And once Wes buggered off, well . . ."

I nodded. "She must have been glad of the help with the twins."

It came out sounding a little awkward, and Sean seemed embarrassed too. "Yeah, well. 'S family, innit?" He unlocked the door. "Debs? I'm back."

He ushered me through a narrow hallway strewn with muddy boots to a small, squarish living room. It was already occupied. Mrs. Curtis—Debs, I supposed I should start thinking of her as—lifted her gaze from the television, and I faltered at the cold expression on her pale, tired face. Perhaps I'd stick with calling her Mrs. Curtis after all.

"Hey, Debs." Sean put his arms around my waist from behind and rested his chin on my shoulder. "You remember Rob, don't you?"

She raised an unfriendly eyebrow. "Rob, is it? Bet your mum never calls you that. You're slumming it a bit, hanging around with a ratcatcher, aren't you?"

"Debs . . ." Sean said warningly, saving me from the impossible task of coming up with an answer that wouldn't offend either of them. "Be nice."

"*You* be nice. I've had it up to here with sodding *nice*."

Sean's sigh warmed my ear. It was almost enough to make up for his sister's frigid reception. "Rough day?"

"Meaning?" she snapped.

"Meaning you were all right this morning, so it looks like something's happened since I went out."

"For God's sake. Men! Why does there always have to be a bloody reason for everything?" She stood up and stomped out of the room. From the kettle-filling sounds coming from the kitchen across the hall, I guessed she was making tea. Presumably, then, we were supposed to stay?

Sean and I looked at each other. "Shit," he said. "Look, don't take it personally, right? Sometimes she just gets days like this. I'll see if she wants a hand."

"No, let me." I couldn't bear the haunted look in his eyes.

"I'm not sure that's—"

"I'll be fine," I said firmly, and strode into the kitchen.

Mrs. Curtis—Debs—was blowing her nose on a piece of kitchen roll.

"Can I help?" I asked.

"I'm not dead yet." She didn't quite look me in the eye. "I can manage a cup of tea."

"Ah, but many hands make light work, as I'm always telling 2E at tidy-up time. Although come to think of it, most of the time many hands just make even more of a mess." Spotting a fridge, I got out the milk. "Mugs?"

"I'll get them." She did so, hesitated for a moment, then reached to the back of the cupboard and got out a china teapot. "There's some loose tea in the cupboard by your head. I won it on the tombola at the school summer fair and never got around to using it. You look like the sort who likes loose tea."

"And loose men," Sean's voice came from behind me as I ferreted in the cupboard, eventually coming out victorious, holding a cellophane-wrapped box of English Breakfast.

"Better hope I don't get them mixed up when I'm pouring on boiling water," I said drily, turning.

"Ouch." Sean moved his hand protectively in front of his groin. His sister, surprisingly, smiled.

She watched me fumbling unsuccessfully with the cellophane for a moment. "Come on, give it here."

I surrendered the tea. The kettle had boiled by this time, so I set about warming the pot to prove I wasn't totally useless, then refilled the kettle with fresh water and set it on to boil again. In no time at all (well, seven minutes actually; the kettle could have done with a good descaling) we were sitting down in the living room with our mugs of tea. Debs was curled up in the armchair she'd been occupying on our arrival, while Sean and I took the sofa, sitting with a two-inch buffer zone between us. I wasn't sure if it was his subconscious or mine that had been responsible for this.

Thinking back to him embracing me in front of her when we first got here, I realised it must have been mine.

Debs had even supplied a plate of biscuits—rather soft digestive biscuits covered in indeterminate dribbly icing designs, presumably by the twins, but it was the thought that counted.

"Is it George H.'s party the twins are at?" I asked when conversation didn't seem to be forthcoming.

"Yeah." Debs sounded surprised. "Over at the soft play in the sports centre. They're going for a pizza after."

I nodded. "Ah, the standard plan of wearing them out with energetic activity, then feeding them junk food until they're bouncing off the walls again just in time for parent pickup, yes? It was a bit hard to miss him handing out invitations to the whole class. And Charlie was talking about it before half-term." Actually, he'd voiced his concerns that it might be all a bit rough for him. I'd encouraged him to accept the invitation on the basis that what doesn't kill us makes us stronger, and it would at least make George H. happy even if diving into ball pits wasn't precisely the sort of thing Charlie would prefer to spend his time doing.

I hoped none of us were going to regret it.

Debs looked at me. "I can't work you out, you know?" She laughed to herself. "Sod it. Wills and Harry like you, anyway. And *obviously* you do," she added, turning to Sean.

Sean gave me a sardonic look. "He's all right, I s'pose."

"Likewise, I'm sure." I smiled at him, my heart melting at the way his answering smile made his eyes soften and glow in the artificial light.

"So where are you from, then?" Debs asked, breaking the spell.

"I grew up in Surrey, but Mother moved to Wiltshire when she and Peter got married."

"Yeah? What's he like, your stepdad? You get on all right?"

"Oh, absolutely. He's been so good for Mother. And so good to me too."

"You got any stepbrothers and sisters?"

"Three, but they're all rather older than I am. The elder two are in their forties with children of their own. To be honest I don't really know them very well—they'd all moved out and got homes of their own already when Mother and Peter first got together."

She nodded. "He's older, then. You were an only child before that?"

Sean leaned forward, looking uncomfortable. "Debs, I brought him round for a cup of tea, not an interrogation."

Debs didn't give an inch. "I'm just showing an interest, all right?"

"It's perfectly all right," I assured them. "And yes, Peter's in his sixties, but he's very active. And I was indeed an only child."

"They okay with you going out with blokes?"

"Perfectly," I said with confidence.

Her tone sharpened. "What about blokes from the council estate?"

Sean shifted in his seat again. "That's enough. Give the man a break, okay?"

She *humph*ed. "There any tea left in that pot?"

I picked it up. "A little, but it'll be very stewed.

"Doesn't matter." She held out her mug, and I poured out a tannin-thick stream until she said, "When."

"More milk?" I offered.

She shook her head. "Sorry for being a bitch," she said abruptly, leaning back in her chair with a sigh. "I just get so sick of it all, sometimes, waiting to find out . . . you know. And that cow next door going on about how it must be a comfort to have Sean so good with the kids. Yeah, right, it's such a sodding *comfort* to know I might not see my boys grow up."

"Debs . . ." Sean started.

"And it's not fair on you either, is it?" She cut him off. "Why should you have to look after my kids just because I got knocked up, married a loser, and got ill?"

"Because they're my nephews, and I love 'em, all right? Anyway, you're gonna get better." His expression was fierce, and it caused a strange pang inside me.

"And then, *then* she goes on about how it's a shame you can't seem to settle down with a nice girl who could be a mother to them."

I assumed the *she* in question was Debs's bovine nuisance neighbour.

"Yeah? What did you say to that?" Sean asked with a tone of grim amusement.

"I told her to mind her own effing business, of course. What's it to her if you go out with girls or blokes or the queen of bloody England?"

"Well, she might have a point if she disapproved of the last option," I said. "After all, that would be adultery, on Her Majesty's part, at least. And age differences of that extent rarely work out."

Debs looked at me and laughed shortly. "God help me. I'm starting to work out what he sees in you."

CHAPTER FIFTEEN

W e didn't stay long after that. The twins would be arriving back from the party soon—one of the other parents was giving them a lift—and Debs insisted she wasn't going to inflict their post-party behaviour on me when I was going to have to deal with them all day tomorrow.

As I strongly suspected she was desperate to have her house back to herself before they arrived, I didn't put up too much of a protest.

When we got back outside to where the weeds were making a valiant attempt to turn the driveway into crazy paving, I paused for a moment, helmet in hand. "Um, if you don't mind my asking, *do* you feel tempted sometimes to only go out with women?"

Sean frowned at me and put his own helmet back on the seat of his motorbike.

"I mean," I hurried on, "wouldn't it be less bother in some ways?"

"What, so I'd fit in and no one would have to know I wasn't straight? Sod them. It's none of their business. I go out with whoever I want to." His eyes narrowed as he looked at me. "You wouldn't go out with a girl to make other people happy, would you?"

He seemed to have an awful lot of confidence in me. "No . . . But that's different, isn't it? I'm not attracted to women. At all. It just seems, if you actually do have a choice . . ." I trailed off, intimidated by his hard expression. It looked all wrong on Sean's face. "I didn't mean to offend," I said weakly. "I suppose I'm just finding it hard to imagine myself in your shoes."

Sean's lips tightened, then he nodded. "Yeah. I know what you mean. It seems weird to me sometimes, how everyone's not bi. I mean, fit's fit, innit?" He grinned suddenly. "So seriously, if you went upstairs one night and found Scarlett Johansson and that girl who played Clara on *Doctor Who* naked in your bed, you'd kick 'em both out on their cute little arses?"

"Well, of course not. That would be rude. I'd just go back down and sleep on the sofa."

Sean laughed, shaking his head. "Should have known you'd be the perfect gentleman."

"So . . . Scarlett and Clara are, as you put it, *fit?*"

"Too right."

"Why? I mean, neither of them has got particularly large breasts, as I recall."

Sean's laugh this time was so loud that an elderly couple on the other side of the street stopped to stare.

I frowned, hurt. "Did I say something amusing?"

"Sorry. It's just, there's a bit more to it than that, yeah? I mean, don't get me wrong, boobs are good."

Damn it, Rose was right. My shoulders slumped.

Sean stopped laughing and pulled me to him. The elderly couple, I noticed out of the corner of my eye, walked away hurriedly. "Hey. Other bits are good too, yeah? I just mean, that's not what it's all about. See, you like someone, there's bits of them that turn you on particularly, right, but they wouldn't work without the rest of them. It's the whole package." He stroked my hair and smiled. "Any bits of me that really turn you on?"

I was so rattled by all the public affection, I blurted out the truth. "Your hair. And your eyes."

"Yeah? Seriously? You got a thing for gingers? Hey, I'm not judging. But think about it. If I dyed my hair and got some blue contact lenses, you'd wouldn't go off me totally, would you?"

I stared at him. When he put it like that, it all seemed so absurdly simple.

Sean coughed. "You're supposed to say no. In case you were wondering."

"No!" I yelped. "I mean, to both. I just . . . I never really thought about it like that. It actually sort of makes sense."

"Well, there's got to be a first time for everyone," Sean said with an easy smile.

I blinked, my mind rushing headlong into visions of *first times* with Sean. But that couldn't have been what he was referring to—could it? "Pardon?"

"Making sense."

"Oh!" Of course.

Sean's smile broadened. "Why? What were you thinking of?"

"Nothing." For such a cold day, my face was feeling quite extraordinarily hot.

He leaned close to whisper in my ear, so close his stubble rasped against my cheek. "Mr. Emeny, you've got a filthy mind."

Oh God. He wasn't wrong.

The ride back to the Old Hatter's Cottage was some kind of torture, with my arms snug around Sean's waist, my chest pressed to his leather-clad back, our thighs touching and a powerful engine throbbing between them. There was no *possible* way Sean could be unaware of what he was doing to me.

Clambering off the bike once we'd *pulled* up in *mi entrada* was somewhat awkward. I took off my helmet with clumsy hands and waited while Sean removed his with rather more practiced ease. It was getting dark now, thankfully, so at least any passersby were unlikely to notice and be offended by my no doubt flushed and definitely excited state. "Would you like to—"

"Yeah," he said, not waiting for me to finish. He swung his leg over the motorbike, and I was certain it wasn't my imagination that painted the shadowy outline of a hard ridge at the front of his jeans.

Oh God. We were going to . . . I gazed at Sean, drinking in the sight of him, the way the weakly glowing streetlamp outlined his form.

"You wanna . . ." His voice gruff, Sean gestured towards the door.

"Right. Yes." I fumbled in my pocket for my keys. Pulled them out. Dropped them. Picked them up again, swallowing as my rising gaze tracked the line of Sean's denim-clad legs.

We needed to get in the house. Right now. On the third try, I fitted the key into the lock and turned it.

And nearly wept when Hanne's voice rang out.

"Robert! This is good timing. I was just about to make some deer antlers. Come in, come in. And your friend too." She was leaning out of her own front door with a big smile on her face.

"I, er . . ." I looked at Sean, who seemed as completely thrown as I was by this sudden turn of events. "We wouldn't want to—"

"Nonsense!" she said briskly. "It's no trouble at all. I couldn't possibly eat a whole batch myself, and you need to eat more, so it's perfect. You modern young men—so skinny, both of you. Come on in."

I made a helpless face at Sean. He seemed to be trying not to laugh.

"Come!" Hanne said again, and clearly her practice mastering Milly and Lily had stood her in good stead, as before I quite knew what I was doing, I was inside her house and Sean, behind me, was closing the door.

Sometime later, we were sitting in Hanne's quirkily Scandinavianised living room, drinking hot chocolate and eating freshly cooked deer antlers. I had been relieved to find these were, in fact, just oddly shaped doughnut-like things, and very tasty. Cooking them had been rather fun in the end, although not at all what I'd envisaged doing earlier.

Milly and Lily had flopped down in front of the hearth, between them taking up about three-quarters of the available floor space. Hanne was showing us pictures of her sons, a couple of strapping, bearded Thor look-alikes.

"You must miss them," I said.

"Oh, so much. But I'm only here for a year, and I'll see them at Christmas. I'm going to stay with Andreas, my youngest, and his girlfriend in Bergen, and Christian and his family will visit us there. It's beautiful there, so colourful, and the fish market is very good. You must visit sometime." She smiled. "Will you see your girlfriend tonight? You could take some of the antlers for her."

Ah. "I, er, like I said before, Rose isn't my girlfriend." I glanced at Sean, but his expression was unreadable. Did he want me to say . . .? His hand gripped my knee. Right, then. I took a deep breath. "I, actually, well, Sean's my boyfriend." I forced a smile and grasped his hand, holding it up to show her.

Hanne's hands flew to her mouth. "No!"

My stomach, weighed down by a whole herd of deer antlers, plummeted.

"Your boyfriend?" she went on. "And you let me drag you in here and give you cooking lessons? Oh, my goodness. I'm so embarrassed. You must think I'm terrible. Go, you must go now. I'm sure you have better things to do with your time together than stay here with me." We all stood, and she made shooing motions with her hands, her face a little pink.

"Nah, it was great, wasn't it, Rob?" Sean said, smiling down at her.

"Absolutely," I agreed with perhaps a little more enthusiasm than was warranted. "And the antlers were delicious. Really. I couldn't think of a better way to spend a Sunday teatime."

"You're much too polite. And I'm so sorry I took your time together."

"Not at all. It was fun." I hesitated, then stepped forward to give her a hug. "Thank you."

"Don't be silly. Now go. Go enjoy your boyfriend." Once again, her deceptively commanding tones had us outside the door before we knew what we were doing.

Sean turned to me, a soft smile on his face. "She's nice. And you've only known her a couple of months?"

"Yes—since I moved here. Why?"

He shook his head, still smiling. "No reason. Look, I probably ought to get going. Promised Debs I'd be back in time to help her get the boys off to bed, and I don't want to leave her in the lurch when she's having a bad day."

"No, no, of course not," I said, trying not to let my disappointment show. "Um. Just come in for a minute, though? Just . . . to say good-bye?"

"Okay. But just for a minute, yeah?"

We stepped into the Old Hatter's Cottage, and I closed the door behind us. Sean's arms slid around me even as I turned, and we pulled each other close. The heat from earlier was gone, replaced by a gentle warmth that was even more intoxicating. We kissed, softly but deeply. Sean's lips were sugary, and his mouth tasted of the hot chocolate we'd shared. Our bodies fitted together perfectly.

When I felt things beginning to stir below the waist, I pulled back. I wanted him, yes—but I didn't want him feeling rushed and guilty. "Good-bye," I said.

Sean rested his forehead against mine. "Yeah. See you around."

And then he was gone.

I wandered into the lounge and threw myself onto the sofa, still smiling dreamily—but as the warmth from his touch seeped away, so did some of my good mood. When I was with Sean, everything seemed absurdly simple, but without him to crowd them out of my thoughts, my misgivings about starting a relationship slunk back into the forefront of my mind.

Things seemed to be going so well with Sean—but they'd *seemed* to be going well with Crispin too, until the storm had broken, and then suddenly, they hadn't. All it would take would be for Sean to find out the real reason I'd left my last job. About Oliver.

Oh God. Was I just setting myself up for another fall? My heart clenched.

I had the horrible feeling I might not survive this time.

CHAPTER SIXTEEN

onfire Night being imminent, class 2E and I spent most of the first
week back after the half-term holiday drawing riotously colourful
pictures to display at school assembly, and firmly going over the
firework code. Thankfully, most of the class seemed to be planning to
go to organised displays at the weekend, rather than having fireworks
in their own back gardens. I could still remember the horror I'd felt at
thirteen, when we'd been called into a special assembly on November
the sixth to be told in sombre tones about a boy in the fifth form who'd
lost an eye through larking about with fireworks. While I doubted any
of class 2E's parents would be idiotic enough to let their little darlings
get their hands on rockets and suchlike, there were plenty of people
who seemed to think nothing of giving sparklers to toddlers.

There was even a little time left over to teach those who didn't know
it already the "Gunpowder, Treason, and Plot" rhyme, and explain who
Guy Fawkes actually was. It really was a quite extraordinary legacy, for
a man to still be burned in effigy every year more than four hundred
years after an attempted act of terrorism that hadn't even succeeded. I
wondered if he'd be proud or mortified, if he knew. Class 2E reacted
with predictable glee to the more gruesome parts of the story—the
attempt to blow up King James I and his parliament, and Fawkes's
subsequent capture, torture, and execution—but were disappointed
to hear he hadn't, in fact, been burned at the stake.

Charlie came up to me at the end of Friday. "Does it hurt, getting
torch-ured?"

"I'm afraid that's rather the point of it, young Charlie. But don't
worry, no one's allowed to do it these days," I reassured him, mentally
crossing my fingers behind my back.

Charlie looked thoughtful. "Oh. Good," he said and went back to tidying up someone else's pencils.

The twins hadn't known (or had forgotten) who would be picking them up from school today, so I reminded myself not to look disappointed if it turned out to be their mother, as it had been all week. Debs had been reserved but not unfriendly. She hadn't mentioned Sean at all, in the few words we'd exchanged at the classroom door.

I hadn't seen Sean since Sunday evening. I'd thought about calling him, but, well, he'd said good-bye in such a casual way. I didn't want to come over as some sort of clinging vine or crazed stalker.

As it happened, my acting skills weren't tested. I only hoped the few remaining parents were paying more attention to their offspring than to me as I smiled helplessly at Sean through the open classroom door. His answering smile didn't waver as the twins launched themselves on him with abandon.

"Uncle Sean! Look at my picture!" Harry demanded, holding up a colourfully crayoned rendition of a grossly elongated Guy Fawkes on a rack.

"Mine's better," Wills insisted, thrusting his imaginative interpretation of a blown-up king in his uncle's face.

"Lads! Let me speak to Mr. Emeny for a minute, okay?"

I gave the twins a stern look. "Why don't you go and put those back in the classroom, boys? Seeing as we're *supposed* to be saving them for sharing assembly?"

They bombed back into the classroom, where they'd no doubt get up to further mischief. I didn't care.

"I hear you'll be going to the rugby-club fireworks display tonight," I said, drinking in the sight of Sean with his hair blown by the wind. "The twins told me all about it. Apparently there's going to be a bonfire bigger than the whole school."

"Yeah, I think the lads might have exaggerated a bit there. But it should be good." Sean shoved his hands in his pockets and looked at his trainers for a moment. "Look, I'm going to ask you this, and you're going to say no, and that's fine, okay? Not a problem."

"It isn't?" I blinked. "Don't I get a say in this?"

He smiled at me, a lock of copper hair falling over his forehead as the wind dropped. "Sorry. I was just going to say, if you wanted to come too, that'd be great. But seeing as you'd probably rather hop on the bonfire than spend any more time today with these two tearaways—"

"I'd love to," I said quickly. Then I frowned. "But do you think Wills and Harry will really want me along?"

"We'll ask 'em. Lads," he called, and they left what they were doing (nothing more alarming than an attempt to stack as many chairs as possible on top of one another, I was relieved to see) and came running over. "What would you think about Mr. Emeny coming to the fireworks with us?"

I braced myself for vehement rejection and was unexpectedly moved when they bounced up and down as one. "Yeah! Come to the fireworks!"

Sean grinned. "Right, then. I'll pick you up at six. That okay? They do a barbecue, so we'll be getting our tea there. Oh, and make sure you wrap up warm, and you might want to wear your wellies. It gets a bit muddy out on the field. We'll see you later, all right?"

"All right," I said, as the twins dragged him off, one to each hand. I had two hours and thirty-three minutes. Plenty of time for a dash to a nearby department store for a pair of Wellington boots.

When I opened my front door at 5:59, Sean raised his eyebrows. "That's got to be the cleanest pair of wellies I've ever seen. And that includes in shops. Are you sure you want to wear them out?"

I might have coloured slightly. "I needed a new pair. Anyway, where are your wellies?" A familiar pair of scruffy trainers peeked out from below his jeans.

"In the car. They're not great to drive in." He smiled suddenly. "You look good in a sweater. Weird but good."

"Weird?" I looked down at myself. I'd donned a perfectly unremarkable fisherman's rib sweater in dark green. With my Barbour on top, you couldn't even see the elbow patches. And I'd thought the bright-red scarf I'd wrapped around my neck lent it quite a jaunty touch. Festive, even.

"You know. Casual. Hey, I wasn't dissing it. Told you, I like it." He stepped closer. "If the boys weren't waiting in the car, I'd show you just how much I like it too. Speaking of which, we'd better get going. You got everything you need?"

"I— Yes, I think so," I said, wrenching my thoughts back from where Sean's low murmur had sent them. I stepped outside and closed the door behind me. "Right. Lay on, Macduff."

"Lay on?" Sean's smile turned wicked. "I'd love to, but like I said, the boys are waiting."

I glared at him and strode towards the bright-red Golf that awaited us, a brace of unruly redheads strapped into identical child seats in the back. They greeted me with exuberance, then promptly returned to their noisy game of slapsies and ignored me totally.

I strapped myself into the passenger seat as Sean slid behind the wheel. Despite the change from a two-wheeled conveyance to four, he was wearing his leather jacket. Underneath it I could see a soft-looking sweater in dark red, and a navy-blue scarf was knotted casually around his neck. He looked warm and eminently huggable.

Distracted from my admiration by the realisation that I'd sat on something, I reached for it and found myself holding up a lipstick. "Is this what you drive when you want to feel pretty?" I asked.

Sean laughed, already starting the engine. "Nah, this is Debs's car. I can just about fit the boys onto the van's front seat, but you'd have had to ride in the back. Thought you'd find this a bit more comfortable."

"You're probably right. I'm not sure I'm ready to know what a pest-control technician keeps in the back of his van."

"Yeah, well, given how we have to clean up after ourselves, I'd say that's pretty close to the mark." He pulled out carefully onto the high street, and set off over the speed bumps at a racy twenty miles an hour. "At least I've got the van. It's the poor sods who work in London I feel sorry for. Footmen, they call them, 'cause they travel around, well, on foot. Have to use public transport. I was talking to one of 'em recently, and he was telling me how he was halfway home on the tube the other night and couldn't work out why everyone kept giving him funny looks and changing carriages. He's carrying a backpack, and he's got a beard, and he's thinking, do they all reckon I'm a terrorist? Then it hits him. It's the smell. He's got half a dozen rat corpses in his backpack, all in varying states of decay, and a couple of dead mice in his pockets."

I shuddered. "Oh God. I suppose he'd just got used to it?"

"Probably. Tell you what, though—that used to it I *don't* want to be. Nah, I wouldn't like to work in London even without all that."

"Because of the commute?"

"Nope. Cockroaches. It's like painting the Forth Bridge trying to clear an infestation in London. There's some city areas they're so endemic, the environmental health inspectors have to have a tolerance level. You just can't get rid of them completely. Out here, it's a lot more cut and dried—they find one roach in a restaurant, they close the place down till we've been in and sorted it."

"Ugh. I'll never eat out in London again."

"Nah, don't worry. Just make sure you give me a day or so to get the inside info on anywhere you're planning to go, and you'll be fine." He seemed entirely serious.

"Do you offer that service to everyone you know?"

"Nah." Sean grinned. "Just the ones I care about."

Warmth flooded through me at his words. Although possibly it was just the Golf's heater finally kicking in.

The rugby club was about halfway between Shamwell and the nearest town, Bishops Langley. Cars were queuing to get in from a hundred yards down the road.

"Seems popular," I said.

"Yeah, it's the best display around. And the barbecue's good. They get their meat locally, none of that supermarket value-brand rubbish."

The twins' ears pricked up at the mention of the word *barbecue.* "Are you gonna have a hot dog, Mr. Enemy?" Wills asked.

"With onions and ketchup and yellow sauce and brown sauce?" Harry demanded.

I turned to smile back at them. "I certainly hope so. Although I may stick to just ketchup."

"That's boring." Both of them started chanting, "Bo-ring, bo-ring—"

"Lads," Sean admonished. "*Nobody's* getting hot dogs if they don't behave themselves." The silence was abrupt and absolute. I made a mock-frightened face at the twins, my eyes darting to Sean in alarm, and they giggled.

"Oi, no conspiring with them," Sean murmured when I turned back to the front. "You're supposed to be the *good* influence."

Finally, we were at the head of the queue, and turned into the rugby grounds. We parked at the end of a long row of cars, and got out. The air was chilly and damp and infused with the mingled aromas of cooking meat and freshly churned-up mud.

"Didn't your sister want to come along?" I asked as Sean pulled on his wellies.

"Nah, she said she did her bit pushing them out into the world, and someone else could do the standing around in the mud and freezing to death bit."

It wasn't *that* cold tonight. "Is she, well, feeling all right?"

"Yeah, she's doing okay. She's got a couple of mates round tonight to keep her company." He paused, although perhaps it was just down to a fiddly bit of jeans-tucking. "It was her idea I should ask you along, actually."

I blinked. "Really?"

"Don't sound so shocked. She likes you."

She did? She could have fooled me, the last few days at school drop-off and pickup.

"Right," Sean continued. "We'd better get moving before these two get fed up waiting and do a runner."

Another rank of cars was already half-filled. We walked back down along the line, Wills and Harry urging us to "Come *on*," and Sean and I attempting to hold them back while keeping a beady eye out for rogue motorists.

I soon saw the wisdom in Sean's recommendation of wellies. There were lights around the club house, and the gazebo providing a shelter of sorts to the barbecue, but otherwise the ground was completely in darkness, making it impossible to see what you were stepping in. I only hoped the pitches would still be playable after tonight. At the far end of the roped-off part of the field I could just make out the dim conical outline of what must be the stack of wood for the bonfire.

We joined a good-natured queue to purchase hot dogs, which when they came proved to be unwieldy things, wrapped in a wholly inadequate scrap of kitchen roll. The organisers had clearly splurged on the sausages, which were fat, meaty, and delicious, and scrimped on the bread rolls. They were soft, pallid, and frankly unequal to the task set them, scattering their largesse of fried onions upon an ungrateful field.

The twins tore into their dinner with gusto and total disregard for the consequences to their clothes, while I tried to eat mine with some semblance of politeness. The sparse lighting was very definitely my friend in this endeavour, and I commended myself for my foresight in donning a scarf the colour of ketchup. We walked slowly onto the field, the crowds getting thicker and the dim light fading as we neared the display area. I imagined there must be more people than us from St. Saviour's School, but with everyone bundled up in hoods and scarves against the chill, it was impossible to recognise anyone from more than a few feet away, and difficult even then.

"When are the fireworks going to start?" I asked.

Sean swallowed a mouthful of sausage and licked a bit of ketchup from his lip. "Soon." He grinned, his teeth shining white in the darkness. "You know, usually it's the kids who get impatient."

"I'm not impatient. I'm just keen. Getting into the spirit of things. Actually, I'd have thought they'd have lit the bonfire by now." I took another bite of my hot dog, tasting spiced pork and an alarming amount of ketchup. Yes, definitely a good idea to wear the red scarf.

"Nah, they always do that at the end. Stops the smoke getting in the way of the fireworks, I s'pose. And, well, the darker the better, innit?"

"Uncle Sean! Uncle Sean!" The twins, their hot dogs already a memory, clamoured at him. "Can we go and stand with George and Edward? They're right by the rope and everything." They pointed to a couple of shadowy child-size figures that could have been children, dwarves, or even hobbits for all I could make out in the gloom.

"All right, but no going anywhere else without asking, yeah?"

"Yeah!" they shouted, already running.

"Are you sure we'll be able to find them again in the dark?" I swallowed the last of my hot dog and licked my fingers preparatory to wiping them on the scrap of kitchen roll.

"I've never managed to lose them yet. And they've got their phones on, I made sure of that. Hey, you've got a bit of ketchup . . ." Sean leaned in and swiped his thumb over the corner of my mouth. Then he licked it. His thumb, that was, not the corner of my mouth, although from the way my skin tingled and my libido stirred, one could have been forgiven for thinking the opposite was true.

My mouth was suddenly dry, and I had to clear my throat before I could speak. "I often wonder how previous generations ever survived to adulthood. No mobile phones, only the most rudimentary child seats, and playing in the street."

Sean was looking deep into my eyes and standing so close to me I could feel the warmth of his breath on my face and smell the spices from his hot dog. "Hey, don't knock the safety stuff till you've got kids of your own."

I wanted to step forward and take him in my arms. I had to remind myself we were in public, and furthermore, surrounded by small children and their parents. Some of whom were bound to know me as Mr. Enemy. Even if they could most likely no more recognise me than I could them . . . "I don't mean to disparage. Actually, I'm in favour. It means we don't have to worry." It was becoming absurdly difficult to order my thoughts and hold a sensible conversation.

"Yeah, we can relax and enjoy the show. Hey, I think they're about to start." Sean stepped back and turned, and the spell his proximity had cast on me was broken.

The noise and chatter of the hundreds of people assembled had begun to quieten, and I could make out shadowy figures scurrying around some distance away on the other side of the rope. A taper flared—and the first firework was lit.

Given the budget constraints the organisers must have been under, the show was really quite spectacular. I found myself oohing and ahhing along with the rest of them. I was glad the twins had made a break for the front—what with all the toddlers sitting on fathers' shoulders, they'd have found it hard to get a good view in the thick of things. Especially of the grand finale involving Catherine wheels and fizzing thingummies, spelling out the host club's initials.

As I squinted at the display and finally made it out (BLRFC, which sounded like the sort of noise one might make after indulging in a few too many hot dogs), I felt Sean's arms slip around my waist. My momentary tension melted away when I realised that among all the people here, not one of them was looking remotely in our direction. Relaxing into Sean's grip, I let my head fall back and folded my hands over his. The skies lit up with a final flourish of rockets exploding in ear-splittingly rapid succession that seemed to go on forever, and Sean's embrace warmed me even as a kiss to my neck sent shivers down my spine.

Then the barrage of explosions ceased, and all that was left were the after-images on our retinas and a heavy drift of smoke in the air.

There was a loud silence—and then people began to talk and to move again. Far down the field there was a flare of light as the bonfire was lit. Sean stepped away from me, and the chill of the night made its unwelcome presence known. "Better find the boys," he said, sounding apologetic.

I'd no sooner started to scan the crowd for their matching woollen hats than they were upon us, bursting out of nowhere in a clamour of "Can we go see the bonfire?" and "Please, Uncle Sean, *please*?"

Sean grinned at me. "You don't mind, do you?"

"Of course not." We swam against the tide of the crowd, many of whom seemed to be leaving *now* the main show was over, and neared the fire, which was ringed by another rope for safety's sake. Just as well, I thought, as we could feel the heat from the flames even here, and sparks were flying in the breeze. Sean and the twins and I stood with the other less hurried members of the crowd, and watched as the flames slowly consumed the *now* unrecognisable figure of the Guy.

Was this what it would be like to be a father, I wondered?

No. This was what it must be like to be an uncle. A normal uncle, not the sort of father-substitute Sean was. Being a father—a proper father, the sort Peter must have been to his own children, and had done his best to be to me from the age of fifteen—involved a lot more than taking the children out for a treat. It would include all the small, everyday stuff my own father had never had time for, like telling them off when they were naughty, reading them stories at bedtime, and nagging them to tidy their rooms.

And I needed to remember that the twins were never going to be some convenient, ready-made family for me and Sean in some idealised future together. If I were ever to end up with some sort of parental role in their lives, it would be following the traumatic loss of someone they and Sean all loved dearly. This—tonight—was just a fantasy, no more real than the figure of Guy Fawkes now combusting merrily on the bonfire.

By the time we left, the twins' steps now dragging even though they put up a game plea for hot chocolate (Sean told them firmly they could have some *at home*) the crowds had largely dispersed. It was a much quicker business getting off the field than getting onto it had been, and we were soon driving back into Shamwell.

"I was thinking I'd drop you off first, Rob, that all right?" Sean said. "I'd better give Debs a hand with these two."

"Oh, of course," I said, trying to hide my disappointment.

"Then I thought maybe I could come round to yours after they're in bed?"

This time, it was my elation I struggled to tone down to reasonable levels. "Yes, why not?"

"Are you gonna read us a story first?" Harry butted in.

"Maybe," Sean said over his shoulder as he pulled up outside the Old Hatter's Cottage. "If you're good."

"Maybe your mum would like to read you a story tonight?" I suggested hopefully, only to get shot down in flames more scorching than tonight's bonfire.

"Nah, Mum's bo-ring at stories."

"She doesn't do the voices. Uncle Sean, will you do the voices?"

"Yeah, I'll do the voices. *If you're good.*" Sean turned back to me. "You okay, there? I won't be more than an hour. Promise."

"That's fine, really." I smiled. "Boys, you'll be good for your uncle, won't you?"

Their halfhearted chant of assent as I got out of the car sounded more like "Yes, Miss Anemone" than anything else, but I was sure the intent was there. My heart was light as I opened up my front door. Sean had invited me on a family outing, and it had been a success. He'd held me in public. Had kissed me too.

All right, it had been dark and nobody else had noticed, but if I were brutally honest with myself, that was probably the only reason I was now congratulating myself over the night's events rather than having some kind of anxiety attack. And he was coming back in under an hour. Which meant there would be more holding. More kissing. There would probably be other activities as well. I swallowed. Bedroom activities.

Oh God. I suddenly remembered the current state of my bedroom. I'd been a little lax about tidying up since getting back to work. My bedroom, not to put too fine a point about it, presently bore a striking resemblance to the epicentre of a very small and localised, but unexpectedly vicious, natural disaster.

I sat on the stairs to take off my wellies, which gave me an excellent view of the large clods of mud I'd managed to traipse into the house. Damn it. Moreover, my wellies, which had seemed such an excellent fit in the shop, were now clinging to my legs like a pair of lovesick terriers. By the time I'd struggled out of the wretched things, I had mud on my sweater, my trousers and all over my hands. And seven of my not-more-than-sixty minutes had gone.

I spent the next thirty-nine minutes frantically scrubbing at mud deposits, changing my clothes, washing my hands and, ye gods, face— at least that one had been down to ketchup, not mud—and shovelling armfuls of dirty clothes from the bedroom floor into the washing machine. I hoped I would remember to take them all out and sort them into lights and darks before I actually tried to wash them.

Then I stood in the living room, scanning for anything out of place and/or potentially embarrassing, like the *Strictly Come Dancersize* workout DVD Rose had brought around as a joke, and my *Dirty Dancing* Collector's Edition, her discovery of which had prompted said hilarious jape. No, they were both safely out of sight. I was pretty sure Sean would forgive me the haphazard mountain of journals, paperbacks, and village magazines, so that could stay. Right. Time to relax.

I collapsed onto the sofa but found it impossible to get comfortable. Was I reading too much into Sean coming round here again? After all, it was only 9:27. I'd never been the subject of one of those alarming modern trends, the *booty call*, but I'd always been under the impression they generally, like the witching hour and things turning into pumpkins, took place at or after midnight. Perhaps we'd just chat. Have a cup of tea, perhaps, and make plans for a proper date—after all, this evening could hardly be counted as a date, could it? Seeing as it had involved a brace of seven-year-olds. Yes, that was it. Sean just wanted to talk. Of course he did.

Then again . . . Oh God. I was out of condoms. I'd *meant* to buy some more, but I'd been into the village chemist's shop three times this week, and each time there had been either a child or a parent in there who knew me. I *knew* I should have popped into Boots the Chemist when I went into Bishops Langley to buy my wellies. How could I possibly have forgotten? Wellingtons, Boots—it was practically a mnemonic all by itself. God, I was an idiot.

I pulled a cushion over my face in despair. Then I yelped as there was a knock on the door.

CHAPTER SEVENTEEN

I leapt up from the sofa, took a deep breath to try to calm my pulse rate, ran to the door, and opened it.

Sean was there, the light from the streetlamp turning his hair into a wrought copper halo. He smiled. "All right?"

"Er, yes. Fine. Thank you."

"Sure? You look a bit red in the face."

"I, um, really?" I couldn't think of a single thing to say.

Sean's green eyes crinkled. "Maybe it's just the light. Colours get a bit off." Then he looked down at where his feet were scuffing against the cracks in the concrete. "That wasn't so bad, was it?"

I stared at him. "Bad? No, of course not. It was fun."

"Yeah? That's great." His face lit up.

Had he thought I'd hate every minute? If so, why invite me? He didn't *have* to follow his sister's suggestion. Unless it was some kind of test . . . I was *not* going to ask him, I decided. "Come in, anyway. I don't know why I'm keeping you out here on the doorstep."

"Yeah, I never had you down as an exhibitionist."

A fluttering started in my stomach at the suggestion in his smile—not to mention his words. Did that mean this *was* a booty call? "C-come in," I said again, this time managing to remember to move aside and let him actually do so.

The fluttering had moved to my throat by the time I'd closed the door behind him. "Did the twins enjoy their story?" I asked, then could have kicked myself for changing if not the subject, then at the very least the subtext.

"Oh—yeah. Loved it. But you know, I was hoping we could think about more grown-up stuff now." Strong arms slipped loosely around my waist.

"I haven't got any condoms!" I blurted out. Mortified, I clapped a hand over my mouth. I could almost feel the breeze of the stable door slamming shut as the horse flicked its tail in contempt and cantered merrily down the street.

Sean was laughing at me. "Okay, unexpected but to the point. I like that in a bloke."

Oh God. "I mean, I thought . . . Just in case we . . . Not that I was making any presumptions, that would be, um, presumptuous. And I wouldn't want to, well, presume . . ."

A rough-skinned hand stroked my face. It was blessedly cool against my heated skin. "Got it. No presuming. Wouldn't dream of it. You know. Presuming you'd presumed."

"You must think I'm utterly ridiculous."

He laughed again. "Well, I wouldn't say *utterly*." It had a glottal stop when he said it. *U'erly*. It was grounding, somehow, as if his very down-to-earthiness could tether me, keep me from flying away unchecked in a puff of embarrassment. "I wouldn't say ridiculous either," he added in a lower tone. Somehow we'd become pressed together from chest to hip, and I could feel the rising heat of him through my clothes.

It wasn't the only thing that was rising. For some reason, I seemed to be finding it harder to breathe, and that was before Sean leaned forward and seized my mouth in a kiss. He tasted of hot chocolate and cinnamon, and his lips were soft, a contrast to the stubble that rasped against my chin. His tongue teased my lips, then slipped between them, shorting out my brain entirely. My hand tightened on what it was holding, which turned out to be Sean's arse—well done, that hand—and a hard bulge rubbed deliciously against its twin in my trousers.

A low sound rumbled in my mouth. For a moment, I thought I'd made it, but then I realised it had been Sean. He broke the kiss to lean his forehead against mine. "You want to take this upstairs? Least I'm assuming that's where you keep your bed."

"Oh God, yes," I breathed, not entirely sure what I was answering. "Stairs, yes. Bed. Um."

"This way?"

Thank God one of us remembered which way was up. "This way," I echoed. Then I realised I hadn't actually moved yet and pulled Sean towards the stairs.

"Hang on a mo," he said, his words a cold shower to my libido. Wait? Why? Was he having second thoughts? Was he . . . Oh. I watched, weak-kneed with relief, as he merely kicked off his trainers. "Right, then," he said, his wicked eyes dark with merriment. "Lay on."

"And damned be him that first cries, 'Hold, enough!'" God, I'd never have enough of this man. Did he know what he did to me? I clutched his hand tightly and stumbled up the stairs.

There were three bedrooms in the Old Hatter's Cottage. I was rather proud of myself for remembering which was the right one on the first attempt. Not that the others wouldn't have been more or less adequate, from the point of view of being furnished with beds, but I had a feeling Sean might prefer one with actual sheets as opposed to just a bare mattress. Unless, of course, he had a hankering to reenact some low-budget porn video, which arresting image wasn't exactly helping my mental clarity right now . . . *Focus*, I told myself firmly.

"This is it." I surreptitiously kicked a rogue sock under the bed. I was fairly sure Sean hadn't noticed it.

"Nice," Sean said without so much as a cursory glance around the room. This was probably just as well as I'd just spotted the sock's forlorn mate. His intent gaze in my direction—Sean's, that was, not the sock's; that would have been silly—was having a noticeable effect on my body temperature, and I put my hand up to undo my bow tie.

I was startled when Sean grabbed my wrist. "Oi. None of that. Have you got any idea how long I've been waiting to do this?"

"This?" I repeated intelligently, only to understand when he gently drew on the free ends of my tie, sliding the silk almost noiselessly out of its knot.

Sean's eyes glittered as he laid the two ends flat upon my shirt front. "Black tie," he murmured, his voice husky. "I don't care where we go, but I'm gonna take you somewhere you get to wear black tie and a dinner jacket. And then I'm going to take it off you. Piece by piece. You got one of those shirts with the studs instead of buttons?"

I nodded, my throat dry. "And a detachable collar. Wouldn't wear any other kind. Not to a formal event."

Sean closed his eyes briefly. "Bloody hell." He put his hands under my jacket, I assumed so he could ease it off my shoulders, but instead of completing the motion he froze.

"Sean?" I asked a little breathily.

Two strong thumbs thrust themselves under the straps of my braces. "You been wearing these all night?"

I nodded. "All night."

"Under your sweater?"

I nodded again. I'd removed the sweater before his return, of course, as it had become a little soiled in the welly debacle. And then donned my jacket because, well, sometimes a gentleman doesn't like to give away all his secrets at once.

"Fucking hell . . ." Sean took a deep breath, seeming to compose himself. "Right. That jacket's coming off right now."

I was half expecting him to tear it off and damn the tailoring, but in fact he slid it from my shoulders with infinite gentleness and laid it carefully on the end of the bed before returning to me.

I took my chance to seize the initiative and tugged at the hem of his sweater. "Off," I said in eloquent clarification.

Sean went one better and pulled off his T-shirt as well. His bare chest was unexpectedly muscular, given his leanness, and lightly furred with copper. I ran a hand up and down it, my fingers catching in the wiry hair. His nipples hardened at my touch. I wanted to bite them, taste them, suck them into points. I wondered what Sean would think of me if I told him so.

"Like what you see?" he asked with a grin. "My turn now."

I drew in a sharp breath as he began to undo the buttons of my shirt, starting at the collar. Would he like what he saw? I'd always been rather lacking in the chest hair department, and while it could be argued that there wasn't an ounce of fat on me under my clothes, it could also be argued, and with at least equal justification, that there weren't all that many ounces of muscle on me either. But then, if he liked girls too, hairlessness and lack of a body-builder's physique shouldn't be a turn-off—or was it only appropriate when accompanied by breasts?

I realised Sean's hands had stilled, and he was looking at me in fond amusement. "Oi. I can hear the cogs turning. Stop thinking so hard, yeah?"

"Easy for you to say," I muttered, and startled as he laughed.

"Did you just insult my intellect?"

I thought back in alarm. "Um. Possibly? Sorry. Carry on."

Sean's fingers tickled my stomach as he undid my trouser placket. I swallowed—but all he did was pull out my now open shirt to let it hang loose, confined only by my braces. It felt as if those twin lengths of elastic were all that was holding me together. "That's a good look on you," he murmured.

"Really?" My voice was shaky. "I think Mother would be horrified if she saw me like this."

I let out an undignified yelp as Sean's hand wrapped around the tent in my boxer shorts, which was poking rather insistently out of the front of my trousers. "Think we'll leave your mum out of this, if that's all right, yeah?"

"Probably for the best," I agreed breathlessly—and then he knocked the wind right out of me by shoving me back onto the bed with both hands.

"Whoops! Sorry about that." Sean's expression held not a shred of remorse. "Sudden attack of the klutzes."

I pushed myself up on my elbows and mock-glared at him. "Don't think I don't know you meant to do tha . . . aaa . . . Oh dear Lord," I finished, as Sean, who'd dropped to his knees while I spoke, freed my achingly hard cock from the confines of my boxers and wrapped his mouth around it. "Oh God, don't stop."

Sean immediately raised his head. *Bastard.* My cock twitched as he licked his lips. It quite understandably wanted to be back on the receiving end of those oral attentions. "Pardon?" he asked, his eyes wide and anything but innocent.

"You absolute—" I broke off with an undignified noise as he fondled my balls, all without changing his expression.

"Did you want something here?" He let go and rocked back on his heels between my legs, now not touching me at *all.* The air was chill on my poor abandoned cock.

"You utter, utter bastard . . . Come back and finish what you started."

Sean was openly laughing at me now. "Sorry, feeling a bit challenged in the intellect department. You're going to have to remind me what that was."

I glared at him. "You know very well . . ."

"Mind's a complete blank."

"Oh, for . . . Suck it." I was getting desperate.

He frowned in a parody of confusion. "Suck what?"

"My cock, you absolute bastard. *Please.*"

Sean was still laughing as he bent his head to his task, and the vibrations sent tingles down through my balls and back up my spine. Oh God. Had anything ever, *ever* felt as good as his mouth on me felt right then? Helpless on the bed, trapped by his ministrations, all I could do was feel the warmth of his mouth surrounding me and the rasp of his tongue on my most sensitive area. He varied his attentions, now sucking hard as if he wanted to swallow me down entirely, now pulling back to repeat the torture of his tongue.

It was sheer, unadulterated ecstasy. The blue touch paper had been lit, and while I did my best to warn Sean to stand well clear, eloquence seemed to be in short supply right now. "N . . . stop . . . going to . . . Oh. Oh God. Oh Lord . . ." Sean was still fanning the flames as the explosion hit. I went off like a rocket, soaring high into the moonlit sky. What little power of speech I had left utterly deserted me as I took in the heady sight of Sean swallowing as I spent in his mouth, his gaze all the while fixed firmly on mine.

Then my elbows gave way and I collapsed on the bed, my chest heaving as if I'd run all the way to London and back. Warmth flooded me like a shot of brandy to the heart, and I felt as heavy as lead and lighter than air at one and the same time. Sean rose from his knees to appear above me, his expression smug as he wiped his mouth with one strong forearm. "Sorry, couldn't quite work out what you were trying to tell me there, so I had to wing it a bit."

I reached up spaghetti arms to pull him in for a kiss. The taste was, as expected, highly salty, and his mouth seemed softer now. I found it curiously difficult to stop kissing him, but duty called. "Mmm. You winged it very nicely. And if you'll just give me a moment until I can actually feel my legs again, I'll be happy to return the favour."

"Oops."

"Oops?"

"Bit late for that. And just to warn you, you might want to sponge those trousers off before you send 'em to the dry cleaners."

Oh. "You, ah . . . ?"

"Jizzed all over 'em. Sorry," he added with a wholly unrepentant smile. Parts of me I'd thought utterly sated twitched at the thought of his impressive multitasking skills. Also, it had to be said, at the image of the debauched state of my trousers.

Then Sean shivered. It *was* getting a little chilly.

"We should get under the duvet. Um. Unless you have to get back?"

"Nope. Not going anywhere tonight," he assured me with a yawn. "We probably ought to lose a few more clothes first, though." He pushed off his jeans, which landed in a messy heap on the floor, and I began the somewhat fiddlier task of disengaging myself from braces, shirt, trousers (slightly foxed), underwear, and socks. After carefully considering the options and deciding I greatly preferred the ones that didn't involve moving from the bed, I gave my trousers a cursory wipe-down with my boxers and decided to worry about them in the morning.

Sean watched me with a smile. "Hey, you ever wear sock suspenders?"

"Ugh. No." I shuddered. "Don't tell me you find *those* sexy?"

"Well, you know. On the right set of calves."

"Which, I regret to inform you, will never be mine," I said firmly. He pulled me into his arms, and I laid my head on his shoulder.

"Oh? Have a bad experience with 'em when you were a kid?"

"As a matter of fact, yes. One of the masters at my old prep school was a firm proponent of the ghastly things." I snuggled closer to Sean. Our legs fitted together extraordinarily neatly, I thought.

"Yeah?" Sean prompted. "So, what? Did he have horrible skinny legs? Gout? Varicose veins?"

"None of the above, as far as I recall." I blushed with remembered embarrassment, glad Sean couldn't see my face. "But, well . . . You have to remember, it was a rather old-fashioned place. I don't think the library had been updated since about 1948." Sean made a puzzled sound, and I hurried on. "So anyway, my friend at the time—Archie, his name was; goodness knows what he's doing now—we'd been reading a lot of old school stories. *Just William*, that sort of thing. And we got it into our heads these sock suspenders might make rather good catapults, not that we'd ever seen such a thing. So Archie dared me to, ah, liberate a couple from Mr. Winters's rooms."

"Let me guess—you got caught?"

"In the very act of reaching into old Frosty's underwear drawer."

I winced.

"God, did you get the cane?"

"Worse. I had to spend two hours writing out the lines *Purloining underwear is not the act of a gentleman.* And after it got around the school, which of course it did within *minutes,* I spent the rest of my time there known to all and sundry as "Undies." And if you breathe a word of this to *anyone,*" I growled as his chest shook with not-very-well-stifled laughter, "this is the last time you'll be getting your hands in *my* underwear."

"Don't worry. Your dark secret's safe with me," he said, his voice warm with amusement. "Honest, Undies."

"I feel I should point out I have a knee extremely close to your testicles right now."

"Yeah, but I'm pretty sure kneeing me there wouldn't be the act of a gentleman." His arms tightened around me. There was a long, cosy silence, and I began to drift off to sleep.

Sean's voice rumbled in my ear. "You didn't mind, did you?"

I blinked bleary eyes. "Mind? Mind what?"

"Going out with the kids earlier. Wasn't too much like work for you, was it?"

"Of course not. It was fun."

"Good." Sean squeezed me just a little bit tighter.

CHAPTER EIGHTEEN

After a long, lazy Saturday morning in bed I had to say a reluctant good-bye to Sean. He'd promised to take the twins to a football match in the afternoon, and while I was tempted to suggest he take me as well, common sense asserted itself. It wouldn't do to make him feel suffocated.

"See you tomorrow?" he said with what I chose to interpret as a hopeful lilt to his voice as we shared a last embrace.

"Definitely," I assured him.

Sean smiled, straightened my bow tie for me in a touching if superfluous gesture, and left.

I flung myself onto the sofa and beamed at the ceiling for a goodly while. Having been constructed in the seventeenth century, it beamed right back at me. Then I got changed and went for a run. The ground, so muddy last night, had been hardened by an overnight frost that lingered in the shade and thawed as the sun hit it, leaving a clean, fresh scent in the air. The whole area around the village seemed extraordinarily beautiful this morning, and I ran for miles, the sunlight almost painfully bright as it glinted off the clear water of the river. I could hardly believe I'd been so lucky as to find this place, having chosen Shamwell purely on the basis that it was quiet, far enough from Potter's Field, and had a vacancy in the local primary school.

By the time I got back, I was ravenous. I called up Rose.

"Pub lunch?" I asked when she finally picked up.

"You what?"

"Lunch. In a pub," I clarified. "Fancy it?"

"Hang on a mo." There was a slurping sound, as of someone drinking from a bedside glass of water. Then there was a swearing sound, as of someone spilling said water on the duvet. All conjecture, of course, but Rose certainly sounded unwontedly surly when she spoke again. "We don't all get up at the bum-crack of dawn, you know."

I frowned. "It's 1:27 in the afternoon."

"So?"

"So you're a little late for dawn. I thought we could try the one down by the river."

"Try what?"

Really, she was being unusually slow today. "The lunches. In the pub. By the river. They're supposed to be quite good. How soon can you get down here?"

"God, you don't give up, do you? Give me half an hour to put my face on." At least she sounded somewhat more awake now. "The Tickled Trout, yeah?"

I beamed. "That's the one! So I'll see you there just before two?"

"Something like that."

I made a mental note not to expect her before half past. Fortunately the pub advertised that food was served all day.

In the event, Rose made it to the Trout at 2:17, catching me in the guilty act of staving off the hunger pangs with a packet of salt-and-vinegar crisps.

"You'll ruin your lunch," she said by way of greeting, and hitched a hip onto the barstool next to mine. "What are you drinking?"

"Lime and soda," I said abstemiously.

Rose's lip curled. "Well, at least you're a cheap date. I'll have a medium white wine. Large," she added as the barmaid turned to fill our order. "So what are we celebrating, anyhow?"

I blinked. "Celebrating? Nothing. I just thought as it was such a marvellous day we should make the most of it. If we go on through to the restaurant, they're keeping a table by the window for us." I smiled encouragingly at her.

She frowned with a touch of suspicion but followed.

Lunch was excellent—admittedly on the hearty end of the scale, rather than anything the *frères* Michelin might have felt tempted to write home about, but I had no complaints about my steak-and-ale pie, and Rose certainly polished off her lasagne with appropriate gusto.

"Dessert?" I asked as the waitress hovered with menus.

"Gawd, no, I'm stuffed. Well, maybe the cheesecake." The waitress gave her a knowing smirk and swept away. "Now, are you going to tell me what this is all about?"

"Why on earth does it have to be about anything?" I cast a glance around the pub, which was crowded with other late lunchers. Mrs. Nunn was at a nearby table, picking at a salad and gesticulating with her wineglass at the tennis coach, while Destinee scribbled industriously on the tablecloth with a ballpoint pen that looked uncannily like one I'd mislaid at school. I smiled genially at them all. "I just fancied lunch out. And it's been splendid, hasn't it?"

A sort of weary comprehension seemed to dawn on Rose's face. "Oh God. You finally got your end away with Sean, didn't you?"

I blinked. "That's . . . something of an assumption to make."

"Not really. If I hadn't been so hungover from last night out with the girls, I'd have spotted it a mile off." She grinned. "So go on, how was he?"

"A gentleman would never kiss and tell." Particularly not when Mrs. Nunn wasn't the only parent from 2E potentially listening. I was almost certain Emily G.'s gran was sitting with her back to us on the next table. Her monochrome curls were somewhat distinctive, and there was a certain attentiveness about the back of her head.

Rose apparently didn't care about my reputation. "So leave out the kissing bit, and get straight on to the shagging."

"I really don't . . ." I cast my gaze around for possible sources of distraction. "Oh, look—they've got a piano here. Do you think they'd mind if I tickled the ivories a tad?" The piano was roughly in the centre of the restaurant and was a baby grand rather than an upright like I had at home.

"Thought it was the trout that was supposed to be tickled here. Nah, save it to impress the boyfriend, I've still got a headache." She smirked. "Did you impress him last night?"

"I didn't ask for a performance appraisal. But he seemed well satisfied," I couldn't resist adding.

I might just possibly have mirrored her smirk, although my conscience pricked as I recalled it had been Sean, in fact, who'd done all the work. Still, I'd been there in a supervisory capacity. Providing, as it were, inspiration . . . I realised Rose was waving a hand in front of my face and had apparently been speaking to me. "Pardon?"

"I'm not going to ask where you drifted off to. There's kids around. So are you seeing him tonight?"

"Tomorrow. He's busy tonight."

"What are you going to do?"

I sent her an evil smile. "That's a rather indelicate question for a lady to be asking."

"Good job I'm not a lady, then, innit?"

I pointedly failed to contradict her. "He's coming over around teatime. We'll probably just have a quiet evening in." I gave her my sternest stare, the one even Destinee paid attention to occasionally (and which had almost had Charlie in tears when I'd inadvertently turned it on him). "So no popping round because you just *happened* to be down in the village."

"Huh. Catch me playing gooseberry to a couple of lovesick loved-up lovebirds. Even *thinking* about it's putting me right off my food."

"Oh dear," I said in mock distress as the waitress arrived with Rose's cheesecake. "Looks like I'd better eat this for you."

For a moment, I thought she was going to stab me with her fork.

My evening with Sean got off to something of a shaky start. He turned up on my doorstep with a hangdog expression and a spare motorcycle helmet.

"Um. Hope you're not going to be mad, but I sort of double-booked myself tonight."

My mood flattened, like a piece of bubble wrap that had had all its little pockets popped. "Oh. Well, if you've got a prior engagement, then of course you must—"

"Nah, I didn't mean I can't see you. Just, we sort of have to go out? One of the lads at work is in a band, and I totally forgot I'd promised to go to his gig tonight. I know you wanted a quiet night in, so I'm sorry about that. We don't have to stay all through it or anything."

"What kind of music is it?" I asked a little dubiously. I could generally find something to engage me in most types of music, but there were limits. Punk and I were not exactly bosom friends, and I couldn't even count heavy metal as a nodding acquaintance.

"Just old covers and stuff."

"That doesn't exactly tell me anything, you know."

"Uh . . . Undertones, Stranglers, The Damned . . . That kind of stuff."

Lovely. Punk it was. "Should I acquire some jeans and rip them? I'd offer to spike my hair, but I think I'm fresh out of eggs."

"Well, that's not the *only* stuff you could use. We could always improvise . . ." He winked, leaving me in absolutely no doubt he'd seen the same film I had. "Nah, you'll be fine as you are. They don't do the real hard-core stuff. Just the popular ones. You'll be fine."

"The fact you felt the need to repeat that isn't exactly reassuring me. So where is this gig?"

"Pub over in Bishops Langley. They do a sort of open mic thing, where local bands can go along if they book up ahead. I mean, they don't get paid for it or anything, but it's all about getting known, innit?"

"Is it? I thought it was about making a living."

"Nah, they've all got day jobs. Just do it for fun, really. And the free drinks, of course. Look, we don't have to go," Sean said with a grimace. "I'll just tell him I couldn't make it."

Guilt twisted inside me. "No, it's fine. We'll go. I'm sure it'll be . . ." Imagination failed me. "I'll just get my coat."

As I swung my leg over Sean's motorcycle, I wondered if turning up to a punk rock gig in bow tie and Barbour was a lynching offence.

I needn't, as it turned out, have worried. The pub was crowded not with the sneering, multiply pierced teenage underclass, but with the Boden-clad, middle-aged middle class. There were several families with children running around, and the "lad" Sean worked with turned out to be pushing forty, which made listening to him sing about "Teenage Kicks" a somewhat unnerving experience.

I didn't even have to use the headache pills I'd carefully stowed in my pocket, and ended the evening pleasantly tipsy on the none-too-shabby pinot grigio a guilty Sean had kept plying me with. There were several of his colleagues there, all supporting the band, and they proved surprisingly congenial company, seeming to accept me without question. One of them even regaled me with a rather amusing story from Sean's early days in his job, involving a rat, a bookcase, and a large wooden mallet. Swiftly followed by a bucket of soapy water for cleaning the bloodstains off the walls before the customer could see them.

The incongruity of it all striking me as rather amusing, I couldn't resist texting Rose: *At punk rock gig with a party of ratcatchers.*

Unfortunately, when the answer came back, *Should your father and I be concerned?* I realised I'd sent the text to Mother by mistake, but all things considered, it wasn't the *worst* thing I could have texted her by accident. Or, indeed, had done in the past.

There was, however, a frustrating downside to spending the evening out instead of in. If the company of Sean's workmates hadn't rendered any public displays of affection unthinkable (not that he wasn't *out* to them, but, well, it just hadn't seemed right), the presence of not a few St. Saviour's School parents—and one or two children—certainly had.

It was late when we roared back up at the Old Hatter's Cottage. "You're coming in," I said as I swung my leg off Sean's motorbike with considerably more grace than I'd managed the first time I'd dismounted from his powerful steed.

Sean grinned. "That didn't sound like a question."

"It wasn't." An evening spent keeping my hands off Sean, coupled with the ride back, had left me rather desperate to get him into the house.

"If this is the effect it has on you, I'm having you on my bike more often," he said as we shut my front door behind us. "Or is this just the wine talking?"

"The pinot grigio would be far too well bred to even allude to any of the thoughts I'm having," I murmured into his ear, having slung my arms around his neck.

"Oh yeah?" He squeezed me tight, causing rather delicious sensations in certain parts of me, then stepped back with an air of regret. "Think I'll put the kettle on, though, just in case. You're up for a coffee, yeah?"

I was up for something else entirely, but he'd already bypassed me, and I could hear him filling the kettle. It seemed futile to argue, so I settled for throwing myself on the sofa to await his return. Possibly with the suspicion of a pout. "That would be lovely," I said, remembering my manners, although somewhat insincerely.

"Sorry about tonight," he said, walking in with two steaming mugs much more quickly than I would have expected. Perhaps the wine *was* making me a little woozy. A certain amount of mental fog did seem to clear as I sipped my coffee. Sean had made it strong but added plenty of milk to take away the bitterness, and the temperature was just right.

"No, don't be silly. Actually I quite enjoyed it. They're very, um, enthusiastic, aren't they?"

"What, Mike and the band? Yeah, just a bit. Good, though, aren't they? Kept the crowd entertained."

"Mm. Although I felt a little bit on the spot when he came over to our table and started singing 'My Perfect Cousin' directly in my face."

Sean grinned. "Could have been worse, you know. Some gigs, they do a cover version of the Sex Pistols' 'God Save the Queen.'"

I shuddered and drank some more coffee.

"S'pose classical music's more your thing?" Leaning back on the sofa, Sean gestured towards my piano. "That yours? Or did it come with the rest of the furniture? You do rent furnished, right?"

I could have done with him waiting until the caffeine had completed its work before firing *quite* so many questions at me all at once. "Um, right. I mean, yes, I rent furnished, but the piano is mine. It was a moving-in present from my stepfather—I always played on the school pianos when I was living in, of course." Mindful of Rose's comment yesterday about impressing the boyfriend, I dived straight in. "Would you like me to play you some *real* music?"

"Go for it." He gave a rueful smile. "Although, maybe not anything too heavy, yeah? Be wasted on me."

I stood and stretched my fingers. "Oh, I'm not really into the heavier classics myself. Too many hours practising that sort of thing as a child, when Mother still had the idea of making a concert pianist out of me. No, I prefer more lighthearted pieces when I'm playing for fun." I pulled out the piano stool and launched into "Fat Sam's Grand Slam" from *Bugsy Malone*, and glanced over my shoulder to see Sean grinning in recognition.

"Pretty good," he said when I'd finished. "You ever sing as well?"

I made a face. "Slightly lacking in the vocal talent department, I'm afraid. But sometimes, yes."

"Go on, then. Let's hear you."

Emboldened by his enthusiasm (and, I'd have to confess, by the lingering effects of the pinot grigio) I went straight into Tom Waits's "The Piano Has Been Drinking," and sang along to this one. Well, spoke along, as the lyrics were more of a rambling commentary than an actual song. I'd always loved this one. There was something remarkably freeing about deliberately playing badly out of tune.

Sean was laughing helplessly by the time I'd finished. "Oh my God. That song, in your accent . . . Have you heard yourself? Bloody fantastic."

"Thank you," I said modestly. "It always seemed to go down well when I was at school."

"Man of many talents, aren't you?" Sean said, getting up from the sofa. "Budge up. Nah, shift back from the piano a bit." As I did as he'd asked, he joined me at the piano stool, but instead of sitting beside me (which would have been something of a tight squeeze) he swung a leg over my lap to straddle me and squeezed me tight in a rather more pleasant way. A growing hardness in his jeans left me in no doubt he'd found my performance stimulating.

Good. Determined to take a more active role in today's proceedings, I slid my hands up under his shirt, tracing the flat, muscular planes of his back. Sean made an appreciative sound and pressed closer to me.

"C'mere," he said, using one hand to cup the back of my head and angle it up for a kiss. It was slow and deep.

"I'm already *here*," I pointed out a bit breathlessly. "If I was any more *here*, we'd merge into one."

"Mm, that sounds good. Ever had sex on a piano stool?" Sean raised a copper eyebrow suggestively.

"Erm . . ." My face grew unaccountably heated. "Possibly."

He laughed, clearly delighted by the thought of my debauchery. "You dirty bastard."

"It's a lot less fun than you'd think. Not enough room to do anything properly, and they're usually placed on very hard floors. Agony on the knees. And elbows too, if you should happen to tumble off. We should go upstairs. I, er, went shopping this afternoon. For, um, supplies."

I'd made the trip into Bishops Langley specially. It hadn't been that I'd been too desperate to wait another night without condoms (or at least, it hadn't been *just* that). Something had told me that waiting until Monday and paying a visit to the village chemist would just be asking for embarrassment. I'd probably have turned around from my purchase to find the Head looking over my shoulder. And half of class 2E peering underneath my arm.

"Yeah? Surprised I didn't bump into you." Sean reached into his pocket and drew out a slim pack of condoms. "Snap."

"Lube?" I challenged.

"Other pocket." He gave me a triumphant grin.

I frowned. "I see how it is. One blowjob and now you're taking me for granted."

"Would I?"

"Well, I was hoping you were planning to eventually," I huffed. "But we still seem to be sitting on this piano stool. Up," I added, lifting him with both hands to encourage him off my lap.

Fortunately for my pride, he took the hint and scrambled off me, then took my hand to yank me to my feet. I followed him upstairs with alacrity—in fact, it turned into a sort of race which ended in us trying to barge through the bedroom door at the same time. We were both laughing when we flopped onto the bed.

"Seeing as I won, I get to choose who does what, yeah?"

I rolled over on top of him and pinned his shoulders with my hands. "You did *not* win. I was ahead of you by a nose."

He rolled me off him and onto my back with embarrassing ease. "Yeah, right. Sorry if this is a blow to your ego, but it's not that big, you know."

"You'd better be talking about my nose," I warned.

"Why? What else would it have been?" Sean belied his ignorance with a press of his hips that drove his erection against mine with delicious force. "Nope. Nothing small about that."

"I think you should take a closer look to be certain. It might have shrunk since last time."

Sean raised himself up onto his hands and knees above me and peered for a moment at my groin. "Can't see a bloody thing," he announced finally. "Too many clothes in the way. Shit."

"What?"

"You're wearing a belt."

"And?"

"No braces." He pouted ridiculously.

"Well, I wouldn't want to risk you getting bored with them."

"Huh. Still don't like it. Nope, it's gotta go." He undid the buckle with deft fingers, and slid it out of the loops with a sensuous slithering sound. "Yeah, that's better." He raised an eyebrow. "Course, these things have their uses too."

"Sounds kinky."

"Good kinky? Or bad kinky?"

"Depends. A little light bondage: fine. Beating me on the arse until I can't sit down? A little too reminiscent of the horror stories the older pupils at prep school used to scare the new boys with."

Sean looked alarmed. "Yeah, definitely thinking on the light bondage side, here. Um. Maybe not this time, then, yeah?" He chucked the belt over his shoulder and onto the floor without waiting for a reply.

I laughed. "You do realise they were only stories? Nothing like that actually went on."

"Glad to hear it. Seriously." He sat back on his heels and ran his hands up my legs, ending with a squeeze. "Don't like to think of anything like that happening to this arse."

"Mm, why not? Have you got plans for it?"

"Thought I didn't get to choose?"

I raised an eyebrow. "Depends what you'd choose."

"Think you know what I'd choose. What'd you choose?"

"I'd choose this," I said, leaning up on one elbow so I could massage the appropriate part of him through his jeans. "In me."

Sean shuddered. Hopefully not in revulsion. "You're gonna kill me," was all he said, so the jury was still out. Then he pulled off his shirt with one swift motion and unbuttoned his jeans.

Revulsion was probably not a problem. I struggled to get out of my trousers, hampered partly by my supine position and partly by the strapping young man seated on my calves.

"Want a hand?" Sean scrambled off me, grabbed the ends of my trousers, and whipped them from my legs with impressive sleight of hand. Or, as it were, of trouser.

"You're supposed to wait for an answer," I complained, clambering to my knees to work on his jeans. "And stand up, damn you. Or I'll never get these off."

He stood, and in seconds I had him naked but for his socks. "Your socks have cartoon mice on," I pointed out, momentarily distracted from the matter in hand.

Sean shrugged, his face a little pink, and started toeing them off. "Gag gifts, what can you do?"

The matter in hand having been Sean's cock, which, as I was still seated on the bed, was bobbing nicely in my eye line, I had to think for a moment before I could remember what we were talking about. "I like them," I said, taking hold and enjoying the velvety feel of him in my hand.

"Yeah?" Sean sounded distracted too. Good.

"Mm. I like this better, though." To prove my point, I plunged my mouth over it. The drop of moisture on the tip was an explosion of saltiness on my tongue, a piquant contrast to the musky maleness of the rest of him.

"Fuck, yeah," Sean gasped, encapsulating my own thoughts succinctly. His hands were on my head, fingers combing through my hair. "God, the way you look doing that—I mean, fuck, still in your shirt and that bow tie . . ."

I'd have thought I looked faintly ridiculous, but clearly it was a matter of opinion. I peered up at him, still sucking, and something stuttered in my chest at the raw emotion in his eyes. I was releasing him from my mouth and standing before I'd even registered consciously just how imperative it was right now to kiss him on the lips.

Sean's tongue invaded my mouth as if seeking out his own taste in there, and his erection jabbed insistently into my belly, aided by my hands on his arse, drawing him in close. We broke apart, panting, and he reached up trembling hands to pull at the ends of my tie. This time, he kept tugging on one end, sliding it from my shirt in a susurration of silk. We both worked on my shirt buttons, I from the bottom and he from the top, until our hands met in the middle. Slowly, Sean reached up to push the garment from my shoulders. "God, you're gorgeous," he breathed, as it fell to the floor.

He cupped me through the cotton of my boxers, squeezing gently, making me moan, then carefully eased them off me, over the head of my erection and down thighs that tingled where he touched. Crouching down, he removed my socks one by one. I let out an undignified yelp as his fingers brushed my sole.

Sean grinned. "Ticklish?"

I eyed him warily. "If I say yes, are you planning to take advantage?"

His smile turned devilish. "Trust me, I'll be doing that anyway."

"Oh. Good," I decided, then immediately regretted it as he licked the bottom of my foot, causing me to yelp again and fall on the bed. "Bastard!"

Sean clambered on top of me, his erection tantalising inches from mine. "You love it really."

"*Smug* bastard."

"So where's all this stuff you bought, then?"

I raised an eyebrow. "I thought you'd brought your own?"

"Yeah, but it's down on the floor now, buried under a heap of clothes, innit?"

"Fair point. Bedside cabinet. Top drawer." I inclined my head in the appropriate direction.

Sean leaned over. "Aren't you worried I'll find something embarrassing?" he asked, opening the drawer.

"Such as?"

"I dunno . . . Mills and Boon medical romances?"

"*No.* They're in the bottom drawer," I couldn't resist adding. Mendaciously, in case there should be any doubt.

"Prefer the historicals myself," Sean said, returning with condoms, lube, and a triumphant look. "All those tight breeches."

I had a retort on the lines of *breaching something tight* right on the tip of my tongue, but the words flew out of the window as he reached one slippery finger behind my balls. "Oh God!"

How long had it been since anyone had touched me there?

Well, technically, Sean had touched me there only yesterday, but this was different. This was touching *with intent*. This was— "Oh, God," I said again as his finger penetrated me.

"Okay?"

"O-okay." It was good, but it was so very much *not enough*.

"I'll go slow—"

"Don't!" I flushed. "I mean, you don't need to, go slow, I mean, don't. That." Sean was laughing at me. "*Please*," I said, pulling him closer.

"Yeah? Something you want?"

"You. In me. *Now*."

I seethed in frustration as he insisted on stretching me out a little longer, then rolled on a condom with glacial slowness. "Sure?" he asked, as he lined himself up, the tip of his erection rubbing tantalisingly at my hole.

"No, I've taken a vow of chastity. Yes, of course I'm sure." I pulled on his hips—then he breached me, and all I could do was let out a long, low sound. The stretch was incredible, and I felt every contour, every vein of him as he pushed into me. "Oh Lord."

"Okay?"

"Very much. Yes." Bent almost double, my legs high around his back, I pulled him down for a kiss. It was perfect.

Sean thrust in and out a few times, his pace cautious—and then he changed the angle, kneeling up and placing my left ankle on his shoulder, and then, God, *then* it was perfect.

He played me like a Stradivarius, with long, smooth strokes and gentle fingering, and far too soon I felt the crescendo building towards a rousing finale. My climax slammed into me with Wagnerian intensity, all complex harmonies and crashing chords, and when I looked at Sean's face I saw he'd let go too. He was beautiful, his expression heady and abandoned and somehow surprised, as if he hadn't believed sex could be like this.

I hadn't either.

We fell into each other's arms, trembling with a subtle vibrato. Sean was the first to recover the power of speech. "God, that was . . ."

"Yes," I agreed.

We lay there for a few minutes longer, and I could feel myself slipping towards sleep. "Will you stay the night?" Knowing it was unlikely, I tried to keep hope from my voice.

"Wish I could. Nah, I'd better be going. Early start tomorrow." Sean stroked my hair. "But it's been a great weekend. You know, the bits I spent with you. Really enjoyed it."

"So did I. When are we going to . . . um, assuming you'd like to, of course . . ."

"Friday night," Sean said firmly. "Wish I could make it before then, but I've got a heavy week coming up. I'd only end up having to cancel. But we'll do whatever you like. Got any ideas?"

"How about the evening in we didn't get tonight?" I suggested sleepily. "Maybe with a takeaway? Fish and chips, perhaps. After all, it is traditional."

"Sounds great. I'll see you then, yeah? I could make it early, if you like. Six o'clock okay?"

"Perfect."

We kissed one more time, slowly and languorously, and then he got out of bed.

After he'd gone, I rolled over into the warm patch he'd vacated. It still smelled like him. Comforted, I drifted off to sleep.

CHAPTER NINETEEN

The week passed in something of a happy blur. Sean's week must have been as busy as predicted, as he didn't appear at the classroom door to pick up the twins even once, but we exchanged texts and the odd phone call—although the latter had to be kept strictly suitable for any prying childish ears. Debs, when I saw her at school, was almost friendly. Rose's complaints about my obnoxious good humour became a daily occurrence, although, as she still shared her lunch with me, she couldn't have been too put out about it.

Friday afternoon, it was, as usual, just Charlie and me left at the end of the day. He stared at the open door with his clear blue eyes as if he could conjure up his father simply by wanting him desperately enough, and swallowed.

I crouched down in front of him with a determined smile. "Right, young Charlie—"

I broke off as the classroom got suddenly darker. Were we experiencing an unplanned solar eclipse? Apparently not, as a deep voice rumbled out, "All right if I have a word?"

I turned my head to see Charlie's father standing in the doorway, the proximity to child-height coat pegs enhancing his already marked resemblance to a giant. He had his sleeves rolled up to display his muscular, hairy forearms, and the buttons of his worn, somewhat grimy work shirt strained to contain his bearlike paunch.

From my position on my haunches, I felt in imminent danger of being stepped on and crushed like a bug. I straightened hurriedly.

Charlie's pale face split into a smile, and he ran to fling himself on one tree-trunk leg. "Daddy! I got a gold star for my writing today. And we had fish fingers for lunch. And George H. was sick, and Jodie trod in it."

Mr. Mason—who did, as it happened, work in the building trade—folded his bulk with obvious difficulty into a crouch. Together, they would have made a perfect illustration for a cautionary tale concerning a small boy about to be eaten by an ogre. I'd always presumed Charlie took after his mother but, as I'd never met her, couldn't be sure. Perhaps he was just a slow starter and would one day reach his father's epic proportions, which was an alarming prospect.

"That's great, Charlie-farley," Mason père said gruffly. "Why don't you go and run around the field a bit while I talk to Mr. Enemy?"

Charlie's lip trembled. "But I'll get muddy."

"Tell you what, young Charlie," I broke in quickly. "Why don't you pop into the library and check that Mrs. Blundell's shelved all the reading-tree books in the right order? And when you've done that, you can pick out a book to read while you're waiting."

"Can I?" Charlie beamed and scurried off.

"Right," I said as the door closed quietly behind him and Mr. Mason heaved his way back up—and up—to standing. "What seems to be the problem?"

Mr. Mason coughed. Then he wiped his size fourteen feet very thoroughly on the door mat.

Then he coughed again.

"Shall we, er, sit down?" I suggested, thinking that might put him at ease. Any considerations of evening up our height difference were purely secondary, of course.

"No. Thanks. I'll stand." Actually, given the relative size—and weight—of Mr. Mason and the classroom chairs, that was probably just as well.

He fell silent again.

"Has Charlie been having some problems with his reading?" I asked to prompt him, knowing full well that Charlie was streets ahead of most of his classmates.

"No, no. He's doing great." Mr. Mason heaved a sigh and scratched the back of his head, his triceps bulging.

I blinked and looked away, hoping he hadn't noticed me staring. It wasn't that I found him attractive, per se, but there was undeniably an earthiness about him that never failed to fascinate. "Has there been a problem with one of the other children?" I'd hoped Destinee had finally seen the error of her Charlie-baiting ways, but perhaps she'd relapsed?

"No, no. It's, well, it's a bit of a . . ." He trailed off, and looked at his feet.

I waited.

Taking a deep breath, Mr. Mason looked me straight in the eye. "You're one of them gays, ain'tcha?"

"Er, yes." Did the entire village know my sexual preferences? The pink bow tie was going to be taking a one-way trip to the charity shop, soonest.

"Charlie, he talks about you a lot. Always going on about you, he is. Mr. Enemy this, Mr. Enemy that."

I went cold. Was this going where I thought it was going? "He's, ah, an affectionate little chap." Oh God, had I just made things worse? "Not . . . not in a physical sense, clearly."

Mr. Mason frowned. "I mean, he looks up to you."

That was better, wasn't it? No harm in a child looking up to a teacher, was there? "I, ah . . ." My mouth seemed to have somehow become filled with cotton wool. Mr. Mason was still frowning. Oh God. It was going to be just like with Oliver all over again. Except *worse*, because while the thought of any impropriety with a seventeen-year-old pupil was morally repugnant, any suggestion of such a thing with a seven-year-old was utterly unspeakable. "I think . . . Please tell me what it is you wanted to say," I managed.

It occurred to me Mr. Mason might, in lieu of accusations, prefer to just thump me. It further occurred to me I might even prefer that myself. He could probably knock me out with a single blow. A nice long stretch of unconsciousness wasn't totally unappealing right now.

Mr. Mason shoved his hands in his pockets and looked at my brogues. "Do you wear, like, dresses and stuff?"

What? I choked off a laugh as the icy feeling inside me was washed away by a heady surge of relief. "That's a, ah, quite a personal question. Can I ask why you feel it necessary to know?" Oh God, I was still fighting the urge to giggle. If he was about to ask me to don a suspender belt and stockings for him, he was in for a disappointment. Fascination only went so far.

Besides, I'd looked ridiculous, the one and only time Fordy persuaded me into drag.

"Charlie. He . . ." Mr. Mason scratched his head again.

I was in a fever. Charlie *what*? Had been telling his dad I taught in women's clothing? Thought I'd look pretty in a frock?

"He likes to wear girls' clothes. I mean, just when we're at home, mind. He don't wear 'em out the house."

Oh. "*Oh*." I wrestled my thoughts back to an appropriate level of sobriety. "And, er, can I ask how you've been handling this?"

Mr. Mason heaved a mountainous shrug. "Well, I've not been *encouraging* him. Just, you know, he had his heart set on that Snow White outfit for his birthday . . . I told him straight, if he wears it around the village, he's going to get teased. I don't want my lad getting bullied," he finished, glowering.

"No, of course not. St. Saviour's has a strict policy against bullying." Except, of course, of the teachers by the Head and, on occasion, Mrs. Ormley. "Well, I'm sure you're doing the right thing here— letting him express himself but warning him it could have adverse consequences."

He frowned. "Yeah, but what I want to know is, what's it mean? Is he going to do it all his life? Is he going to be wanting a sex change when he's older?"

I thought about Charlie as I knew him. "He's never said anything to me about feeling he's really a girl," I said slowly. "I mean, he mostly plays with the girls, but I think that's more to do with not being fond of rough games. And, obviously, enjoying dressing up and playing with, ah, more traditionally feminine toys. But it doesn't have to *mean* anything, except that that's the kind of boy Charlie is."

"So was that what you was like?" Mr. Mason's weathered face reddened. "What I mean is, is Charlie going to be one of them gays too?"

"How would you feel about that?" I asked cautiously.

Mr. Mason's face got, if possible, even redder. "Well, it's up to him, innit? Who he wants to go out with. I don't want my lad getting beat up for it, mind," he added in tones that would have put the fear of God into any possible gay-bashers who might have been listening.

"I'm glad to hear it. It's good to know Charlie will have your support if and when he decides that's where his, ah, interests lie. But don't you think it's a bit early to be worrying about that?"

"I just want to know how to treat 'im, that's all."

"I think, really, you have to be guided by Charlie here. I mean, you seem to be doing a good job so far," I said encouragingly. "Although perhaps you could work on getting to school to pick him up a few minutes earlier? Charlie can be an anxious little chap."

Hammer-like fists shoved into trouser pockets, and Mr. Mason looked away. "Yeah. I'll work on that."

"And maybe try and give him as much of your attention as possible? He obviously adores you, and the more you strengthen that bond, the more able he'll feel to talk to you when he's a little older and might have questions about, well, things."

The deep-set eyes looked hunted. "Can't you do that?"

"Mr. Mason," I said firmly. "I'm very fond of young Charlie, and I'll be very happy to help in any way that's appropriate. But I'm not his father. In a few short years, he's going to be moving on to secondary school, and I won't see him again. And that's the time he's going to need your support the most. Whatever his eventual conclusion about his preferences."

Mr. Mason nodded slowly, still looking unhappy. "What's it like?" he asked finally.

"Um, meaning?"

"Being gay. What's it like?"

Oh God. Was he actually asking what gay men did in bed? "I think I'm going to need you to be a bit more specific, Mr. Mason." And I was absolutely reserving the right to refuse to answer any questions I chose.

"Well . . ." He turned and stared out of the window for a long moment. "You get beat up and stuff?"

Oh. Thank God. "I haven't been that unlucky, no." Although there had been one or two terrifyingly close calls. "It does happen, but please try not to worry too much. After all, we don't even know if Charlie's actually gay yet. He may yet surprise you and bring home a girlfriend."

Mr. Mason looked frankly dubious. "He brings home a girl, it'll most like be so they can paint each other's nails. Well, I won't keep you, Mr. Enemy. Thanks for, well, you know."

"You're welcome. I'll go and see if Charlie's finished in the library."

I found him curled up on a beanbag, frowning at a copy of *Princess Smartypants*. "Ready to go home, young Charlie?"

He nodded and clambered to his feet. "I'll put the book back, Mr. Enemy."

"You can take it home with you, if you like."

"No, thank you. I don't like it much."

"Oh? Why's that, then?"

He held out the book, and we both stared at the jolly-looking princess on the front, her blonde hair streaming behind her as she rode her motorbike, clad in bizarrely frumpy black leathers. "She's weird," Charlie said firmly. "And silly."

"Why do you think she's silly, young Charlie?"

"Well . . . she's a princess, but she just wears jeans and does gardening and stuff." He shelved the book decisively.

"Well, not *all* princesses like keeping clean and wearing pretty dresses," I said, as I shepherded him back to the classroom.

"But why not?" Charlie's eyes were round, and he sounded as if his world view had just been shaken to the core.

"You know, that would be an *excellent* question to discuss with your father." I smiled and pushed the lad firmly towards Mr. Mason.

Once they'd gone, I sank onto a table, my knees suddenly more than a little wobbly.

Oh God. I felt like a cricket ball that had been launched from the arm of a spin bowler on steroids, knocked for six by a gorilla, and was now lying trembling in the grass, waiting for a fielder to scoop it up and lob it back into the fray. I'd thought for a horrible, gut-wrenching moment my life here was over.

My hands still shook as I closed the classroom door behind me and set off home. Sean. I was supposed to be seeing Sean tonight. In two hours, in fact, when he'd come round for our cosy fish-and-chip supper. I'd been looking forward to it all week; now it loomed ahead of me like my impending execution. Self-doubt gnawed at my innards like a particularly vicious rat. Or squirrel, as it might be. Had I been mad to think I could have this? Would I *never* escape my past?

I couldn't let Sean see me like this. He'd be bound to ask what was wrong, and if the truth came out . . . But I couldn't cancel either. That would look even worse.

I'd just have to pull myself together, that was all.

And make absolutely *certain* Sean didn't suspect a thing.

The evening went about as well as might have been expected. Which was to say, not well at all.

When Sean turned up on the dot of six o'clock, he found me still edgy, nervous, and in the throes of a severe headache. I should have cancelled, or at the very least suggested we go out where there would have been some distraction, but I'd been too bloody weak. I'd wanted to have his strong arms around me, reassuring me that all was well.

Instead, after I'd mangled my fish, dropped half my chips, and ruined my shirt with ketchup, I got his large, troubled eyes gazing at me, and his sombre voice asking me what was wrong.

"Rob? Come on, you can tell me."

I couldn't. How could I possibly explain I'd thought I was about to be accused of improper relations with a pupil—for the second time? "It's nothing. Really. I . . . I just have a bit of a headache, that's all. Been a long day."

I wasn't looking at him, so I couldn't see his expression as he stood up. "Right. Well, it's getting late anyway." It was 7:18, actually, which wasn't even late if you were a seven-year-old, but I didn't point that out. "I'll leave you in peace."

"All right, then," I said, judging it the lesser of two evils. I wanted to ask him to stay—but I knew it'd be better to let him go. Less risk I'd crumble and tell him what he thought he wanted to know. I was a little hurt he hadn't even offered to fetch me an aspirin, though.

"See you," he said, and left without kissing me good-bye.

CHAPTER TWENTY

I spent a restless night, alternately dozing off in exhaustion and then waking up again with a start. Deep sleep must have finally overtaken me sometime in the not-so-early hours of Saturday morning. At least, I felt incredibly groggy when I woke up at 10:23 to a barrage of knocking on the front door.

Too sleep-fuddled to register at first that the aggressive summons wasn't Sean's casual knock, Rose's sharp rap, or Hanne's soft rat-a-tat-tat, I staggered downstairs in my dressing gown to open my door.

And stared at the boyishly handsome if somewhat chubby face in front of me. "Fordy?"

He looked tired but still larger than life, with his beaming smile and mismatched yet expensive clothes that, as usual, strained to contain the breadth of his shoulders. I tried to blink some clarity into my vision and my mind.

"What are you doing here?" Oh God, he hadn't left Linette and the baby, had he? No, that was ridiculous. For one thing, he didn't appear to have any luggage.

Fordy laughed, his dark hair flopping over his eyes. He tossed it back again in a bizarre imitation of a shampoo commercial. "Well, there's a charming greeting. Aren't you going to invite me in?"

"Oh—of course. Sorry. Come in."

Fordy strode into the Old Hatter's Cottage, glancing from right to left, visibly sizing the place up. Somehow it seemed much smaller with him inside. "Very quaint around here, isn't it? What on earth do you find to do with yourself? Still, I suppose London's close enough. You know, I could murder someone for a coffee."

I stared at him, then straightened my thoughts out with an effort. "Excellent idea. The coffee, I mean. Not the murder. I'll put the kettle on."

"No, no, don't bother. I'll pop down the road and get us a couple. The baker's shop was advertising them. I'd have gone there first, as a matter of fact, but I wanted to be sure you were in." He laughed again. Good old Fordy, I'd forgotten how easily he laughed. "In bed, by the looks of you. So come on, how many cups do I need to bring back?"

"Just the one. For me, I mean." My face grew hot, to my intense annoyance. Surely *one* day I'd be able to allude to matters carnal without turning incandescent.

"Right-oh," Fordy said, unconcerned by my embarrassment. Still, if anyone ought to be used to it, it was he, after all. "Won't be a minute."

Fordy's departure seemed to suck all the vitality out of the house. I stared at the front door for a moment after he'd left, half thinking I might have dreamed him. Then I pulled myself together and raced up the stairs for some clothes.

When the peremptory knock came again, I was at least more properly attired for answering the door. Fordy beamed at me. "That's more like it. The Emsy I know and love, bow tie and all. Brought you breakfast, seeing as I dragged you kicking and screaming from the duvet." He handed over a large takeaway cup of coffee and a paper bag which, upon inspection, proved to contain an enormous almond croissant. "Go on, dig in. I ate earlier. Much, much earlier." Fordy shuddered. "Georgie's clearly planning to be a farmer when he grows up. Or a postman, or one of those godawful people on breakfast television who have the nerve to be cheerful after getting up in the middle of the night to go to work."

"How is he?" I seized the chance to get a word in as I led him to the living room.

Fordy flung himself down on the sofa. "Oh, he's fine. Thriving, as they say. You must come down and meet him over Christmas. Get to know your godchild. Did I mention we were going to ask you to be godfather? It'll be in the spring, haven't set a date yet. For God's sake don't say no, or we'll be stuck with some awful friend of Linny's."

"Um, thank you. I'd be honoured. Unless you think it'd be a bit—" I'd been about to say awkward in view of our mutually exploratory past, but Fordy interrupted me.

"Funny having a *literal* fairy godfather? I doubt that'll be a problem. You should see our vicar. Well, you will, anyway. Queer as a three-pound pilchard. Offered to take me up the back stairs to the bell tower. I told him I'm a married man these days." He sighed rather theatrically and took the lid off his coffee.

"Is everything all right?" I asked cautiously. "With Linette and, well, things?"

"Oh, she's fine." He sipped from the cup, closed his eyes briefly, and sighed again. "Oh yes. That hits the spot. Linny's fine, baby's fine, everything's sodding fine."

"But?" I prompted. I took a bite of almond croissant, which, I decided, was the crack cocaine of baked goods. One flaky, almondy hit and I was hooked.

Fordy put his cup down. "Well, you know. It's as if I've ceased to exist. Except when a nappy needs changing, or we've run out of baby wipes or that revolting stuff in jars she insists on feeding him. It's all Georgie, Georgie, Georgie. No, we can't go skiing this year because airline travel is bad for babies' ears. No, we can't have a night out, because she's breastfeeding. And God forbid I ever try and get frisky with her these days. I tell you what, when they cut that umbilical cord, they might as well have cut my bloody prick off at the same time. Linny's certainly got no more use for it." Fordy blew out a disgusted breath. "So how's your sex life going? Found yourself a rustic bit of rough out here in the sticks? Been rolling in the haystacks, making babes in the woods, all that sort of stuff?"

"Um. I am seeing someone. Sort of." I winced. Sean didn't deserve a *sort of*. Even after last night. I hoped.

"Oh? What does he do? I take it it's a *he*. If you've finally seen the light and come over to the distaff side, I'm telling you straight, it's not bloody worth it. Breasts are all well and good until she drops a sprog and takes out a bloody restraining order to keep you from coming within three feet of them. So what is he? Another teacher?" He grinned. "Got the Head giving you head?"

I'd been dreading this. "Sean's a, um, pest-control technician." I turned my attentions to my croissant, but despite having excellent qualities in other respects, it failed to ward off Fordy's remarks.

"A what? Christ, Emsy, when you're after a bit of rough, you don't piss about, do you? A bloody ratcatcher. What did you do, go cruising in the sewers?" He laughed out loud.

I didn't. In fact, the paper bag crumpled in my hand as I barely restrained myself from walloping him.

Fordy snapped to attention, leaning forward and resting his elbows on his knees. "Oh. *Ohhh.* Stepped on the old toes there, have I? Pierced a nerve and shredded a something-or-other? Well, I'll reserve judgement, then. Far be it from me to criticise an ancient and no doubt honourable profession. So what's he got that the PE teacher didn't have? He was all right, he was. A bit too obsessed with fresh air and exercise, but then you like that sort of thing, don't you? Can't think why. Didn't you get enough of all that when we were at school?"

"I like him," I ground out, concentrating hard on picking fallen almonds out of the base of the paper bag and not, say, kicking Fordy out of my house. Figuratively speaking, obviously. Attempting to do it physically would have been rather akin to a gnat trying to steamroller an elephant. "He's got twin nephews in my class, and he looks after them as if they were his own, and he never complains."

"Where's their father, then? Over the hills and far away, I suppose?"

I nodded. "And their mother's got cancer. It's so unfair; she's ridiculously young to be thinking about dying. Maybe she's not the, well, *friendliest* person in the world, but she doesn't deserve to die. *They* don't deserve to lose her."

"Well, of course not. Poor little sods. Still, mustn't give up hope. Miracles of modern medicine and all that rubbish. I mean to say, they're still managing to patch my old man up just fine every time he has a heart attack, and I've lost count of how many hips Mother's been through. By the way, and while we're on the subject, your absence *was* noted from the old folks' ruby wedding do last month." He stopped talking and fixed me with a reproachful look.

I cringed a little. "Sorry about that. I mean, I did send your mother my apologies, of course, but . . ." I simply hadn't been able to face fifty or so well-meaning acquaintances I'd seen neither hide nor hair of since the Fordhams' last Boxing Day Brunch, all of them with nothing more to say to me than a polite enquiry as to how the job at Potter's

Field was going. Or, for that matter, my mother's attempts to persuade me to give Crispin another chance, as if he'd actually wanted one. I wouldn't have put it past her to have invited him along, come to that, but as her affection for him was completely unrequited, I sincerely doubted he'd have turned up.

"Oh, I know, I know. Linny found the whole thing a terrible bore too, and at least she had Georgie to keep her amused. No, no—no reproach there. But the reason I bring it up is, I got talking to your mother, and she mentioned one of your old students was asking after you. Rang her up right out of the blue. She thought he was selling something to start with and nearly hung up on him, but they managed to get it all straight in the end. One of the young men from Potter's Field, before you had your brainstorm or mid-youth crisis or whatever it was that made you leave a perfectly good job teaching A levels to come and wipe bums and noses in Ye Olde Village School. And honestly, Emsy, you can't *still* think that's a good career move, can you? I mean to say, the salary must be abysmal. Thank God *your* partner of choice isn't likely to suddenly start breeding. You'd be back sponging off your parents before you could say *Knightsbridge*. And then—"

"Fordy," I interrupted with some force. "Who was asking about me?"

"I don't know, do I? I never met any of your students."

"What *exactly* did Mother say?"

He shrugged. With some effort, I forbore to throttle him. "Not a lot. Simply that she'd given out your new address to some young man or other, and wasn't it marvellous that he'd been so inspired by your teaching as to want to write and thank you personally?"

Oh God. I felt sick. The almond croissant seemed suddenly to have left a bitter aftertaste in my mouth.

Fordy frowned. "Are you all right? You're not going to upchuck, are you? I get quite enough of that at home, believe you me. Nine months of Linny throwing a rainbow every time I looked at her, and as soon as she'd stopped, the baby started. Use the paper bag from the bakers, it'll probably hold. Or if you can hang on long enough, I'll fetch something from the kitchen. Got any least favourite saucepans?"

"Fordy, please stop talking. It's really not helping."

"Huh. Funny, that. Just what Linny says." He beamed. "And here I was thinking you two had absolutely nothing in common. You know, you really must come and visit. The house is an absolute pigsty, reeks of sour milk and shit, but Georgie's a fabulous little chap. You'll love him. Well, you'll have to, being his godfather, it's one of the job requirements, but—"

"*Fordy*," I said warningly.

He frowned. "What? Oh, right." He mimed zipping his lips, turning an invisible key, and chucking it over his shoulder. And looked at me expectantly.

"Oh God." I put my head in my hands. Moments later, I heard Fordy moving. My chair shifted, not without protest, as he perched on the arm and began to pat me on the shoulder. It was so *Fordy*. I had a vivid picture of him offering the same awkward comfort to Linette as she panted in agony during childbirth. I wondered if she'd walloped him, and tried unsuccessfully to stifle a somewhat hysterical giggle.

"Um," Fordy said. "Can I speak again, yet? Because I may not be the sharpest log in the watershed, but I've got the strongest feeling something's amiss. If you don't want to talk about it, that's fine, obviously, but, well, if you *do* . . ."

I looked up. "I don't. Really."

"Oh. Fine, fine. Fine." His expression was a curious mix of relief and disappointment.

"It's just . . . There's someone from Potter's Field I'd really rather not see again."

"Ah." Fordy scrunched up his eyes. "But won't that Quentin Crisp fellow already have your address?"

"*Crispin*. And no. Or yes, possibly. But it doesn't matter. It's not him."

Fordy's always rather exuberant brows had now entirely met in the middle, like a couple of very small, coy ferrets exchanging a kiss. "No? Who else were you shagging, then?"

"No one!"

"Oh." Fordy looked honestly baffled. The ferrets parted, as if surprised by the younger ferret's father coming home unexpectedly early and catching them at it. "Then why don't you want to see him again?"

"It's complicated. And I really don't want to talk about it."

"Problem shared, problem halved?"

"Not this one. More like problem shared, problem squared. Or problem to the power of n, where n equals infinity."

"Fair enough, then. I'll take your word for it. Never was that good at maths. As you know, of course. Don't know how I'd have got through the GCSE without you helping me. Sure I can't return the favour here?"

I shook my head.

"Is that a no, I can't, or no, you're not sure?"

"I'm sure. You can't." I took a deep breath. "I just wish I could forget it ever happened. Not that anything actually *happened*," I added hurriedly. "Anyway, how come you've been let off nappy duty to come here?"

"Linny's mother is staying. I'm a total spare part. Worse than. Not even fit for purpose, from the way *she* looks at me. You know she never wanted Linny to marry me. Wanted her to get back together with the theology student. Think she fancied being mother-in-law to a bishop someday. Being able to mention casually to her friends that she'd be visiting the palace, that sort of thing. And she's desperately fond of purple. Ghastly colour. Makes her look like an alcoholic; though, between you and me, she's always been fond of a glass or six. So I skipped out, said I'd come over and ask you to be godfather to the sprog. I *did* ask you to be godfather, didn't I?" I nodded. "Good. Expecting a delivery, are you? Only there's a chappie in a motorcycle helmet coming to the door."

I twisted around to look out of the window. Oh God. It was Sean. I hadn't even heard the bike. Should I ask him in to meet Fordy? Well, quite clearly I *should*. But what if Fordy said something about me leaving Potter's Field? Or, to be blunt, put his foot in it some other way? Fordy *meant* well, but he had an unfortunate way of making Prince Philip look positively tactful.

Sean's knock sounded loud and clear while I was still debating furiously with myself. "I, um. I'd better answer that."

"Unless it's likely to be a summons. They have to deliver those into your hands or the whole thing's invalid. Less use than a bicycle in an arse-kicking contest." He frowned. "Or do I mean a fish? Anyway, I could tell him you're out, if you like."

"No—it's not a summons. It's, well. It's someone I know." Avoiding Fordy's eye, I hastened to the front door.

Sean had taken off his helmet by the time I opened it. "Hi," he said, with a hesitant smile. "You all right?"

"I— Fine. I, er, wasn't expecting you." I hung on tight to the door handle with one hand and the frame with the other.

"Yeah, well, thought I'd just drop by. See if you were around." He glanced at his feet. "Wanted to apologise for last night. Think I was a bit, well, you know. Might have overreacted a bit."

"Oh—no, that's fine." I smiled at him, but it felt forced, and Sean was giving me an odd look. I abandoned the attempt.

"How's the head?" he asked.

"The Head?" I queried, confused.

"Yeah. You said you had a headache last night." Sean was frowning now.

"Oh—yes, of course. Much better, thank you." Damn it. Why hadn't I remembered that?

"So are you going to let me come in?"

"I . . . Well, I was just about to go out, actually," I improvised hastily, my stomach tying itself in knots. The weather forecast had said it would be mild today, but there was a definite chill in the air on my doorstep. "Maybe we could get together later? Tomorrow, even?"

"Right. Guess we'll have to. If you're busy now."

"Yes. Sorry. Really do have to dash, I'm af—" I stopped abruptly. Sean's expression had changed. The knots tightened as I realised he was looking over my shoulder.

To my utmost horror, Fordy clapped me on the back. "All right here, Ems? Thought I'd better come and see what was keeping you. This fellow giving you any trouble? Told you, you should let me answer the door." His voice turned brisk, obviously directed at Sean. "Well, what is it? What seems to be the problem?"

Sean's eyes narrowed. I suddenly had a horrible insight into how Fordy must come across to people who didn't know him. With his plummy vowels and self-important manner, he probably sounded like a member of the House of Lords addressing a tradesman. Worse—a member of the House of Lords upbraiding a tradesman for the shoddiness of his service. And most likely calling him a pleb, to boot.

"There's no problem," I said quickly, half turning to him. "Fordy, this is Sean Grant. My... friend, here." I knew Fordy would understand what I meant. "Sean, this is Malcolm Fordham. We were at school together."

"Right," Sean said slowly, his expression not softening. "Fordy, right? Yeah, you mentioned him."

Oh God. I'd told him we'd slept together, hadn't I?

"Delighted to meet you," Fordy said, shouldering me out of the way as he thrust a hand towards Sean. "You're the rat man, yes? Hah, sounds like something from a comic book. Can't stand the things myself. Rats, not comic books. Not particularly into those either, to be honest, but given the choice, I'd take them over vermin any day."

Sean had looked at Fordy's hand, given it a brief shake, and dropped it. I could feel the weight of his gaze on me. "Fordy just popped round," I explained. "Didn't even phone to say he was coming." Which, of course, Sean hadn't done either. Would he think I was criticising him?

"Right. So where are you two off to, then?"

"Off to?" Fordy asked in a baffled tone. "Are we going somewhere, Emsy? You didn't mention you were taking me anywhere. Not that I mind, of course not. You know me. Always happy to be taken up the garden path."

Oh God. I'd told Sean I was going out, hadn't I? "Er..."

"Yeah, well, never mind," Sean cut me off, his voice hard. Brittle. "You can tell me all about it some other time. Or not. Wouldn't want to keep you, anyhow." He jammed his helmet back on his head and stalked back to his bike, swung his leg over it, and roared off up the high street at significantly more than twenty miles an hour.

CHAPTER TWENTY-ONE

My heart was heavy as I closed the door behind Sean.

"Oops," Fordy said behind me. "Trouble in paradise?"

"*Fordy.*" I spun to face him, about to tell him in no uncertain words to *shut up*, but the worried frown on his face forestalled me. I sighed. "He knows about us."

"Us?"

"You know. That we were . . . *friends* at school." I sank down to sit on the stairs.

"Well, for goodness sake, Ems. You were at boarding school. He can't have expected you to emerge *virgo intacta* after all those years. Or should that be *intacto*? Funny, that, isn't it? All those years having Latin crammed into the old brain with a metaphorical sledgehammer—wouldn't have put it past old Pickles to use a *real* sledgehammer, mind, if he'd thought he could get away with it—and the one time I actually need it, I'm clueless. Of course, I was pretty much clueless all through school, come to that. God knows why you ever put up with me, I'm a hopeless case, really." As usual, Fordy beamed as if proud of that fact. I'd always used to find it rather endearing. "Anyway, he can't seriously believe we're still carrying on. Can he?"

"I don't know, damn it." *Had* Sean jumped to the conclusion I was cheating on him? That would be ridiculous, surely. He had no evidence whatso—

Oh. Apart, that was, from the way he'd caught me lying to him about why I didn't want him coming in the house. Oh God. I jumped up. "I need to talk to him. Explain." I grabbed for my Barbour and started looking around for my car keys.

"Whoa, there, Ems. *Ems.* Hold the horsepower." Fordy was making *calm down* gestures—at least, I guessed that was his intention. It came across more like someone trying to bat away a particularly dozy fly. "If you go haring after him now, guns blazing, headlights, well, blazing, isn't it going to look rather like a guilty conscience? Linny explained all this to me. Said coming home late from work and starting the conversation with, "I'm not squiffy, darling," just screams out *drunk as a lord* to a woman who's in the know. Not that your rat man is a woman. Didn't mean to imply that at all."

"I wish you'd stop calling him my rat man," I muttered. I leaned against the wall and massaged my temples. "You really think I should wait?"

A large, heavy hand landed on my shoulder. "Absolutely. Trust me, Emsy. I'm a banker."

Manfully, I resisted the urge to weep.

I took Fordy for a brief tootle around the villages in Portia and then for lunch in a pub we'd spotted en route, but it was just a quick sandwich and soft drink. Fordy kept looking at his Rolex, and I had a feeling that guilt over abandoning the family had set in.

After we'd hugged and I'd waved him off in his Audi (which I'd been mortified, earlier, to find he'd parked right outside the lych-gate of St. Saviour's, meaning the driver of a hearse had had to double-park when he'd arrived for a funeral), I slumped, depressed, onto the sofa. Fordy had spent the last couple of hours trying to cheer me up, but he'd been visibly struggling to find positive things to say about my local area, careers in primary education, and young men who worked in pest control, with the net result that I was now wondering if I'd made a ghastly mistake moving here.

"Are you sure it's really you?" he'd asked seriously. "It's not just some kind of rebound thing?"

Well, that had been the gist of it. There had been a lot more words involved when Fordy had said it, of course.

Was he right? While he didn't know the whole story, Fordy did know Crispin had let me down somehow. Perhaps Sean was simply a reaction to the breakup—someone very different, and, not to put too fine a point on it, someone to whom I could, in some ways, feel superior? To make up for all the ways in which I wasn't fit to . . . to bait one of his mousetraps?

He was probably better off without me.

And as for the job—I'd *thought* I'd been enjoying teaching younger children, relishing their fresh, imaginative outlook and spirit of fun, but had I simply been glad of the relative lack of pressure of a much lower-flying career?

The sick knot in my stomach tightened. I closed my eyes in despair.

Then I opened them again. "Oh, bloody hell," I said out loud. "Emsy, stop wallowing in the sodding misery mire. Time for a run."

I didn't precisely leap off the sofa and into my running gear with a single bound, but I managed to shake off the sloth well enough to get out and about while it was still light.

It had been a mild day, but there was a cold snap in the air, and my breath steamed as I jogged down the familiar road to the park. There were few people around, making it easy to avoid the gaze of anyone I knew. I upped the pace and sprinted down to the river, where I slowed once more.

The rabbits were chomping in the fields, the sky was streaked a lazy orange, and there were little rustles in the hedgerows that betrayed the presence of furred and feathered companions on my run. The air was almost painfully fresh with a hint of coming frosts. It was a beautiful late-autumn afternoon. And I was being an idiot.

Filled with sudden resolve, and despite the fact I'd only been out for fifteen minutes, I turned my steps back towards the Old Hatter's Cottage.

Should I change? I wondered as I approached my front door. But if I changed, I'd have to shower, which would take far too long. And Sean had said he liked me in my running gear, hadn't he? I gathered my car keys from the house, whispered a heartfelt apology to Portia for inflicting my unwashed self upon her pristine white leather interior, and set off up to Sean's. It really wasn't all that far, up the hill and nearly at the farthest expanse of the village in that direction, which was probably just as well for the avoidance of second thoughts.

I had a moment's doubt when I reached the house he shared with his sister, fearing Sean might be out, but the motorbike was parked outside, so he couldn't be too far away. I pulled into a space a little way down the road, between a once-white van and a Robin Reliant three-wheeler I could only assume was an ironic statement of some kind. I breathed a silent prayer that they'd look after my girl and went to knock on Sean's door.

Debs opened the door, a plain red scarf on her head and an incredulous look on her face. "Bloody hell, trying to blend in with the natives, are you?"

I blinked, then recalled I was still in my long-sleeved T-shirt and jogging bottoms. "I've been for a run," I explained. "Is Sean in?"

"He's in." Her tone was flat. "I'll go and see if he wants to talk to you."

I swallowed, a little of my optimistic buzz dissipating in the chilly twilight air. As she hadn't invited me in, I scuffed my trainers on the doormat while I waited.

Sean's face, when he came to the door, was wary. "Yeah?"

"I'm sorry," I said. "I was an idiot. I was so worried you'd get the wrong impression earlier that I, well, I think I gave you *entirely* the wrong impression."

"Yeah? So I was wrong about you not wanting your posh mates to know about me?"

"What? That's ridiculous! Um. Sorry. It's just . . ." I couldn't believe he'd thought that. "Absolutely not. Really. I mean, I'd already told Fordy all about you, anyway. Um. Sorry about him, by the way. I mean, when you get to know him, you'll love him. Really. It's just he has a bit of a tendency to talk without really thinking about how he comes across."

There was the merest suspicion of a lightening of Sean's frown. "So why'd you make up all those excuses to stop me coming in and meeting him?"

"Because I'm an idiot? I, well, I was worried you'd think there was something going on between us. Fordy and me. Because I told you we'd been, ah, close before." I felt a little uncomfortable, because it wasn't *completely* the truth, but it was true enough, wasn't it? I *had* worried he'd thought that.

"So how come you told him I was just a friend?"

I frowned. "I didn't."

"Yeah, you did. You said, and I quote, I was your 'friend' here."

"No, I didn't." Here, at least, I was on firm ground. "I said you were my *friend* here."

"That's what I just said."

"No, it— Oh. Um. Yes, I can see why you might think that. I was using *friend* euphemistically. There was absolutely no intent to deceive. Honestly. Fordy knew exactly what I meant. He could hardly *not* know, given how much I was droning on about you."

"You were droning on about me, were you?" There was a definite lessening of hostilities coming from Sean's direction now. One might even go so far as to call it an armistice.

"Incessantly," I assured him. "Well, when I could get a word in edgewise. You know what Fordy's like. Well, you don't, but you will. If you want to," I amended hurriedly. "I mean, a certain amount of him is probably going to be unavoidable, as his parents and mine are friends, but he's very easily distractible if he starts becoming a bore."

Sean's smile bloomed like a poppy upon Flanders Fields, only with far fewer sombre connotations. "So did you run up here after he'd gone, then?"

"No, no. I came in Portia." I beamed back at him, glad to find the subject was apparently closed.

Sean's mouth quirked. "You've got a Porsche?" He didn't pronounce the final *e*. "Might have guessed."

"No, *Portia*. It's her name. I forgot you hadn't met her yet. Come on out and I'll introduce you."

Sean looked down at his feet, which I noticed for the first time were clad in alarmingly large, furry slippers. With claws attached. I raised an eyebrow.

"Present from Wills and Harry. Don't even *think* about saying anything, yeah?"

"My mind is a perfect blank," I assured him.

Sean gave me a teasing smile, then ducked out of sight, returning moments later in a pair of trainers. "Come on, then. Show me your girlfriend."

"Fiancée, actually. She's an old-fashioned girl."

"Wouldn't let you in her before you put a ring on it?" We rounded the hedge, and Sean laughed out loud. "You weren't joking, were you? She's beautiful. Nissan Figaro, right?"

I nodded, smiling at Portia, pretty as a picture under the streetlamp with her retro sixties lines, pale-aqua paint, and retractable white top. "She was a twenty-first birthday present from my stepfather. It was love at first sight."

Sean shook his head. "Right, that's it. I'm out of here. No way can I compete with a girl like that."

"Oh, I, er, think she might be persuaded to share her affections." I was glad of the gathering darkness; my face felt like it was on fire. I tried to push away all unfortunate thoughts of threesomes.

"Yeah, but it's your affections I'm worried about."

"You really don't need to be," I said softly. Sean looked at me, his face in shadow but his hair ablaze in the glow of the streetlamp, and for a moment I thought he was going to kiss me, right there in the street. In the middle of a council estate. My heart stood still while my thoughts raced—was it safe? was it even *sane?*—and then the moment passed. "You should come for a drive," I blurted out.

"Yeah, all right." He laughed. "Although I feel a bit underdressed."

"*You're* underdressed? Look at me, for heaven's sake." I gestured down at my running gear. Sean might only be in jeans and a sweatshirt, but he scored over me in not having mud splatters on his trainers, not to mention the cuffs of his trousers.

"Don't worry. I have been," Sean said in a low voice that reverberated through my libido.

I suddenly remembered just how little jogging bottoms tended to conceal. "Drive?" I said hurriedly, opening Portia's passenger door for Sean. "Or do you need to tell your sister first?"

"Nah, I'm a big boy. She won't send the tracker dogs out. Least, not as long as you have me back in time for tea." He hopped into the seat, and I rounded Portia and joined him. "So where are you taking me?" he asked as I buckled my seat belt.

"Haven't the foggiest," I admitted. "Over towards the Ayots?" The Ayots were a cluster of small villages with a common name: Ayot St. Peter, Ayot St. Lawrence, and Ayot Green. The last was presumably not important enough to warrant a church of its own and therefore would more properly be known as a hamlet, not that anyone ever actually used the word these days. "I keep meaning to pop in on George Bernard Shaw's house."

"You'd be better off doing that while it's open, then. Most of these National Trust properties close at dusk."

"You've been there? To Shaw's Corner?"

"Yeah, back in the summer. They had one of these activity days for the kids, and I took Wills and Harry along." He grinned. "They had a go at hoop-rolling. Don't think they were too impressed with the nineteenth-century alternative to the Xbox."

"No, I don't suppose many modern children would be. Actually, that's unfair; I very much doubt I'd have been too excited about hoops at that age either."

"God, I can just imagine you as a kid. I bet you dressed like something out of the nineteen fifties, in shorts and a sleeveless sweater. And never, ever swore."

"I refuse to answer on the grounds I may incriminate myself. Anyway, are you telling me you *didn't* wear shorts as a boy?"

"Two words: freckly knees."

"Ah. Yes, I can see that would be something of a disincentive. But what about nowadays?" I gave him a sidelong look. "Do you go to the beach in a burkini?"

"*Nowadays*, I've discovered sunblock, thank you very much."

There was a short silence while I negotiated a particularly narrow part of the lane, having to stop a couple of times to allow other vehicles to pass.

"So this Fordy bloke, he's a good mate of yours?" Sean asked when we'd reached a wider stretch, his tone mild and curious rather than condemnatory, thank the Lord.

"Absolutely. We've been friends since the term I started at Loriners." I hesitated. "It was midway through the year, which didn't help, and some of the other boys were a little . . . disparaging about the fact that I only had a place at the school due to Mother's job there. Fordy never cared a jot about that."

"Bad, was it?"

I darted a glance at Sean and was unnerved to find a deep frown on his face. I shrugged. "These things happen," I said vaguely. The last thing I wanted to do right now was to go into a detailed list of all the many ways certain of my schoolmates had done their level best to make my life a living hell. "And once we were friends, the worst of it stopped—well, you saw Fordy. He's filled out a little since he was thirteen, but only a *very* little. And he was always good at rugger, which helped immensely, of course."

"That was before your mum got married again, right? The other lads looking down on you, I mean."

"Before and after, really. Mother stopped working when she married Peter, but it was a bit too late to matter by then. They met at Loriners', by the way," I added, glad to get onto a more cheerful topic.

"Yeah?"

"Mm. On Speech Day. Peter's eldest grandson had just started there, you see, and he won the prize for physics the year I won the prize for maths. They got talking over sherry afterwards, widower to widow, and the rest, as they say, is history."

Sean nodded. "What about your mate Fordy? Did he win the prize for anything?"

"Trampling the opposition into the dirt on the rugby field, mostly."

"Yeah, I can imagine that. You ever play rugby? 'Cause I've gotta say, I can't picture it."

I shuddered. "*Everybody* played rugby at Loriners'. But cricket was more my game. I was in the first eleven, my final year," I added with some pride. I hadn't thought I stood a chance of getting in, but Fordy had badgered me to try out for it. Then got me hideously drunk on illicit gin after I'd been selected, but the less remembered about that, the better.

"You've got to get onto the village team, then. I could come and watch you play in the summer, bring a picnic, that sort of stuff."

"Sounds good." It sounded idyllic, actually. Even as I pictured sunny days together, my heart clenched at the thought of Sean so casually planning so far ahead. Would we still be together then? I'd be an idiot to build my hopes up. Once bitten, as they say . . . I *was* being an idiot. It was just one of those things people said. It didn't mean anything. I needed to remember the literal definition of *Utopia* was *nowhere*.

"I'd better get you back to your sister's," I said. A weight seemed to have descended upon me.

Sean glanced at his watch. "Shit, yeah. Listen, I'd ask you in to have tea with us, but I don't reckon it'd go down all that well. Debs won't have cooked enough for five. And I'm going to be out with some mates later—it's Chris's birthday, so I don't like to cancel, you know?"

"Chris?" I queried, my voice coming out more sharply than I'd intended. "Another ex?"

"Just cos I'm bi, it doesn't mean I go out with everyone I meet, you know." Sean's tone was mild, but I could sense an underlying exasperation. "We're capable of making friends, you know. Just like normal people really."

I winced. "I was only asking. Sorry."

"'S okay. I'm used to it. And no, he's not an ex. He's a bit of a lager lout, Chris is, which you may have noticed isn't really my type."

"Definitely not," I agreed with a smile, my heart significantly lighter.

CHAPTER TWENTY-TWO

Things settled down after that.

Sean and I spent most of our weekends together, which meant my weekday evenings were largely taken up with marking and lesson planning, sometimes in Rose's company and sometimes not. I got to see a lot more of the local countryside, quite a bit of it from the pillion of Sean's motorbike.

Rose treated my conversion to enthusiastic biker with hilarity, particularly when she challenged me to tell her what model Sean rode and I had to confess I hadn't even noticed what make it was. It was a Honda, I informed her stiffly the next time I saw her, and had to endure her cackles once again.

Remembrance Sunday came and went, with its solemn procession through the village of all the local guides, scouts, Cubs, and Brownies, and a surprising number of village elderly wearing medals, their backs for once straight and proud. Towards the end of November, there was the grand turning on of the village Christmas lights, an evening event with carol singing and fairground rides for the smallest of the children. As I sipped my mulled wine, I realised I was beginning to finally feel part of village life.

There was still the nagging fear over what Fordy had told me—but if any students had asked Mother for my address, they hadn't made any noticeable use of it. Which argued strongly in favour of it *not* having been Oliver who'd asked, I thought. I *did* broach the subject on the telephone with Mother, but she was able to tell me frustratingly little. Her description of a half-remembered young man could have fitted Oliver but equally could have applied to around two-thirds of the boys I'd taught. He hadn't, she said, impressed her as particularly good-looking, but then Mother and I had always had very different opinions about men.

With the arrival of Advent came the arrival of the St. Saviour's School Christmas tree. This was a monstrous thing, sourced by old Arfur Minnit from who knew where—certainly, most of the staff seemed to agree it was better not to ask. I had visions of him chopping down some ancient sentry to one of the grand homes in the more well-to-do part of the area and hauling it away cackling. "Like a Krampus," I mused aloud, as we waited for the other classes to finish filing into the hall for whole school assembly.

"What's a Grampuss?" Destinee demanded. She'd taken to shadowing me closely this half-term, and her behaviour had improved markedly as a result, apart from the odd initial scuffle with Charlie. Eventually they'd seemed to come to a tacit agreement that while he was, and always would be, my right-hand man, she was now very definitely my left-hand young lady. I had an uneasy suspicion that following the altercation at the school gates, Mrs. Nunn had charged her daughter with acting as a sort of protection detail.

"The Krampus, young Destinee, is a sort of Alpine anti-Santa. You know how your mother warned you if you didn't behave yourself, you'd only get coal in your stocking at Christmas?"

"*No,*" she said scornfully. "I'm getting a new phone for Christmas. And a TV in my room."

"I'm getting some fairy wings!" Charlie put in excitedly. Then his little face fell. "But I'm not s'posed to tell anyone."

"Never fear," I said soothingly. "Your secret is safe with us—isn't it, Destinee?"

"S'pose," she muttered with a huff and a pout. Then she turned on Charlie with a mercenary glint in her eye. "*If* you let me play with them."

Charlie nodded enthusiastically, bless him.

"Anyway," I continued. "Back to the Krampus. When *I* was your age, coal was customarily threatened if I wasn't a good boy. But children in the Alps—that's Austria, Switzerland, and southern Germany, mainly—are warned about the Krampus. He's a rather hairy sort of chap, with horns and hooves like a goat, and if you're a bad little boy or girl, he'll take you away in his sack."

Destinee's little eyes narrowed. "Why don't they get the police on him? That's illegal, and they put you on a register."

"Is that like our class register?" Charlie frowned, clearly puzzled.

"No, stu—" Destinee caught my eye and amended what she'd been about to say. "It's a special register for bad men and pee-dohs."

It wasn't the first time I'd found the extent of Destinee's knowledge and vocabulary somewhat alarming. "Has your mother explained what a, ah, *pee-doh* is?" I asked cautiously.

She nodded confidently. "They offer you sweeties in the park and ask you if you want to see their kittens, but they haven't really got any. You have to shout *no* really loud, and if they don't go away, you have to kick them in the balls and run back home."

Charlie's eyes were like saucers, and he edged towards Destinee as if for protection. "Is that true?" he whispered.

"It's a, ah, reasonable summation," I said. "Although I'd prefer to emphasise the running-home solution rather than escalating to violence." Perhaps I should check the school's current teaching on Stranger Danger and suggest some reinforcement. "Now, shush, assembly's about to start."

Assembly, led by the Head, consisted of announcements, a brief and pointed prayer about remembering people less well-off at Christmas, and the singing of a couple of traditional English carols such as "Rudolph the Red-Nosed Reindeer" and "When Santa Got Stuck up the Chimney." As I'd only just begun teaching them to the little darlings, neither was exactly a bravura performance. I found my piano playing becoming louder and louder as the piping voices faltered and faded. Thank God there were still a couple of weeks to go until the carol service.

One announcement which was particularly well received was the apparently traditional invitation to each child to bring a Christmas-tree ornament from home to bedeck our magnificent Christmas tree—here, the children were invited to applaud Mr. Minnit's efforts in supplying such a specimen, and he bowed graciously.

Less well received—by me, at least—was the news that all ornaments should be given to Mr. Emeny, who, as the tallest person on staff, would be responsible for hanging them up. The fact that the wretched tree was at least twice as tall as I was, and decorating it would therefore involve a stepladder no matter who did it, didn't appear to register.

I'd hoped to have at least a day to prepare myself for the task, but straight after assembly, the Head confronted me with an emphatic hope that the children's singing would improve in the coming weeks. While I was still on the defensive from that, she directed me to go to Mrs. Ormley's office after dismissing my class for the day, where, apparently, I would find tinsel, lights, and the ornament for the top of the tree. Lucky me.

Mr. Minnit, helpful as ever, offered to "gerra ladder" for me. There was, it seemed, no escape.

It wasn't, I thought half an hour later as I gingerly scaled the promised stepladder, that I had a particular problem with heights. Flying held no terrors for me; neither did cliff tops or tall buildings. I'd even been known to scale a tree or two in my time. It was just something about ladders, specifically, that unnerved me. Perhaps I'd watched too many black-and-white comedy films with Peter, which often featured the wretched things collapsing under their hapless users. Or maybe it was just a balance thing. Whatever the reason, I was not enjoying my ascension to the dizzying heights of the school hall, burdened with an angel that had frankly seen better days. Not that anyone would be able to see, once it was in position, just how tarnished his (or possibly her; the figure was defiantly androgynous) halo was, nor that various limbs had been snapped off and inexpertly glued back on.

I stood staring at the top of the tree, and wondering how on earth I was supposed to get the angel to stay there. From the state of the thing, I suspected this dilemma was not a new one.

"Ooh, look, Evie," I heard Rose's voice from far, far below, "our tree's got a fairy on top."

I glared down at her, then wished I hadn't as vertigo assailed me and my intended retort dried up in my throat.

"No, miss," the girl with her said seriously. "It's an angel. You can tell cos they wear longer dresses. And they got haloes instead of wands."

Rose cackled. "Oops, sorry. My mistake. You all right up there, Mr. Emeny? Looking a bit wobbly on that ladder."

"I'm perfectly fine, thank you," I told the tree. "Just need to get on with it."

"You sure? Wouldn't want you coming down the quick way."

"I'll be fine," I reiterated through gritted teeth, and concentrated on getting the wretched angel to stay where I put it. For something with wings, it was showing a marked affinity for plummeting to the floor.

Another thought I *really* wished I hadn't had.

Rose didn't speak again, and must have left the hall. I could faintly hear the voice from before asking with apparent relish, "If Mr. Enemy fell off the ladder, would he die?" and then there was silence. I breathed a sigh of relief and willed my legs not to tremble.

I nearly fell off the ladder when a gruffer voice asked, "Yer want me to take over?"

God, I was tempted. "No, thank you, Mr. Minnit. I'm sure I'll manage," I said firmly. I was *not* going to be beaten by a bloody Christmas tree. My pride simply couldn't stand it. "You go on home to . . . er, *Is* there a Mrs. Minnit?"

"Suit yerself," he said and clomped off without enlightening me as to his marital status, leaving me ample solitude to reflect on the literalness or otherwise of the old saying *pride comes before a fall.*

Having finally got the angel to stay where it was put, I had to wrap an industrial-length string of lights around the tree—fortunately, they were modern LEDs rather than actual lightbulbs, but it still took forever to get a uniform effect—and arrange fourteen garishly coloured tinsel garlands in artistic fashion. By the time I'd finished, my arms were ready to fall off my shoulders. I climbed off the hated ladder for the last time with a sigh of heartfelt relief.

"Bloody 'ell, you still 'ere?"

I turned wearily to see Mr. Minnit. "Yes, but I'm all finished now. What do you think?"

He stared at the tree for a long moment. Then he shrugged. "It's a tree. You going to eff off so I can lock up proper, then? I only come back in 'ere cos I saw the lights was still on. Thort someone was robbin' the ICT suite."

"Ah. Sorry to, er . . ." Mr. Minnit tapped his watch. I gave him a weak smile. "I'll be, ah, effing off, then."

He nodded, and I left.

Or, indeed, effed.

CHAPTER TWENTY-THREE

I didn't know who I was expecting, when there was a knock on the door early on Advent Sunday morning. Hanne, perhaps. Or the Jehovah's Witnesses. Beside me in bed, Sean mumbled something incomprehensible. I didn't want to move from the warm circle of his arms.

"They'll probably go away if we ignore them," I muttered sleepily into his largely unresponsive hair.

The knock sounded again, louder this time. I heaved a put-upon sigh and hauled myself out of bed, just in case it proved to be important. Sean mumbled again as I slipped from his grasp. Or possibly snored. I ran down the stairs, hoping whoever it was wouldn't be too scandalised by my bare legs sticking out from the bottom of my hastily flung-on dressing gown.

I fumbled with the key and opened the door.

It was Oliver.

An ice-cold bolt of lightning shot through me, freezing every vein in my body. Oliver stood on the doormat in jeans and a heavy peacoat, his light-brown hair blowing in the breeze. There was a hint of stubble on his jaw. Had he grown taller since I'd last seen him? I couldn't be sure. At any rate, his gaze met mine squarely. "Can I come in?"

I struggled to form words. "I— No— What are you doing here?"

He shrugged. "Your mum told me your address."

I should have known. "Yes, but what are you *doing* here? Oliver, for God's sake. After what— After you—"

"I'm sorry, all right?" He stared at his feet. "Didn't mean to make you lose your job."

"Didn't mean . . .? Oliver, *you went to the headmaster*. You told him I'd . . . Oh God." I wanted desperately to sit down, to not be clad only in a dressing gown, to wake up out of this nightmare. "Oh God," I said again. "We can't—not out here. You'd better come in."

I stood back and let him enter my house, fighting the urge to run. Sean was still asleep upstairs. Please, God, let him still be asleep.

Oliver walked straight in, his shoes leaving damp marks on the hall tiles. It must have been raining outside, I realised, and yes, his coat was wet.

"I never thought he'd believe me, all right? I was just— Sod it, you know. The scholarship boy. I never thought he'd believe me over you."

"Why the bloody hell did you do it, then?" Were we speaking too loud? "Come into the living room," I urged him in a lower voice and shut the door behind us.

Oliver sat on the sofa without invitation, his long legs taking up more space than I remembered. "I was mad at you, okay? You never took me seriously. Just wanted to show you . . ." His face twisted. "You were never supposed to lose your job over it."

"Never supposed . . . Oliver, for God's sake, what did you think the headmaster was going to do in the face of allegations of that nature? He couldn't just ignore them, could he?"

"Yeah, but it wasn't like there was any proof or anything. Couldn't have been, could there? Just my word against yours. I didn't think he'd believe me, okay?"

"And that's why you came here? To apologise?"

"Yeah." He bit his lip. "And— Shit." He stood up, and I followed suit automatically.

"What?" I prompted when he remained silent. I tried to keep my impatience out of my voice, but I just wanted him to *go*.

Oliver took a deep breath. "I'm eighteen now. Not at school anymore."

"I know," I said. At least, I'd assumed, barring resits, he'd have left by now. "You're at uni?"

"Yeah. Got into Cambridge."

"Congratulations," I said with as much warmth as I could muster. "You're enjoying it?"

"'S okay. They're all a bit posh at my college." He gazed down at his feet, then lifted his eyes to stare at me with disconcerting intensity. "Got holidays in a few weeks. I thought we could, well, you know. Be together."

Apparently there was something colder than ice, and it was running through my veins right now. Then abruptly it boiled. "You thought *what*? You honestly thought we could just *get together* as if nothing had happened? As if you'd never lied about me, lost me my *job*, my boyfriend . . ." I was hot and shaking, and my throat hurt.

And then the door to the living room opened, and Sean stepped through. "Heard shouting," was all he said, as his gaze took in Oliver, and me, still in my dressing gown.

"Who the fuck's this, then?" Oliver demanded. He took a step forward. So did Sean. I realised Oliver was the taller of the two, although admittedly he had shoes on. Sean's bare feet peeped out from the bottom of his jeans. He'd pulled on a T-shirt as well but still looked vulnerable next to Oliver's peacoat-clad bulk.

I had to say something, anything, to defuse the tension. "This is Sean. My fr—my boyfriend." I swallowed. "Oliver is . . . Oliver is someone I used to know at Potter's Field. He just came round to . . . to see how I was doing, but he can't stay." I took hold of Oliver's arm and urged him towards the door. "You have to go," I whispered urgently. "Please, for God's sake, just *go*."

Oliver didn't resist, thank God. Blinking rapidly, he looked almost as if he were about to cry as I hurried him to the front door. "I'm sorry," I found myself saying. "But we can't . . . Not ever. I've got a life here now. I'm sorry."

He nodded and was gone.

When I turned from closing the door, Sean was standing in the hallway, his arms folded. "Seemed like a bit more than just coming over to see how you were," he said.

I forced a smile. "No, no. He's just a bit . . . volatile, that's all."

"Funny, that. Seeing as it was you I heard shouting. Something about losing your job, was it?"

Oh God. "No, no, I think you must have misheard. Thick walls, these old houses." I couldn't tell him the truth. I couldn't face it. Not with Sean—watching his face as the wheels turned in his head, and he wondered how far he believed me and what it might do to his own reputation. Running through my head over and over, its rhythm tolling a death march, was probably the most hateful phrase in the entire English language: *no smoke without fire*. I couldn't cope with it. Not again.

I could call Oliver back, I thought feverishly. Get him to explain... But would he? He'd lied to the headmaster at Potter's Field. Maybe he'd lie to Sean. Maybe he'd *want* Sean to split up with me.

"It's nothing," I said again. "Really. Maybe you, um, misheard? We were just talking about, um, old times."

Sean said nothing for a long, long moment.

I thought it was going to be okay. After all, it wasn't the first time he'd, well, seen or heard something that appeared to put me in a less than flattering light. He'd always been so understanding. So ready to forgive. Surely this time would be no different? He'd accept my explanation, and we'd be fine.

Wouldn't we?

There was a lump in my throat that was making it hard to swallow, and I found my fingers crossing themselves furtively without even a by-your-leave.

Then Sean spoke, his tone bleak. "You know what my last memory of my dad is? Him telling me and Debs we've got to lie to our mum so she won't find out he's having an affair."

"But I'm not having—"

He held up a hand. "Never said you were. I told him I wasn't going to lie for him, and he gave me a clip round the ear. Still didn't do it. I didn't like lies when I was a kid, and I don't like them now."

"I'm not lying..." I couldn't continue. Because I *was* lying to him, wasn't I? If not precisely by commission, then certainly by omission.

My silence, I suppose, was as good as a confession. Sean's face closed off, his eyes hard. He jammed his bare feet into his trainers and grabbed his jacket from the banister.

"I don't think this is gonna work." His voice was jagged, and so quiet I could barely hear it. "I'd better go. See you around."

And then he was gone, and the chill of the hall tiles seeped up through my bare feet into my very bones.

After Sean left me, I did the only thing that made any sense. I went back to bed, dressing gown and all, and pulled the duvet over my head. Surrounded by his scent, cocooned in warmth, I could almost believe it hadn't happened. That he'd just slipped out of bed to make a cup of tea and would be back with me any minute.

Only the raw, searing wound in my chest called me a liar.

I wallowed in self-pity rather longer than was probably healthy, but eventually even I had to admit I'd be better off getting up. My head was throbbing with a fierce ache, and my empty stomach rumbled queasily. I stumbled out of bed, burnt myself some toast, and ate it all as a kind of penance. I was almost disappointed to find I actually felt a little better once I'd choked it down.

I still felt in need of a shoulder to cry on, so I called Rose. She came bearing a half-eaten box of Quality Street, a tub of homemade pasta salad, and her own particular brand of sympathy.

"Robert, you moron. What the bloody hell were you even thinking?"

Rose's sympathy tended markedly towards tough love. "I'm not sure I *was* thinking," I muttered, cuddling a cushion and picking through the brightly wrapped sweets. All the purple ones had gone, which was my life in a nutshell.

"Yeah, you got that right. Telling Sean it was *nothing*. Like he was ever going to believe that!"

"I suppose you'd have come up with a perfectly plausible story on the spot." Sod it. I was having a toffee, fillings be damned. I unwrapped it, popped it in my mouth, and chucked the gold paper over my shoulder like a pinch of spilt salt, uncaring where it might land. Perhaps I'd just let my house fill up with rubbish, like one of those people they showed documentaries about on Channel Four. Invite in the rats and the cockroaches. After all, it wasn't like Sean would ever come here again to see *me*.

"Or," she said pertly, "and I realise this is a *totally* radical idea, I might have told him the truth."

I stared at her and opened my mouth to speak—only to find my teeth had gummed up. "Damn it," I cursed indistinctly and tried to discreetly dislodge the toffee with my tongue.

"Use your finger, it's only me here," Rose said helpfully.

I glared at her and finally freed my jaw. "I can't tell him the truth."

"Why not?"

"*Why not?*" I stared at her in disbelief. "What if he doesn't believe there was nothing in it? What if he actually thinks I might have been capable of . . . of that?"

"Yeah, but if you look at it this way, he's dumped you already. What have you got to lose?"

"What if he then goes round telling everyone about it? I'd have to leave my job." Again.

I'd miss Charlie, if I had to leave. Damn it, I'd even miss Destinee.

"Sean wouldn't do that. Not without any evidence you'd ever actually done anything. He's not like that."

"Would you risk it, though? He might . . . he might think it's the public-spirited thing to do. To warn everyone about me. And anyway . . . I couldn't bear it. To think that 'he is alive in the world and thinking ill of me.'"

Rose looked up. "Lizzy Bennet in *Pride and Prejudice*. That's what she said. Don't look at me like that. I've got the DVD, you know."

I was too dispirited to point out it was from a book. There was a fair chance Rose knew that anyway and was just trying to cheer me up. Well, fairish.

"So you'd rather stay dumped," Rose continued, "than take a chance he might actually believe you?"

"Why *should* he believe me? He dumped me for lying to him, Rose. Why would he imagine I'd suddenly come over all truthful?"

"Yeah, well, there is that." She sighed. "Maybe you just need to chalk this one up to experience, then. Find yourself someone a bit more trusting."

"A bit more . . . Rose, I *lied* to him." I stood up in my agitation, and Quality Streets cascaded to the floor to lie like scattered fairy lights on the rug. "I tried to keep him from even *meeting* Fordy, and when Oliver came over—the boy who pretty much *destroyed my life* last year—I told Sean it was nothing. *Nothing!*"

I realised I was shouting in her face and backed off a bit. "Sorry."

Rose had her hands held up. "All right, all right. You're a shitface. I get it. So-*rry*. Jeez."

I slumped back onto the sofa, dislodging the last few Quality Streets, and put my head in my hands. "He's better off without me."

"Meh."

I looked up. "*What?*"

"I said, 'Meh.'" Rose leaned forward, her gaze piercing. "Look, I get it, all right, but if you look at it another way, you've known him a couple of months, that's all. What gives him the inalienable sodding right to know all your deepest darkest secrets anyway? If he really cared about you, he'd wait till you were ready to tell him all that stuff, wouldn't he?" She popped a sweetie in her mouth in triumph, I assumed, at a point well-made.

The wrapper she discarded was purple. I narrowed my eyes at her.

Then I sighed and closed my eyes. "It doesn't matter, anyway. Who's right or wrong. He's gone."

"Never mind, eh? Come on, cheer up. Christmas is coming."

"I'm not *five*, Rose."

"Exactly. You're an adult. And what's Christmas when you're an adult?" She looked at me expectantly.

"Do elucidate," I said in my driest tones.

"Nah, I've been trying to give that up. Christmas, you numpty, is the world's best excuse to spend most of the time pissed off your face." She beamed.

Well, there was that, I supposed.

CHAPTER TWENTY-FOUR

On Monday, to put the powdered cyanide icing upon the botulism-laced cake, when I slouched wearily into the St. Saviour's School hall for morning assembly, I was greeted by two hundred and fifty children all thrusting their prized Christmas ornaments into my wholly inadequate hands. I tried to look enthusiastic as I resigned myself to an evening spent up Mr. Minnit's blasted ladder hanging the things.

In fact it only took me an hour and twenty-seven minutes, which meant there was at least some benefit to being too dispirited to care overmuch how the myriad ornaments were arranged, aside, of course, from basic considerations such as size and colour. I was even starting to feel a little cheered by the result of my efforts. Then when I collapsed the ladder, I managed to trap my finger painfully in the process, and as I swore and lost control of the thing, it knocked against the tree, causing the sodding angel to fall off. It nosedived into the branches, where it took me twenty-three blasted minutes to locate it, and a further nine to get it fixed back into position with the aid of half a roll of sticky tape, a fistful of paper clips and a rubber band.

"Let's see you fly out of that one," I muttered grimly to Our Lord's herald.

Then a previously unseen Mr. Minnit yelled up, "Ain't you done yet?" and nearly made me fall off the ladder.

It was a long, weary walk back to the Old Hatter's Cottage. As I passed the Chinese takeaway, I paused, recollected the contents of my fridge (a half-eaten salad, some mouldy cheddar, and a microwave vegetarian tofu thing that had seemed like a good idea at the time) and headed in.

Sean was there. Oh God.

I'd been prepared, at the end of school, to meet him at the classroom door. Not that I had; Debs had arrived to pick up the twins with her face carefully arranged to express her hopes I would die horribly in a fire, to which event she would be pleased to bring a gallon of gasoline.

I wasn't prepared to meet Sean here, when I was tired, hungry, and even more off-balance than I had been at the top of that wretched ladder.

"Oh," I said intelligently.

"Yeah," he replied. He looked . . . he looked even better than I remembered him, although there was tiredness in his eyes. Maybe he'd been busy at work.

Maybe he'd had trouble sleeping last night. Like me.

Maybe . . . maybe he'd had time to have second thoughts?

"I just came to . . ." I waved in the general direction of the Chinese lady at the counter, who was watching us with interest.

"Yeah. Me too." Sean shoved his hands in his pockets.

"Are you, um, eating alone?" I asked. It was almost eight o'clock, and I couldn't imagine Debs making the twins wait that long for their tea.

"Yeah. You?"

"Yes." I took a deep breath and stepped off the metaphorical ladder, adrenaline fizzing through me almost painfully. "Maybe we could, well, share?"

Sean looked away. "Prob'ly not a good idea," he said.

"Oh."

"Order for Grant," the lady interrupted, holding up a plastic carrier bag.

"Cheers," he said and took it. He sort of shrugged in my direction. "I'll see you around, yeah?"

Watching him go was every bit as painful as it had been when he'd walked out on me last night. Worse, even, as this time he took every shred of hope with him.

"You want to order?" the Chinese lady demanded, not unkindly.

I turned back to her. "I—I'm sorry. I'm not hungry anymore."

I fled.

CHAPTER TWENTY-FIVE

Whoever had decided it was appropriate to make the St. Saviour's School end-of-term carol service a candlelit one had, I felt, not been quite right in the head. Or possibly they just didn't like children very much. Two hundred and fifty excited children, each holding a naked flame, were just the sort of thing I thought Health and Safety regulations existed to prevent, but apparently not. Every child in the school had been issued with a six-inch red candle, with a rough-cut disc of cardboard pushed onto the bottom to keep wax from dribbling onto little fingers. And then some idiot had gone around and lit the wretched things.

True, Mrs. Ormley had been stationed at the entrance to the church, forcibly handing out elastic bands to any child with long hair that wasn't tied back, but it was a little like applying a sticking plaster to a severed head.

"It's beautiful, innit?" Rose whispered in my ear. "I love the carol service. Makes you think they're not all that bad, really, the kids. And the church looks lovely, all candlelit."

Et tu, Rose? "Have there been many fatalities over the years?"

She gave me a pitying look. "They're only candles, you know, not flamethrowers. The kids know they've got to be careful."

"They *know* they're supposed to wipe their feet when they come in from outside too, but that doesn't stop the classroom from being knee-deep in mud by lunchtime."

"Stop being an old humbug. Everyone else thinks it's lovely. And it's only an hour. What can go wrong in an hour?"

"You just had to jinx it, didn't you?" I muttered.

"Stop being a worrywart and get up there and strut your stuff, all right? The eyes of the village are upon you. So, you know, no pressure." She grinned.

I was really rather proud of the way the children had shaped up as a choir, over the last couple of weeks. The Head had even been seen to smile at the last rehearsal, or so I'd been told. "All right, wish me luck."

"Break a leg. Or an arm, whatever."

I stepped up to the ranked children and frowned. Wills and Harry had shuffled their way out of class order and into the front row, which did not, I felt, bode well. The fact that they had somehow got hold of a brace of candles apiece boded so far from well that world health authorities should probably start getting concerned.

"Wills, Harry, have you got somebody else's candles?" I asked sternly.

"They gave them to us."

"We're just looking after them."

I frowned, hoping there would be an innocent explanation, such as an urgent toilet break. "Who gave them to you, and why?"

"Destinee and Charlie."

"Charlie's crying."

Oh dear. I looked around quickly and found the two of them sitting on the stone surround of one of the pillars. Charlie was, indeed, in tears.

This was not, in itself, unusual, sad to say. What was slightly more alarming was that Destinee had her arms around him and was glaring fiercely at anyone who dared approach.

"Destinee?" I said cautiously, crouching down to their level. "What's the matter?"

"It was her. Mrs. Ormley."

I blinked. "What on earth did she do?"

"She said I had to tie my hair back." Destinee, ever the rebel, had complied with the spirit if not the letter by scraping her long hair back into what was, for a seven-year-old, a disturbingly sophisticated Essex updo. "Then she gave Charlie a band and said he should too, cos he was just a big girl anyway."

I felt a brief and, given that we were in God's house, wholly inappropriate urge to introduce Mrs. Ormley to the sharp end of my

baton. How *dare* she upset a child like that? I swallowed my rage—
the vicar was starting to cast anxious glances in our direction—and
considered my words.

"Charlie, do you think being a girl is a bad thing? Destinee's a girl,
and she's, ah, really quite a strong character."

Destinee preened.

"But I'm not a girl," Charlie sobbed. "I'm a boy."

"Quite right, young Charlie. And do you know what difference
anything Mrs. Ormley or anyone else might say makes to that?" I
leaned closer. "*Not a thing.* Charlie, I'm sure you've sometimes said
silly things. I know I have. Quite a lot of them, probably. But just
because someone says a silly thing, it doesn't make it true, does it?"

"I told him," Destinee said proudly. "I told him she's a stupid fat
old cow who dun't know nuffing."

I winced but decided now was really not the time to deal with
that seething tangle of issues. "We all think you're a fine young man,
don't we?"

I stared the children down until a halfhearted chorus of "Yes,
Mr. Enemy" ensued.

I handed Charlie my handkerchief. "Come on, you have a good
blow. Er, gently, mind, we don't want any nosebleeds. Now, why
don't you take your candle back from Wills or Harry—no, no, keep
the handkerchief, you can put it in your pocket just in case—and get
back into line, and show everyone what a marvellous singing voice
you've got?"

He nodded bravely, and the twins, thank goodness, handed over
their borrowed booty without complaint.

I looked around. Mrs. Nunn and the tennis coach were taking
their seats—just a few rows away from Sean, not that I'd been looking
out for him, obviously—so it was definitely past time to start. I
nodded to the vicar, and he stepped into the apse with visible relief,
clasped his hands, and welcomed us to the church in ringing tones
that effectively silenced the parental chatter. "And without further
ado," he finished, "I'll hand you over to the St. Saviour's School
musical director, Mr. En—er, Mr. Emeny."

I took a deep breath, planted my reindeer antlers firmly on my
head, affixed my red nose to the appropriate organ, and stepped
forward, baton raised.

The children were magnificent. Their little voices filled the huge church building with a joyful sound, and together with the candlelight, the effect was both reverent and magical. I was sure there couldn't be a dry eye in the house. I was particularly pleased with "It Was on a Starry Night," which had some awkward timing that had puzzled them at first, and they managed to sustain their enthusiasm all the way through the carols, interspersed with readings, to "Calypso Carol." As the last chords died away, there was tumultuous applause. I gave the children an emphatic thumbs-up, then turned and bowed to the congregation. There was a smattering of laughter as most of them noticed my red nose for the first time.

At least, I presumed that was what they were laughing at. I'd checked to make sure my flies weren't undone before the service commenced; that was the sort of mistake one didn't tend to make twice.

The Head was very definitely smiling now. And, I realised with some amazement, not a single person had begun to smoulder. If that wasn't a Christmas miracle, I didn't know what was.

As the vicar said a few words to close the service—including the pointed suggestion that it might be nice to see a few of those assembled at some of the *other* Christmas services this year—I pushed down any thoughts of other Christmas miracles my foolish heart was hoping for.

Rose joined me to help take charge of the children as they filed out of the church, still clutching their candles. Mrs. Ormley stood guard by the door to retrieve her elastic hair bands, though why she wanted them back was beyond me. Did she save them and bring them out again next year? Was that really hygienic?

"Shouldn't she wait until the children have blown their candles out?" I wondered aloud. "And shouldn't they be doing that now, anyway?"

Rose looked at me as if I was a particularly dim reception-class child. "Don't be daft. They look really sweet, going through the churchyard in their little lines, all lit up by candlelight. Sort of like a mini torchlit procession."

"As long as nobody *actually* gets lit up like a torch," I muttered.

"God, you're wasted as a teacher, you know that? You could've had a glittering career in Health and Safety, going around making sure no one plays conkers without protective goggles and a suit of bloody armour. They've been doing this service for fifty years or more, probably even a hundred, and nobody's *ever*— Oh, bloody hell!" Her eyes widened, but my head was already turning at the panicked, matronly scream and the tumult it provoked.

"You just *had* to say it, didn't you?" I cried, scrambling over the pews and one or two startled parents to get to Mrs. Ormley. She was shrieking like a banshee, which was an entirely sane and sensible reaction given that the bottom of her long woollen coat was *on fire*. The children who had been en route to the door pressed back the way they'd come, not so much frightened as ghoulishly fascinated. What with all the excitement, I could foresee the whole lot going up in flames like a box of matches. "Everyone blow out your candles!" I yelled, dropping to my knees at Mrs. Ormley's feet. I tore off my jacket and flung it around her legs, beating out the flames that licked upwards from her coat hem.

A jet of water hit me in the face, and I spluttered and gasped, blinded. Hands helped me to my feet, and I wiped my eyes, dizzy with adrenaline. When I could see again, the first thing to meet my eyes was Rose, brandishing a fire extinguisher like an offensive weapon. I blinked, but the vision remained the same. She made an apologetic sort of face.

The vicar, meanwhile, had managed to make his way to us. He took hold of Mrs. Ormley's arm. "Are you all right? Dear me. Still, accidents will happen."

"Accidents? *Accidents*? They did it on purpose, those little monsters!"

Oh God. Had Destinee taken revenge on Charlie's behalf?

"Are you accusing the children?" Rose said sharply.

"Surely not . . ." The vicar wrung his hands.

Mrs. Ormley might no longer be burning, but she was still seething. Spitting fire looked like it might be on the horizon too. "Children? Little devils, more like. And look at me! This coat is ruined!"

The scorched patch actually looked ridiculously small now the danger had passed, but the soaking hadn't done the heavy garment any favours. I stood, dripping, and thought resentfully that at least she still had several layers to keep her warm. With my jacket on its way to the great jumble sale in the sky, the chill from the ancient stones was seeping into my bones with cheerful alacrity.

"Ah, which children?" the vicar asked *most* unhelpfully.

"Those Curtis twins. Little redheaded tearaways!"

"It wasn't us!"

"We never!"

I looked around and saw the twins were, in fact, suspiciously close to the scene of the crime, wearing identical expressions of outraged innocence. Since I'd seen them wear those expressions before when I'd caught them in the very act of some misdemeanour or other, I wasn't fooled.

"Boys," I said, shaking my head sadly.

"Something ought to be done about those two," Mrs. Ormley ranted on. "If it's not one thing, it's another. They shouldn't even be in a mainstream school, with all their behavioural problems."

"Oi." Sean's voice in my ear startled me, and I spun around to see him standing behind me, his face red.

I pulled myself together. "*Mrs. Ormley*," I said firmly. "I understand you're upset, but please refrain from making judgements about the children's educational needs. You are a receptionist, not a medical professional."

"I've been working in St. Saviour's school a lot longer than you have, young man, so don't you *dare* tell me you know children better than I do. You come in here thinking you're God's gift, with your fancy education, your posh accent, and your ridiculous outfits—"

"Oi!" Sean said again, which cheered me. I'd been a little hurt by that last remark.

Mrs. Ormley turned on him. "And you! You're not even the boys' father, so I suppose I shouldn't be surprised you can't control them. If you ask me, a bit of time in foster care would do them the world of good."

"*Oi!*" This time, it was me. I cleared my throat. "I mean, Mrs. Ormley, this is *not* the time or place. I think you could do with a nice cup of tea back at school . . ." I took her arm.

She shook me off angrily. I was pleased to see I'd left a damp handprint on the sleeve of her kitten-print sweater. "I'm going home.

And I shall be thinking *very strongly* about handing in my resignation in the morning."

She stalked off.

I stood there, dripping, in the silence that ensued. Everyone, it seemed, was staring at me. *Sean* was staring at me. Then with a collective effort, the parents, staff, and children remaining in the church seemed to rouse themselves. Noise levels rose quickly as raucous chatter struck up once more, and diminished with equal speed as the carollers followed Mrs. Ormley out through the heavy wooden door.

Sean and the twins were among them.

"That went well, then," Rose said brightly, still holding the fire extinguisher. Catching my gaze, she propped it up against a pew, where it promptly fell over with a resounding clatter. She shot the rather dazed-looking vicar a guilty smile and scurried out.

I glanced at him, realising the usual *Excellent service, vicar!* probably wasn't appropriate in the circumstances. "Er, sorry about that," I said, as I picked up the soggy remains of my jacket and squelched after Rose.

"Robert?" The voice had come from the shadows by the west door, from which I'd just emerged.

Sean was there. Alone. My steps faltered. "Are . . . are you waiting for me?"

He nodded. Shrugged. "Just wanted to say, you know, thanks. For sticking up for Wills and Harry. And I thought you might want to borrow this."

He slid his leather jacket off, leaving him clad in a cosy-looking sweater that made my arms ache to embrace him. I had to be content with slipping the still-warm leather jacket around my shoulders and breathing in deeply. Despite myself, I smiled.

"I don't like to speak ill of anyone, but she's a dreadful old harridan. Made Charlie cry before the service out of pure spite. I don't blame the twins for retaliating on his behalf." I thought about what I'd said. "Only, for God's sake, please don't repeat that. Especially anywhere Wills and Harry might hear you."

"Yeah. Prob'ly best not to encourage 'em." His face turned sombre. "They gonna get into trouble? She's not going to get the police on them, is she?"

"Well, they're below the age of criminal responsibility, and I think it'd be very hard to prove malicious intent in any case. I'd appreciate it if you gave them a good, stern talking-to on the dangers of fire, however."

"Oh, they'll be getting that all right. And then some." Sean fell silent but made no move to go.

"I should—"

"You busy for Christmas?" he asked abruptly.

My heart clenched. Did he mean . . .? No. That was the sort of thing people said all the time, wasn't it? Just to be polite. "Actually, I'm going down to stay with Mother and Peter. There's a big family dinner planned. Well, Peter's family. You know." And the Fordhams' Boxing Day Brunch, no doubt, but I didn't think bringing up Fordy would be the best idea.

"Yeah?" Sean scuffed his feet. "Seeing that Oliver bloke too?"

"God, I hope not," I said fervently, then flushed as I realised how it must sound to Sean. "Er, no. And you? Do you have, um, plans?"

"Just the usual. Be going out with the lads from work Christmas Eve. I'll be home with Debs and the boys for Christmas Day."

"How is Debs? Any news?" I desperately hoped it would be good, if so. I hadn't dared ask her myself—I very much doubted she'd have thought it any of my business.

"Yeah, actually." He smiled, looking suddenly younger. "Course, sod's law, she's come down with a real stinker of a cold now. It's why she's not here today, but the chemo worked, they reckon. She's gonna have to keep having checkups, of course, but no more treatment unless they find something new."

Relief flooded through me. "That's fantastic. I'm so glad."

Sean nodded. "Yeah. Best Christmas present ever for Wills and Harry, not that they know it. Or deserve it, right now," he added darkly.

"And for you," I said, certain of it. Debs might be prickly to outsiders, but it was obvious how close she and Sean were.

"Yeah." He looked at his feet. "I'd better let you go and get dry. You . . . you take care, yeah?"

"And you," I said, but he'd already disappeared.

I pulled his jacket more closely around my shoulders, and sighed.

CHAPTER TWENTY-SIX

Christmas Eve dawned bright and frosty, and the drive down to Wiltshire was easy and pleasant, considering the time of year. Peter's house was on a road known simply as "The Lane," which had wooded common land on one side and rambling houses of a certain age on the other, guarded by tall cypress and ancient yew. All the houses had large gardens, and moss was a perennial problem on the extensive lawns.

I'd barely parked on the gravel drive and got out of Portia when Peter opened the front door and stepped out, beaming. He must have been watching for me. "How's my beautiful girl?"

"She's doing splendidly," I assured him, smiling back.

"I thought *I* was your beautiful girl, Daddy." I looked over Peter's shoulder at the ringing, slightly nasal Godolphin School tones and tried to muster a smile for my youngest stepsister, Laetitia.

As a child, she'd been known as Titty. Apparently nobody had thought this in any way odd, but it possibly accounted for her tendency to take offence at the slightest provocation even at thirty-four.

Possibly.

Peter was quick to reassure her. "Of course you are, my dear. And getting more beautiful every day—"

"Oh, *Daddy*." Her expression was smug.

"—but I don't leave you in the care of this young rapscallion, do I?"

Laetitia and I eyed each other with shared horror at the prospect. "Oh, I'm sure I could manage to look after her for you," I said with a touch of malice. "It can't be that different to looking after Portia—take her out every weekend, keep her clean, and make sure she doesn't take her top off around disreputable young men."

She gave me a poisonous smile. "No, I'll leave all the disreputable young men for you. Did you bring one, by the way? I can't see him, but perhaps he's in the boot?"

"Children," Peter chided. "Behave. Robert, your mother should be somewhere around. I'm sure she'll be delighted to see you."

"I'll just get my bag, then. My old room?"

"Of course. I've told you before, it's still your room. And it's always open to you, any time you need to come home. No need to ring ahead."

I winced internally at the gentle implication of filial neglect as I fetched my bag, then crunched across the thick gravel to the front door.

Peter's house—I still found myself thinking of it as that, even though it had been my home during school and university holidays ever since I'd been fifteen—was much like Peter himself: getting on in years but still spruce and sprightly, although perhaps not very modern. His daughters, Laetitia and her older sisters, Camilla and Beatrice, had all grown up here, so I supposed it was natural to resent the interlopers, at least to some degree. The elder two having families of their own, they wouldn't be staying with us, I'd been told, but we'd see them all for Christmas dinner, although they'd been excused attendance at the dreaded Boxing Day Brunch.

Perhaps Fordy could be persuaded to slope off to the pub with me—Lord knew, we'd done it plenty of times before. But I somehow doubted Linette would allow it this time.

Inside, the house showed clear signs of Mother's touch. After years of living in work-provided accommodation, she'd leapt at the chance to flex her interior decoration muscles—perhaps another cause for resentment. Personally I thought she'd brightened the old pile up tremendously.

And the house as well, I reflected with a mental snigger that turned to a pang of regret as I thought how Sean would have appreciated the joke.

My room was on the top floor, under the eaves and facing towards the back garden. Birds always nested there, and as a teenager I'd spent many hours lying on my bed, listening to them scratching around and chirping tirelessly. Unsure of my place in this unfamiliar, overlarge house—not to mention frankly alarmed by the lovesick cooing of my mother and Peter—I'd tended to escape upstairs whenever I could. I'd filch battered, well-read paperbacks from Peter's extensive shelves downstairs and lose myself in the crime-fighting exploits of Lord Peter Wimsey or the wartime adventures of "Biggles" Bigglesworth of the RAF.

Up here, at least, there had been something to remind me of our old house, way back before Father had died. It had already been a fading memory by the time Mother and Peter were married, but I recalled there had been a tree just outside my bedroom window that usually held a nest or two in the spring.

I dumped my bag on the bed and then jogged back downstairs to find Mother.

Christmas dinner, as usual in recent years, was had at Brodgingly Hall, a local stately home-cum-golf course with a Michelin-starred restaurant. It was a far cry from the days after Father and before Peter, when Mother and I had stayed in her flat at the school and shared the smallest turkey that money could buy (actually, I suspected her of substituting a chicken on the sly some years, but wouldn't have dreamed of calling her bluff). All the other boys went home for the holidays, of course, and it would be just the two of us, with one or two of the masters of the confirmed-bachelor variety popping round for sherry.

I remembered those days rather fondly, but Mother, not to put too fine a point on it, did not.

Our table at the restaurant was easily the largest, as Camilla ("Cami, darling, please," *mwah*) and Beatrice ("Bea," barked in parade-ground tones, and no air kiss) had both brought their broods. Bea's eldest, Rufus, who had been the one who'd more or less brought Mother and Peter together, was absent, however. Now twenty-two, he was Christmassing in Tibet with his girlfriend. There had been a gap of twelve years between him and his nearest sibling, ten-year-old Philip, and although Bea's marriage now seemed happy enough, I strongly suspected it had at the time been a shotgun wedding.

Bea, I was certain, had wielded the shotgun. Expertly.

I caught Mother eyeing her stepdaughters assessingly.

"Don't worry, Mother," I whispered. "You're still the thinnest of them all."

"It's not their fault. They have young families," she whispered back with the smug air of a woman who'd pushed my pram in a size eight Chanel skirt and had the pictures to prove it.

I was seated at Mother's left, and as the other unattached junior family member, Laetitia was at *my* left. Peter had, in fact, suggested she might prefer to sit farther down the table with one of her sisters, but she'd made some scathing comment about being forced to talk about potty training over the turkey. Apparently she found my conversation, such as it was likely to be, preferable to that. I wasn't sure whether to be flattered or simply incredulous.

"Daddy, when are we going to the Fordhams' this year?" she asked, speaking across Mother and me as our starters were served.

"Ah . . . When is it again, darling?" Peter asked Mother with a smile, although I strongly suspected he knew perfectly well. All Peter's marbles were present and correct, and arranged with military precision.

"The twenty-seventh," Mother said. "I'm rather looking forward to seeing the latest addition—have you met little Georgie yet, Robert?"

I swallowed my wine hastily. "No—only seen pictures."

"Does he take after Fordy?"

"Er . . . Difficult to tell, really. Although I hear he eats a lot, so possibly, yes."

"I remember you and Fordy when you were at school," Laetitia put in loudly. "Always going off alone together when he came to stay in the hols. I always wondered what you got up to. Still, he obviously grew out of it."

"Titty," Peter said warningly.

"*Daddy.* I'm not a little child. Anyway, if Fordy can settle down, I don't see why Robert can't—"

"*Laetitia.*" Mother so rarely raised her voice to any of Peter's children it caused a hush all down the table. Even two-year-old Henry at the far end paused in shock, tiny spoon midway to mush-smeared mouth. "Would you mind passing the water, dear? Thank you so much."

I intercepted the carafe en route and filled Mother's glass for her. She leaned in and whispered, "Boyfriend trouble," all while smiling sweetly in Laetitia's direction.

I winced, reminded with a pang of my own difficulties in that area.

Like a lioness, Mother was quick to pounce at a sign of weakness. Although perhaps the protecting-the-cubs instinct was the more apt analogy. Maybe. "Darling, is there someone you haven't told us about?"

"Is he very disreputable?" my sharp-eared stepsister put in.

"He's . . ." I sighed. "He's not anyone. Not any longer. Well, he *is*, obviously, but, well, I think it's over." I managed a wonky smile in Mother's direction. "You wouldn't like him anyway."

"Why not?" Mother frowned. "He's not a socialist, is he? Or does he have one of those terrible regional accents?"

"No, no. It's his job."

"His job? Well, at least he has one. And as long as he's not a dustman." She laughed, but something in my expression must have alarmed her, as her forehead took on a tense look. "He's *not* a dustman, is he?"

"No. He, er, he works in pest control."

"A *ratcatcher*?" Laetitia's voice was loud, ringing and derisive.

"Really?" Peter put in enthusiastically. "I remember when Uncle Alastair had rats in the stables and brought in men to deal with it. Absolutely fascinating. Peanut butter, that's what they used. Rats go wild for it, apparently. I wonder if they still use it? Used to put some stuff in that turned it bright blue. You ask your young man if they still use peanut butter." He beamed at me.

"Ugh," Laetitia said, putting down her knife and fork. Her mostly untouched whitebait, perhaps sensing their sacrifice had been in vain, gazed at her in mute, glassy betrayal. "I can't imagine a worse job. Sewer worker, I suppose. I mean, God, the *smell*. Does he—"

"*Laetitia*," Mother and Peter said together.

Little Henry's lip quivered. Bea's husband, Gordon, jumped, winced, glared at his wife and engaged Laetitia, who was on his right, in hearty conversation, all in the space of six seconds.

Mother patted my arm. "Darling, you know I wouldn't care about something like that."

I pointedly looked behind her.

She narrowed her eyes.

"Just checking to see if you had your fingers crossed behind your back."

She sighed. "Darling, I know I *used* to be a little more concerned about such things, but I really do just want you to be happy." She glanced, as if involuntarily, at Peter, and her face softened. "I still don't understand what went wrong with Crispin. Even *Laetitia* liked Crispin."

"Hmm, and what does that tell you?" I muttered to my asparagus terrine.

"And you had *such* a good job at Potter's Field . . ."

"*Mother*. Please?"

She cut herself another tiny sliver of smoked salmon, then laid down her cutlery. "I do understand it's been hard for you, you know. I only ever wanted the best for you."

I looked at her in concern. "Mother? Well, of course you did. I've never doubted that for a second."

"I just wish you'd, well, *confide* in me a little more. I *am* your mother." She sighed. "Robert . . . You were *happy* at Loriners', weren't you?"

"Of course I was," I lied heartily and with the ease of long practice. "And I really do appreciate all the sacrifices you made for me. Honestly, Mother. Now, more wine?"

"Well, maybe just half a glass," she said, smiling a little mistily. "I do have to watch my figure."

After lunch, we all went out for a walk in the grounds. While the younger children ran wild and their fathers improvised games of cricket for the older ones using sticks and fir cones, Peter detached himself from Mother's side and came over to talk to me. I glanced over in Mother's direction, but she'd be fine with Bea. Somewhat surprisingly, they'd taken to each other like ducks to water the first time they'd met. I couldn't imagine what they had in common.

Peter and I talked about all the usual things—cricket, Portia, Mother, Portia, politics, Portia—and then he surprised me by mentioning Sean. Not by name, obviously, because I hadn't told him Sean's name. But it was fairly clear who he meant by "your young ratcatcher."

"You do realise we'd be very glad to welcome anyone you'd care to invite along to visit us, don't you?" he said with paternal firmness.

"I'm not sure Laetitia would agree," I muttered, kicking a fir cone ahead of me as we walked.

The fir cone veered over Peter's way, and he passed it adroitly back to me. "Hah. Your sister, I'm afraid, is very rarely pleased about anything approaching a change to the status quo. I don't suppose you noticed at the time, but it was three years before she'd say a civil word to your mother."

I'd noticed, as it happened, only too well. "Oh, really?" I said politely.

"But," Peter continued, "I made up my mind when I met your mother, I wasn't going to let Titty rule my life"—heroically, I managed to keep a straight face—"and I'm damned if I'll do it now. Now, I don't know what's gone on between you and your young man, and I'm not going to pry. But if there's any suggestion it's to do with how he feels he might fit in here, you can tell him from me, that is *not* a consideration."

I didn't quite know how to reply. Peter seemed to understand and gave my shoulder a fatherly pat. "Now, come along, let's join the others and show 'em how the game's *really* played, what do you say?"

"Absolutely," I agreed, and we jogged back over to the impromptu cricket pitch together.

Presents were exchanged once we'd said our good-byes to the extended family and returned to Peter's house. Both my married stepsisters insisted their children's bedrooms were already bursting at the seams, and there was a tacit agreement that they and I didn't know each other well enough to make the exchanging of gifts either meaningful or advisable.

Laetitia, however, being unavoidably present at Peter's house for the duration, had to be provided with a gift. I'd thought long and hard, panicked briefly but thoroughly, and eventually gone for a hand-painted silk scarf from a craft stall on the Shamwell village farmers' market. Even if she hated it (which she would, as it was from me) it'd make a nice gift for someone else. Or, as might be, the local charity shop.

Predictably, she received it with a cry of, "Oh, how *sweet*. Did one of your class make it?" but I noticed her trying it on in front of a mirror later on when she thought I wasn't looking.

Mother seemed pleased with the scent I'd bought her, and Peter professed himself delighted with his book on local history. For my part, I was equally happy with my beeswax polish and bottle of brandy (Peter) and pair of pyjamas and new bow tie (Mother). I was hopefully not too visibly irritated with Laetitia's gift of a garish, trendy-looking designer shirt that was worlds away from anything I'd have worn, and in any case two sizes too large.

As dusk fell, Mother, Peter, and I settled down to play cards, while Laetitia had a loud, bitter-sounding telephone conversation in the next room. When she returned to the lounge, Peter made a point of making space for her on the sofa, which seemed to comfort her. She still spurned my offer of a jellied orange with a comment tarter than a candied lemon, so she couldn't have been feeling too bad.

At breakfast on Boxing Day, my phone rang, and I excused myself to answer it when I saw who was calling.

"Rose? Merry Christmas."

There was no answer, save a loud, drawn-out sniff.

"Rose?" I repeated, alarmed.

"'Snuffing," came indistinctly down the line, followed by another sniff.

Initially confused, I managed to translate after a moment. "It clearly *isn't* nothing. What's the matter?"

"Shitface."

I felt I deserved some sort of prize, perhaps from the cipher people at Bletchley Park, for working out she wasn't, in fact, insulting me. "Your ex-fiancé? He's been in touch?"

"Came to Mum and Dad's." She made a strange noise, sort of halfway between a hiccup and a snort.

"What, for breakfast?"

"Last night, you twat. I'm back at home now. Couldn't stay. Didn't want to see him again."

"He's got family near yours?"

"Well, *duh*. How'd you think we met?" There was a withering sniff.

"*I* don't know, do I? You never mentioned how long you'd been together. I suppose I thought you'd met at uni. But what did he want? To get back together?"

There was a louder sniff. "Bastard brought me a *present*. From Dubai. Said he hoped we could still be friends, oh, and he's met this really great girl out there, here's her picture, isn't she fucking lovely? She's round at his parents' house *right now*."

"Oh, Rose . . ." I entertained brief and, to be honest, probably entirely unrealistic thoughts of going round to wherever the man lived and thrashing the living daylights out of him.

"Three months since we split up. *Three months* . . ."

Perhaps Peter might have an antique tyre iron he could lend me . . . "You're better off without him. Quite clearly. Anyone who could treat you like that is *not* worth wasting tears over."

"Too sodding right," she agreed. Then sniffed again. "When are you coming home?" Rose's tone was more akin to one of her pupils enquiring after a much-missed parent than to her usual happy belligerence.

I grimaced. "It'll be a couple of days yet. I've got to go to the Fordhams' Boxing Day Brunch tomorrow."

There was another sniff, this one slightly puzzled. "Boxing Day is today."

It took me a moment to work out what she was getting at. "Ah. I know, but it's still called the Boxing Day Brunch. Apparently a slight temporal displacement is immaterial to the spirit of the thing. Like May Balls in June. You know."

"No, I sodding don't. We didn't all go to uni among the glittering spires of Oxbridge."

"I was at Durham! But, anyway, you've got other friends . . ."

"They're all away at their families'. Or being all loved up with their husbands." The way she said *husbands*, one might have thought it a euphemism for *serial killers*. "Can't you miss it?"

"I . . ." I thought about it. It was tempting to make an early return to Shamwell, avoiding any awkward questions re career choices, no doubt about it. But Mother would be upset, Fordy would be hurt, and Peter would be disappointed. Laetitia would probably be delighted, but I felt that wasn't really a consideration that should factor into my decision.

An idea formed in my mind. "Why don't you come down here? Peter and Mother have got plenty of spare rooms, and I'm sure they'd love to have you. You can save me from my evil stepsister," I added deviously but also hopefully.

"Won't the roads be really busy? Christmas, and all that?"

Hah! She was wavering. "Shouldn't think so. They were fine on Christmas Eve—it only took me two hours fourteen minutes door to door. And if you're worried, take the train. Portia and I can pick you up from the station. It's not far."

"You do realise your car isn't actually a person, right? Sod it, all right. I'll come. Always wanted to find out how the other half lives. Do I need to, like, dress for dinner and stuff?"

"This isn't Downton Abbey. Just wear your normal clothes."

"And you're sure it'll be okay with your mum?"

"Mother will love you," I said confidently. After all, Rose was at least three dress sizes larger than Mother, which pretty much guaranteed a warm reception. "Now, you go and pack, and I'll tell Mother you'll be here for dinner."

CHAPTER TWENTY-SEVEN

R ose arrived, in fact, in plenty of time for dinner, and despite my protestations, insisted on changing. Laetitia greeted her appearance downstairs with a friendly, "Oh my God, he's brought a bloody tranny."

To be fair, Rose *was* looking a little overdressed for a family dinner, and the leopard print really wasn't doing her any favours, but I couldn't see anything remotely masculine about her. And in any case, there was no call for that kind of language.

I bristled on her behalf, and Peter made warning noises, but Rose just stepped up to Laetitia with a smile. "Lovely to meet you too. Robert did tell me your name, but I've got a brain like a sieve, me. Is it Anastasia, or Drusilla?"

"Laetitia," I corrected, stifling a laugh. "But you can call her Titty."

Rose snorted. Laetitia, for once, was speechless.

"Drinks, anyone?" Peter said loudly and poured himself a large one.

Mother didn't appear to be watching her figure this evening, either. But then, it *was* an awfully nice Chablis.

It was fun, having a friend to stay. Rather like being at school again. Particularly when Rose knocked on my door at midnight with a bottle of sherry and some mince pies she'd liberated from the larder.

"Always fancied having a midnight feast," she said with a shrug.

"Rose, you live alone," I reminded her. "You can eat anytime you want to."

"Not the same, though, is it?" She grinned. "If we make too much noise, will your stepdad come and tell us off?"

"Probably. But he'd be very polite about it. And probably join us." Surrendering to the inevitable, I downed the water from the glass by my bed and let her refill it with sherry. "So what do you think of the old place?"

"Seriously?" Rose frowned, her expression curiously at odds with the gambolling sheep on her pastel-pink pyjamas. "It's a lot less grand than I was expecting. I mean, I could actually see me living in a place like this. When I win the lottery, obviously. And your mum cooks and everything."

"It's Mrs. Patmore's week off," I said drily.

"You ought to watch that, giving the servants time off. They'll only start to expect it *every* year."

"Shocking, isn't it? They'll be wanting to be paid next. The audacity of the lower orders is astounding."

Rose laughed. "Speaking of which, you heard any more from Sean?"

My levity evaporated like expensive brandy. "No. Not since the carol service. I've still got his jacket at home."

"Holding it hostage, are you?"

"Not exactly. I might have been sort of hoping he'd pop in to retrieve it on his way through the village sometime."

"You could actually take it back yourself."

I gave a short, mirthless laugh. "With my luck, I'd just run into Debs."

"Oh, come on. You can't be scared of *Debs*. Not after facing down Mrs. Ormley like that. She *has* resigned, you know. Lucy Kemp told me. She's thinking of organising a collection for a thank-you present for you."

"I'm sure the twins deserve far more credit than I do. Then again, thanking them for setting someone on fire would send out *entirely* the wrong message. But anyway, Debs is very protective of her brother. And, well, if I have to hand the jacket over to her, it's gone, isn't it?"

"Oh my God. You've been sleeping with it, haven't you?" She cackled. "Better make sure you sponge it off before you return it."

"I have *not* been sleeping with it. Either literally or euphemistically." That one time I'd dozed off on the sofa while wearing it *definitely* didn't count. "I just meant, once I've handed back the jacket, the excuse for talking to Sean is gone. That's all."

"You could always go and talk to him *without* an excuse, you know."

"No, I couldn't." He'd think I was needy and clingy and one step up from a demented stalker. And I'd been *so* careful to try to play things a little bit, well, cool, to use the common parlance. *Clingy* was desperately unattractive. Crispin had made that abundantly clear. "I, um. I don't suppose you've seen anything of Sean, the last week or so?"

"Nope. Sorry. Haven't been around, have I?" She patted my knee. "But you must be in his good books at least a little bit, after the carol service."

I nodded. "We . . . Well, we did speak, a little, after the service. And it seemed . . . *He* seemed . . . Oh, I don't know." I drank some sherry. It didn't mix well with the minty flavour my toothpaste had left in my mouth. "You probably don't want to talk about this, anyway."

"Course I do. Go on, tell me everything."

"That's just it. There's nothing to tell, really. Just that he seemed . . . regretful."

"Yeah? *Regretful* regretful, or *maybe still interested* regretful?"

I traced the lines on the candlewick bedspread with one finger. "The latter. I think. Possibly."

"See? That's the way it goes with you two. You screw up, he storms off, then he regrets it and comes back. It's your thing." She gave a satisfied smile and slurped some more sherry.

Oh God. My heart thudded into the pit of my stomach. She was right. Every time we'd had a misunderstanding, I'd just left it up to Sean to make the first move towards a reconciliation. I'd been an idiot. Sooner or later, he was going to just stop bothering.

Looking back, I was amazed it hadn't been sooner. "I need to do something," I blurted out. "Oh God. What should I do?"

"Well, it's not rocket science. Have you tried, I don't know, *phoning* him?"

"What, phone him from here?" Laetitia might be listening.

"No, I thought you could go round his house and *then* phone him. Duh." Rose refilled her glass of sherry. "On the other hand, you're probably better doing it face-to-face." She sniggered. "Pun not intended."

"What— Oh." I took a too-hasty gulp of sherry and suffered a minor choking fit that left tears in my eyes.

Rose thumped me painfully on the back. "Yeah, see, he obviously fancies the pants off you, so you want to focus his mind on what he's missing. So face-to-face." She nodded. "Wear something sexy."

I sipped my sherry more cautiously this time. "I'm not sure I own anything sexy."

"Yeah, I was just thinking that." She grinned. "You could turn up on his doorstep in a bow tie and *nothing else*."

"Because *that* wouldn't get me arrested. Not to mention, frostbitten in unfortunate places, this time of year."

"All right, then—you ask him round to yours, and you open the door in your bow tie and the altogether. Or, you know, you could even put your bow tie on your—"

"And if it turns out to be the postman at the door?" I cut her off hurriedly. "Or Hanne? Or you, even." I narrowed my eyes.

"Yeah, time to confess. I'm just *that* desperate for a glance at what you keep in your paisley pyjamas. Speaking of which, you don't actually wear those at home, do you? 'Cause I gotta say, they're not going to do a lot for the get-him-back-and-keep-him cause."

I might have coloured faintly. "These were a Christmas present from Mother."

"That figures."

"What do you mean?" I bristled on Mother's behalf.

"Well, you're her little boy, aren't you? Even if it's all subconscious, she's going to want to keep you all sweet and innocent in bed, isn't she?" She cackled. "And trust me, those pyjamas are going to do the trick."

"And sheep are just *so* seductive," I retorted.

Rose held up a hand. "I'm a city girl, all right? I don't want to hear about what you get up to in the countryside."

"Actually, there are very few sheep around here. More dairy cattle. Some of them have very fine eyes . . ." I sniggered at Rose's shudder and had some more sherry. It was starting to taste a lot better, which was probably a bad sign. "What's it like, growing up in a city?"

"I dunno. Normal. What's it like growing up here?"

"Dunn— I mean, I don't know. I mean, I didn't actually move here until I was fifteen. And even then, I spent half the year at school."

"So what was it like in the holidays?"

I shrugged. "Rural?"

"Wasn't it dead boring?"

"I used to spend a lot of time reading or practising the piano, and Fordy was near enough to visit quite a bit, so no, I don't remember ever being bored, really." Lost, perhaps—or at least misplaced—and alienated by my stepsister's hostility, but never exactly *bored*. There had always seemed to be plenty of things to do. "Peter used to give me driving lessons on the common," I remembered with a fond smile. "And teach me golf."

"You get on all right with him, don't you?"

"Shouldn't I?"

"Well, no. He took your mum from you, din't he?"

"Perhaps being gay preserved me from any Oedipal leanings." I leaned my head back against the wall and closed my eyes. "He made her happy, anyway. You don't know what it was like, when Father died and the whole ghastly mess got revealed. She had to go through a hell of a lot, and it showed. Then she met Peter, and, well, she was happy again. Still is." I opened my eyes. "I'd have loved him for that even if it hadn't turned out that we get on all right."

Rose looked at me mistily and gave a loud sniff. Then she downed her sherry in one and refilled her glass. "More?" she asked, holding the bottle out to me.

"Thank you." I suddenly realised how much the conversation had revolved about my family. "Do you want to talk about, um, Shitface?"

"No." She took a hefty swig of sherry. "Not now, not ever."

"Okay."

"I mean, Christ, how much of a bastard could he be? Turning up at my mum and dad's on *Christmas* sodding *Day*, just to tell me how fucking happy he is without me? I mean, seriously, is he a wanker or is he a wanker?"

"Wanker," I agreed solemnly and wondered if I might perhaps have had a tad too much sherry. I took another sip while I thought about it.

"And then he gives me a present. A sodding *present*. Bastard."

"Bastard." I nodded. "Was it a good one?"

"What?"

"The present. Was it good?"

She shrugged, and spilled some sherry on the bedspread. "Oops. Sorry. Nah, it was all right. 'Spensive stuff from the duty-free shop."

I frowned. "So, not even from Dubai?"

"No. Bastard."

"Bastard," I agreed. "Is there any more sherry left?"

"Bit. Here you go. Oops. No, so no, he didn't think of me *at all* while he was out there. Only on his way home. Like, mixed in with the guilt about not calling his mum every week, he gets the guilt about totally fucking over his fiancée, and buys a couple of scarves and some perfume. As if that's going to make it all better."

"As if." I frowned again. Or possibly I hadn't stopped since the last time. "He could have got you a handbag. Some Louis Vuitton luggage. A . . . a watch. Not just a cheap scarf."

"It was a Lanvin scarf. One of 'em was. And an Alexander McQueen."

I snorted dismissively. "As if the cost had anything to do with it."

"*Yeah.*"

"Yeah." We clinked glasses, causing yet another spillage to the bedspread. I considered laundering the bedclothes tomorrow, but Mother would most likely misinterpret my motives, which might be embarrassing all round.

Rose downed her sherry and stood, wavering a little in the dim light. "I'm gonna bed. Nigh."

"Night." I toasted her with my sherry, put the glass carefully back on the bedside table, then flopped back on my sherry-sodden bedspread and went to sleep.

CHAPTER TWENTY-EIGHT

The Fordhams' house in the New Forest was only twenty-two minutes away by car. We *could* all have piled into Mother's Range Rover, but as that would have put Laetitia and Rose a little too close together for comfort, I ended up taking her in Portia.

This meant, of course, that I wouldn't be able to drink at the brunch, but as I seemed to be suffering something of a sherry hangover this morning, I wasn't particularly bothered.

Rose, annoyingly, seemed unaffected by the previous night's libations. Once arrived at the Fordhams', she got out of Portia and whistled. "Did I say your parents' place was posh? I take it all back. Your mum and dad are just one step up from a council flat. This? *This* is posh. I mean, look at it! It's got *wings*."

"Well, yes, but they haven't used the west wing in years. Decades, even. It's all closed up—dust sheets on furniture, that sort of thing. Fordy and I used to frighten the life out of each other by creeping in there at midnight looking for ghosts."

"Ever see any?"

"No, but according to family tradition, some nights you're supposed to be able to hear a baby crying. Apparently it's a young Fordham of generations ago who died in infancy. And Fordy swears blind he's stayed here sometimes, and either he or Linette have got up in the night because they thought they heard little Georgie cry, only to find him fast asleep."

Rose shivered. "Okay, if I had a baby, I would *not* want to stay here with it. We're not going to be staying here after dark, are we?"

"Hardly. It's brunch, not supper."

"You say that, but the invitation was for twelve. To my mind, that's lunch. No *br* about it."

"No, lunch would be an entirely different affair. The menu would be completely different, for a start."

"Whatevs. Come on, I'm starving."

I rolled my eyes and offered Rose my arm. She accepted with a strange expression which I think was supposed to be a simper (after all, she hadn't eaten yet, so it couldn't *really* be indigestion), and we crunched across the gravel to the stone steps of Copse House (or Corpse House, as Fordy and I had liked to dub it in our more ghoulish days).

Having Rose with me, I soon realised, was a *godsend*. Instead of asking awkward questions about my career choices, all the old acquaintances and not-quite-relatives occupied themselves with getting introduced to her and wondering what on earth our relationship was, and if there was a possible polite way to ask if I'd moved on from Greek love (if there was, nobody managed to find it). It left me free to actually enjoy my quails' eggs mini muffins and prosciutto crostini for once, with attention to spare for avoiding the infamous squid fritters. (They appeared without fail every year despite the fact everyone loathed them; I was convinced they were Mrs. Fordham's idea of a joke.)

I caught sight of Fordy and Linette over on the far side of the room with some university friends I'd met once or twice before. I waved and Fordy detached himself, beaming, to come and welcome us. Mother and the others had arrived only moments after we'd gone in, and still lingered at the entrance. Fordy greeted her with an affectionate kiss, Peter with a hearty handshake, and Laetitia with polite forbearance.

I was enveloped in one of Fordy's trademark bear hugs. "Finally! It's about time you got here. I was beginning to think you weren't coming."

"We're only six minutes late. Sorry."

"Yes, but six minutes late for you is the equivalent of about a decade and a half for everyone else. Trouble on the roads?"

"No," I said with an involuntary glance at Rose. "We just left a little late."

She rolled her eyes, unabashed. "Yeah, right, blame it all on me. Just cos I couldn't decide what to wear."

"Well, you look absolutely delightful in that dress, I must say," Fordy said with one of his most charming smiles, and in fact it wasn't empty flattery. I'd finally persuaded Rose into an understated wrap dress that showed off her curves, and even Peter had cast her an admiring glance that had lingered until Mother raised a single eyebrow that sent him scurrying, shamefaced, back to her side.

"Fordy," I put in, mindful that I was neglecting my manners. "This is Rose Wyman, a colleague and friend of mine. Rose, this is Malcolm Fordham, my old school friend."

Rose went faintly pink as he kissed her on the cheek.

"Delighted," Fordy said. "Now, why don't you come and meet the sprog?"

One arm thrown casually over my shoulders, Fordy ushered us through the mostly aging throng to be introduced to my godson elect, who was presently sucking lustily on his mother's finger. The university friends nodded a greeting and dispersed, presumably in search of food. Most of them being built on similar lines to Fordy, they tended to descend on buffet tables like a plague of locusts.

"Linny, darling, look who's here. It's Emsy and Rose, his er . . . Sorry, what did you say you were again?"

Halfway through mouthing *Emsy?* at me with a wide-eyed look that promised a great deal of teasing later on, Rose turned back to Fordy and smiled. "Colleague, friend, and saver from starvation."

Linette gave her a wan smile. "I don't know what they teach them at Loriners', but it certainly isn't cooking. I can't even get Mal to make beans on toast."

She looked tired. Of course, I'd barely seen her since she and Fordy married, when she'd been radiant in yards of silk and lace.

Rose shrugged. "Yeah, well, at least you don't need to worry about this one wasting away." She angled her head at Fordy, who blinked and then laughed with the rest of us. "How old's your little one, then?"

"Five months." Linette jiggled Georgie proudly. "So are you two . . .?"

"Gawd, no." Rose's reply was a shade more emphatic than was flattering. "Can you imagine Robert with a girlfriend? It'd be like watching David Attenborough try to snog a squirrel. And I'm off men, anyway. Think I'll become a lesbian. Or a nun. Maybe a lesbian nun," she finished thoughtfully.

Linette looked like she didn't quite know what to make of Rose but was far too well-bred to say so. She glanced at Fordy, who still had his arm around me in avuncular fashion. "I think Georgie needs changing. Do excuse me."

She left. Fordy drooped, rather, and dropped his arm from my shoulders. "I'll, ah, go and see if she needs a hand."

I stared after him, feeling a little like I'd just been watching a foreign film without subtitles.

"She thinks you're shagging her husband," Rose murmured.

I spluttered on my orange juice. "Rose! I can assure you I'm doing nothing of the kind."

"Bet you used to, though. I mean, come on, the way you two are with each other."

"I . . . What way? And, anyway, even if we did use to, well, you know, we were younger then. A *lot* younger."

"Are we talking jailbait here?"

"No!" I looked around guiltily. "Well, maybe. But only by a few months. Fordy was sixteen, and we were in the same school year. It was just that my birthday wasn't until the summer. But what do you mean, the way we are with each other?"

She raised a knowing eyebrow. "All touchy-feely."

"Fordy's always been a tactile person," I protested.

"Yeah? Didn't see him giving anyone else a quick grope on the doorstep."

"There was no groping!" One of Fordy's uncles turned to give me a *very* disapproving stare. I cringed, mortified.

Rose was giggling. "Keep your voice down, you numpty."

"But there *wasn't*," I hissed. "It was just a hug."

"Yeah, and how many other people got one? I was watching him when he came over to say hello. Me: kiss on the cheek. Your mum: kiss on the cheek. Various interchangeable men: firm, manly handshake. *Laetitia*: firm, manly handshake. Robert Emeny, old school pal, dorm mate and one-time bum chum: a nice little cuddle with optional wandering hands."

"There were *no*—" I lowered my voice. "There were no wandering hands. Fordy *loves* Linette."

"Maybe, but I bet he wouldn't say no to a bit of the old extramaritals from you."

"No," I said uncertainly. "You're wrong. Fordy wouldn't do that."

"Well, you know him best," she muttered in a tone that implied I most certainly *didn't*.

My face growing hot, I thought about how Fordy had been when he was chatting to his university friends. There *had* seemed to be rather more in the way of personal space involved than was customary between the two of us.

Could Rose possibly be right? This would put Fordy's visit to me last month in a wholly new and not altogether comfortable light.

"Would you?" she asked.

"What?"

"*You know.* If he offered."

"You obviously don't know me very well," I retorted stiffly, "if you think I'd consent to being someone's dirty little secret."

Rose opened her mouth—then her expression altered subtly, as if she'd been about to say something and then changed her mind. "How well does Linette know you? Not very, I'd have thought."

I blinked. "Not really, no. They met at Oxford. Fordy didn't introduce us until they were already engaged."

"Yeah, well, look at her." Rose nodded to where Linette had returned to the room far too quickly, I would have thought, to have reasonably performed any sleight-of-nappy. She was over by the window now, handing Georgie to his grandmother.

Linette did, in fact, look a little strained, and I said so.

"That's cos she doesn't know what's what. So she's just imagining it, which is always way worse. Like in horror films, when they don't show you the worst bits. If you and him is all over and done with, he ought to tell her about it. Or you ought. Oh, I know *you* won't, 'cause of the old school tie, honour among gentlemen, blah-di-blah-di-blah, but he ought to."

I took a sip of orange juice and wished fervently for vodka. "I don't know. I mean, I see what you mean—but I'm not sure he'll go for it." I wasn't even sure how one might attempt to persuade him. I had an uneasy feeling I wouldn't be terribly convincing in the role.

God, what a mess. I felt my shoulders slump.

"Yeah, me neither, now I've met him. But I'll tell you what, if he doesn't, he's going to regret it." She hugged me, which was so unexpected I nearly dropped my glass. "Look, just 'cause Fordy likes to have his cake and eat a bit of buttered stud muffin on the side doesn't mean Sean's like that."

"That wasn't—Rose," I said carefully. "Do you think I ought to tell Sean the whole story about, well, about Oliver?"

She stepped away from me, looking shifty. "I never said that. Don't even know if *I* know the whole story, do I? But I do know that woman's not happy." She nodded in Linette's direction. "And if Sean's like her, he's not happy either. Probably imagining all kinds of stuff."

I winced. "You really think so?"

Rose cocked her head to one side. "Well, maybe not. He is a bloke, after all. But yeah. I mean, I'm not all honesty-is-always-the-best-policy, 'cause sometimes, what you don't know doesn't hurt you, does it? Let's face it, I was a whole lot happier before I found out about Shitface and Skinny Cow. But if someone knows there *is* something, and they don't know what it is, then they're probably better off knowing the truth." She frowned. "Or, you know, a really convincing lie. And face it, sweetie, you've got the world's worst poker face, so you'd probably better stick to the truth."

Was she right? After all, Mother and Peter had never suspected I'd been unhappy in my teens . . . Had they?

The mini muffins from earlier sat like a leaden lump in my stomach, the ghosts of unborn quails fluttering feebly in my intestines.

"You all right? You look like your stomach's just realised one of those canapés was off. It'll be one of those fishy ones, I bet you. God knows what they put in those. Tasted like rubber bands. Probably *was* rubber bands."

"I'm fine," I managed. "I just had a rather uncomfortable epiphany."

Rose frowned. "Isn't that not till January?"

"Not that kind of epiphany. This sort involves rather less in the way of gold, frankincense, and myrrh, and rather more in the way of unpleasant truths."

"Oh. So are you going to tell Sean about your sordid past?"

"I'll . . . think about it. Damn it. I'd better go and speak to Fordy, hadn't I?"

Fordy hadn't been any keener on the idea of spilling all to Linette than I'd thought he would be, but he hadn't rejected it out of hand, so perhaps some good would come of the exceedingly awkward three-way conversation he, Rose, and I had ended up having.

At least, I *hoped* if he told Linette about us, it would be a good thing.

"You're quiet," Rose commented as I drove her back to Peter's house. "Brooding about Sean?"

"About Fordy, actually." I sighed. "But now you've mentioned Sean, I expect I'll start brooding about him too."

"Well, yeah. I mean, come on, Fordy's the past, in't he? You've got to start thinking about your future."

"Do you really think Sean and I have a future together?"

"Course you do. *If,*" she said, and looked at me significantly. "*If* you get the past sorted out so Sean doesn't think it's the present." She blinked. "Huh. That was actually pretty good, wasn't it? 'Specially considering how much shampoo I've drunk."

"Prosecco," I corrected. "Mrs. Fordham thinks champagne is common."

"How can it be common when it costs a bloody fortune?"

I shrugged, my hands still on the wheel. "Apparently it's been cheapened by conspicuous consumption."

"Posh people are weird. Are we there yet? I'm getting desperate for a pee." She giggled. "Don't want to turn your car into a Portia-loo."

Alarmed, I put my foot down.

CHAPTER TWENTY-NINE

Dusk had descended by the time Rose and I got back to Peter's house, so we spent the remainder of the day indulging in the traditional post-Brunch activities of drinking coffee and staring blearily at old films on television. Rose had vetoed *It's a Wonderful Life*, calling it the single most depressing film ever made—"*I mean, seriously, he has this completely shit life never getting to do anything he wants to, and it's supposed to be* uplifting?"—so we were currently watching *Goldfinger*.

Rose sipped thoughtfully at her coffee. "Sean Connery, Roger Moore, and George Lazenby. Shag, marry, or shove 'em off a cliff?"

I rolled my eyes "Easy. Shag Sean, marry George, shove Roger."

"You sure about that? George hasn't got a good record with getting married. Look what happened to Diana Rigg. And anyway, what's wrong with Roger? If, you know, he was about a hundred years younger."

I stared at her, nonplussed. "What's right with him?"

She stared back, then shook her head. "All right, Timothy Dalton, Pierce Brosnan, and Daniel Craig."

"Again, pitifully easy. Shag Tim, marry Dan, and shove Pierce."

"Weirdo."

"Why? What would you go for?"

"Shag Dan, marry Pierce, and shove Tim so far off that bloody cliff he'd end up in France. Ugh. Just something about that face." She shuddered, while I looked on, bemused. "Right. Time for a tougher one. Pussy Galore, Solitaire, or Whatserface Onatopp?"

"*Is run screaming from all of them an option?*"

"Nope. Rules of the game. You've got to choose."

"Well . . . wasn't Solitaire the one with the tarot cards, who had to stay a virgin so she could keep her powers of prophecy? And Ms. Onatopp was the madwoman who killed men with her thighs?"

"Think so."

"Then I'd enjoy a chaste marriage with Solitaire and hire a professional to shove Ms. Onatopp, ahem, off the top." I sniggered. "So I suppose I'll have to shag Pussy."

There was a startled noise behind the sofa. "I'm sure that sounded *entirely* different in context," Mother said, regaining her composure. "Now, I just came in to ask if you'd like any Christmas cake?"

"Um, no, thank you," I said, my face no doubt doing a sterling impersonation of one of the bright-red baubles on the Christmas tree.

Rose, having descended into helpless giggles, simply shook her head.

"How would you feel about not staying until New Year?" I asked Rose some time later. "I'm not sure I can wait any longer to try and sort things out with Sean."

We were sitting in our pyjamas by the fireplace and attempting to toast marshmallows, because apparently that had been a lifelong ambition of hers, goodness knows why.

"Gutted. I'm hoping if I hang around here long enough your stepdad will adopt me too." Rose shrugged. "Nah, it's okay. Whenever you want to get going. I was running out of Titty-based digs anyway."

"Oh, I'm sure you could think of a few more if you put your mind to it. But wouldn't your parents have something to say about the adoption thing? Oh, and watch it, your marshmallow's caught fire."

"Bugger." She blew on it until the flames expired, then grinned. "What, like offer him my brother on BOGOF?"

"Bog off?" I queried, baffled. I took a cautious bite of my blackened marshmallow. "Are they supposed to taste of charcoal?"

"Don't ask me. And, just when I think you're starting to live in the real world . . . *BOGOF*'s short for *buy one, get one free.*"

Oh. "I knew that really. I was just distracted by the idea of having you for a sister." It was curiously attractive, in a masochistic sort of way. Laetitia had certainly been a lot less voluble in my direction since Rose's arrival. I popped a thoughtful marshmallow in my mouth straight from the bag. They were a lot nicer this way.

"I make a brilliant sister. I never forget an embarrassing incident."

I gulped, swallowed my marshmallow in one, and stared at her in theatrical horror. "Pack your bags. We're leaving tomorrow."

Rose cackled and lit up another marshmallow.

Mother proved to be surprisingly relaxed about me leaving the next day, although I suspected that might have been because I would be taking Rose with me. Rose, regrettably, wasn't really Mother's sort of people, although Peter had quite taken to her. Fortunately, I felt reasonably certain she wouldn't have a similar problem with Sean. *If*, that was, I managed to straighten things out between us. Mother always got on well with men; women, less so. It was just one of those things.

"Are you going to ring him before we go?" Rose asked as I hauled her perplexingly large suitcase down the stairs.

I put the case down on the hall carpet and flexed my fingers. "Um, no?"

"But you *are* going to ring him when you get back, yeah?"

"Probably?" I *wanted* to talk things out with Sean. It was just that the thought of actually doing it was rather daunting. "But what do you think I should say?"

"Just get him to come and see you. Or meet you somewhere. Probably best not to go round to his. You want a bit of privacy, not the twins jumping up and down on top of you."

Not to mention Debs glaring at me like I was the anti-boyfriend.

"What if he doesn't want to?"

"Trust me. He wants to." She gave an exasperated sigh. "Look, he's at least going to give you a chance to explain, isn't he? He's that sort of bloke. Now are we going to get a shift on, or are you waiting for that case to sprout legs and carry itself to the car?"

"Slave driver. I *could* leave you to get a taxi and take the train, you know, rather than driving you back home."

"No, you couldn't. It'd offend all your gentlemanly instincts. You'd come out in a rash or something."

Sadly, she was probably right. I sighed and picked up her case once more.

CHAPTER THIRTY

t felt odd coming home after even such a brief stay at Peter's house. The Old Hatter's Cottage seemed overly quiet, and with Hanne away visiting her family, that wasn't likely to change unless I did something about it myself. It also seemed sadly unfestive—as I'd planned to be away until after New Year, I hadn't bothered with a Christmas tree, although I did at least have my Christmas cards up on the mantelpiece and windowsills. The ones from the children at school, mostly from cheap multipacks purchased in the village post office and featuring such traditional Christmas animals as hedgehogs and meerkats, were already curling merrily at the corners.

Rose's parting words to me, as I'd dropped her off up The Hill and heaved her luggage across the threshold, had been "Ring him."

Should I? Or would a chance meeting be preferable? Less forced?

No, I told myself firmly. This time, *I* was going to be the one to close the gap between us. It was the least of what Sean deserved. I'd find him, speak to him, and lay all my cards on the table.

I swallowed. Even if I *was* only holding a fistful of deuces.

My hand hovered by my phone but still somehow failed to come in to land. What if he didn't want to speak to me? Didn't want to sort things out?

Oh God. He'd had some kind of a works do on Christmas Eve, hadn't he? And those things were notorious for starting ill-advised romances between colleagues. What if he'd met someone else? Or, well, not *met* them, because obviously if they worked together they'd already met, but what if he'd got together with them? After all, he had a much wider pool of potential lovers than I did. What, not to put too fine a point on it, if it was already too late?

What if I just rang, and found out? I told myself firmly, and dialled his number.

It rang several times. Just as I was preparing a voice mail message in my head, a voice said, "Hello?"

Debs's voice.

This was *not* good, and why on *earth* was she answering his phone in any case? "Er, hello. It's Robert."

"Yeah. I know."

If she'd realised it was me, why had she answered? "Um, is Sean available?"

"He's taken the boys down the park to play football."

Couldn't he have taken his phone with him? "Er, right. Would you mind telling him I called?"

"All right." There was a pause, and I was about to thank her and ring off when she spoke again. "Look, don't mess him about, all right?"

"I wouldn't—"

"If you're just going to dump him for some posh bloke who went to the right sort of school—"

"I'm not," I said firmly, hope beginning to flare. If Debs thought he still cared for me . . . "Could you tell him I'm back home, please? Just in case . . . in case he'd like to come and get his jacket back? I mean, I'll be home all day . . . if he's, well, passing."

There was a beat. "I'll tell him. Look, thanks for what you did at the carol service. It could have been a lot worse, from what Sean said."

"Oh—it was no trouble. Really. And, well, I'm glad to hear you've had some good news, healthwise."

"Thanks. Look, I've got to go. I'll tell him what you said, all right?"

"Thank you," I said, but she'd already hung up.

Nothing to do now, I supposed, but wait patiently for Sean to get in touch. I put on a CD, flung myself on the sofa, and opened my copy of *Our Man in Havana* to the soothing tones of Bach's Cantata no. 156. No reason I couldn't relax while I waited.

Seven minutes later, I threw the book down in disgust and jumped back up. Relax? I was wound up tighter than the strings on a school violin after reception-class music lessons. And why on earth hadn't it occurred to me earlier that if Sean was at the park with the twins, I could go for a run and just happen to bump into him? It would be the best of all worlds: the appearance of a casual encounter, without the need to wait for fate to smile upon me.

I ran up the stairs, threw off my clothes, and changed into my running gear.

Halfway down the stairs, I paused. What if Sean called when I was out?

I ran back up and grabbed my phone. Oh hell, where was I going to put it? What on earth had possessed me to buy jogging bottoms without that most basic of practical features, a zip pocket? In the end, I put the phone on vibrate and shoved it in my sock. Hopefully I'd manage not to step on it in the likely event it fell out. It felt overly large and obtrusive there, as if I were a criminal who'd been electronically tagged. I hoped that wasn't a bad omen.

Right. Time to go and find Sean. I reached out to open the front door—and nearly jumped out of my skin when there was a loud knock upon it. My mouth went dry. Oh God—could it be Sean? Already? Was seventeen minutes long enough for him to get back to Debs's house and come back out again? I hadn't heard the motorbike pull up, but perhaps he'd had other business in the village and had parked elsewhere? It was surely too late for the postman, Hanne would still be in Norway with her family, and Rose wouldn't be visiting so soon after we'd got back . . .

And whoever it was would be walking away if I didn't get a move on and answer their knock. I smoothed down the front of my T-shirt, combed my fingers through my hair, peeked in the mirror and flattened down the resultant mess, had a moment's panic I should run upstairs and change—perhaps into my bow tie with TARDISes on it—told myself firmly there was no time, and opened the door.

I blinked at Mrs. Nunn, Destinee, and the tennis coach, all standing there solemn faced. Seen out of school uniform, and in an outfit that closely resembled her mother's, Destinee looked more like thirteen than seven. "Oh—hello," I said uncertainly.

"Destinee's got something to say to you, Mr. Enemy." She nudged her daughter. "Go on, then."

Destinee took a deep breath. "I'msorryIgotthetwinstosetMrs. Orribleonfire."

"Pardon?"

She served up a heavy sigh, with a side order of eye roll. "It was me what told the twins to set Mrs. Orr"—she caught herself—"Mrs. Ormley on fire."

I blinked.

Mrs. Nunn prodded her daughter. "*And?*"

She shoved her hands in her pockets, looking mutinous rather than penitent. "And I'm so-rry," she chanted.

"Oh . . ." This definitely made more sense, and I was heartily relieved to hear the twins hadn't, in fact, simply succumbed to sudden and random pyromania. "Because of what she said to Charlie? But you know, you really ought to apologise to Mrs. Ormley."

"What, that 'orrible old cow?" Mrs. Nunn was frankly incredulous. "Deserved all she got, she did. But I rung Debs and told her it wasn't her boys what came up with the idea, and I thought you ought to have an apology too, seeing as you was the one what got most of the water from that fire extinguisher. And we got you this," she added, thrusting a bottle-shaped object wrapped in cheap Christmas gift wrap at me.

"Oh . . . Thank you. But you really needn't."

"Go on, take it. It's Tesco's finest, so it's good stuff. We got it special. I'll drink any old rat's piss, me."

"Well, in that case, thank you very much." I bowed to the inevitable and took the bottle, hoping to God they wouldn't be expecting an invitation in to sample the contents right now. "Have you been having a good Christmas?"

"Well, you know. Kev turned up pissed Christmas Day, din't he, Ry?" The tennis coach nodded and looked as if he'd gladly deliver a forehand smash to Mrs. Nunn's former husband's nose. She gave him a fond smile in return. "Then that cow he's living with—her with the cheap hair extensions, you remember her, don't you, Mr. Enemy?—came to drag him home, and they had a screaming match out in the street, but it's all good entertainment, innit? Anyway, mustn't keep you. Dest has got Charlie coming over to play with their Bratz dolls, haven't you, love?" The tennis coach winced but forbore to comment. "You take care," Mrs. Nunn finished with a beaming smile.

"Ah, you too. And have a happy new year. Good-bye, Destinee, enjoy the rest of your holiday."

"Bye, Mr. Enemy."

I closed the door and looked at the bottle of wine. Tesco's finest? I could always find someone to give it to, I supposed.

Or, I told myself with a mental slap on the wrist, I could stop being such an inveterate bloody snob and just drink it and enjoy it in the spirit in which it was intended.

I put it carefully in the fridge and took a deep breath.

Oh God. What to do now? Would Sean still be at the park? It was twenty-nine minutes since I'd called him. Football might be a game of ninety minutes, but how long could a mere kick-around last? Would it be safer to stay at home and wait to see if he turned up?

The prospect sounded about as appealing as taking up the offer from Ruby's Waxing to get my bikini line done. Sod's law, I'd have the whole village knocking on my door if I stayed in—all but the one person I was desperate to see. Hanne would prove to have returned unexpectedly early from Norway. Rose would pop round to suggest a takeaway, now that we no longer had Mother's cooking to sustain us. Or God forbid, Mrs. Ormley would turn up to demand recompense for her ruined coat. Anything was possible.

I pulled up my socks and set out on my run before anyone could turn up to delay me further.

We'd had a few windy days, and the trees on the back lane that led to the park were now almost fully bare, just a few obstinate leaves clinging on to their branches. The chill breeze sent them trembling one minute with a gentle feint, then the next minute mustered its forces in a heavy gust. The leaves, for the most part, rattled like flags on poles but still stood, defiant, when the exhausted wind dropped once more, like lone soldiers who knew the end would come but were determined to fight to the last breath of life and drop of blood.

There were few people about. Perhaps they were put off from venturing out by the heavy, grey clouds and the bite in the air that promised frost tonight. Perhaps they'd simply over-indulged over the last few days, and were trapped indoors by inertia and the lure of new electronic toys. Some of them, perhaps, had returned to work for the few days between Christmas and New Year; after all, *somebody* had to be manning the tills for the plethora of sales we'd been bombarded with advertising for since Christmas Eve.

Come to think of it, *that* was probably where everyone was: out shopping. Rose had spoken with enthusiasm of "hitting the sales" once we got back, but personally, as I'd informed her, I'd rather eat my own liver than join in the mad rush for bargains on consumer goods I neither needed nor wanted.

She'd replied, "That's because you're a boring old fart—sorry, young fart—who doesn't have to worry about money and wouldn't know a fashionable outfit if it turned up naked in bed with you," which statement I felt wasn't *entirely* justified. Or, for that matter, logically sound, but I felt Rose might not respond well to me pointing this out.

A dapper magpie was strutting on the path a short way ahead of me. It looked startled at my approach and flew away with an affronted flutter of wings which only emphasised the quiet. All I could hear as I swung around the corner towards the park was the sound of my own footsteps. It was eerily reminiscent of the establishing shots of some postapocalyptic filmic nightmare, and for a moment the cold bit more deeply into my limbs. Then a childish shout rang out, and the spell broke. I jogged on into the park, the ground now soft and damp under my feet but, thankfully, no muddier than the last time I'd been this way.

I could tell at a glance that Sean and the twins weren't in the upper part of the park. Not a single redhead was to be seen—in fact there were only three other people here: a couple of pink-cheeked toddlers on the swings and a cold-looking mother pushing a pram back and forth. I ran on, down the hill towards the river, my anticipation rising. Surely they'd be there?

They weren't. I'd missed them. Disappointment settling like a leaden Christmas pudding in my stomach, I ran over the bridge without pause. Damn it. I'd been so *sure* they'd still be here.

I needed to get home, I realised. I'd said I'd be home all day—if Sean turned up and found me out of the house, it'd be . . . well, not good. He *probably* wouldn't think I'd done it deliberately, but simple thoughtlessness wasn't going to endear me to him either.

Then again, what if he never came? What if he decided a lost leather jacket was a small price to pay to be rid of my secrets and evasions? What if he was even now sitting at home thinking the very worst of me?

Damn it all to hell and back. Time for Mahomet to gird his loins and pay a visit to the mountain. Or, as might be, The Hill. I turned and retraced my steps through the park, then picked up speed as I hit the streets.

I soon realized why The Hill merited its capital letters. The gradient, at the start, was deceptively low but soon rose sharply. I overtook a couple of old ladies I knew by sight, gaining a new respect for their daily trundles to and from the village shops with their tartan shopping trolleys, and swerved around several clusters of council-estate mothers pushing double and even triple buggies. Most of them—the mothers, not the old ladies—smoked like tracksuit-clad chimneys as they walked, yet still somehow had the breath to chat loudly in between admonishing their offspring; they must have had lungs of steel.

Even Rose, who lived less than halfway up, must be fitter than she looked from her trek to and from the school. No wonder Sean often preferred to ride his motorbike into the village. Reaching the peak and turning left onto the council estate was a blessed relief, but despite the relatively flat path from here, I was still breathing heavily as I neared Debs's house, and my pulse was so rapid that it would have caused any passing doctors to worry for my health.

Although I strongly suspected the latter was not due to my run alone.

My steps faltered as I reached my goal. Upon the following conversation could rest the whole of my future relationship with Sean—or the lack thereof. I could hear Rose's voice in my head, ringing out with a breezy *So, no pressure, then.*

Taking a deep breath and plucking up my courage, I approached the front door, knocked, and braced myself for more of Debs's disapproval.

But when the door opened, I found myself gazing into Sean's wary eyes.

CHAPTER THIRTY-ONE

Sean couldn't have been home long—he was still pink-cheeked from the cold, his copper hair fluffing up in the breeze that stole through the open door. He was heart-stoppingly gorgeous.

"Robert?" He seemed to gather his wits. "Debs told me you wanted to talk to me."

"I— Yes." I was still panting from my run, and my breath fogged in the frigid air. I couldn't stop simply drinking in the sight of him.

"So . . . do you want to come in?"

"Oh God. Yes. Please." He stood aside to let me enter. The moment of almost-contact as I brushed past him was torturous.

We didn't move on, just stayed in the narrow hallway after he'd shut the door. "So, um . . ." he said, looking at my feet.

I looked down automatically to see what was wrong with them, caught myself, then kicked off my muddy running shoes onto the doormat, abashed. "Sorry."

"What? Oh—yeah, don't worry about it. Um. The lads are in the living room. Playing Xbox." Sean nodded down the hallway, but even if I hadn't already known where the living room was situated, the high-pitched—and high-decibel—shouts of alternate glee and frustration ringing out from that direction would have told me. "Do you want to come upstairs?"

Oh God, yes. Even if it did feel a painfully awkward to be going to his bedroom, the way things stood between us. "Yes, please." My voice caught, and he frowned.

"Get you a coffee first? Cup of tea?"

I didn't think I could bear waiting for the kettle to boil. "No, I'm fine. Really."

Sean nodded and led the way up a toy-strewn trip hazard of a staircase, negotiating the obstacles without appearing to notice them. I picked my way with care—it would be just my luck to get so close to him again and then break my neck before we'd had a chance to sort things out.

I'd never seen his bedroom before. We'd always, for obvious reasons, preferred my house for our intimate encounters. It was a small room, more suited to a child, but he'd told me the twins shared the largest bedroom in the house. There were probably all sorts of insights to be gleaned from its furnishings and contents, but right now all I could focus on was its inhabitant, who seemed to fill the space between the dresser and the bed.

And who was currently holding out a plastic carrier bag he'd taken from the top of the dresser. It wasn't from Tesco, so I couldn't see what was inside.

I stared, nonplussed.

"I got you a present," Sean explained, not meeting my gaze.

"You shouldn't have," I said awkwardly, and then he looked at me. Finally. Something twisted inside me at the tension around his beautiful eyes.

"Yeah, well. I did anyway."

I hesitated, then took the bag. "I, um . . . Should I open it now?"

"Up to you. It's not wrapped or anything. S'pose I'm a bit crap at presents. Don't tell Debs, she'd kill me. But, um, sit down." He gestured at the bed and sat. I joined him, my heart thumping so loudly, I half expected Debs to come upstairs and complain about the noise. Then again, she'd probably been deafened by the twins' games.

Piquantly conscious that our thighs were now only inches apart, I reached a hand inside the bag. I felt something fuzzy, like felt, perhaps? Even before I drew it out into the light, I realised what it was.

I smiled helplessly. "You got me a fez."

Sean shrugged. "Yeah, well. Thought you could wear it next Halloween, like the bloke said. Wills and Harry might just be planning to give you a sonic screwdriver at the end of the summer term too. Probably shouldn't have told you that."

"I'll act surprised, don't worry. And thank you. It was really thoughtful."

"There's something else in there too."

"There is?" I plunged my hand once more into the bag. The shape I felt was very familiar indeed, and my head felt curiously light as I pulled out the bow tie Sean had got me. Then I saw the design, and the twisted thing inside me snapped in two.

Bow Ties Are Cool. It was embroidered in red, on dark-blue silk.

"It's . . . it's perfect." I cleared my throat. "Thank you. Where on earth did you find it?"

Sean rubbed his hands on his denim-clad thighs. "There's this girl I know who's into making stuff. So. Yeah. We should talk, right?"

My guts discovered auto-origami and set to it with gusto. "I need to explain things to you," I said quickly, before I could lose what little nerve I had. "About Oliver."

Sean tensed at the name. "Go on, then. I'm listening."

I was glad I was sitting next to him. That way, I wouldn't have to look him in the eye. Wouldn't have to watch his face change as I told him my last secrets.

"Oliver was . . ." I sank my head into my hands. "Oh God. You're going to hate me. But I swear nothing happened."

"So go on. Tell me what didn't happen."

"He— I— Well, he was such a bright young man. *Is* one, I mean. Really bright. He wanted to go to Cambridge. I mean, he's there now, but back then he was still trying to get in . . . Anyway, that's not important. The point is, he needed some extra tutoring. So we had extra lessons. Four till six, Tuesdays and Thursdays." Almost against my will, I found myself searching his face, desperate after all to see his reaction. "That was all it was. Really."

Sean cocked his head. "Yeah? Doesn't look like it from where I'm sitting."

I stood up. "That was the whole problem, really. Oh God. I'm explaining this all wrong." I took a deep breath and stared at my sports socks, my toes sinking into Sean's soft blue bedroom carpet. "We got on a bit too well. He's, well . . ." Intense. Different. Dangerous. *A bit like you.* "Not that I ever even dreamed of acting upon it," I added quickly. "I mean, I was with Crispin." Perhaps that had been part of the attraction too—I'd *known* it would never go anywhere, so I'd felt safe to enjoy it.

I risked another glance at Sean's face. He was frowning. "So this Oliver, he was the lad I met down at your place? How old was he? Can't have been younger than sixteen."

"God, no!" Nausea rose in my throat. "Seventeen. He was seventeen."

"He was legal, then. If he hadn't been your student, it'd have been fine, right?"

"But he *was* my student. And . . . that wasn't the only thing. He didn't have the best of backgrounds. I think that was partly why he got a bit of a crush on me." It didn't excuse my behaviour, though. Nothing did. "I should have stopped giving him private lessons at once, persuaded one of the other teachers to do it, but . . . I *liked* him, you know? Liked spending time with him." If I was brutally honest with myself, I'd enjoyed the ego boost too, the way he'd seemed to look up to me, even though I was barely six years his senior. "But it would have been totally unethical for me to go out with him, even if I *had* been free."

"What happened?"

It wasn't as hard as I'd thought it would be. "He . . . well, he didn't want to take no for an answer."

"He tried to force you into something? That bastard." Somehow, Sean was standing behind me, his arms around my waist. Solid bands of comfort, where I'd thought I'd never feel them again. I looked down at his roughened hands, the jagged nails, and tried to draw strength from them.

"No—God, no. At least, not like that." I swallowed. "He said if I didn't agree to go out with him, he'd tell the headmaster I'd—I'd molested him."

"So what happened?" His voice was a growl. I ought to find it sexy, I supposed, but right now I was just numb.

"I didn't. And he did."

"Bastard," he said again, and his arms tightened around me. "And they believed him over you?"

"The headmaster was really good about it. He thought it'd be best if I just left quietly."

"Oh yeah, I'm sure he had your best interests at heart. Nothing to do with not wanting his precious school in the papers."

I spun in his arms, pushing away from him angrily. "You think *I'd* have wanted to be in the papers? No anonymity for the accused, remember? And people always say there's no smoke without fire. Do you honestly think I'd ever have got another teaching job?"

"So what happened to the bloke you were with?"

"Crispin. He . . . Well, we split up." I managed a wobbly smile. "Couldn't run away from me fast enough. And he was a PE teacher, so, well, obviously pretty quick on his feet."

"God. The one bloke you'd expect to believe you when you said nothing had happened."

"I think . . ." I couldn't say it. But I had to say it. Had to be honest with him, or it would fester forever. I stared at Sean's feet for a change. He was wearing thick woolly socks—a Christmas present? They were black, to match the jacket I still hadn't returned to him. "I think . . . it didn't really matter to him whether I was telling the truth. About nothing having happened between me and Oliver. He was just worried he'd be tarred with the same brush. And I wasn't w-worth risking that for." It was so humiliating, admitting it to the person I wanted most to think well of me.

"Fucking . . ." Sean trailed off, glaring to one side. My chest tightened painfully, and a heavy weight thudded into my stomach, bringing a swift end to the hundred or so paper cranes that had hitherto flitted queasily therein.

Then Sean's arms were around me once more, pulling me close. I stumbled, but he caught me and held me in his strong arms.

"God," he breathed into my hair. "Why didn't you tell me? Did you seriously think I'd act like that prick? Fuck, don't answer that. I'm not like that, okay? He was a fucking idiot."

My heart twisted, but I had to say it. "But . . . you left. Just like he did."

"I know. I'm sorry." Sean still held me tight for a moment, then he loosened his grip to look me in the eye. "Look, sometimes I get a bit . . . Well. You know. It's not easy, sometimes. I mean, you're used to all these posh blokes with high-flying careers and degrees coming out of their ears, and I'm just a bloody ratcatcher. I mean, fucking hell, what did your family say when you told them about me? *If* you told them about me," he added more quietly.

I was hurt. "Of course I told them about you. I'm not ashamed of you. Far from it. Peter said to ask about blue peanut butter," I remembered.

Sean gave a surprised bark of laughter. "Yeah? God, we haven't used that stuff in years. Bloody EU regulations. Mice used to go wild for it." His gaze dropped. "Shit, I'm sorry. Should've trusted you. And I shouldn't have got mad at you for not telling me everything. I mean . . . Well, it's your life, innit? Not mine. Up to you what you tell people. I shouldn't have dumped all my dad's crap on you. Just cos he was a tosser, it doesn't mean you are."

I blinked. "Have you been talking to Rose?"

Sean directed a sheepish smile at my socks. "Yeah, well. It's possible she might have called me out this morning to deal with a rat in her bathroom that turned out to be a spider."

"A spider?"

"It was a pretty big spider, mind. Took a few tries to get it down the plughole. She gave me a cup of tea afterwards. And a proper talking-to. So anyway . . . You've probably noticed I'm a bit of a dick sometimes. And I'm sorry I left. Really sorry." He pulled me back into his arms. "But I'll always come back to you. You know, if you want me to?"

I couldn't believe he thought there was any doubt about it. "I want you to," I said, my heart unclenching itself into an almost painful lightness. "Always." And, well, if he didn't, I'd just have to make sure I went looking for him.

Sean smiled, his green eyes bright and that roguish look upon his face that had always drawn me to him. He stroked my hair, and it occurred to me for the first time just how unkempt I must look after my desperate sprint to reach him. A second later, it further occurred to me that maybe he didn't mind that one bit—maybe even found it attractive—and I couldn't have kept an answering smile from my lips even if I'd wanted to try.

"Right, then," Sean said, his voice fond. "That's a promise."

EPILOGUE

The Easter end-of-term service at St. Saviour's Church was predictably less well attended than Harvest and Christmas, but I was heartened to see most of the children in my class had at least one parent in the pews. Destinee's mum was there, with the tennis coach, both of them lean, tanned, and probably Botoxed as well, although it was possible the vacancy in their expressions was due to boredom rather than cosmetic treatments.

Mr. Mason was there too, for a wonder. This was the first time I'd seen him on hallowed ground. Although perhaps I shouldn't be surprised. His punctuality when picking up Charlie had improved markedly since our little chat, which helped me remember it—and its consequences—without total mortification.

Even Hanne had turned up, having told me she wanted to hear "my" children singing. She was standing, beaming with maternal pride, next to a tall, rangy Viking I recognised from the photos she'd showed us of her younger son, Andreas. I suspected there might have been a subtle hint intended that it was time he thought about providing her with some grandchildren to spoil when she returned to her native land. She'd be moving back in the summer. I was going to miss her.

I glanced in Sean's direction, only to find him frowning in a sardonic way that somehow managed to fully communicate *I saw you eyeing up the hot bloke, and don't think you're getting away with it.* I widened my eyes in mock trepidation, and he immediately ruined the stern effect with a grin. Smiling back helplessly, I caught Debs's exaggerated eye roll and turned hastily back to the children in my charge.

Debs was still cancer-free, and the prognosis was apparently good. She still wore headscarves out in public for now, not liking how her vivid red hair looked at its early stage of regrowth, but was looking forward to dispensing with them by the summer.

The ponderous tones of the organ rang sonorously though the church, and the congregation launched into "There Is a Green Hill Far Away," some more enthusiastically than others. Destinee, at the end of my pew, looked bored out of her sophisticated little mind but perked up when Harry nudged her. I pretended not to notice the four heads (Wills, Harry, Destinee, and Charlie) bent over whatever they'd found to distract them. They'd been fast friends this term, and the other teachers and I had taken to calling them The Fearsome Four. Not that young Charlie, bless him, was the least bit fearsome even now, but his confidence had certainly come on in leaps and bounds of late.

The vicar said a few words (actually, he said a few *more* words; I'd been so distracted, I'd entirely missed the start). Then it was time for class 2E to perform "He's Alive," an upbeat modern hymn whose chorus—at least in the version we were using—consisted solely of the words *he's alive* repeated fourteen times, presumably on the basis that even the most dense listener would get the message by the end.

I stepped out of the pew to shepherd my little charges into the apse, and the vicar moved to one side to let us pass, giving us a beatific smile. The Fearsome Four were still gleefully furtive, and I gave them my sternest look as the class lined up. Free this time of any seasonal accoutrements (Rose had suggested bunny ears and a tail, but I'd strongly suspected the Head might fail to see the joke), I raised my hands to bring them in.

"He's Alive" rang through the church at a creditable volume. Destinee had an impressive pair of lungs on her when she condescended to use them, and clearly she was in a condescending mood today. As the last chords died away, a sudden and very localised burst of applause drew my attention, and I turned to see Mrs. Nunn on her feet, clapping enthusiastically.

"Ah, excellent, excellent," the vicar said. "But, ah, we don't normally applaud during the service," he added in conspiratorial tones, as if the entire congregation couldn't hear his amplified voice perfectly well.

Mrs. Nunn made an *ooh, get him* sort of face, but at least she sat down.

As the children filed back into their pews, I noticed the twins hanging back a little—and then Wills crouched down for a moment behind the vicar. When he straightened, I caught a glimpse of a matchbox before it disappeared into his trouser pocket. Wills glanced up and met my gaze with a curious mixture of defiance and worry.

Should I say something? Warn the vicar there was now in all likelihood some leggy creepy-crawly climbing up his cassock? I hesitated, and the vicar looked at me, his lips tight-pressed. "*If* we could get on, Mr. Enemy?"

Ah, well. The chances were he'd find out for himself. I meekly joined class 2E in the pews, and the vicar began his sermon.

Georgie's christening earlier in the month had gone well. Sean had accompanied me, and I'd taken care to make it quite plain where my affections lay. Certainly Linette had seemed much more friendly towards me at the end of the day than the beginning. Come to think of it, Sean had been in rather a good mood too. The ensuing night had certainly left me in no doubt of where *his* affections lay.

The air in the church was still chilly with winter's damp, but outside in the churchyard and, indeed, all over the village, daffodils had sprung out in full force to herald the warm, sunny days to come. I was looking forward to them. I'd joined the cricket club—we both had. Sean, despite his lack of experience with the sport, had proved in training to be a very passable batsman and, of course, an excellent fielder. He also cut a rather fine figure in cricketing whites, despite his initial doubts. And training together naturally gave us an ideal opportunity to shower together afterwards . . .

I cut off that train of thought sharply. It was veering into territory not *entirely* suitable to dwell on in a church.

I was under strict instructions to take Sean to visit Mother and Peter in Wiltshire during the summer holidays, but it would only be for a few days and there was every chance Laetitia wouldn't be there. Her on-off relationship with the boyfriend was currently back *on*, and they'd booked a fortnight in Tunisia. Sean and I had a tacit understanding that he would, when it came down to it, prove completely unable to get any time off work that wasn't during those dates.

There would be plenty of time for leisurely drives in Portia, rides on the back of Sean's motorbike, and lazy evenings together. And then, of course, it would be time to start teaching St. Saviour's little darlings the official school harvest song all over again. Funnily enough, I couldn't seem to bring myself to mind.

Even as I smiled to myself, the vicar's drone faltered, and he scratched behind his ear. Only to find Wills's little gift, presumably having made it to collar height under its own steam, had now hitched a ride on his hand.

My word, that *was* an impressively large spider.

The drone turned into a high-pitched shriek, and the vicar flicked the spider away in horror—only to have it land smack in the middle of the reception class, half of whom scrambled out of the pews in mortal terror while the other half yelled "Don't kill it!" and set about trying to rescue the thing.

I caught Sean's eye—then had to look away rapidly. The sight of his handsome, well-loved features, creased with laughter, was *not* helping me in my struggle to keep a straight face.

And Fordy thought the village was a boring backwater? Well, it *was* something of a backwater, perhaps. But boring? Maybe it would be, for him.

I only knew there was no place on earth I'd rather be.

Explore more of *The Shamwell Tales* at:
riptidepublishing.com/titles/universe/shamwell-tales

AUTHOR'S NOTE

"I Like Baked Beans" is not, alas, a real song. But if it were, these would be the lyrics:

I like baked beans
Brussels sprouts and tangerines
Cabbages and carrots
And peppers red and green.
Alphabet spaghetti, pick and mix
Chocolate muffins and sesame sticks
Tins of soup and frozen food
Let's thank God for all that's good.

Dear Reader,

Thank you for reading JL Merrow's *Caught!*

We know your time is precious and you have many, many entertainment options, so it means a lot that you've chosen to spend your time reading. We really hope you enjoyed it.

We'd be honored if you'd consider posting a review—good or bad—on sites like **Amazon, Barnes & Noble, Kobo, Goodreads, Twitter, Facebook, Tumblr,** and your blog or website. We'd also be honored if you told your friends and family about this book. Word of mouth is a book's lifeblood!

For more information on upcoming releases, author interviews, blog tours, contests, giveaways, and more, please sign up for our weekly, spam-free newsletter and visit us around the web:

Newsletter: tinyurl.com/RiptideSignup
Twitter: twitter.com/RiptideBooks
Facebook: facebook.com/RiptidePublishing
Goodreads: tinyurl.com/RiptideOnGoodreads
Tumblr: riptidepublishing.tumblr.com

Thank you so much for Reading the Rainbow!

RiptidePublishing.com

ACKNOWLEDGEMENTS

With grateful thanks to all who helped with this book: Kristin Matherly, Susan Sorrentino, Josephine Myles, Bruin Fisher, Rhys Ford, Verulam Writers and of course, Linda Ingmanson.

ALSO BY JL MERROW

ABOUT THE AUTHOR

JL Merrow is that rare beast, an English person who refuses to drink tea. She read Natural Sciences at Cambridge, where she learned many things, chief amongst which was that she never wanted to see the inside of a lab ever again. Her one regret is that she never mastered the ability of punting one-handed whilst holding a glass of champagne.

She writes (mostly) contemporary gay romance and mysteries, and is frequently accused of humour. Her novel *Slam!* won the 2013 Rainbow Award for Best LGBT Romantic Comedy, and several of her books have been EPIC Awards finalists, including *Muscling Through*, *Relief Valve* (the Plumber's Mate Mysteries), and *To Love a Traitor*.

JL Merrow is a member of the Romantic Novelists' Association, International Thriller Writers, Verulam Writers and the UK GLBTQ Fiction Meet (ukglbtfictionmeet.co.uk) organising team.

Find JL Merrow on Twitter as @jlmerrow, and on Facebook at facebook.com/jl.merrow

For a full list of books available, see: jlmerrow.com or JL Merrow's Amazon author page: viewauthor.at/JLMerrow.

Enjoy more stories like *Caught!* at RiptidePublishing.com!

Adulting 101
ISBN: 978-1-62649-450-3

Too Stupid to Live
ISBN: 978-1-937551-85-8

Earn Bonus Bucks!

Earn 1 Bonus Buck for each dollar you spend. Find out how at RiptidePublishing.com/news/bonus-bucks.

Win Free Ebooks for a Year!

Pre-order coming soon titles directly through our site and you'll receive one entry into a drawing for a chance to win free books for a year! Get the details at RiptidePublishing.com/contests.